THE SECRET INHERITANCE

RACHEL LYNCH

Storm

This is a work of fiction. Names, characters, business, events and incidents are the products of the author's imagination. Any resemblance to actual persons, living or dead, or actual events is purely coincidental.

Copyright © Rachel Lynch, 2024

The moral right of the author has been asserted.

All rights reserved. No part of this book may be reproduced or used in any manner without the prior written permission of the copyright owner.

To request permissions, contact the publisher at rights@stormpublishing.co

Ebook ISBN: 978-1-80508-558-4
Paperback ISBN: 978-1-80508-560-7

Cover design: Eileen Carey
Cover images: Shutterstock, iStock

Published by Storm Publishing.
For further information, visit:
www.stormpublishing.co

ALSO BY RACHEL LYNCH

DI Kelly Porter

Dark Game

Deep Fear

Dead End

Bitter Edge

Bold Lies

Blood Rites

Little Doubt

Lost Cause

Lying Ways

Sudden Death

Silent Bones

Shared Remains

Helen Scott Royal Military Police

The Rift

The Line

The Rich

ONE

Clara

'It won't be long now,' the doctor whispered.

Clara dipped a mouth-swab into a bowl of cold water and was reminded of giving out lollipops to the children when they were small. But Jude didn't acknowledge his treat with a giggle or a glance, as she ran it around the inside of his mouth to bring him some relief for his murderous thirst. He didn't even open his eyes.

The doctor packed away his things, his moment of compassion gone. He'd practically camped here for a whole week.

In the end, the descent into nothingness had come quicker than anyone expected. It was as if Jude had given up. After a lifelong quest to soldier on, no matter what harshness was thrown his way, he'd accepted his mortality and regressed to being a child.

Clara had witnessed only the second half of that journey, from Jude's supreme eminence as a successful businessman through to his current decline. She'd watched his tragic depreciation from vital master to atrophied dependant.

She leaned over his face as he stirred gently and tried to speak.

'Hush now,' she said. 'There, you don't want to waste your energy.'

The doctor stopped what he was doing and stared at Jude, who he'd known for fifty years or so. Clara thought she detected water in his eyes, just at the corners, but he looked away and resumed his fussing. Observing the diminishing potency of his client had taken its toll on him.

Clara took the change in behaviour to signal the end. She didn't expect verbal confirmation of her suspicion, but she sensed the conclusion to Jude's long story was near. Oncologists, like most medical doctors, found real, human communication awkward but she could tell by the doctor's behaviour that Jude was losing his final battle.

'Let him speak if he so wishes,' the doctor said.

She nodded and went back to refreshing Jude's mouth which must have felt like the Sahara Desert to him. He opened his eyes and swallowed, though the tumours in his neck made this difficult to achieve and he winced in pain. Clara reached over to his syringe driver and pumped some more morphine into his arm like she'd been shown.

The doctor waited. He'd finished packing away his things and held his bag, ready to leave. Clara looked at him and he nodded to her.

'Goodbye, Jude. I'll see you tomorrow,' he said.

Jude's breathing eased as the drugs kicked in and Clara stared deep into his eyes. They were like pits of despair and she could tell that he read their thoughts.

There would be no tomorrow.

He grabbed her arm.

It was wholly unexpected, and Clara gasped. She softened and gathered herself quickly.

'They get stronger at the end. It's a little flourish of energy. Expect him to become agitated later today,' the doctor said.

Clara stared at him.

'He can still hear us,' she told him, glaring.

Jude squeezed her arm tighter, and she sat back down on the bed beside him to soothe him. She heard the door close and felt a wave of disappointment wash over her. The caring profession had just left the room.

She stroked Jude's head. His eyes flickered open at her touch and she remembered a time when her fingers caressed his face in a loving embrace, not one of pity. Those days were long gone and after everything, they had nothing to show for it. But his eyes sparkled just as brightly as they had forty years ago, when she'd begun working for the family at Warbury House. Mrs Fitzherbert had passed ten years ago now, and the house had been empty like a mausoleum ever since, despite herself, Michael and Jude still existing inside its walls.

After Beatrice's death, Jude had slumped into a deep despair. His body had begun to degenerate, though he fought on, despite his heart being sliced in two by life's cruel plan. Even now, he still wasn't ready to give up his last breath and leave this world. He had too much to do.

Too much to apologise for.

Clara pondered on his children and stared at her employer, who mumbled under his breath. He was settled now, and she saw that his eyes were still open, as if he was fighting something. They were like portals to a past universe. She saw that he was still in there, perhaps weaker and smaller, but he remained, proud and keen-eyed, like the man she'd known. A father, a grandfather, a husband, a master and a lover.

Some part of her believed he'd never fade away. His spirit was too powerful, his energy too vital, but as she sat here, watching him descend into nothingness, Clara realised that even Jude Fitzherbert was fallible, and he was indeed going to die.

Panic gripped her for a second and she leaned over his face and put her ear close to his mouth to check he was still breathing. She felt a faint rhythmic breath, which tickled her skin and told her he was still holding on.

'I'm cold.'

It was a whisper.

'I'll fetch a blanket,' she said, rubbing her hands up and down his arms to warm him up but taking care not to break his fragile body.

He was a bag of bones.

He'd worked in his study until he could no longer walk to his desk, and then he'd moved his trade to his bed. Then his writing failed him, and after that, his eyesight. The phone still rang. People demanded his attention even as the cancer spread through his body and he stopped functioning. Money didn't stop going round and round because one man got ill. Investments – whatever they were – didn't stagnate because one person couldn't come to the phone. The world carried on.

He was helped by friends and associates to make the most pressing decisions about his business, and she knew at least one of his children helped him via email and telephone. She supposed that's how business was done these days. It meant they didn't have to travel all the way out here to Oxfordshire to make a decision. Jude wasn't as quick as he used to be, but the old Jude was still inside the shell she saw before her now.

But Clara's world had changed forever.

She didn't care for stocks and shares. High risk or low risk to her was more about children's games than business. Her interest was in real people. Those whom she'd loved and cared for. Money couldn't love you back. But people would sure enough kill for it.

She stroked his face gently and then got up from the bed to

find a blanket. She saw one discarded on the chair, put there for herself to keep her comfortable when she dozed off in the middle of the night, unable to leave him.

She unfolded it and spread it across his body, tucking in the edges. In a moment, he'd be too hot again, so she prepared to whip it off as quickly. It was all part of the pattern of life when it lapsed into chaos. Nothing lasted forever, she thought.

Clara considered Jude's descent into a child's form. We come into the world unable to control our bodies, and we depart it the same way, she reflected. When she'd gone through the change of life some ten years ago, she'd suffered with hot flushes one minute, and freezing chills the next. But Jude wasn't transforming. He was the main star in his own finale. For a second, her memory flashed up scenes from when they'd first met: how his hand brushed hers as he pretended to search for titles in the library, or when dead-heading dahlias in the garden. Any excuse to touch.

'Children,' she heard him murmur, and once again she leaned closer to him, feeling his body diminish underneath her as if by the very second.

'Whose children, Jude?' she asked.

'My fucking children, whose do you think?'

None of them had come to visit.

She rolled her eyes at the profanity. The cancer certainly hadn't reached his mouth.

'Where are they?' he continued.

'I'm sure they'll come,' she said.

'Don't lie to me, Clara. I can tell when you're lying. I have four fucking children and none of them can be bothered to watch me die.'

This led to a coughing fit and his body moved back and forth. Clara was reminded of the children she'd tended to, when coughs and colds had banished them to their beds many years ago.

'Three children, Jude,' she corrected him.

He stopped wriggling.

'Three children, yes.'

He was silent but she could see his face flushing and knew that he was overheating. It was a never-ending cycle of discreet guardianship, though she never thought she'd be coddling him like the babies she'd raised and lost. She wafted his face a little with a hand-held fan on the bedside table. It had belonged to Beatrice.

He became alert once more and stared beyond her to the window, which overlooked the great trees, which in turn led down to the perimeter.

She'd had his bed moved into this room so he could enjoy the view, and from it, he could see all the way across his estate to the fields beyond, and even to the driveway, which languished empty these days. Warbury House sat atop a small hill and commanded an excellent position to survey all four thousand acres. Jude preferred the view to the front because the back faced the lake, and he didn't want to be reminded about what had happened there. Of late, though, he couldn't even sit up enough to see out of the window, so she stood by it for him and described what she saw.

She scolded herself for correcting him. What difference did it make anyway? He was dying. She could have easily ignored him and pretended not to hear, and made herself busy with washing downstairs, continuing with her day.

She was his housemaid and cook, not his wife. She didn't have to listen to his last-minute ramblings about regret and sorrow. But pity – and something else – tugged at her heart.

'They'll come the minute I fuck off,' he said.

'I'm sure they will, Jude.'

'To get my money.'

Clara nodded.

He began to laugh. It started as a chuckle but then worked

its way into a crescendo, causing him to go purple in the face. Clara tried to sit him up, to ease the congestion drowning him from inside his chest, but the jerking prevented her from getting a good grip on him. She panicked. He couldn't get air into his lungs and his eyes were turning red, and his lips blue. He gasped for air, and she shoved her fingers in his mouth to try to open his airways wider.

Suddenly, he took a deep breath and then more followed and his body stopped rattling like an old coal cart. She set him back down and mopped his brow with a flannel.

'Don't do this to yourself, Jude. Leave it be. You can't get all excited,' she soothed.

He rested a hand on her arm and nodded.

She held his hand.

'If they turn up now, before I'm dead, kick them out with the trash.'

'You mean the rubbish? We're in England, remember?' she said.

He glared at her.

'The world has changed. Catch up! We're all American now!'

Jude had invested much of his money in the markets over the pond. The ones she knew about and the few she overheard him speak about were in Central and South America, which she thought was just full of heat and animals that could kill you, but what did she know? Money, and what it did to people, was something she avoided.

'Should I put a movie on?' she asked him.

It would be a Hollywood film, obviously. They watched them together, and commented on how perfect all the actors looked, even when they were over fifty. She'd had Michael, Jude's butler, set up a projector in his room.

He smiled.

'I'm sorry, Clara,' he said.

'Don't be, Jude! I love a good movie.'

'No, I'm truly sorry.'

She patted his hand. An understanding passed between them, and she saw that he was confessing his sins to her, expecting forgiveness.

She left him and took a pile of last night's bed linen with her. It'd all be thrown into the washing machine, not like when the children were small and she boiled bed clothes and scrubbed them by hand.

Nothing was hard work anymore. Jude was right when he said that value earned had lost its sheen.

By the time she returned to him, armed with several choices of movie, all from the 1970s, Jude was still and at peace.

She placed the DVDs down gently and went to him to check he was comfortable, or if he'd nodded off in an awkward position.

But when she got to his side, she felt something was different. He looked completely at rest, as if all the lines on his face had melted away, and the grimace in his jaw had disappeared. She touched his cheek and knew from the lack of energy emanating from his body, before she moved her finger down to his carotid artery, that he was dead.

A wave of electricity assaulted her abdomen as she experienced an overwhelming sense of guilt that he'd died alone. Soon after that, hot anger burned inside her and made her neck flush.

After all this time, and the thousands of times she'd reassured him, promised him, lied to him, that his children were coming, they still hadn't and now it was too late. But she knew, as sure as the rising of the sun in the east, over the island in the centre of the lake –

where Jude would be buried – that they'd come for their money.

TWO

Rosie

Rosie stared out of the conservatory window, across her small garden, watching greedy summer birds with their fat bellies pick at treats she'd left out for them. In seven years, she'd transformed the place from a mass of weeds and empty containers, into a cosy retreat, full of aromatic perennials and flowering shrubs together with a pergola which she could escape to whenever she pleased. A perfect haven for her writing.

The arbour wasn't anything like the grandstand which languished on the island in the middle of the lake at Warbury House, but still, it served the same purpose. It was a place just as magical and where anything was possible. Inside her imagination, she could create any characters she liked and direct them to her bidding. They could love, laugh, cry and kill.

The birds outside sang of happier times, or so it seemed. Their warbling made her think of tragedy, and memories being laid down for future generations. Even when birds were caged they sang, and she didn't know if that made them stupid or admirably faithful.

Her house was overlooked by other townhouses, and the distant traffic could be heard as it crawled through London, but clever planting and high walls at least gave the impression of privacy. In reality, any number of nosy neighbours might watch her coming and going, through binoculars perhaps – studying her habits, preparing for the exact moment they'd be required to bear witness to her last movements on this earth. Though she was only thirty-eight, Rosie knew she would die alone.

She shivered.

Somebody walking over her grave.

Rosie had always been plagued with an overactive imagination. It was what made her books so popular. She wrote crime novels for a living.

Her daydreaming had been used against her at school. She'd been described by her teachers as a simple child – inadequate and mediocre. All the girls had been brainwashed into believing that fantasy was useless, and aspirational thinking was for those who denied reality. Thanks to the blessed Sisters of St Mary's, she'd quickly found herself unemployable after graduation, due to her clumsiness and absentmindedness.

Until, that is, she discovered she could sell her stories, and she could break free of her father's shackles.

Now she peered over the cover of her MacBook Pro to pick up her coffee cup and realised she'd been lost in a paragraph so poignant that it had sucked time out of her body and the coffee had gone cold. She must have been daydreaming for twenty minutes or more.

She was stuck on a phrase, and she checked her thesaurus to see if she could word it better. But despite trying her best to replace three words with one, the sentence still wasn't working. She closed the laptop and sighed.

Rosie found it difficult to understand how some writers forced themselves to type a certain number of words per day. She couldn't do it. Her process was organic. She allowed her mind to travel widely and openly, and when she felt ready, she transferred it all to the page without stopping. The kind of people who set targets and stuck to them were not like her. For her, it was important to resist rules, not be bound by them.

Bobby – her border terrier crossed with something else, perhaps a Jack Russell – languished lazily beneath her feet, yet even in his sleep he was still on guard, pointed towards the garden in case she was overcome by robbers. He licked his lips and twitched inside his doggy dream. Perhaps he was chasing squirrels. Rosie had saved him from the kennels three years ago, after realising that life in London was consummately lonely. No matter how hard she tried (or didn't) to connect with people, she simply couldn't force herself to like them. Bobby did just fine and was all the company she needed. He was the perfect companion: quiet, loving and loyal; three things she'd yearned for, ever since finding the courage to leave Warbury House for the last time.

Catching a series of words on the moment, she tutted with a jolt of recollection and reopened her Mac. The arrangement had been staring her in the face all along. It wasn't difficult after all. She'd just needed space to think. Silence to breathe. Room to pause.

The mail dropping through the letterbox startled her, and she turned quickly towards the front of the house. Bobby woke, poked his nose into the air and sniffed, eyeing her through sleepy dark balls of wisdom. His eyes were sunk into their sockets and seemed to disappear forever.

She got up and placed her Mac on the table. She reassured Bobby by giving him a pat behind his ears, and he rested his head back on the blanket she'd laid out for him. Then she went to the door, picked letters up from the floor, and sifted through them. Most of her mail went straight into the bin and she marvelled at how utterly pointless it was for companies to send out promotional flyers at all, but then she'd never been interested in business.

But one letter stood out.

Rosie recognised the handwriting straight away, even before she put her glasses on. It was unforgettable, because she'd sat for countless hours alongside her, pretending to be two teachers when they were just girls, calling out imaginary names and marking off absences and lateness. They'd filed these attendance registers with their school reports, written by the lights of secret torches, deep into the night, when the boys played soldiers underneath their duvets in the next room.

But the recollection of the handwriting didn't resurrect the same feelings of exploration and daring from those days long ago; instead it jarred her. Her hand froze, holding the letter addressed to Rosamunde Fitzherbert, and she lost more nuggets of time studying the looped script. It was tidy and formal, which was unlike the sender, Rosie thought. The last time they had communicated was to tell each other they hated one another, not in words, but by text. In black and white; words that could never be taken back. They'd languish in eternity, between them, against them, forever. The loops of the writing reminded her of the marks in the sand, as Michael dragged a canoe along it, leaving welts in it which filled with water and then melted away as if he hadn't been trying to hide anything at all.

When she came to her senses, she'd no idea how long she'd been standing there, but Bobby was no longer on his blanket and the sun's rays had shifted in the conservatory, slightly to the left. Her south-facing garden acted like an ancient sundial at the end of a long summer, casting its warnings over the tiles on her conservatory floor. Motes of dust gathered in the beams and danced there to remind her that time still journeyed on. It hadn't stopped just yet. She looked back down at the envelope in her hand and gently placed it on the side table in the hallway.

The postmark was yesterday, and the stamp was slightly

askew, and her shoulder twitched at the sight of it. It didn't take much to get a stamp straight. A steady hand and a thoughtful eye, that was all.

The sender had clearly taken her time over the words, but not the licking of the stamp, and Rosie wondered if it had lain on her desk for days before she forced herself to send it, then, without thought, shoved the stamp on and let it drop into the post box.

She picked it up once more and turned it over. The sender's address was in Oxfordshire somewhere. *She didn't get far*. Rosie imagined her living in some fine country manor house, smaller than Warbury House, of course, but still luxurious, with servants tending to her every need, and being surrounded by lots of children, her belly swollen with fertility and preparing for the next one.

Hettie, Rosie's sister, was a baby machine. Or at least that's what their brother called her. It had sounded like light-hearted teasing when he said it. Rosie had counted three offspring before she stopped keeping track, and she no longer asked.

Cherry House, Appletree Lane... it read.

Fitting for Hettie, all right, she mused.

A smile curled at the corners of her mouth, and Rosie tried to force it away. Her body had betrayed her like that many years before, when she still hadn't learned to control it, and she was irritated at herself. Her mouth moved without her say so, being simply a bunch of facial muscles connected to fascia and tiny bones all working on the command of the constant electrical signals from her central nervous system. She didn't *make* her mouth curl up. It did it all on its own. Which is what bothered her; it showed her that something deep inside her was happy at the memory of her and Hettie at Warbury House.

But then she remembered the last time she saw Hettie, and what had gone before, and it didn't make her want to smile at all. It made her want to scream, and she tossed the envelope across the floor, as if it was laced with poison. It slid with a hiss across the terracotta tiles, and slithered towards the front door, halting inches from the gap underneath where she could see sunlight taunting her to go outside.

Her heart rate soared, and she knew without looking that her chest had turned pink. She placed her left hand over her heart, and felt heat radiate up to her neck. She placed her index finger on her carotid artery, and the tip of it vibrated like a machine gun.

She tried to remedy the panic by breathing deeply, forcing affirmative thoughts into her psyche, but the crushing negativity of seeing her sister's handwriting terrified her.

The letter had sullied her space and she found herself pinned against the radiator in the hallway, at a loss at what to do about it. She stood, inert, unable to move, until Bobby came to find her. He wagged his tail innocently and tilted his head as if to ask her how she was. She bent her knees and reached a hand down, so she was able to stroke his forehead and he wagged his tail in approval. He stopped whining and opened his mouth into a breathy grin.

All was well.

But it wasn't.

She went into the kitchen, and was vexed to notice that the sun had gone in. Clouds had swooped over the conservatory roof and turned her workspace grey.

She knew she wouldn't get any more writing done today until she decided what to do with Hettie's letter. She could throw it away, thereby cleansing her home and releasing herself from Hettie's grip, which had managed to take hold of her all the way from Oxfordshire. Or she could open it and find out what she wanted.

Hettie knew not to call her. She'd stopped trying years ago. She knew that if she ever had something important to communicate to her sister, she'd write. And she had.

Something important.

Something that needed answering.

Rosie imagined the worst thing Hettie could have to say and kicked herself because she'd gone straight into default mode already, and the letter had only been in her house for ten minutes. So, instead, she thought of all the positive things her sister might have to tell her. But that didn't work either. It must be something bad.

She walked slowly towards the doormat and stopped to look at Bobby. He peered at her hands and then at the door, his tongue lolling out, thinking they might be going for a walk. Suddenly, he barked and it jangled her nerves and her shoulders reared up in shock. Then she laughed, releasing tension from her whole body.

She knelt again to stroke him, and he rolled over expecting her to scratch his belly. His body flopped over the letter, and it meant she didn't have to pick it up just yet.

At least I saved you, she thought.

And it didn't matter anyway, because she already knew what was inside.

Instead, she left Bobby and sat back down with her Mac, opening emails which on any other day could wait. Trash seemed to stream into her inbox all day long. Publishers, publicists, interview requests (all turned down), private messages from fans, and notes from her editor all kept her busy and her mind off the letter. But still it nagged at her, like a throbbing ball of energy, waiting for her in the corner of the room.

It was torture, and all she had to do to make it stop was open the damn thing. But she knew that as soon as she did, time would end, and she'd never be able to go back. What came after would be inevitable and her life would never be the same again.

She then tried to focus on the acknowledgements for her new book, as well as planning a special interest piece for a newspaper, but the unopened letter burned a hole in her head. It sat discarded on the floor, where she'd tossed it, eyeing her in a taunting and smug manner that even Bobby seemed uncertain of. Her dog sensed the air in the room had shifted but was unsure what to do about it, and so was Rosie. She hadn't allowed thoughts of her family to stain her home like this for years.

Hettie had got under her skin, as always.

All she had to do was take the envelope and rip it open, and read what was inside, but her body refused. She got up and scratched the flesh on her arms. Bobby followed her into the kitchen, and she realised, with joy, that he hadn't been fed this afternoon. It gave her something else to do. She apologised to him and stroked his ears. He grinned at her, and his head cocked upwards and slightly to the side as if to ask whether she was back to her usual self.

She smiled fondly at him and took a fork out of the drawer, then a can from the cupboard and scraped out food into his bowl. The familiar sound of the dog eating filled the room and brought calm.

Noise was a rare visitor inside her small house. A selective mute, Rosie had chosen to stop speaking many years ago, too many to count. She anchored the memory of it to the events that led up to it rather than the year, and now those memories flooded back as if emanating out of the envelope on the floor. She imagined a scream, because that's what stressed people did, but her mouth didn't move, and she found no solace in simply imagining the act.

But then she felt her resolve cave in, and her shoulders slump, and she stared at the letter, then swiped it up in one hand and stomped across the room, leaving Bobby to his dinner.

She sat down heavily on a sofa in the lounge, facing the TV that she watched in order to study her favourite subject: the mystery of people.

She could easily go out and meet them, talk to them, watch them at airports, or on trains, and tubes, on buses, or in cafés.

But she couldn't bear them.

They were infuriatingly noisy.

The TV screen – or inside books – was as close as she ever wanted to get to most of them. The electronic world was her barrier between herself and the outside. Inside her home, she was safe from their noise.

She sat back on the sofa and closed her eyes. Thoughts inside her head clanged for attention and wouldn't go away. She peered at the letter in her hand, intimately conscious of the fact that Hettie had taken a pen and touched it, writing her name upon it, and had licked the stamp, sticking it on, leaving her DNA behind. Her saliva was underneath the stamp, and smiling King Charles had no idea how toxic it was. At least it hadn't burned a hole in the paper.

She ripped it open.

THREE

James

As the tube rattled and shook its way out of Stratford station James tried to concentrate on the posters above the men's heads. There were six of them, in all. Men, not posters. Six weary faces across from him, staring ahead into nothing, tarred with tiredness and heat. James wondered where they'd been for the day and what it would be like to exist inside their lives. One wore painter's overalls, splattered with green marks. He had heavy boots on and carried a backpack, resting it on his knee for the journey home. The one to his left scowled sullenly and wore the staple outfit of an East End boy: black joggers, expensive trainers and a black hoodie, despite the temperature inside the metal box underground. He looked in his twenties and took up more space than paint-man, even though he was slimmer. His long limbs and broad shoulders somehow commanded more air, and it was as if paint-man knew it, because he squeezed his shoulders together as tightly as he could. The guy to paint-man's right was older – around fifty – and wore old chinos, dirty shoes and a sorry excuse for a shirt and tie. Teacher, James guessed, or a civil servant.

Or handyman for a country home...

James loved this game.

The trick was, though – especially on the Central line from Liverpool Street to Wanstead – not to make eye contact. This was an old and dilapidated section of the tube, and at five o'clock on a Friday evening, one could never tell what characters would be accompanying him. There was a frisson of Old London, and that brought potential danger. He felt out of place, despite trying his hardest not to be. He forced himself to sit nonchalantly, as if he hadn't a care in the world, sometimes reading on his Kindle, and crossing his legs occasionally to display his casual nature. He was no threat to anyone. He minded his own business. But he couldn't help himself making up stories about his fellow passengers, because that's, after all, why he was here. If he couldn't make up a gripping tale about a stranger, then he didn't deserve to be paid the astronomical amounts he was by his clients. His commitment to his research was nothing if not exemplary. It wasn't just his sister who created fiction.

Juries must believe him in order to convict, or acquit, and research, like this, was vital to his authenticity. He took journeys all over London, piecing together narratives about the nameless masses he saw. It's what gave him the edge. So many lawyers were out of touch with real life and stood in front of a judge and jury puzzled and blinded by the witnesses they examined.

To him, the people sat across from him were case studies; a cross section of the types of people he faced in court. Defending criminals was an art form, and one couldn't go into it blind. It was taxing work, and dangerous at times. He'd once been followed off a train at Cockfosters and held at knifepoint, as a young boy no older than fifteen robbed him of an expensive watch and his credit cards.

Occasionally, somebody might sneak the odd forbidden glance at somebody else's face, and if you made eye contact, they looked away, blushing and mortified by their faux pas.

But James had learned to assess the essence of another human being by not even looking at their face. He could sit opposite somebody and work out their passions and their fears just by sharing their air. And he wasn't often wrong.

James dedicated so much of his time to studying ordinary people because the cops often got the wrong person. Those he represented were fighting against prejudices created centuries before about privilege and propriety. James believed it was his job to throw a hand grenade against such entitlements and expose the judicial system for what it was: a machine that protected its own and cushioned those in authority, like his father. Deceit hid in unremarkable places and James took pride in exposing the layers of lies weighted against those who weren't members of the club, like the men sat opposite him.

Truth and integrity weren't the same thing, and those with advantages weren't necessarily the most honest. Sincerity wasn't born of fortune, just as deviance wasn't always a product of hardship.

Each time James represented an anti-hero, it was another blow for the establishment that had produced his father, and one more door closed to the past that had made him and haunted him.

He felt injustice rise up in his chest and envisaged his father smashing up an outboard motor, with a heavy sledgehammer, inside the boat shed at Warbury House.

James had inherited his temper.

The train shot through a tunnel and the metal against the tracks, along with the air screaming for space, created a high-pitched rush of noise which grated on his nerves, but it was soon over and the train pulled into Wanstead. It was as if somebody had turned a dial and the relief was instant. He stood up and held his briefcase tightly, checking the seat behind him, and holding onto the bar overhead.

The train slowed, and the hooded twentysomething stood up, too, and stepped in front of him, blocking his way. A waft of cologne caught in James's nostrils and he watched the stranger's back move to the door. James looked around and moved himself to the doorway, standing next to the tall man, who peered at him from under the dark hood.

James shifted away slightly, but the man kept staring.

The train stopped, jolting as it did so, and James held onto the rail, balancing his weight perfectly so the momentum made his body sway only slightly. He watched as the other man trotted onto the platform as soon as the doors opened, light on his feet and ready to run. Others followed him and he was taken by the rush to the exit. The train disappeared behind them with a whoosh of hot air. There was only one way to leave at Wanstead. There were no connecting lines here, and the single route led to the long escalator up to the outside world.

The suburb hadn't changed since the last time he'd been here, over ten years ago. The huge Wetherspoons pub on the corner – The George – was full to bursting, inside and out, with punters downing cold pints in the late sunshine, and students smoking and looking cool. He wasn't dressed for it, but his casual attitude more than made up for it. He never rushed anywhere, preferring to saunter and slow down with the waning of the sun.

He waited to cross at the lights and became aware of a large presence close to him. He glanced sideways and noticed the young man from the train standing next to him.

'You staring at something?' the young man asked.

'No, not at all,' James replied rapidly. He held up his free hand as if to reassure the man. Paranoid types were everywhere, it's what got most of his clients into trouble.

The lights changed and the green man beckoned them to cross.

'Loser,' the young man muttered as he walked away.

James would have laughed out loud had he not been so aware of his surroundings. East London wasn't the place to enter into a disagreement with a local youth. He should know. He'd represented a few. There was no money in it, sadly, but occasionally he still considered cases on the basis of injustice. A spot of 'David and Goliath' inspired work satisfied his desire to redress certain hardships he'd suffered himself. Criminal defence did pay handsomely, though, when you represented organised crime or corporate snakes and James happily worked with both.

He watched the man walk away and disappear down Wanstead High Street. Thankful that he'd lost interest in him, he headed to another pub, The Bull, where he'd arranged to meet a friend. A man he considered to be his brother.

He felt his phone vibrate in his pocket and realised that it was probably catching up with all the calls that had been waiting in the ether when he'd been underground, and he ignored it. When it buzzed another four or five times, he took it out of his pocket irritably and glanced at his missed messages.

Most of his notifications were turned to mute – he had no time for LinkedIn, WhatsApp or X if he wasn't in the mood, and he rarely was, though he didn't delete them entirely. Being connected was a double-edged sword, but it was still a novelty for somebody of James's generation and the lure of being needed, even if only a tiny bit by complete strangers, was intoxicating.

But it wasn't social media that caught his attention, it was a series of missed calls that made him stop in the middle of the high street outside The Bull.

He stared at the handset and recognised the number, which coincided with a sinking feeling in his gut.

This was it. It was happening, finally.

He'd only saved her number out of pragmatism – that one day he might need it. He'd told her he fully intended to delete it, and he never wanted to see her again, or hear from her, but he hadn't meant it. He knew that one day, he'd receive this call, and now he had to take it.

It stopped ringing but he wasn't off the hook. Just the name popping up on his screen had knocked him off kilter, sending him sideways into a spiral of discomfort.

It rang again and he almost dropped the damn thing, as if it were rigged to an electrical charge. He felt hot and grubby under his collar, which he tried to loosen. In doing so he dropped his briefcase and the contents spilled out onto the pavement. He knelt and began cleaning up, but suddenly there were hands helping him and he peered up into the face of the young man who'd got off at the tube station. The one who'd called him a loser, a little too aggressively, as if testing the water...

He stopped picking up documents and the man stared directly into his face and thrust something into his hand. At this distance, he was beautiful. His eyes were dark pools of uncertainty and innocence, and they reminded him of somebody else, from a different time. James couldn't speak.

The man got up and walked away. James watched him, then he looked down to see what the stranger had put into his hand. It was a note, and it had on it an address and nothing else. He quickly put it into his pocket and tidied the rest of his notes.

The phone rang again as he entered the beer garden in front of The Bull.

It was her again.

It was clear she wasn't going to leave him alone, so he answered.

'What do you want?' he asked rudely.

'I'm not calling to say hello,' the female voice said.

'So why bother at all?' James asked.

'It's Dad,' she said.

'Dad? What about the old bastard?'

Jude Fitzherbert was a part of his life he'd rather forget, until the time came to claim what was rightfully his. Money was the only form of communication he wanted with the poisonous old bigot.

'He's dead,' Hettie said.

'What? Like... really dead?' James asked.

He stood still, in the middle of the pavement, frozen in time, wondering if Hettie was toying with him. But he could tell by her voice that she wasn't: their father was one topic that Hettie could never bring herself to manipulate or lie about.

'Like, really dead. As in, deceased. The cancer killed him quicker than expected,' she said.

James couldn't speak. It wasn't that he didn't know what to say. There was a lot to say, and he'd planned it a thousand times in his head already. He could have talked for hours about how he'd wished his father dead for years. But no words came to him in that moment because all he could think about was that it had finally happened, and he didn't feel like he thought he would. Not at all. His guts turned over and he felt what could only be described as pain rising up from his belly to his throat.

'James?'

'Yes, I'm here. Fuck. It's so...'

'Unexpected? Well, not really, he was dying of cancer for a year.'

'He choked on his own poison,' he said.

Now it was his sister's turn to fall silent and he wondered if she was still on the other end of the line.

They were both stoic in their bravado, unwilling to break the silence.

Finally, he spoke.

'Thanks for letting me know, I guess. What happens now?'

James said the words to appease his sister. He was already aware of the arrangements from the law firm Dad used. Refusing to use James's own firm was supposed to be a blow to his son's ego, delivered cruelly, typical of his father. In the end – like now – it didn't matter at all.

'Like a funeral?' Hettie asked.

'Yes.'

'No. Things are on hold until we get there. Michael is dealing with the sundries.'

'Michael is still alive?' The butler, Dad's personal manservant at Warbury House, had been in the Fitzherbert employ for decades. 'Are you sure Michael didn't kill him off? Dad always said he'd look after him in his will.'

'On to money already, then?' Hettie asked acidly.

'Whatever, Hettie, I'm not arguing with you, though I know you'd love that. Did you say, "until we get there"?'

'Yes. Michael said Dad's lawyer wants us all there for the reading of the will. If we don't go, it doesn't get read.'

'That's ridiculous. Probate can sort it out.'

'James, don't be a fool. You know as well as I do that Dad will have gone over this to make the terms watertight. And we all have to be there.'

'Rosie, too?'

'Yes.'

'Hettie, don't even bother, you know as well as I do that she won't want to be involved.'

'Have you forgotten how persuasive I can be?'

'No, I'll never forget that, darling sister.'

'I'm relying on Rosie coming back to me today. I want to go ahead this weekend. Get it done. I know it's short notice but I'm sure you can make it work.'

'I wouldn't hold my breath for Rosie's reply,' James said.

'Oh, one more thing,' Hettie said.

'What?'

'Apparently, we must bring our partners and children,' Hettie said.

'What?'

'Do you want the money or not?'

'I suppose he always did make it clear that the family inheritance was reserved for the respectably hitched and abundantly fertile.'

She remained quiet and he fell into the trap of filling the gap. He couldn't bear silence.

'I'm just not comfortable bringing someone to Warbury... it does strange things to people,' he said.

'You're single, then?' she taunted him. 'Well, you'll have to pretend. Pay somebody. Isn't that what you always do anyway?'

'Fuck off, Hettie.'

She hung up.

He put his hand into his pocket and peered at the piece of paper he'd been given by the stranger. He glanced towards the pub then back at the address, which was less than five minutes away, then hailed a cab.

His best friend could wait.

Thirty minutes later, the same cabbie dropped him back in front of the garden at The Bull. The thing with illicit sex was that it needn't take time. He straightened his jacket and walked towards The Bull in a blur of aftershave and body sweat, aromas that James clung to greedily, like a whispered memory. He opened the door for a young couple staring into each other's eyes and giggling, like he had been half an hour ago when the stranger commended the size of his equipment. He smirked to himself as he let them pass and went into the bar.

People thought casual, anonymous sex was perilous, but to

James it was one of the only pastimes that kept him out of harm's way.

He found Donny nursing a pint and he raised his eyebrows at him, acknowledging his tardiness by way of an apology. But timekeeping wasn't something that was serious between them. Besides, Donny knew James better than anyone. He smiled to himself as he ordered a Coke. He paid for his drink, tapping his card, and took it to the table in the corner, next to the jukebox, which looked as though it was placed there merely for appearances, to give the sense of retro chic. Low conversations, mixed with acoustic pop drifting from the sound system above the bar, wafted around the small room, punctuated by the scraping of chairs along the wooden floor.

'You're late,' Donny said. He stood up.

'Hello, Donny,' James replied.

They embraced and James held onto his friend, exhaling deeply as he did so.

'It's good to see you,' James said. They sat down.

'What's up?' Donny said, pre-empting James's thoughts, as always.

James's phone pinged and he checked it, noting that his sister had forwarded him the instructions for the will reading at Warbury House. *Pending Rosie's reply,* it said, which galled him because she wasn't supposed to text him until she'd heard back from their sister.

Now she had an excuse to contact him, he thought, she'd never stop.

He noted that she was moving quickly on the arrangements. Of course, she'd want her money right away, he mused.

'Everything OK?' Donny asked.

A flash of something long forgotten interrupted James's train of thought and visions of the lake entered his head unannounced and unwelcome. The small boat wobbling from side to side and the touch of the water on his skin as it splashed over the side. The rhythm of the movement mesmerised him and he held onto the table as if he were steadying a vessel, with no navigational equipment, lost on the tide of the ocean, vulnerable to the elements and alone in the vast space.

'Hello?' Donny slid him out of his daydream by waving his hand in front of his face. Donny's words hit him like the noise from a speaker test at a concert: staccato and rough. James stared at him.

'My father just died,' James said nonchalantly.

Donny's face changed instantly.

'Already?'

'I know, it was quick.'

'So, it's a good job I'm down here, then. I hate London.'

James smiled and looked around the bar, wondering if The Bull served wine or cocktails. Beer filled him up too much and he hadn't eaten yet. If they'd been in the north, they'd be drinking pints of real ale. The Coke was to quench his thirst after his earlier exertions.

'Are we ready?' James asked him.

'Born ready, just say the word.'

James went to the bar to ask for a wine list. When he got back, Donny was on the phone. After he hung up, Donny asked him again if he was ready to put their plans into action.

'I suppose I am. It's a shock. I don't really know.'

'Are you changing your mind?' Donny asked.

The wine arrived, a bottle of Chablis, and James poured a glass, filling it to the top.

'Hey, go easy, mate.'

Donny wasn't best placed to lecture anybody on alcohol moderation, but James appreciated him trying, nonetheless.

'No, I haven't changed my mind,' he said.

Their friendship, solidified at school from the day Donny had taken a lacrosse stick and beaten James's tormentors, then nurtured through those years getting to know Donny's family, was the only thing in his life he could trust. Everything else was transitory and came and went like fortunes on the wind. Testimony, sworn oaths, investments and capital could all be flipped in an instant. But Donny was solid. If he said he'd do something, then he'd do it.

'So, Donny, you've dragged me out here, almost to Essex, practically an hour out of London, and you haven't even told me about the kids. And Nanny. How the hell is she?'

'It's not an hour out of the city. I chose somewhere... suburban,' Donny whispered. 'And you could ask Nanny yourself.'

Donny's stare made James feel ten years old and guilt swallowed him whole. He'd neglected Donny's mother recently, he knew. Nanny had taken him in when his own family didn't want him and he had fond memories of spending time with them in Merseyside, getting to know the family business.

Donny stroked his pint glass, then rubbed his hand over his mouth, the way butch, straight men do when they're thinking. They say it takes seven seconds to judge somebody, and James had liked Donny Salvatore within two or three. After the lacrosse incident, they'd been inseparable.

They'd do anything for each other. James helped Donny with the legal sticking spots inherent in the running of one of Merseyside's biggest drug rings, and in return, Donny provided less orthodox help to James when he was faced with certain obstacles to justice.

James had been wary of introducing him to his own family, because Jude Fitzherbert could never quite grasp that despite clamouring for the status of old money power, he still derived his fortune from new money graft. He would have doubtlessly looked down on the northern family, with their easy family traditions, accent and dialect. Jude Fitzherbert craved to be accepted into the noble traditions of the country, but in doing so, ignored the fact that all posh people were either gangsters themselves or descended from them. But he had introduced one member of his family to the Salvatores. A couple of summers, he'd taken Rosie up to Merseyside, and even though those memories seemed a lifetime ago, they were still fond ones.

'Rosie is playing hard to get, but she'll come around.'

Donny looked away.

'How long is it since you saw each other?'

Donny smiled, but James knew it was forced.

Donny was the brother James should have had. But in the next few weeks, he'd have to face the ghost of the one he'd lost, as well as his two sisters. The siblings' survival, as far back as he could remember, had been built on a series of alliances formed to fight off the worst cruelty of their father. But James hadn't indulged in childhood ententes since they'd all grown up and put fanciful dreams away, buried in the soil of Warbury House.

The news about his father had elicited a dead, cold nothingness inside his chest but had also awakened something else. He must be prepared to fend off the efforts of his biological family to carve up what was left of the Fitzherbert fortune and be ready to outmanoeuvre his sisters. Then, before too long, he would never have need to return to the place of his childhood again. But first, he must make sure that he got what was rightfully his.

And Donny was going to help him do it.

'I'll stay out of the way, she won't even recognise me now,' Donny said.

'Good point. It's not as if it's going to be a cosy reunion or anything,' James said, sipping his wine.

'No, it's not the time for that,' Donny said.

They chinked glasses and Donny's spilled a little, being the heavier of the two.

'The beer is fucking awful down here.'

'Don't worry, mate, you won't be here long. Once this is over, you can go home.'

'It'll be my first time seeing where you grew up,' Donny said.

'And the last.'

'And you're sure Rosie's OK with it? I mean, me handling everything?'

'Why wouldn't she be?'

'So you haven't told her.'

'Should I have done?'

Donny picked up his pint and drained it right to the bottom.

FOUR

Hettie

Hettie threw her phone on top of the bed and watched it bounce.

This was it, she thought.

Her father was dead. The childish part of her that had believed Warbury House was the whole world was no more. Both her parents were gone now, and she felt lost, as if the thing that anchored her was missing.

But she had her own children to think of now.

Being idle made her uncomfortable and she felt desperate to move her body to expend some of the nervous energy rising up inside it. Perhaps now, she considered, her life could move forward and not remain trapped by what Jude Fitzherbert dictated.

Finally, the time had come for everybody to grow up and to make their own way. They each had a decision to make and they were on their own. Which is why she'd hung up on James. Although she no longer felt responsible for the needs of her siblings, she was still burdened by them, and now,

THE SECRET INHERITANCE 33

with Father dead, she finally had an opportunity to change that.

It was a curious sensation. Part of her feared that she was being premature, hoping it was all over, but she told herself to calm down and focus on facts. Their father was gone. There was nothing left to worry about.

God knows, there'd be enough of that at Warbury House.

Assuming her brother and sister even turned up. But Hettie knew they would. Curiosity, greed, or good old-fashioned morbidity would draw them out of the holes in which they'd chosen to hide. They'd never let an opportunity to get their hands on their father's fortune slide by. Both insisted they didn't need their father's cash, but she knew better. Money was the same colour no matter how mighty your morals.

She straightened her cashmere jumper and ran her fingers through her long hair, which always made her feel better, as if she were pressing the restart button. She looked in the mirror and gave herself a silent nod of reassurance, willing herself to have faith that all would come good.

Taking her little brother by surprise had been deliciously entertaining and it reminded her of when they were growing up together, side by side, at Warbury House. She'd been the dutiful eldest child, fearful of stern reprisals from her father and he'd been a chaotic mess of frivolity and freedom.

She missed him. Her smile faded to a frown and the familiar feeling of discontent threatened to send her spiralling again. But she did, she realised, have something to do now. She needed to pack for a trip to Warbury House, her childhood home. Tingles of electricity coursed through her, and she flung open her wardrobe to search for clothes to pack.

That was better.

She hadn't decided how long she might stay at Warbury House, and assumed it would depend on the contents of her father's will. Still, she'd have to pack several changes of clothes:

there was outdoor wear, dinner wear, and casualwear to think of.

Locating suitcases and deciding what the children would need, too – including Edward – would keep her busy for the rest of the evening, and if she was distracted, then the noise inside her head would subside. It was why she filled her days with incessant chatter and occupation. It was the channel along which she deadened the memories that chased her.

Impressions that sat on top of her chest, like energetic children, couldn't hurt her if they were ignored, or kept just out of harm's way.

At the back of one wardrobe, she tugged on a small suitcase and it dislodged unexpectedly, sending her flying backwards. She sat awkwardly on the floor where she fell and the case landed on top of her. Behind it, she saw a flash of pink silk and a shadow of familiarity settled on top of her.

It was Rosie's blanket. Hettie had claimed it had been taken by another girl at St Mary's. Now she could never admit it was she who took it. The passing of time made it impossible to tell her sister the truth and Rosie would never believe her now. Being the eldest, and all that came with it, had been an unwanted responsibility for long enough.

Which was why she'd received the news first, because her father was a traditionalist. As the eldest, it was her task to inform the others of his death, just as it was her duty to make the arrangements. She'd always been singled out for her adherence to obligation, but inside, all she ever wanted was to play with her other siblings and enjoy their games. Instead, their play remained a secret, Rosie and James having formed a band of two. Rosie had detested her for so long that it was habit to lock horns whenever they were in the same room as one another. And Hettie was unsure if she had the commitment to change it. Too much had happened now. They were grown adults and had been for a long time. She felt that nothing would change Rosie's mind about the past.

The package had arrived by courier and had been presented in an ivory box bearing the Fitzherbert crest. She'd known straight away what it was. There were no more weddings to be celebrated at Warbury House. In fact, hers had been the last. There was only one thing it could be, therefore.

Thirteen years ago, to take away everybody's pain and divert their sorrow, she'd said yes to Edward, after a particularly heavy night out in London, and the rest was taken care of by planners, paid for by her father. It was fortunate for everybody concerned that he'd lost his faith only a year before, else Hettie might have delayed. In the end, there was no insistence on a priest, or a church, and they were married in the garden at Warbury House, and everybody said what a new era of happiness it ushered in.

But it hadn't lasted.

They'd never intended to get married at all. They'd had two children already – who were page boy and girl at their wedding – and they were happy living their own lives, Edward in London and Hettie at home, at Warbury House, where she belonged.

She had done it for her father. The wedding had been a distraction, and it had worked for a time – for the whole family – and the atmosphere at Warbury House had lightened.

For one whole day, Hettie had felt transported back to the time she'd been the centre of the universe and the apple of her father's eye. She had framed photos dotted around her Oxfordshire home to prove it.

The formal notification had been unnecessary and Hettie realised that her father remained aloof until the very end, unbending in his coldness towards his three remaining children. What really hurt was that neither Michael nor Clara had thought to call or visit. A personal message would have been welcome. A telephone call, even. All she had left of him were a few investments that Father had guided her on towards the end. She'd sniffed at first, but became interested when they started to accumulate wealth. It made her father chuckle, but it gave Hettie something approaching pride. After five or so years of investing in her own name, she was independently wealthy, but it was something she wasn't yet ready to share with anybody, not even her husband. It was just a shame she hadn't had the chance to prove to her father that she was a success. Everything was too late.

Edward had found her on the study floor, sobbing over the contents of the envelope, which she'd covered in snot and tears, late in the afternoon, hours after receiving the post. She'd fed and dealt with the children and taken herself off to somewhere she could let go of the frustration that had built up over decades.

So they'd all given up.

The wounds were too deep. The lies too true.

'He obviously left specific instructions for you to organise everything, and that shows that you're still his favourite,' Edward had soothed. '*Was* still his favourite,' he corrected himself. Which had led to another bout of bawling.

Slowly, but surely, Edward had cajoled her into the kitchen, and they'd begun to plan what they should do next. First, they delivered the news to their children, who were suitably bewildered, having not spent any time at Warbury House in years. Then he'd dictated the letter to Rosamunde, and they'd agreed that a quick phone call to James would do well enough.

Now the job was done, and she wasn't sure how she felt about it.

In control... or at least, that's how she'd hoped to feel, but something was slipping away from her even as she enjoyed the power of knowledge over her two siblings.

She'd had a head start, and, with Edward's help, had begun

the planning process. There was only one reason why her father would wish to inform her first and allow her to then pass on the information to her siblings, Edward said, and that was because he trusted her the most. Of course, they all had to be present for the reading of the will. That was to be expected. But it was she who he'd chosen to take charge.

Edward had been a darling. Already, after the shock of three days ago, he'd managed to pour salve on her wounds and allow her to process the devastating effects of the contents of the letter. If it wasn't for him, she'd have allowed the guilt to consume her, and the fact she and her father hadn't spoken in years to chew her up and spit her out. But Edward reminded her that she led a busy life with three children to take care of, and she wasn't the only one who possessed a phone. Her father had her number; all he'd had to do was dial it to speak to his grandchildren. He sent money, of course. But they stopped speaking. She couldn't remember the exact day it had happened, it just had.

Resentment bubbled under her ribcage as she recalled the gargantuan effort she'd expended to keep her family together before her mother passed. She'd tried to provide the glue when she fell ill. The incessant planning for family gatherings, Christmases and birthdays had exhausted her. Edward had finally called time and said enough was enough.

She ran her hands down skirts and jackets in her wardrobes, caressing the fabric and sniffing it deeply, closing her eyes and imagining the garments as outfits for the pantomime that might unfold at Warbury House next week.

The years of longing and waiting would come to an end, and she could finally expel her siblings from her life for good.

Warbury House would be hers, and she had the signed documents to prove it.

It was indisputable. *And yet...* She'd waited for this moment for a long time, but now she questioned if it really was what she wanted.

The sound of her phone startled her, and she scrabbled around, trying to find it, finally laying her hand on it under the as-yet-unmade bed.

It was Edward.

'Has Rosie replied?' he asked. They were both on edge.

She sighed. He was more eager than she was to get this over and done with.

'No.'

'What if she doesn't?'

'She will.'

'If she could speak, we could have just called her,' he said sarcastically.

'Don't forget that she chooses not to speak, Edward, it's a conscious decision. She's a drama queen,' Hettie reminded him. 'Though she might have grown up by now, I suppose…'

'Who might have grown up?'

Hettie spun around to see her eldest daughter stood in the doorway of her bedroom.

'Dear God, Kitty! I didn't hear you.' She told Edward she had to go and hung up, leaving him guessing and, she imagined, as frustrated as she was.

'Hello, darling! How was school?' she asked Kitty.

'I walked home with Ava, her boyfriend's a dick,' Kitty answered her mother. 'What were you talking about? Who might not reply to what?'

Hettie let the bad language go – one had to choose the battles to fight with teenagers.

'Nosy, it was a private conversation.'

'No, it wasn't. You said we must be "open to one another because we're a family". Surely I can't trust you if you don't trust me?' Kitty asked.

Hettie smiled, but not so widely that her daughter could see it. Kitty listened to everything intently and pointed out discrepancies whenever she got the chance.

Like now.

'Good point. Yes, this is an open family and you're right. Still, this is private and it's to do with Grandad's funeral. I'm not sure who will attend, that's all.'

'Was he popular? It'd be embarrassing if no one came, right?'

Kitty flung herself onto the bed and stared at the ceiling. Hettie wished her life was full of such simplicity.

'How was school?' Hettie asked again, to change the subject.

'Boring.'

It was the usual response. Kitty expected more from life in general and Hettie had no idea where the girl's fire came from. She fell silent and a memory of Warbury House fluttered across the room. It was of Rosie flinging herself onto her bed, just like Kitty had, and moaning about Clara missing one of their school plays. She couldn't remember either of them being upset that their own mother hadn't made it.

'I've got homework to do,' Kitty said finally, getting off the bed. 'Do we have to go to the funeral?'

'Yes, you do. Your grandfather wanted you there.'

'Why don't we see Auntie Rosie and Uncle James very much?'

'They're busy people. Rosie has her books and James is a lawyer. They have important jobs.'

'You always put yourself down, Mum. Being a parent is important, too. More important, actually.'

Kitty hovered at the doorway for a second then disappeared, leaving Hettie feeling emotionally raw. The love she felt for her daughter sat in direct conflict with what she felt for her sister, and she wished it wasn't so. She'd shared stolen feasts with Rosie. They'd paddled to the island together, taking baskets of food and ice creams which melted by the time they unpacked them. If only it were still as simple. Raising children had always been straightforward for Jude Fitzherbert, or so it seemed. It was quite simple to him, really: give a child good breeding and solid rules and they became winners. He had no patience for excuses.

Her father loved that she was a breeder of future Fitzherberts and rued the failure of his younger children to produce conquerors. Rosie was unlovable, mute and barren in her obsession with her books and had no room for romance. And James was simply odd, scared of girls since school and a coward when it came to responsibility. Both Hettie's younger siblings had shown utter selfishness when choosing to remain single and childless. It must have broken her father's heart, but then it meant that her own three offspring wouldn't have to compete when the time came. As his favourite, Jude Fitzherbert had promised her that everything would be passed to her and a portion of it held in trust for her children.

Hettie and Edward had already made plans for the lake. Their vision was to develop the island, but every time Hettie thought about it, she questioned whether, when the time came, she'd be able to go ahead with it. After all, it would involve moving the family cemetery and demolishing the ancient chapel.

She left her bedroom and went downstairs, heading outside to the end of the garden. She didn't stop walking until she reached the seat at the end which overlooked the fields behind the house. They'd learned three weeks ago those fields were to be developed into new housing. Jude's death couldn't have come at a better time, really. Moving away from here just in the nick of time was a godsend. She sat down heavily and gazed across the waving grass.

She heard footsteps behind her and turned around. Edward was walking across the lawn towards her. His face changed when he saw that she was crying. He dropped his briefcase and opened his arms for her to fall against his chest.

'This visit to Warbury House... It's all too much,' she whispered.

'I know. Don't worry, it'll all work out in the end.'

'You always say that. How do you know?'

'I don't. Nobody does. You've got the document, signed by your father, and really, Rosie and James shouldn't cause a fuss. If they do, you have grounds to sue.'

'James is a lawyer!'

'He's a criminal one, love, not probate,' he soothed. 'He's not an expert in family law.'

She leaned against him, smiling at the irony. 'I'm the only one who deserves the house. They've always hated it. They couldn't wait to get away. It's mine.'

'Of course it is, my love.'

'They're frauds. They've never loved that house.'

'Or your father,' Edward reminded her.

'Exactly. Or him.'

'What did that lawyer say – Ian Balfour?'

Hettie pulled away from him and gazed back towards the house.

'You had a meeting with him, didn't you?' Edward continued.

She nodded, distantly distracted. 'Yes, he reassured me that everything is in order, but he was cagey. I reckon Rosie and James have tried to get to him.'

'He is your father's lawyer. He must keep client confidentiality.'

'Yes. That's what I said, and I told him I'd never ask him to break it.'

Hettie stared over the fields which were to be developed shortly. 'It'll ruin the view,' she said.

'We won't be here to see it,' Edward said.

FIVE

Rosie

Rosie had read the letter ten times or more.

It sat on the floor, near Bobby, where she'd let it slide from her fingers.

He'd sniffed around it several times but had grown bored and gone back to his bed. Now, she leaned over to get her MacBook from the table.

She knew that Hettie would be waiting for a reply. And she also needed to pack for a journey she'd always wished would never come.

Writing to her sister was a precarious pursuit because, once given words of any kind, Hettie took them for herself and never gave them back.

The light across the city was fading and the streets were waking up to the nocturnal beasts who'd dominate them until dawn. The air was noticeably cooler, and Rosie got up to close the back doors. Bobby stirred and stared at her, sensing something was wrong. They were such simple creatures, dogs, yet it was as if they were plugged in to their surroundings.

They were comrades in quietness, for Bobby couldn't speak either.

She knelt to pet him, and he licked her fingers. It was all the communication she needed right now, in that moment.

She felt stuck between two places, and it was a real dilemma – reflected in her hesitation to flick on a light switch or to leave it and sit in the dark, which is where she thought she was better off. The dark was an unsettling, strange place. Like the dim corridors of St Mary's.

She went to the sink to fill up a glass with water, but her fingers wouldn't work properly. The dark corners played tricks with her mind, and she found herself back in the kitchen at her old school – though it wasn't really a kitchen, more of a room at the end of the corridor where they hid their snacks sent from home. It was next to the grand staircase, and adjacent to that, in the cupboard boarded up like a cell, it smelled like a mixture of vomit, cleaning products and old food.

It was only once inside that small cupboard that the entrance to the cellar and the well beneath was accessed. It was concealed by a trapdoor, through the cellar and past the dripping walls.

It beckoned her back to visit.

'You're so sensitive, Rosamunde,' Sister Agatha told her after freeing her from the hole again.

Rosie called it the hole because that's what it felt like; a pit of despair where things went to rot. It was cold, abandoned, and terrifying to her, and the first time felt like only yesterday. It was as if Hettie's letter had brought it back to her, through the words on the page, and everything threatened to be sucked right back inside it.

She heard the girls' voices, and they screamed inside her head. She felt their hands on her body, too, clawing and shoving. They had always come for her in the middle of the night, when the light outside faded into corners and shadows. In her deep state of sleep, she was always shocked at the rude awakening because even after they did it ten times – twenty, more – she never expected it. The first sign was a rush of cold air to her body and her nightgown, then wafting over her skin as it rode up. Then the hands that pinched and forced her body upright. After that, a sudden realisation that she wasn't in the middle of a vivid dream, but firmly in another reality: awake.

By the time they'd quickly dragged her out of bed and along the corridor, down the stairs, to the end of the hall, she was fully alert but powerless.

The first time had been intriguing, fun somehow. She'd giggled along with them. Along with Hettie.

That first time she'd imagined herself special, or maybe they held some secret midnight ritual where the little ones were woken up in the middle of the night to play and be initiated?

Until they opened the trapdoor, and pushed her into the cramped space under the stairs. Then her inauguration was not fun. It was hell.

Once inside, she examined what she could see – which wasn't much – but what she remembered she could still picture to this day. The underbelly of the wooden stairs, spiders' webs clinging to them, and the scent of wood polish, mixed with the musty odours of things left to die. That and the damp.

The floor was tiled, and the terracotta was always wet in places.

But the hidden tomb underneath was scariest of all. The walls were bare brick and she fancied she saw fingernails embedded in them where others had tried to escape.

Once in the bowels of the school, the gloom was absolute and the glimmers of light she thought she saw were firmly of her imagination and not real. Once submerged, she banged on the door above her, as it slammed shut, begging them to let her out, but the key turning in the lock always came: the scrape of the metal and the click when it met its connection, and she was sealed in there for as long as they wanted.

Her only companions were cold and damp, as well as the ghouls of her imagination. She'd felt her way around the abandoned well many times and discovered that it was bricked up to around waist height. She recalled the other girls saying that Sister Agatha had found the devil himself underneath the school and had ordered the pit be sealed, but there was still room for a small body like hers.

Was she the only one? Doubt crept into her memory and she saw flashes of others being dragged there, too. Had she seen Hettie taken there once?

She fought hard during the first couple of occasions, never giving up hope that she could find her way out. If only she was cleverer, or calmer, then she could figure it out and escape her tiny prison. But it was no use. She soon learned that fighting was pointless. And a waste of the precious energy she'd need to keep herself warm in the hours that followed. The well wall was sharp and bumpy, but she got to know the contours and traced her way along them, finding an indent where she could curl up to sleep.

Sometimes she changed position but mostly she coiled her body up tight into a ball and tried to radiate heat from her core to her fingers and toes. She'd rock back and forth and move her muscles to generate a little warmth, but often, if she couldn't find an old rag to sit on, she'd be on the bare floor and the frigid fingers of ice would penetrate her flimsy nightgown and soak up the damp. She'd count the drips from the nearest corner where groundwater seeped through the brick, and imagined a spider playing a string instrument in time with her breaths. She'd pick her nails and the flesh around them, chewing pieces of her own skin for want of something better to do.

Screaming never helped.

Neither did pleading.

Sound was irrelevant. Begging for mercy was a waste of time. They never set her free. The schoolgirls – encouraged by the nuns – were monsters.

Bobby beckoned Rosie out of her waking dream, and she realised that at some point during her vision of that terrifying past, she'd curled up in an armchair and tucked her feet up. Bobby was huddled up next to her, as close as he could get, keeping her feet warm and telling her she was safe, as if he knew how cold it had been in the hole, and had been with her the whole time she'd been sitting there, locked inside her nightmare.

Her arm had gone numb where she'd been laying on it, and she tried to wriggle free from the inertia to pump blood back into it so she could open a notification on her phone. The noise reminded her that she was grounded in the present and Hettie couldn't hurt her... yet.

The attachment was a royalty statement from her agent. The unfinished email to Hettie taunted her from the next line.

The royalty payment into her account had been seven figures again and the news made her smile. But it wasn't in a smug way, more one of relief that chipped away at her self-doubt, deposit by deposit, to bolster her sense of worth. Breaking free from her father's money was all that mattered. Curiously, it gave her the energy she needed to carefully word a response to her sister.

Dear Hettie…

She felt no emotion and abandoned the email as soon as she started, going back to her royalties. For a professional writer, she was hellishly avoidant when it came to putting down words. Melodies from the radio in the kitchen filled the rooms downstairs and she tapped her finger on the side of the MacBook.

Dear Hettie…

    She pressed delete.

Hettie…

    She deleted that, too.

Henrietta…

    That was a little better. Formal and distant.

Dear Henrietta,

I received your letter with surprise, I thought Pa would last a little longer, despite his illness.

    She was aware of every word she typed because she knew that Hettie would keep it and file it along with the others, for the future unknown, to use against her when the time came.

I will attend Warbury House for the reading of Pa's will, and be present for the hearing of his testament. I've been in touch with Radcliffe & Sons Solicitors, though why you haven't used James's firm, I'll leave to your good judgement.

    It wasn't a condemnation of her sister's acumen, just a reminder that James's work was as good as anyone's. She was also letting her sister know that she fully understood why she hadn't used them. Her email was physical proof that Rosie wasn't aware of the connection between James and Radcliffe & Sons.

    Hettie would know full well why Rosie had written it. And Rosie knew that Hettie knew she knew. It was a tedious game.

As you might be aware, I will travel alone. I remain single and I believe that Pa accounted for that in his final wishes, not expecting my coupling with another due to my current affliction, which is ongoing.

Pa's request for Kitty, Benji and Pippa to be present is odd and I wish he'd spared them such a trial, though I do look forward to seeing them.

Best wishes…

> She deleted the valediction.

Condolences…

> Too insincere.

Faithfully, Rosie.

> She sat back and congratulated herself. She was nothing if not faithful. Her devoted loyalty to her family had been tested several times and had never wavered, despite not sharing the family home for as long as Mother might have wanted. Rosie had covered all bases and pre-empted Hettie's arsenal of attack. *A weapon discovered is a weapon blunted…*
> She pressed send and a flush of adrenaline hit her stomach. She gulped her coffee to counter the hormone. Coffee killed anything.
> She closed her laptop and accepted she'd get no more writing done until this was all over, except in her notebook, of course, which she kept daily. It had started at St Mary's, and she'd found comfort in it when she was ostracised by the other girls. It had been her constant companion and her tower of strength since deciding to stop speaking.
> Some people sang to themselves in the shower, or exclaimed

when surprised, even if they were all alone. Others chatted incessantly on the phone, or online to strangers. Rosie found no need for any of that, and once she'd embraced silence, she'd felt relief, pure and simple. Eloquence didn't have to be noisy, and she spoke through her books.

Her house wasn't quiet, anything but; she had Bobby's whimpers and barks, and the radio and TV. But it was other people's voices that she had fled from. People spent so much time speaking, that real things – the things that truly mattered – got forgotten, and society was all the poorer for it.

In her writing, thousands of words converged on the page to create a story of depth and wonder, and it was her fingers creating that harmony, not her vocal cords, though she listened along to the narrative inside her head. Besides, being mute had honed her other senses. Her hearing, taste, touch and smell were extraordinarily sensitive and picked up signals that others often missed because they were too busy talking. Chatter confused the mind like a drug.

And that's what scared her about returning to Warbury House.

Next week promised to be so full of babble that it would take her a long time to recover, and she needed to preserve her strength. There would be lawyers, house staff – Michael and Clara – sympathetic locals, baggage carriers, caterers and taxi drivers. She knew her eyes must remain firmly on the prize, nothing could deter her from that. She was suitably prepared, and she wouldn't let anyone stand in her way. Hettie would assume that she'd want the house for herself, but nothing could be further from the truth. In fact, she wanted to witness its destruction, just as James had promised.

Her laptop pinged and she saw a reply from Hettie in her inbox already. She opened it and read that it was an out of office notification. Rosie couldn't help but snigger at the thought of Hettie having a real job that might necessitate an office. Her pretentiousness knew no bounds. Rosie had never met somebody so idle and yet so entitled. As she read it, another popped up, and this time it really was her. Like most people who set their emails to OOO, they checked for the important ones, and she imagined Hettie checking her inbox every five minutes to see if her little sister had contacted her.

Dear Rosie,

Thank you for your reply, I'm so looking forward to catching up with all your news. Are you still writing? It must be a terribly tough job, with all that wonderful competition out there! I'm currently reading *The Bones of Cameron Beck* by C.J. Dark and it's excellent – have you heard of him? Apparently, it's going to be made into a TV programme! The children are looking forward to seeing their auntie after so long.

With love,
Hettie x

Rosie reckoned her sister must have written the email in under a minute, and yet she still managed to squeeze in two exclamation marks and a kiss, as well as a dig at her lack of literary success compared to someone famous. She felt instantly fatigued. Her sister had always sucked up all the energy in a room, even when she wasn't in it. Her voracious appetite for mindless prattle could be felt hundreds of miles away inside Rosie's kitchen. It was as if Hettie hoovered up words, then regurgitated them, like some kind of sweet, syrupy glaze over a fat cake. She couldn't help herself. None of it was sincere, yet it read like a note from a sister who lived down the road and shared regular family dinners with her.

Next week would be hell.

Rosie's eyes lingered on the word *love* and the small x at the bottom of the email; an afterthought, no doubt, but a huge one and it marked the spot where Rosie had once been branded with her sister's endearment. But rather than make her softer, the words stiffened her resolve to see this out to the bitter end. Soon it would be over, and she would have triumphed without so much as a sound, or even half a word.

She closed her computer and went upstairs to pack.

SIX

James

James and Donny stood face to face in front of Wanstead tube station, swaying slightly and oblivious to passersby, who trickled slowly towards buses and cabs, making their plans to get home. They'd drunk far too much and James felt slightly wobbly.

Donny wrapped his arms around his surrogate brother and slapped him on the back.

'You need to call Mum,' Donny said. 'She misses you.'

James nodded. He'd thought of Nanny Salvatore as his own 'mum' since he was at school with Donny. She'd been more of a mother to him than anyone related to him through biology. Nanny regarded her sons as equals whether they'd been created inside her or not. James wasn't the only waif who'd been cast aside that she'd picked up over the years and taken home, fed and nurtured back to life. But James was acutely aware that he'd neglected her of late. Over the last few months, he'd withdrawn from everything he held dear, in preparation for what he knew was coming.

He giggled and hiccupped at the same time.

Donny rolled his eyes and supported the younger man. 'You OK to get home?'

'Of course!' James slurred.

'Listen, James, I know how you felt about your dad, but if it was me, I'd want to know what was in that will.'

James swayed slightly. 'I hated him.'

Then he straightened, as if his own words surprised him. The booze, and lack of food, had made him emotional but he knew his true feelings were safe with Donny.

'I know. Here's my ride... are you sure I can't drop you somewhere?'

James put his finger to his lips and hiccupped again.

'You know we're not supposed to be seen together,' James said, and giggled.

'Don't worry, I'm always discreet, you know that,' Donny said, slapping James on his back. They shook hands, and James pulled him in for another bear hug. Donny held him and James sighed as stress left his body.

He turned and walked to the tube entrance and didn't look back. Pressing his debit card against the pad, he went through the barrier, taking the lift down to the bowels of the earth, feeling the heat rising with every inch he descended.

The train was virtually empty, and James looked at his watch. It was gone eleven o'clock at night and he realised he was ravenous. The long journey seemed endless and when the train finally arrived at St Paul's, he felt weak and dog-tired. The ancient city centre was quiet as he emerged at ground level. The area thrived on day workers and hardly anyone lived there, but that's why he liked it.

He stared up at the dome of St Paul's Cathedral and felt a pang of nostalgia for the scripture that had been shoved down his throat at school. A good Catholic education was a double-edged sword, he'd worked out. It gave those who were subjected to its brainwashing an impressive bank of ancient knowledge of things that were once important, such as Latin, sin and purgatory. But it also left its students with an aching cavern of moral emptiness which was almost impossible to fill.

James was in a melancholy mood, and he realised that it had become a habit lately. He was plagued by the dilemma of if he was doing the right thing. He couldn't confide in anyone, because there was no one close enough he could trust; only his partner in the mission. And Donny.

He headed back to his flat, which was a short stagger from the station, with no eateries open in between, so he called Uber Eats and ordered a kebab to be delivered. The concierge let him in as he fiddled with his keys.

'Evening, Mr Fitzherbert.'

James saluted in return, followed by a wink, then he fumbled his way to the lift.

'I've got food coming,' he informed Eustace, the guard, who nodded. It was a regular occurrence after all.

His flat was in darkness, and he went straight to the kitchen tap and filled a large glass with water, gulping it down and contemplating what Donny had said.

He felt a little less inebriated and flicked off his shoes and undid his tie. He stared out of his large window, over the river, mesmerised by the lights of the city. They were a source of security for him, as a Christmas tree might be to a child. There was something comforting about the cleanness of them. From his insulated cocoon he couldn't hear the city, so he just watched her.

His mood was gloomy and he stared at his phone, looking for a connection that never came.

Nanny stayed up late. Like him, she was a nocturnal animal. Darkness masked their hunting patterns, but also gave the predator peace and quiet to perform necessary tasks.

He called her number.

Sweat clung to his body like a cheap nylon vest and he

unbuttoned his shirt. His eyes wandered to a fat legal binder on the coffee table in front of him. It had languished there for weeks, though the case was closed and had been successfully defeated. It wasn't one of his cases. He'd borrowed it from the department of family law. It was a probate case, where two siblings had fought over their mother's estate. Each had sabotaged it, through various subterfuge and sheer spite, in such a fashion that it was worth nothing after they'd fought over it in an open court.

It had been such a waste. A needless exercise in malice, driven by an insatiable appetite for vengeance. It still chilled him to think of the warring family, and how far they were willing to descend into their own hate to simply say they'd won.

The only winners were the lawyers and James had made around two hundred grand from it, simply by consulting on the potential criminal aspects of it.

Nanny operated through the use of burner phones, even though her work in the family business had slowed down.

She answered straight away.

'James! I saved your number. I knew you would call me. You still refuse to close your eyes?'

Her Naples accent skipped through the phone, and he couldn't help but smile. Her voice always did this to him. There was something magical about the maternal attention of a nurturing voice, and it was magnified by the low melodic vibrations of a foreign accent. Her Italian inflection made him think of freshly baked bread and homemade pasta lathered with lashings of tomato sauce.

'When are you coming to see me? It has been so long. Donny has been ill, did he tell you? The summer is long and hot this year for England and reminds me of Napoli. James, tell me your news.'

The machine gun assault was just what he needed, and he imagined that folk with real parents got this intravenous hit every time they spoke to one another. It felt like what he assumed home to be.

He felt his body relax, and he put his feet up on the low table.

'I've been busy at work, it's been crazy.'

'I know, you saved me five million last year!'

'Nanny, not over the phone,' he shushed her, and she laughed deeply.

They weren't an accountancy firm, but Nanny had never understood that. The legality of some of her dealings enabled him to cut corners to pass on to the team who dealt with her finances. It wasn't done purely out of love, though, she paid him a handsome cut.

'I have some news,' he said.

'You are getting married? You have a boyfriend, and you didn't tell me? You know I want to be the first to meet him!'

'No, Nanny, I don't have a... partner.' His mouth couldn't get around the shapes needed to verbalise the word boyfriend or husband. Years of shame and indoctrination at the hands of his father had rubbed out his innate ability to articulate such things.

'My father died recently.'

For once, in hundreds, if not thousands of conversations with Nanny, the phone went silent, and he could hear her breathing.

'My poor boy. The bastard is dead and still you grieve. I know. Old habits do not die, and he is your flesh and blood. I understand. Will there be a funeral? Will you go, my darling boy?'

'I actually have no idea. I need to attend the reading of his will first.'

'His what?'

'*Ultime volontá*. His wishes. His estate...'

'Ahhh, now I understand. You want to make sure those

blood-sucking sisters of yours get nothing. Good boy. Can I help?'

James conjured images of Nanny Salvatore arranging vans of black-clad assassins brandishing Uzis, jumping out to ambush his family at Warbury House, and their bodies strewn across the lawn down to the lake, bullet ridden, and crying out for mercy. But the vision disappeared as he came to his senses and admitted there had been enough tragedy at Warbury House to last a lifetime.

Nanny wouldn't understand that he saw sufficient retribution on a daily basis to prevent the urge to commission it for himself. He was leaving that to his sisters.

'No thank you, Nanny, it will be fine.'

'Fine is an English word that was invented to paper over the cracks. So, who will read his... what did you call it?'

'His will.'

'Ah, who will read it?'

'Lawyers.'

'*Mamma mia*, do you trust them? You're the only lawyer I ever trusted.'

'They're my lawyers.'

'Ah. Clever boy. Do your sisters know?'

'They will soon.'

'*Mi piccolo*... You need to make sure you eat before you go, build your strength, like for a war. Garibaldi didn't fight on an empty stomach.'

'I will. Nanny, can I ask you a question?'

'*Ovviamente!* You need money? A car?'

'Nothing like that. It's about Donny. Is he fully better?'

James tried to hide the fact that this wasn't the first he'd heard that Donny had suffered with his health lately. Tonight, he'd found him his usual self, if a little overweight and tired. He admonished himself for not paying more attention.

Another silence sat between them.

'It came back, and I don't know this time. He's keeping it from me. A mother knows.'

Her words were crushing. People only spoke like that when they referred to cancer, the disease with no name. James wasn't superstitious but understood why articulating something brought bad luck. It was the same with voicing words that referred to sexuality, or a man loving another man. He'd thought taboos were for old people until he learned the value of keeping quiet. The irony that forbidden subjects were usually linked to the sacred, traditional or familial was lost on those who avoided speaking about them.

'I saw him tonight, he looked well,' James lied. He'd noticed Donny's sickly pallor and the shadows under his eyes, and he'd felt guilty about expecting so much from him. But James himself was too wrapped up in the drama created by Hettie to be aware of anybody else's suffering. It made him awash with guilt.

'Ah, good! My boys together like the old days.'

Nanny's deep chuckle made him smile and he didn't even notice his other phone flashing, so comfortable he was with her, and happy he'd called. Time stood still when you were inside her love.

She had six children. Donny was the eldest, with James fitting in somewhere in the middle. A straggler. Nobody had invited him to join the family, it had just happened organically, and their generosity had sustained him through some of the worst times with his own blood relatives. They'd embraced Rosie for a time, too. The times she'd accompanied him on visits to the north, they'd visited the beach and spent days hanging out together. He'd even thought Donny and Rosie close at one point, but it all ended abruptly after a summer he'd rather forget.

Some people didn't deserve to have children.

'Donny spends too much time at work,' Nanny said.

Knifepoints of guilt stabbed at him.

'OK, I hear you. I'll try to talk him into slowing down.'

'In my day, I had no choice, but Donny has a family and a good life. Talk some sense into him, James.'

He hung up with a promise to make a journey up to Liverpool to see her sometime soon and also to get Donny to take a break.

After they'd finished what they were working on.

A light tap on the door told him his food had arrived, and he tipped the delivery driver generously. Then he devoured the contents of the yellow box. It was still warm, and the aroma of fat, cumin, chilli and grilled meat filled the room. He wiped his mouth with a paper towel supplied inside the box and sat back, then he stared at the door.

Sarah would still be up. She always was. Like he and Nanny, Sarah was a creature of the night who struggled to sleep during the hours of rest for everybody else. He got up and went to the door, opened it and walked across the hallway to the only other apartment on his level. There were six in total over three floors. His and Sarah's were at the top, and as a result of having premium views, were the most expensive. He didn't ask how she afforded it on her own and Sarah didn't inquire after his financial security either. Their friendship was based on less serious things.

He knocked lightly on her door, and it didn't take long for her to answer.

'Late one?' she asked him, standing back, allowing him in. He'd sobered up somewhat since leaving Donny and walked in a straight line into her apartment, going straight to the window. The view was almost identical to his and he stared at the lights.

'You OK?' she asked, closing the door.

'I've got a huge favour to ask.'

'Fire away.'

'I want you to pretend to be my fiancée.'

Sarah laughed out loud. 'What?' She sat down and he joined her and took her hand.

'You like adventure, right?'

'Of course.'

'I need to present a stable and respectable front to my hideous family, and I can't think of anyone better than you.'

'How exciting. Will I meet them? For real?'

'Yes, and I trust you entirely.'

'When?'

'Next week?'

'Where are we going?'

'Oxfordshire, all expenses paid.'

'Do I have to kiss you?'

'Ugh, no.' James slapped her thigh. 'We just need to be close and loving, I suppose. Happy couples don't kiss in public, do they?'

'I wouldn't know, I've never been in a relationship that lasted more than three months.'

'We can talk about the details before we go. There's one more thing.'

'Yes?'

'Can you pretend to be pregnant as well?'

SEVEN

Hettie

The microwave pinged and Hettie removed the bowl, checking that all the kernels of corn had popped. Sometimes they didn't and it irritated her because they were supposed to. She poured syrup, covering the pieces liberally, then took the bowl to the lounge, where Edward and the children were waiting to start a film. Her husband had complained of a hard day and was virtually asleep on a large sofa, while the children snuggled under blankets on their own individual couches. The blinds were closed, and the only light was cast by a small lamp. The kids liked it dark on cinema night, though Kitty reminded her mother that she wasn't a kid anymore and was attending family movie night because she had no choice. Hettie winked at her. They'd agreed together that if Kitty at least pretended to watch the movie, she could catch up with her friends on her phone, under the blanket, out of the sight of the younger two.

Their bags were packed for the short journey to Warbury House tomorrow, and it was all Hettie had thought of. It was a little like Christmas Eve when a child desperately wishes the hours to disappear.

She tried to distract herself with her children. She studied them one by one. At sixteen, Kitty fancied herself as much older and Hettie watched her profile as she gawped at her phone. Kitty suffered from the common teenage affliction of antisocial arrogance and reminded Hettie of Rosie at the same age. The thought invaded her head before she could control it and the vision took her by surprise. She'd always felt responsible for her siblings, like a mother should. A dark shadow interrupted her thoughts, and she imagined Kitty locked in a dark damp hole, screaming to be let out, and how she might cope with it. She tore her eyes away from her eldest daughter and instead looked at her son Benji, who, at fourteen, still secretly enjoyed being a part of something if it involved treats. Pippa was the youngest, at twelve, and the most enthusiastic. Benji and Pippa dug their hands into the bowl of popcorn and Hettie marvelled at how naturally comfortable they both were with each other as brother and sister.

'What have we chosen?' Hettie asked.

'*Ice Age 4*,' the two youngest announced.

Hettie stole a glance at Kitty, who rolled her eyes and studied her phone under her blanket.

'What about Dad? He's asleep,' Benji said.

Hettie glanced at Edward and saw his eyes closed and heard tiny purrs coming from his nose. She threw a cushion at him, and he woke with a splutter, which made the children laugh.

'Right then, shall we start?'

Edward coughed and sat up, dazed. Benji and Pippa fed themselves popcorn and smiled as the credits whirred. Scrat filled the screen and chased his beloved acorn, and laughter filled the room. Even Kitty chuckled, and Hettie saw that she was secretly watching, too. Edward drifted back off to sleep.

THE SECRET INHERITANCE 63

Hettie watched the images on the screen but didn't follow the story. Instead, her mind drifted to Warbury House. The sound of Edward's dozing, as well as her younger children's tittering, faded into the background as her eyes fluttered closed and she found herself transported back in time, to a less settled period, when neither she, Rosie nor James ever curled up on sofas to watch a film with their parents.

She recalled how she and Rosie, at the same age as Kitty, had lived away from home for over a decade and had been forced to grow up before was natural, relying on their wits for survival.

It had almost broken Rosie, and Hettie knew her little sister still blamed her for that.

Hettie shifted her weight as if she could still feel the sting on her backside from the cane that had swung across it, leaving red welts across her flesh. The scars were no longer there but the humiliation still burned.

'I'll beat respect into you.' Sister Agatha's words stung her memory and she twitched, her hand going to her thigh and stroking it as if applying the salve that never came.

Hettie closed her eyes, and the spectre of St Mary's filled her vision. The dark menacing turrets above a cathedral-like structure, their windows fast closed, keeping silent secrets, and the sound of the wind howling along the corridors. Sister Agatha believed in the educational value of severe hardship. Punishments were dished out like cold soup and none of the girls ever knew what they'd done to deserve it. Rosie was so tiny and young that at first, she'd thought Sister Agatha's orders a game. From then on, Rosie was the Sister's first choice when seeking a girl to hurt.

Hettie had tried to protect her, but she knew it hadn't been enough.

She reached across to the small table and picked up her wine glass, sipping the cool liquid, which reminded her of summer days at Warbury, once they'd grown up and were allowed to run free. They stole bottles of booze from the cellar and chased each other around the lawns. Her Chardonnay was the colour of straw, the same colour as the beds they made in the haystack. Their father bought the stuff every year from a neighbouring farmer who'd fallen on hard times and who Dad took pity on. They didn't need it, but every year trucks of it arrived and Michael shovelled it into pens that he'd built from felled trees. It made an excellent hiding spot.

She watched Benji and Pippa screaming at the TV when the mammoths slipped on the ice shelf. *No wonder they became extinct.*

Hettie took a minute to marvel at Benji's innocence. She recalled James at that age suddenly and remembered his eyes filling with tears the first time she'd seen her father's hand slicing through the air to strike him.

She flinched and bit her lip.

The darkness of the room concentrated the energy inside her head as it conspired against her and threw up images that she didn't want to face. She'd buried so many memories that the resurfacing of them since her father's death had taken her by surprise and hijacked her peace. If only she could see some shaft of light, other than from the TV and the make-believe, two-dimensional monsters on the screen.

The flickering images lit the faces of her family and cast shadows across the room.

'*Let me out!*' she heard inside her head.

It had only been in the last couple of years – when the savages inside her own head had come alive – that she acknowledged what Rosie must have felt when she was locked underneath the stairs, all alone, desperate and terrified, abandoned and forgotten, in the hole.

It had seemed so innocent at the time.

A prank. Some harmless fun.

But Rosie hadn't even been Pippa's age when it had started and when Hettie looked at her youngest daughter now, and how tiny she was, how in need she was of safety and security, Hettie could hardly stand the burning guilt that raged inside her body.

It hadn't been her idea to lock her sister in the dark, but that wasn't why she felt the sting of contrition. Passersby and those who watched were just as culpable as the ringleader, wasn't that what she said to the children when they saw somebody being picked on?

Every child who'd stood on top of the locked trapdoor, listening to Rosie's screams – as Sister Agatha stood idly by, pretending not to hear – was to blame for the wickedness shown those long nights.

The burden on Hettie felt heavier by the day as news of their father's death brought her period of hiding to an end and the time to face her sister ever closer. But Hettie believed she'd had no choice, because if it hadn't been Rosie, it would have been her, and perhaps she'd be the one now mute, or worse, lying under the earth on the island in the middle of the lake at Warbury House.

The face of her youngest brother filled her vision and suddenly his face merged with Benji's. But it wasn't a moment of nostalgia. The appearance of Christian's face in her head reminded her not of all the good times with her brother, but augmented the fact that she was lucky to survive, when he hadn't.

Growing up at Warbury House had been like natural selection in its plainest form, and Hettie was a fighter. Christian had been a pacifist. A conscientious objector, felled in the act of crisis when faced with a mightier enemy.

Clara had said he was too perfect to live, too sweet to survive the excrement of toil. He died unsullied and never grew old.

Whatever the reason, it was just as hard to accept today as it had been then. Maybe that's why she found herself so protective of her own children, Kitty in particular; her daughter approaching the age Christian had been when he died could be triggering hidden anxiety that she'd shut out. She was aware of the dramatic nature of her drifting thoughts, but she'd been encouraged by her therapist to follow emotions through when they arose.

Had her own mother ever looked at Christian the way Hettie did Benji? Had she felt any kind of love or affection towards her children at all? Hettie had no idea and would never know now. It wasn't something they'd ever discussed as a family. Conversation was something that belonged to people who were open to negotiation. Her family was past that. Perhaps she could piece together answers from signals given in other ways but when she looked at the evidence – being sent away to school at five years old until the age of eighteen, the military style practices in their home, the silence, the lack of physical touch – then it was difficult – impossible even – to find ways in which her parents might have loved her.

Her phone vibrated and she peeked at it in the darkness, not wanting to disturb the kids.

It was a reply from Rosie.

Henrietta,

Yes, I've heard of C.J. Dark, like everyone else.

Please give my love to the children.

Rosie

Curt. Aloof. Jealous. She put the phone back down by her side, tucking it between her thigh and the sofa, as if it'd be safe there and no more words could escape from it and disturb her.

She'd hit a nerve. Rosie hadn't mentioned anything else. Nothing about Warbury House. Nothing about her family, or James, or even Christian. All she'd done was acknowledge a great novelist. A competitor, if Rosie was even still writing. Her little sister was struggling – Hettie could feel it through the airwaves, or microwaves, or whatever made the internet work.

Rosie was desperate.

And still angry.

Her little sister's quest to amount to something in the face of her father's disapproval had come to nothing after all this time, and Rosie, she realised now, would be desperate for money.

EIGHT

Rosie

Early the next morning, Rosie listened to a podcast on meditation techniques and clearing chakras, but nothing could wash away the feeling of dread that sat under her ribcage after yesterday's news. And the brief communication with Hettie had rattled her.

C.J. Dark was indeed a celebrated crime author, and one who, when Rosie had been starting out, she'd have looked up to. Hettie was goading her, like she always had. Even before she set off to travel to Oxfordshire to face her older sister, Rosie realised that the game had already begun. They'd both been waiting for this moment for a long time. It was nothing new, but still, the thought of battling with her sister made Rosie feel sick. She recognised her malady as fear and tried to work out the source of it. She knew that recognition of a trigger was halfway to dealing with it, but Hettie's words – and the sound of her voice in Rosie's head – had got under her skin. Her nerves were shot to pieces.

What was she scared of?

She'd loaded the washing machine with a final wash and prepared Bobby's last meal before she took him to Nellie's house – a fellow writer who she'd met online, and who happened to live close by. Rosie had introduced herself to Nellie with her pseudonym – Roberta Todd – and that's what Nellie had always known her as. Nellie was a struggling author, with the same literary agency as Rosie's, and they belonged to the same writers' Facebook group, as well as one on Instagram and X.

But, so far, Hettie hadn't tracked her down. When Facebook first started, Rosie knew that it had thrilled Hettie and satisfied her voyeuristic tendencies with more information than she could ever know what to do with. The potential pool of information for gossip, slander and stalking played into the hands of people like her sister who loved to live their lives through others. Her sister even had her own fake persona online, and Rosie had scrolled through it, snorting at some of the things she claimed, such as being a champion kayaker. Hettie had no privacy settings on her profiles, just as she had none on her mouth.

As a result of what was available online, Rosie knew more about her sister now than she had thirty years ago, when they'd shared a bed, or played in camps on the island in the middle of the lake. Or pretended they were champion kayakers going to rescue stranded puppies. But then it had been all made up, like one of Rosie's novels. For children, and authors, reality was whatever you made it.

Since growing up and becoming a writer, Rosie had been anonymous and unavailable. She didn't share photographs and her profile pictures were of scenes found online. Nobody except Nellie, Bobby and her agent knew what she looked like, not even her publisher. Even on Zoom, she blanked out her face, which she was perfectly entitled to do, and with today's obsession with personal prerogative, no one questioned her. She'd made it clear from the outset that she wasn't interested in promoting herself, which, she was initially told, was a mistake. To get anywhere in a cut-throat industry, they said, she had to thrust herself into everyone's homes via their gadgets. But she didn't want to. And, thanks to healthy sales, she could afford to avoid those functions that made her feel uncomfortable. She did plenty of articles and Q&As online, which kept interested parties at bay. She'd been asked to attend libraries, bookshops, and parties, like all authors at some stage in their careers, but she politely declined. She didn't appear on panels or at festivals. She wasn't concerned what people thought of her. She was not her books, and they were not her.

It also meant that she could decline the offers of cash from her father. What she really craved, and protected fiercely, was her anonymity.

Nellie also wrote under a pseudonym, and she was quite happy remaining anonymous, too, which was why Rosie knew she could trust her with her own privacy, or rather, Roberta Todd's.

She'd bathed Bobby earlier, in preparation for his own little mini break. He'd stared at her, fluffed up like an Ewok. She smiled as he shimmied his backside around the house, trying to shake off the scent of cleanliness, before she walked him the short distance to Nellie's house. Nellie always loved having him, and he'd have a wonderful holiday with her, though he'd certainly be ruined with cooked chicken and sharing her bed. But it was one less thing for Rosie to worry about when she was away.

When she returned from Nellie's, the nerves had kicked in and she checked off her list of things to do before it was time to leave. She'd cancelled the milk delivery, as well as her fresh organic vegetable box. She'd also informed her agent and publisher that she'd be unavailable unless it was an emergency.

Now, before setting off, she stared at the dresser in her

kitchen. She'd been avoiding the drawer where she kept an envelope full of photographs. It was all she had of her time at Warbury House, when she had still carried the weight of the Fitzherbert name. She approached the drawer and opened it, rooting around until she found it, reaching for it and taking it to the kitchen table, where she sat down and sipped the last of her coffee. If she was going to travel back to where it all started, she needed to be prepared.

His photo was on the top and she remembered the last time she'd gone through them. She'd left this one there, in prime position, on purpose.

His face was bright and round, tanned by a long summer, and his golden hair framed his face. He was on a boat, on the lake, at Warbury House. His body was becoming hard and muscular, and his athletic build was visible underneath his adolescence. He must have been fifteen years old, growing into a tall and lean young man.

His eyes pierced Rosie's soul and she wiped away tears that formed at the corner of her own eyes. She sniffed and her throat betrayed her. She made sounds, even though she did not speak. She was still allowed to be a noisy crier. She always had been, which is why Sister Agatha got so much enjoyment from her torture. She enjoyed her screams. Rosie also sighed occasionally, she could laugh and tut, too. There was a thousand ways for humans to communicate, and only one involved words. The face and respiratory organs could make up for a whole catalogue of phrases unspoken – it was how humans got along while speaking different languages, after all.

She recalled, on holiday once in France, Mother imitating a chicken to the local butcher because she couldn't remember the word. Christian had reminded her.

'Mother, it's *poulet*.'

They'd all rolled around laughing.

Rosie had always preferred non-lexical sounds to real words. They said so much more to her.

She and Christian had had their own language. They communicated in non-verbal signs, late at night, inside camps built in their bedrooms or out amongst the trees. Their long summers were filled with transmitting signals that nobody else understood. When those moments, stolen in time, abruptly ended, cruelly ripped away, when school terms restarted, they promised to write letters, but it wasn't the same. Their stories were whispers and dreams, never put into formal language.

Instead, they had waited, and now she wished they hadn't.

Her tears dripped onto the photograph, and she went to get a cloth to wipe it, careful not to damage the pictures or make their colours fade. She kept them in the drawer to protect them, fearing that if she framed them and decorated the house with them, the sun would take him away from her all over again.

She flicked through the other photos.

Another showed all the siblings lined up together, as if on a military parade. It was taken on the shore of Lake Königssee in Germany. Their parents had been wanderers and they'd wanted to instil the love of travel in their children. The problem was that if a child is unhappy at home, then they won't be happy anywhere else either. Their smiles were forced, despite the wondrous vista in the background. The staggering command of the Bavarian Alps behind them, and the clear blue water, popped out of the scene, but their eyes were dead.

She touched her finger carefully to Christian's face and tried to remember his smell. She put the photo to her nose, but it had no aroma at all, just the inside of a musty drawer.

I'm coming home, Christian...

The echo of the words in her head startled her and for a second she wondered if she'd articulated them out loud, but she hadn't. She felt almost ashamed of having nearly caught herself out. The words were so deafening inside her head that she still felt a buzzing sensation behind her ears.

She shuffled the photographs to see if any more of them spoke to her, and stopped at another one of Christian in his school uniform. The boys had hated St Christopher's as much as she hated St Mary's.

At this, her thoughts then turned to James.

Soon, she'd see the faces of her siblings in the flesh, and she had no idea how she'd react.

Fear gripped her and for a moment she doubted she could pull it off... then James's words soothed her. They'd planned this for so long, now wasn't the time to crumble, but she questioned if she could go through with it.

Then she heard Christian's voice, as clear and emphatic as if he was standing right next to her and was holding her hand.

Of course, you can. Do it for me.

She snapped out of the grip of self-pity that had imprisoned her momentarily and looked out of the window for her taxi. She checked the prompt cards she carried with her on the rare occasions she ventured outside. She relied on them to be her voice. She used them and text messages to get her message across, but it was only very occasionally that she was challenged on her choice not to speak. One man on a publishing call once had acted offended as if her preference was somehow personal. Another time, on a dash to a supermarket to buy coconut milk for a Thai curry, the woman at the checkout had made her ordeal excruciating, by pretending to be baffled when she showed her communication cards. In the end she'd opted for her emergency card, which stated she was stricken by throat cancer. That usually did the trick and shut inquiries down. Still, on that occasion, she'd left the supermarket red-faced, and had forgotten her coconut milk and had to go back for it anyway.

She pulled on her coat and listened to the house, which was ready to remain silent in her absence, quite devoid of life. Bobby wasn't in the habit of growling or barking much, but his sabbatical was still felt keenly. She sensed a shift in the mood of the walls and noticed a gap in her universe where his warm body should have been. She sat waiting for the taxi at the window seat in her small conservatory at the back of the house. Hettie would have called it an *orangery* and it rattled Rosie that her sister entered her head so easily. She was doing that a lot lately, and it was as if Warbury House was reaching out to her because it knew she was almost home. Soon, she'd have to listen to her sister's voice running riot through her head, pitching and wailing like an international freight train, and she knew she'd want to speak even less. She'd believed once that, at some point, she'd feel compelled to talk again, but even when she'd met James in London recently, it hadn't been like that. It had been quite the opposite, and she hadn't felt the need to fill any gaps at all.

James's voice was altogether less offensive than Hettie's. At Warbury House, he'd been overpowered. Hettie had done enough talking for all of them. Rosie had almost forgotten what it sounded like, until he'd offered to take her to lunch in London ten weeks ago. She'd met a man in place of the boy she'd left. But he was still the same inside. He spoke quietly, putting in little effort, and studied all those around him in an attempt to read them. On the outside he looked like a hotshot lawyer, but in the caverns of his eyes, it was obvious he was just as scared as she was.

But the thought of seeing Clara calmed her. After all, she'd been with Father when he finally passed. Then Rosie panicked: what if she wasn't there? Michael, too, might have decided to move on. What if the house was now completely devoid of real life and truly empty, and there were only lawyers to talk to?

She opened her phone and texted James, asking him if he was aware of Clara or Michael's plans. He replied straight away, understanding her deep anxiety and matching it. She

THE SECRET INHERITANCE

imagined him commanding an office overlooking the Thames, dishing out orders and saving people's lives, for what else does a criminal lawyer do? But then she also envisaged him biting his nails or talking to himself like he used to in his sleep. They were similar beasts: easily spooked, though it didn't mean they weren't brave.

Nervous?

She sent back a thumbs-up emoji.

He reassured her that Clara and Michael were still at Warbury House, for now.

She fiddled with her bags and got up to walk to the hallway, in case she'd missed a car pulling up outside. There was still half an hour to go before her allotted ride showed up, and she felt silly worrying so much. She checked her hair with her fingers and imagined that it looked just fine. She applied her lipstick in the reflection from the kettle's surface. Rosie didn't own mirrors. She hated them as much as others detested monsters and ghouls. They had a habit of shining back trickery and nonsense, and not telling the truth, and she didn't trust them.

Her clothes suddenly felt uncomfortable, and she shivered. Her shoes were newly polished, like Clara had taught her, and she'd matched a summer dress with a green cardigan and bag. She hadn't wanted to pack too many changes of clothes because of the impression it could leave with everyone. She neither wanted to give the image of showiness, nor austerity – both encouraged animosity.

There was no draught coming from outside and the sun was shining so there was no good reason for her to have goosebumps, except the sinking feeling she had in her gut, which had already caused her to miss breakfast.

She'd tried to come up with a new storyline for a book to fill some time, but it had been no use. Her thoughts were dragged back to Warbury House, as surely as she was destined to step foot inside its creaking walls in a couple of hours.

That's what she remembered most of all: the noise.

She realised that her memories were old. They were outdated. Everything might have changed. Even the lake could be overgrown with plants and bushes encroaching from the edges, a thousand secrets disappearing forever in the depths. She understood that her shiver was likely her body's response to venturing into an unwelcome situation where she had little control. In the coming hours and days – if she had any knowledge of lawyers at all, and her father – she'd know soon enough. Her greatest fear was that going back there would betray her very soul and she'd find herself throttled by the urge to speak. She recalled cracks and whispers along the corridors, and the gravel outside shifting under the weight of people's feet, and the dragging of a dead animal.

Father's sobbing before Christian's funeral.

The scrape, scrape of metal and wood as a rusty old plough, connected to a wheelbarrow, was hauled back and forth, up and down to the lake, taking bits of waste to be sunk to the bottom. The plop of a police diver jumping in from a boat, descending with dredging equipment...

But most of all, she was terrified that she'd hear Christian.

NINE

James

Reluctantly, James packed his computer away into his laptop case and rested it on his desk. He went to the window and stared out over the city. The magnificent buildings and bridges looked like toys from where he stood, only the movement of people all around them, on top of them, and inside them, made them real.

In here, he was the boss. Out there, he was just another person, wandering along London's lonely streets, looking for something.

His phone buzzed and, seeing it was Sarah, he answered.

'So, I've packed skirts and blouses, seeing as I'm a respectable fiancée now.'

'I asked you to be my fiancée, not respectable.'

'Ha. Very funny. What are they like? You said be grey, but what does that mean? I don't know how to be grey.'

It was true. Sarah normally wore bright colours. Her body sang in greens, yellows and oranges, partnered with garish jewellery bought at Camden market.

'I was thinking kind of...'
'Heterosexual?'
'Yes.'
'Bland?'
'Kind of.'
'To fit in?'
'Yes.'
'God, James, who are these people? Do they have sexual organs?'
'I'm not sure.'
'What will happen if you just turn up as yourself?'
Silence.
'Sorry.'
'Don't be. If it's too much...'
'No. You're not getting away with self-pity. I've said I'll come and I'm going to do you proud. I will look out my most insipid belongings and watch back-to-back episodes of *The Good Life* on UK Gold until I get it right. I won't let you down.'
'Maybe I *should* just be me.'
'And let them eat you alive? Like you said, you risk being cut out altogether if they think you've erred from your father's wishes. It's only a few days. Will we sleep together?'
'Ugh.'
'Thanks a lot. I was rather looking forward to that bit, actually. We can gossip about them until the small hours, under a duvet, with a bottle of vintage wine from your father's cellar.'
'Now you're talking.'
'I'm almost done. There's just one more thing.'
'What's that?'
'What if I fancy one of your sisters?'
He hung up. She'd at least made him smile.

Christian had always turned up as himself. Even from birth, he'd managed to just be. He'd appeared into their lives, as if by magic, after one summer term. They'd been delivered back to

Warbury House from their respective boarding schools, and there he'd been, in mother's arms: a new baby.

'Look what I've got,' she'd said.

James had returned home first, from St Christopher's. The girls had come back that evening and he'd been holding Christian, on his lap, staring at his tiny fingers and toes.

'What's that?'

It had been Hettie who was most curious. Rosie had been distracted. Moody. Discontent.

Hettie had burst through the doors, full of life, demanding to know what their new gift was. She'd poked the baby and made him cry and their mother had laughed. James had found it curious behaviour, as he'd always thought that babies were fragile creatures to be cared for. Why else were they all wrapped in blankets? But his mother and sister had scared it by shouting into its face and dropping things close to where he was sleeping.

James had thought little of it until Rosie – who was only seven years old at the time – had told him in secret later that she'd asked Clara what babies needed, and she'd told her they required love, and that was all. Rosie spent the whole summer tending to the baby's needs after that, asking to feed him from a bottle and change his nappies, which were tricky because Clara insisted on using the old-fashioned cloth ones. James would sit and watch, and they made up games pretending that they were Christian's parents. James carved a stick from the forest and smoked it like a pipe and asked when his dinner was ready, whilst Rosie wore one of Clara's aprons and stirred food on her toy cooker.

They didn't play their game in front of Mother and Father, but in secret.

No one knew, except Clara, and she would never tell, because she loved Christian like they did.

That's when they'd first made up their coded language, to

only be spoken to each other. It had been a collection of noises rather than words, and they added to their vocabulary each night, after saying goodnight to Christian.

One day they caught Hettie taking Christian down to the lake in her doll's pushchair. At eleven years old, Hettie was allowed to wander off and play on her own, whereas Clara kept a strict eye on the younger two, and now the baby, who Mother wasn't very interested in. That summer, Mother and Father had travelled to Paris, where Rosie said people fell in love. But it didn't work for Mother and Father because they came back miserable. They told everybody, including Clara and Michael, that they'd been blissfully happy in Paris, so James didn't understand why they looked sad on their return.

They arrived home just in time to say goodbye to their children before they were herded back to boarding school. Christian was three months old, propped up in a bouncy seat and babbling words in Rosie's secret tongue.

It was one of the nicest summers he could remember at Warbury House.

Shadows crossed his desk and he realised he'd been daydreaming for a good forty minutes. It was the telephone that jolted him.

Donny had returned his call.

'Hey, how's things? I spoke to Nanny like you asked.'

'Thanks, pal, she misses you. I take it you were able to avoid questions about me and you?'

'Just about. I do need to go up there to see her, though. She sounded different. And she's worried about you.'

'She's getting old, James. We're not teenagers anymore. She's in her late seventies. She can still make a man shake with fear but putting her socks on is a bit of an effort these days.'

James laughed at the thought, but inside it made him feel wistful that Nanny was aging. It was never meant to be. They were all supposed to live forever, frozen in time, like they were when they spent long summers together. James realised that if Nanny was growing old, then so, too, was he, and he wasn't ready. Donny completely avoided the reference to his own health, like James knew he would.

'I'm all sorted,' Donny said. 'Ready to go.'

'Look, if you want to stay with your family then I understand,' James said.

'Are you kidding? I love getting away from the noise. I live for my work, so change the record, James. More importantly, how are *you* feeling?' Donny put the emphasis back in his court. James knew it was pointless to push him.

'Surreal.'

'Because the old bastard is finally gone, and you can get on with the rest of your life?'

'Something like that. I think. Maybe I'll get there and realise that it wasn't worth it. That I made a mistake. What if I should have given them another chance?'

He was babbling, thinking out loud.

'Bullshit. You got this. We haven't been preparing for this for nothing. Have you changed your mind? You're going soft on me?'

James didn't reply straight away.

He heard Donny sigh. This was all so straightforward for him. If somebody crossed you, and harmed one of your own, then retribution was swift and effective. No discussion. Donny's ethical boundaries were as clear as his pure-grade cocaine, which he then had cut with talc. Donny had never struggled with right and wrong. Morally, he'd known his path all his life and never wavered from it, but James had always wrestled with finding it in the first place, and then sticking to it. His experience of reward and punishment was so random, like the time his father told him he was proud of him for punching a boy at school in the face, but then got mad when he stuck up for Rosie. None of it made any sense and it had always been a battle for him to adhere to a path of any meaning. He made his decisions on the spot – except this one – and then fretted about it.

'You're panicking,' Donny told him. 'Which is also part of the plan. You must get this out of your system and then you'll see it's the right thing to do.'

'But what if I get there and change my mind?'

'You won't.'

'But I might.'

'Then I'll bang your head against a brick wall until you stop doing it and remember what we agreed. If you don't throw the first punch, they'll tear you to pieces.'

'I must face it.'

'That's better. You can do this. Be proud and strong.'

'I wish I could do it as myself,' James said. 'I want to go there and tell them all who I am.'

'Burst in there in a cape and a wand and make everything better, and you'll all get on happily ever after?'

'I know it's bullshit.'

'You only have to pretend for a little longer, then it'll all be over.'

'I'm taking my neighbour. She's agreed to be my fiancée for the week.'

'What? Holy shit, James. Can't you just do anything slowly? Does everything have to be so dramatic. Jesus. Who is she?'

'You've met her. She lives in the other apartment on my floor. Sarah.'

'Oh, that woman, she's gorgeous, she'll do a cracking job. Can she be my fiancée, too? Do you realise how risky it is, though? Why put yourself through it just for those bastards who deserve nothing?'

'My father made very clear the terms under which he'd bequeath his money. Gay and unmarried didn't make the cut.

Or childless. Except Rosie, of course. He made an exception for her.'

'So she never married and had kids? I remember her saying that's what she wanted,' Donny said.

'She told you that?' James asked.

Donny backtracked. 'It was a long time ago. Maybe I was wrong. I thought she was the marrying type, you know?'

James paused before answering. A memory jumped into his mind, but he pushed it away just as soon as it had come.

'When was the last time you saw each other?' James asked instead.

Donny sighed audibly and blew out air. 'Can't even remember, mate.'

James waited.

'Anyway, how will you tackle the marriage-and-kids thing?'

James was brought firmly back to his present dilemmas and hesitated.

'Sarah is going to pretend to be pregnant as well?'

James could never lie to Donny, who knew him so well. He'd always been terrible at it.

'It'll be fine,' James said.

'James, nothing in this life is ever fine when dealing with other people's money. I should know. I've had brothers, sisters, aunties and uncles turn on me over the stuff. It's toxic. It eats away at the mind. They'll smell a rat.'

'No, they won't. They can't hurt me anymore. He's dead and my sisters are just as terrified as I am. Everybody will be on their best behaviour.'

He'd known Sarah for four years. It was long enough, surely? He was only fooling his sisters. They were so taken up with their own self-obsession that they'd never notice.

But Michael would know...

He told himself to stop punishing himself. He and Sarah had sat up until the early hours researching the symptoms of pregnancy for the first three months. It wasn't practical for her to fake a pregnancy later on in her term, as it would involve stuffing cushions up her shirt and that was just stupid. This way, she could say she was only just past her first trimester and still not have a 'bump'. They'd discussed it so much they almost believed it themselves. They were well-rehearsed and prepared, he told himself. He even thought Sarah might be getting a little too excited about the whole affair.

'I've always wanted a baby,' she'd told him.

It was just what Rosie had said to him, years ago, by the lake, after their mother's funeral. She was buried alongside Christian on the island.

His sister's experience, and the resulting loss, was so long ago it was as if it had never even happened. Nobody ever talked about it. Not even Rosie anymore.

The boy had been taken away from her, after she'd laboured to give birth to him for two days. Father said she'd ruin her life if she kept him. Giving him up was non-negotiable.

Fear gripped James. What if his impending fatherhood brought back terrible memories for Rosie? Then he realised his foolish mistake. Maybe asking Sarah to fake a pregnancy had been a step too far. He suddenly felt like a child who'd been scolded for stealing something from the kitchen. They were all adults, yet their father's grasp still haunted them from beyond the grave and he wasn't even buried yet.

Women got pregnant every day, he told himself; Rosie must be surrounded by them on the street in London, or through work. He wondered if she lived a glamorous life as a writer or if she was an introvert. He couldn't imagine her going to glitzy parties or rubbing shoulders with famous authors. He'd looked up her name and couldn't find any of her books, so he assumed she wrote under a pseudonym. Clever.

Melancholy tugged at him as he realised they'd spent so much time over the last few months discussing their family history but not the son she'd lost. But sometimes he felt as though dwelling on the past sucked the life force out of each other, instead of getting to know one another all over again and building a new future.

That would come in good time. For now, they had a job to do. He'd approached her with the proposal, and he'd been surprised how quickly she'd agreed. For now, it was their secret. Only Donny and the lawyer, Ian Balfour, knew anything about what they intended for Warbury House.

He and Sarah had run through their story several times. They didn't have trouble forging a history of shared likes and dislikes, because they knew those already. It was one of the many reasons they were friends.

James had shrunk inwardly at the thought of a neighbour initially. He'd enjoyed having the floor of his building to himself for a few years before Sarah moved in. He'd marked the date of her arrival as the end of his splendid isolation on the calendar as if it were the funeral of a loved one.

But Sarah had proved him wrong. They appreciated the same music – 80s pop and rock, as well as modern rap, and they booked tickets for the same plays – Berkoff, T.S. Eliot, Arthur Miller and the odd Shakespeare tragedy. His comedies were farcical, they both agreed, and they'd laughed out loud at the irony. They shopped in the same places and were culinary snobs. Sarah existed courtesy of her father's generous allowance, as far as James had pried, and she had a complicated family, but they wouldn't divulge much of that on their trip. Suffice to say, that they each felt confident – about as confident as any young couple – to cover for each other's story if they had to. They probably knew more about each other than the average lovers about London, that was for sure. The only thing they didn't know was what it was like to make love, and stare into each other's eyes at the point when adoration is all consuming and pulls on the heart like the claw of an eagle, but that wasn't for polite discussion anyway.

'Can you trust Sarah?' Donny pulled him out of his melancholic spiral into the past.

'Absolutely. She can't wait to meet them all.'

'That sounds a little premature to me,' Donny said.

'But genuine. My sisters are incorrigible gossips and they'll all be competing, even Clara.'

'Especially Clara, from what you've told me,' Donny said. 'If I was wanting to find out all your darkest secrets, I'd put my money on her. I bet that housekeeper of yours knows everything.'

James laughed.

'She certainly thinks she does.'

TEN

Hettie

Hettie watched Harold, her children's pet rabbit, hopping about the garden. His fur was pure white and it contrasted with the foliage under the bushes and trees. He wouldn't last a day in the real world. She reckoned white rabbits were bred for homes such as hers, without consideration for their true heritage. It stopped and munched silently, ignoring its surroundings. If a fox jumped out now and grabbed it, Harold probably wouldn't even squeak. She marvelled at how innocently it assumed its nonchalance would keep it alive and she wished she enjoyed the same luxury.

Rosie was a white rabbit.

But was she like Harold, trusting and harmless, or like the famous friend of *Alice in Wonderland*? A nervous fraud. Either way, Rosie no longer chattered.

She closed the door on Harold and walked towards the oven, where a loaf of soda bread was baking. It wasn't her recipe, and she hadn't even made it from scratch; it was a shop-bought pre-packed mix, which she had only to combine with water and bake. The kitchen smelled divine, like Clara's used to. The loaf would provide a simple lunch before setting off for Warbury House. Much-needed sustenance for the trials ahead.

She flicked on the radio, never having been able to feel settled in silence. Their luggage had sat in the hallway fully packed since last night, and the car was refuelled to maximum, not that it needed it for an hour's drive across Oxfordshire. She tried to will time to move quicker, but it refused, and she watched the bread in the oven. The radio was set to chill music, because she couldn't bear the news. It was so depressing. The brutality of London was spreading to the counties and into homes like hers. Only last week, a respectable boy from a wealthy family had been stabbed to death at a party in Norfolk. The offender had been in a drug-fuelled rage, apparently. Nowhere was safe.

She fussed around the cooker, peering inside, ready with oven gloves to take out the bread when it was ready. She opened the door and decided it was the right colour and removed the tin.

'Shit!' She threw it onto the countertop with a clatter and ripped off the oven glove. It had a hole in it, and she'd burned her thumb. She put her hand under cold water, with the tap gushing, and her erratic movement made it splutter all over the floor. The cold water didn't help and a blister was forming already. She kicked a cupboard in frustration. The day was slowly turning to disaster. Nothing was going right.

A tiny voice in her head told her that it was punishment for ignoring Harold the rabbit. She'd been cruel to the animal by locking him outside and this was karmic transference. She heard the nuns tutting and swishing their skirts in disgust and she could almost feel their scratchy habits glancing against her body. It's why she used expensive softening products in her washing machine and had done since leaving the hellish place. Hettie couldn't stand stiff, rough cloth.

She glanced over to the kitchen door and spotted Harold peering in at her. He nibbled whatever he'd found in the garden and sat patiently waiting to be let in. He wasn't used to having to wait, though. She stared at him through the glass and he munched away, on the other side of the closed door, oblivious to her pain. She turned her back on him and went to the drawer where she kept the medicines and pulled out a plaster to wrap the end of her thumb. The pain was excruciating, and a thousand needles travelled up her hand to her wrist. It throbbed and she fastened the plaster tightly, hoping the wave of pain would subside. She glanced at the bread, regretting the effort, and admonished herself for trying to be perfect at everything. It didn't change anything.

She'd never agreed to be a housewife. She couldn't recall the day, or the year it had happened, but it had. One day, she realised her life was full of children and her own dreams were lost. She had assumed that looking after children, as well as a man, would be easy. They'd planned to have nannies – like her own parents – but could never seem to afford it. The allowance from her father, along with Edward's wage, was eaten up by life. But as time went by, she lost the confidence and the skills to search for a real job. And Edward spent more time in London.

It turned out that staying at home wasn't very satisfying at all. In fact, it was dull, mundane work. But now she was too far down the pit of uselessness to ever train for anything or get a decent job. She'd toyed with the idea of getting a local part-time position, simply to stave off the boredom once the children went to school, but when she'd looked at what was on offer, she'd turned up her nose at the secretarial positions that required computer efficiency, or the work for the library. The pay was awful and akin to slave labour. She wanted something where she could converse with people who were like her, but there was nothing.

'That's unskilled work for you,' Edward had said nonchalantly, making her blood boil over.

She knew he was secretly relieved that she was unemployable, knowing full well how hard she'd find it to secure something suitable for an educated woman of her standing and background. Men like Edward needed to have their women stuck at home to make themselves look better.

Now, as she dried her hands, she realised, with horror, that she'd done exactly what she said she'd never do: turn out like her mother. She felt as though she was rotting away, having used up the best part of her life raising children, and now she was in her forties, approaching forty-five, with no skills, no ambition, and no prospects.

She felt trapped, and she realised that she'd been looking forward to her father dying more than she cared to admit. It was a real chance to change. Edward wanted another baby, but it was the last thing she desired. It was just what her mother had done. She'd given in.

Three was plenty.

Everything had changed when Christian came along. Her mother should have stopped at three.

She'd hated him.

He took everything away.

She and Rosie spent their school terms dreaming of coming home to freedom, some kind of love, at least from Clara, and long holidays doing whatever they pleased.

Christian changed all that.

Mother became deeply depressed, and Father disappeared for long chunks of time. Nothing was ever the same again.

Hettie recalled one day when she had locked the door while Christian had been outside in his pram, underneath the huge cherry tree, for fresh air and a nap, and she'd been tasked with keeping an eye on him. She'd bolted the utility door and leaned against it, feeling a delicious satisfaction that she no longer had to look at him. Just like she was doing to Harold now.

She glanced at the kitchen door, and he was gone, and she sighed with relief. She was glad that he wasn't still sat there, staring at her with accusing eyes telling her she was an appalling guardian.

Back in the grips of that day, she remembered Rosie's scream from outside in the garden and James joining her in shouting for Clara. Then the fuss and drama which followed. The commotion outside the back of the house reached a shouting crescendo when the gardener joined in and she remembered holding her hands over her ears, shutting out the cries for help. Instead, she ran up the stairs and to her room, and dived under her pillow, forcing it over her head. Then, on second thoughts, she'd run her hot water tap in her bathroom, and wet a flannel, then held it to her face, producing fat round cheeks, so by the time mother found her, she was in bed, complaining of a fever, and denying that Clara ever asked her to watch the pram. She must have been confused, she told her mother, and asked Rosie instead.

Mother believed her and Rosie spent the afternoon and evening in the hole: the space between the utility and the cellar where Mother put them when they were naughty. Usually, Clara let them out to give them bowls of soup and drinks from the larder, but not that night. Rosie stayed in there until the next day when Clara was instructed to let her out and give her something to eat.

It had been a silly punishment in Hettie's view. Christian was fine. A big fat crow had sat on his pram and pecked at him, making him cry, and Clara had panicked. Still, Hettie never came clean and told the truth, and allowed Rosie to suffer the torture of the hole.

Rosie spent her life being terrified of confined spaces and all the time she was locked in there, like at school, she'd never uttered a sound. Which only made Hettie want to see her in there more.

Her telephone ringing from inside her bag caught her attention. She took it out with her good hand, and answered. It was Ian Balfour, Father's lawyer.

'Ian? I didn't expect you to call today.'

She was flustered at the intrusion and tried to still herself.

'I know I shouldn't be calling you like this, but I couldn't help it. I've been thinking about it all week, since—'

'When I saw your number, I assumed it was business.'

'Like I assumed it was business when you came to my office last week?'

Hettie grimaced, but kept her voice light. It had been an innocent mistake, but now he wouldn't leave her alone.

'We shouldn't talk like this over the phone,' she said.

'No one will know,' he breathed. 'I can't wait to see you again.'

'We must be careful,' she told him.

'Don't worry, I can do that for you.'

Hettie felt queasy, but her attention was taken away from the prospect of keeping Ian Balfour at bay by the squawking of a bird. She glanced at the back door leading to the garden.

'Oh God, I need to go.'

She threw her phone down on the kitchen counter and rushed to the back door, flinging it open, and ran across the garden, flapping her arms up and down at the huge bird. It was a kite – or even a bloody eagle – and it was gigantic, and it had Harold in its claws. Its wings flapped and swished the air around her ears, but she wasn't perturbed, taking off her shoes to throw at it. Finally, it dropped the poor rabbit and flew away, looking back at her with its prehistoric eyes bleeding menace from the sides of its head, as if warning her that he'd be back. She stood in the middle of the garden and panted, her chest heaving up and down, then looked for Harold.

The poor bunny lay on his side and stared blindly up at her, terribly wounded, blood seeping through his fur. His nose was still, though his heart thumped fast in his chest. She sank down to her knees and lifted him gently, resting him on her lap. Blood oozed from his neck and soaked into her skirt, but she comforted him and ignored the mess. She rocked him and said his name, willing him to show her some sign that he was OK. His nose twitched from side to side.

She swallowed and forced herself to examine his wound. It looked a lot worse than it really was. She carried him into the kitchen and ran water in the sink, then took a clean cloth and bathed the cut. It cleaned up well and she caught her breath, staring at him and telling him she was sorry.

'Oh, Harold, please don't die,' she said.

You can't even be trusted to look after a rabbit.

It was Sister Agatha's voice she heard rattling around her head.

Harold made a noise, and she watched him return to his senses. She held him to her face and felt his heart beating.

Sister Agatha was wrong.

But perhaps it was a sign? She questioned if she could go through with the ruse of deceiving her siblings out of the Warbury Estate. But then she dismissed her panic as nerves. She found a bandage in the medicine drawer and wrapped it around Harold's neck.

She'd have a hell of a story to tell the kids when they returned from school.

When they did, it was Benji who noticed the cut on the back of her arm. The bird's talons had scraped her and she hadn't even noticed. Wasn't that what good mothers did? Ignore their own wounds for the sake of those around her? Didn't that prove she was a loving mother, unlike her own? All three children had taken turns comforting poor Harold, who was bandaged and nonchalantly contented, chomping on a carrot, before they piled into the car. The rabbit was a stoic sufferer and they stuck to their original plan of Harold being looked after by the neighbours. The dramatic story about the bird had also served to distract Hettie, but as they set off for their journey into the countryside, Hettie felt her mood shift and she didn't look back. Benji was engrossed in YouTube or TikTok on his phone and Pippa read a book about some Korean love story that was all the rage. And Kitty was like a padlocked chest, perhaps considering a new love interest. She certainly had been grumpy about having to take time off school and it had to be because of a boy. Hettie studied her daughter's face, which was covered in shadows, and tried to remember what it was like to be a teenager. It was so long ago, and she'd spent most of it at St Mary's.

As Edward drove, Hettie breathed a sigh of relief that they were finally on their way. Her guts were a torrent of slush and she stared out of the window looking for a sign that everything would turn out the way she wanted. Edward reached over from the driver's seat and patted her hand – the one she'd hurt – and she pulled it away. He recoiled, looking offended. She'd been promising him the estate their entire marriage, but now she wasn't so sure she could go through with it.

Suddenly, her desire to share Warbury House with him disappeared, and she'd found herself dreaming about the refurbishment without Edward in it.

The sun shone through the windscreen straight at them and they lowered the visors to protect their eyes, until they turned west and hit the country roads leading to Hettie's childhood home.

'I've had confirmation from Clara that dinner will be served at seven sharp,' Hettie said, pulling away from Edward's hurt stare.

'Why does your family have servants, Mum?' Kitty asked.

Hettie laughed.

'They're not servants, they're staff. They have well-paid jobs and enjoy their work.'

'Did you ever hear them say that? I think service work is demeaning and those who do it are desperate with no other choices. Therefore, those who employ them are exploiting the lower social classes.'

'It's not exploitation. Clara has been with us since I was born, and Michael came to us from a minor royal household – he preferred it at Warbury House.'

'How do you even know? I bet they hate their jobs. I would.'

Hettie's face turned pink. She glanced in the passenger-side wing mirror and caught Kitty smirking. Pippa watched her older sister and smiled, too. Benji remained oblivious in the middle. They were good questions and Hettie realised she couldn't answer them. She'd always assumed Clara and Michael to be part of Warbury House and in truth had never questioned if they enjoyed it or not.

Kitty wasn't letting go. 'It's no different to slavery, really. The domination of one group of people over another, simply because they have more money.'

'Kitty, that's enough, you really don't understand these things. Slavery indeed! Goodness, whatever next.'

'Execution, usually. In a normal job, employees have certain rights, such as the right of complaint and the right of fair working hours and conditions. I bet if Clara ever complained, she'd be sacked or, worse, banished to the cellar.'

'Really? The cellar?' Pippa asked, with a worried, small voice.

'Kitty!' Hettie scolded.

'Is there really a cellar, though, Mum?' Kitty asked.

Hettie fell silent.

Edward missed a turn, and he swore, indicating to take the next left.

'Are we nearly there yet?' Benji asked, taking his headphones out of his ears.

Hettie turned around, reached out to pat his arm and caught sight of Pippa's face. Her expression was a mixture of confusion and fear.

'Don't worry, Pippa, there's no dark, scary cellar, your sister is winding you up.' Hettie glared at her eldest daughter.

Hettie's guts turned over as they approached the stone gates of Warbury House. She sat up and peered ahead, desperate to catch the first glimpse of her home. She turned back to watch the road and Edward swerved to miss an oncoming tractor.

'Christ!' he shouted.

It did nothing for her nerves and the sun shone into her eyes, momentarily blinding her, but not before she imagined a black space under the house, where she and Rosie had played dare. Hettie recalled their screams when as a joke, James hid in there and jumped out at them. 'It's an old house, but there's nothing to be frightened of, I promise.'

'It's huge. Grandad was so rich,' Kitty said.

Hettie followed her daughter's gaze and saw Warbury House in a different light to the one she'd grown up with. She accepted that it must look like the setting of an awesome and wondrous childhood, but the truth was much darker.

'Shona sent me an article on the estate, Mum. She said it was in a magazine and the money came from slavery. God, that's so embarrassing.'

Kitty finished reading from her phone and put it back in her pocket, as if from there it couldn't embarrass her. She stared out of the window. Hettie felt sorry for her. Privilege was something that people thought made things easier, and she never expected sympathy for it, but in reality, all it meant was that there was more to lose.

The driveway was wide and lined with high trees and flowers adorned the bushes all the way up the hill until the main house came into view and Hettie found herself holding her breath. She'd forgotten how vast it was, because she'd never had a reason to question it before now. She'd taken it all for granted. Kitty, too, had fallen silent, overwhelmed by Warbury House.

Hettie felt like a dead man walking to his execution, and as they neared the entrance, and she spotted Clara and Michael standing ceremoniously at the bottom of the stone steps, all she wanted to do was run away.

ELEVEN

Rosie

Rosie had been fortunate with her taxi driver. She was a woman who was quite as happy to chat as she was to stay quiet. At first, the driver had asked a few questions, before realising her mistake and apologising, to which Rosie had smiled sweetly. Now, she was quiet, and Rosie stared out of the window at the static London traffic, wishing she could stay in the thick of it, behind the throng of vehicles, safely encased in metal from behind which she didn't need to emerge into the open. She took the private cab all the way to Paddington, so she didn't have to negotiate the tube. Crowds made her nervous. The jostling and shoving reminded her of St Mary's and the way the nuns used to push the girls ahead of them in the chapel, as if into the jaws of the devil himself, to save themselves.

Memories of those times flooded her brain occasionally, and they were as intense as they were unwelcome, but she couldn't escape them, so she allowed them to swirl around her head. She made storylines from them to make them fictional so they couldn't cause her any more harm. It was her way of making sense from chaos. If she could conjure up characters and scenarios that made up a familiar tale, with a beginning, middle and an end, then all the better. If it sold, then she'd done her job.

She'd never set a story in an actual nunnery or a school because she feared that doing so might give vitality to the terror and make it come true all over again. She couldn't gamble with the life she'd created away from all that, so she kept it hidden, but she could feel the outlines of long-hidden ghouls emerging from the shadows as she journeyed towards her childhood home, and the closer she got, the nearer they became.

And the more she felt Christian by her side.

It had started with the camping trip.

He was eleven years old, and she was eighteen. The boys' schoolmaster had arranged to take the boys to a beach in Wales, where they were to camp, forage, walk and cook, and generally bond with the great outdoors. She recalled packing Christian's bag for him. James had turned twenty but often helped with the younger boys at his old school, in between his university terms, just down the road, at Oxford. Christian was beyond excited that weekend, as she'd loaded chocolate and sweets into secret compartments of his bag so Mother wouldn't find them.

'It'll make a man of him,' Father said.

Christian didn't know how a man was supposed to behave, and Rosie's experience was tainted with disappointment so she couldn't tell him either, though now she wished she had tried. She'd hugged him close as the driver came to collect him, and she'd walked him to the car. Mother and Father weren't there to wave goodbye. She recalled her sense of desolation on Christian's behalf, but he didn't seem to notice like she had.

By the time he arrived back, everything had changed.

Rosie remembered waiting at the stone gates for his return,

but the car drove straight past her, with Christian staring dead ahead, not even acknowledging her running behind them. When the car stopped, he'd got out and slammed the door shut, running into the house and locking himself in his room. He seemed to know that Mother and Father wouldn't be there to greet him, and she recalled the sound of her breath as her lungs heaved when she climbed the hill and tried to run as fast as she could. She'd got back to find Christian's bag abandoned at the foot of the grand staircase, and the driver nowhere to be found. She'd banged on Christian's door, on and off, for four hours, but he wouldn't let her in.

She'd come home specially for his return, but he'd ignored all her requests to be allowed into his room. Clara delivered his meals to his door. Not even Michael, offering to take him boating on the lake, got him to come out.

James hadn't answered his phone all weekend and when she finally got hold of him, he'd said he had no idea what she was talking about, that she was overreacting, and when he'd left him at camp, Christian had been fine.

'What did you do to him?' James had asked her in the edgy legal tone he was quickly picking up at Oxford. The place suited him. He was turning into Father.

'Nothing! I wasn't there holding his hand! Something happened at camp.'

By the time they discovered what had happened to Christian, it had been too late, because by then, Father knew.

The taxi lurched forward, and she wished she'd brought tissues. Her eyes were moist, and she wiped them with the back of her hand. They'd arrived at Paddington station and she couldn't remember the journey. She looked at her watch and realised that she'd lost an hour of her life, but couldn't recall it. She paid the driver with her card and got out. She didn't have long to wait for the Oxford train and from there, she'd be collected by another driver from Warbury House. There was no turning back now. She wondered if their cars would smell the same, and if the drivers had changed at all. She imagined, in her silliness, that nothing would have changed, but at the same time, she knew that everything had.

The train was packed, and her head throbbed as she found her seat and forced herself to smile politely each time she was asked a question by a member of the public. They were everywhere, crawling over her skin like ants. She scratched her forearms when she sat down and wriggled out of the coat she'd worn, wishing she'd paid for a car to take her all the way to Oxford. After all, she could afford it.

She was desperate for water, space and air – the basic things that kept her alive. Her head banged with a brewing migraine and her throat felt dry – and to top it off, a gentleman in tweed sat opposite her. She reckoned he was in his seventies or eighties, and he wore a flat cap but not in the country bumpkin style, classier than that. He wore a signet ring, too. He was just like her father, and she closed her eyes and tried to imagine herself somewhere else, but all she saw behind her eyelids was the island in the middle of the lake, and Christian's grave next to her mother's.

TWELVE

James

'So, this is where you grew up,' Sarah said, staring out of the car window at the Oxfordshire countryside.

'I think "grew up" is pushing it a bit. I did that after I left.'

'Come on, James, help me out. I'm trying to get to know you better, like lovers do. I'm your fiancée.'

James sighed.

'I was sent away to school, to a hideous place run by monks, and I rarely came here, apart from for the holidays. My parents were hardly around, they were always off on a trip somewhere.'

'Without their kids?'

James nodded.

'Cruel. So, tell me about school.'

'Do I have to?'

'Of course, it's part of you, good and bad, and ugly. Warts and all.'

'St Christopher's was a boys' school. I was sent there when I was four years old.'

'Holy shit. Is that even legal?'

James laughed.

'It depends on how much money you have, I suppose. Private schools are businesses, like Microsoft or Cadbury's. They make profit. They take the raw material, as young as possible, and turn them into masters – and mistresses – of the universe. Hey presto. *Moi.*'

Sarah sat quietly pondering.

'I went to private school, but it didn't feel like that. And Donny isn't like that at all.'

'Aha, but there are varying degrees of indoctrination,' James joked.

His two closest friends had met once or twice, in James's apartment, for dinner and polite conversation. Sarah had told James after that she'd found Donny fascinating, all business and ball-breaking, full of mystery and promise. And it was true – Donny wasn't a stereotypical public-school boy. For a start, his Italian twang – even though he was English born and bred – peppered his Merseyside accent like currants in a Chelsea bun. But that was one of the many things James loved about him; the fact that he was a living, breathing example of the hypocrisy of the British class system. Money was the passageway to everything and even manners could be bought. James had secretly longed to take him home to meet his father to show him that his hard-earned cash was just the same as a drug dealer's from Liverpool, but he couldn't bring himself to do that to Donny, whom he loved.

'You were a day girl, not a boarder. And Donny is... a fighter. Besides, there are different types of private school. The Catholic ones use whips and chains to hammer you into shape. His family is Italian, so they believe in all that crap.'

'Was it that bad?'

'Worse.'

'Maybe we shouldn't talk about it then.'

'Suffice to say that it will explain why Hettie and Rosie are the way they are.'

'They went there, too?'

'No, they went to St Mary's. It was run by nuns.'

'Real nuns?'

'No, pretend ones, like Whoopi Goldberg. Of course, real ones.'

'I thought they didn't talk.'

A shadow crossed James's face, but he forced a smile. 'I think you're thinking about the Middle Ages, my darling. Their vow of silence.'

'Is that why Rosie doesn't speak?'

James laughed. 'No! She hated the nuns as much as I detested the monks. It's a personal choice.'

'God, there's so much to learn about your family.'

'Can you try not to blaspheme so much?'

She stared at him. 'Really? You just asked me that? Is this for my own safety, in case I grow horns, or to keep up appearances?'

'I'm sorry, it's just... swearing and blasphemy were frowned upon in my house.'

'But your parents are both dead. Who is there left to be scared of?'

'I'm not scared of anyone, it's just the normal conversation I think might take place between a man introducing his fiancée to his family for the first time. Isn't that pretty standard? Don't say *fuck* too much, and that sort of thing.'

'I guess so. Best behaviour. I can't help feeling it all sounds so... well... repressed.'

'Bingo. It was. Exactly.'

'It's no wonder your sisters are so fucked up.'

'I suppose not.'

'How did you turn out so well?'

James stole a glance sideways, and his cheeks felt hot. He smiled. 'This is why they'll believe us. You're perfect for me.'

They laughed.

'So how did we meet?' he tested her. They'd discussed the details late into the night and had been over them several times.

'At the office. I was a client of a colleague of yours, and you caught my eye. We weren't allowed to date to prevent conflict of interest, even though you were representing my father, not me, but I asked for your number after it was all over. We've lived together for four years.'

'That part's kind of true. What was your case?'

'Burglary. My parents' house was terrorised by thugs from the local council estate for months before they broke in and my dad fought them off with a stool, harming two of them, and he was facing charges of assault.'

'That'll create enough drama for a diversion.'

'And a great conversation about why I was living so close to a pesky council estate.'

'Now, now. This isn't the time for your social warrior to come out, but good point, Hettie will pick up on it.'

'And grill me about my humble roots?'

'They're not that humble but yes, she will.'

'Am I allowed to have some fun?'

He grinned.

'Is it odd, Rosie not talking? I mean, doesn't she even say hello, or goodnight, or answer the phone?'

'No. She's mute.'

'But you said it's selective, so she is able to talk?'

'Oh, undoubtedly. Hettie always said she was faking it.'

'It must be hell trying to keep it up.'

'She's very good at it.'

'How does she communicate?'

'With notes.'

'So what kicked it off?'

'I guess it was gradual. She vowed never to speak to our father when she left Warbury House, but then it extended to everyone else as well. Rosie is a drama queen.'

He concentrated on the road. Betraying his sister behind her back felt wrong. And using the same insult as Hettie did made him squirm but he didn't have time to explain his relationships with his sisters deeply now; the important thing was to turn up with an ally.

'That's some promise. She must be exhausted. Why did she leave?'

James grasped the steering wheel tighter. Suddenly, the Maserati wasn't as comfortable or luxurious as usual, and he might as well have been sitting in a Ford Fiesta. He thought of the small bundle that Clara had carried out of the bedroom, after Rosie had spent the night screaming in her bed. He supposed it was one reason he never wanted kids, that and the fact that he thought himself incapable and utterly unsuited to fatherhood. It terrified him.

'Sorry, I just think I should know as much as possible.'

'Well, maybe you could find out for us all.'

'Holy fuck!' Sarah breathed. Her eyes were glued to the scene ahead as they entered the gates of Warbury House. James spied Rosie's profile in the back seat of a Rolls-Royce in front of them. But Sarah wasn't exclaiming at the car. The whole of Warbury House, sat atop the hill, had just come into view and he had to admit, it was something to behold, even if it made him want to kill someone.

THIRTEEN

Hettie

Hettie waved enthusiastically when she saw Michael and Clara waiting on the stone steps of Warbury House. They were both dressed in black.

'Dramatic,' Edward commented.

Hettie slapped him on his thigh playfully.

Michael stepped forward, once Edward had parked, to open Hettie's door and she slid out, taking his offered hand and grinning widely at him, before peering up at the splendour of the house. Edward got out of the driver's side and strode around to shake Michael's hand.

'Sir,' Michael uttered.

The children got out reluctantly and stared at the house.

'It's bigger than I remember,' Pippa said.

'Is there a football pitch?' asked Benji.

'I can carry my own bags,' said Kitty.

Hettie smiled at them, hoping the experience of staying here wouldn't be too traumatising for them. She willed her siblings to behave. She looked up at the façade of the great stone house and caught Clara smiling conspiratorially at Kitty.

Divide and conquer, just like she used to, thought Hettie. Clara had no such smile for her, and she guessed that they were still not forgiven for not visiting her father before he died.

'I've made a cake,' Clara said to Kitty. 'Are you hungry?'

Kitty nodded. Hettie noted that Clara still behaved like the matriarch of the house, and it made her miss her mother, not because she was a good mother, but because she'd been a limiting influence on Clara's hold over her father. She thought about what Kitty had said about servants and felt struck by the irony. Clara behaved nothing like the paid help.

'Cake!' Pippa said excitedly.

'I hope you're not going to make us fat, Clara!' Hettie said.

'Mum!' Kitty hissed. 'Nice one, after all we've talked about.'

Hettie looked at her feet, remembering the conversation about the pressure on teenage girls to look a certain way and suspecting, months ago, that Pippa wasn't eating properly. The youngest girl took Clara's hand and was led away. Kitty followed. Benji found his football and began kicking it along the gravel. Hettie sighed and sniffed in the air, despite it being the same as the stuff that swirled above her own house. She'd screwed up already.

'Can I go over there?' Benji asked his father.

'Go wherever you want to, son,' Edward told him.

Michael busied himself with the bags from the boot. Edward and Hettie walked up the steps, hand in hand, pausing at the top to turn around and view the estate from their elevated position. Edward squeezed her hand.

'This will all be ours,' he whispered.

'Are we the first, Michael?' Hettie asked, dropping Edward's hand.

'You are, madam. I believe young James and his fiancée are driving, and Rosamunde is enroute, too. She was collected from the station – ah, here they are,' he said, peering down the driveway at two cars.

Edward glared at Hettie. She shook her head, to tell him to calm down, and they walked inside.

'Don't you think we should be outside to greet them?' Edward asked.

'Why? I'm not their mother.'

'Fiancée?' Edward whispered in a derisory snort.

'Likely story,' Hettie said.

The house was cold, just as Hettie remembered it, but the cool temperature was welcome in late summer, though there was a whiff of damp and decay in the air.

Hettie walked around the grand entrance hall scowling. Her will to remain positive deserted her and she felt her shoulders sag, just a little, enough to affect her mood and for Edward to notice. He peered at the stained wallpaper, and the dark brown furniture and the ancient paintings adorning the walls. The house was tired and dated, and she calculated that it'd take a stack of money to bring it up to date. It also smelled rotten. She walked into one of the reception rooms and he followed her, clinging to her, clearly not knowing what to say. In the moments it had taken to come inside, her dreams had soured, and she turned to him with panic in her eyes.

The place was a relic. It was like looking forward to a slice of a luxuriously decorated cake but cutting into it and finding it dry and unpalatable.

But it was theirs. It might take time and effort, and a lot of money, but they had all three in abundance, or would have once they got rid of her siblings. He went to her and put his arm around her waist.

'Mr Balfour will be arriving at three sharp and I've readied the library,' Michael said from behind them, making Hettie jump.

'Of course.'

'Should I show you to your rooms?' Michael asked.

'You go,' Hettie said to her husband.

'Are we in the south wing, Michael?' Hettie then asked. She and Edward had already discussed their presumption that they'd be staying in the finest set of rooms in the house, and the only ones big enough to accommodate a family of five comfortably, with their own sitting room overlooking the deer park.

'I'm sorry, madam, I was told to make up the green rooms. Rosamunde is in the south wing.'

Hettie stared at him.

'And who told you to do that?' she asked.

She felt her decolletage burn.

'Mr Balfour. He was left strict instructions by Master Fitzherbert before he passed. He had everything arranged down to the time of afternoon tea for you all. You know how he managed everything...'

Michael stood in the doorway, with a bag under each arm and a spare football for Benji in his hands.

'If they were Father's wishes, then that is good enough for us,' Hettie said. 'I just wonder if the arrangement is sensible, given that we are a family of five and Rosie is on her own?'

Michael looked at Hettie, who fiddled with her neckline.

She softened. 'It's not a problem, Michael, we'll manage, if they were Father's wishes.'

'Of course,' Michael said and left. They heard him on the stairs.

'How the hell...?' Edward said to her.

'She must have spoken to him before he died,' Hettie said, sitting down on a cold, worn but terribly expensive sofa and sinking straight into it. Dust shot up into the air as her weight displaced it. 'God, this place is vile.'

The smell of must and rot was even worse in there than the hall. She peered around and damp patches caught her attention. The plaster on the ceiling was lumpy and the windows rattled slightly, which made her shiver, though the wind rushing through them was warm.

'How do you know?'

'What?'

'That Rosie had a conversation with him? I thought she was mute.'

'I just know. I mean by letter, or something. She was always deceitful. I wonder what else they discussed. This is to put me in my place – well, I won't stand for it. Ian Balfour promised me we had an understanding. I see Michael is still loitering in dark corners and sneaking about like an uninvited guest. He gives me the creeps, he always has.'

'He's acting upon your father's wishes, so his hands are probably tied.'

'Don't defend him! I'll let this one thing go, I don't want to appear childish. Why is he even still here? There's nothing here for him, unless he was so desperate to see James. It's sad, really, but it will be fun watching his face when James gets out of the car with his fiancée.'

Edward came towards her, but didn't sit next to her. He examined the cushions instead, grimacing at the smell of damp.

'This is going to be hell – I can feel a migraine coming on,' Hettie said, putting her fingers to her temples.

She stood up with effort and brushed off her dress.

'I suppose we better say hello and be civil,' she said, and left the room. Outside, they walked down the steps together to greet her siblings.

FOURTEEN

Rosie

Rosie noticed the car behind them, and she knew it was James. Only he would buy a flashy car like that. He had somebody beside him, and her curiosity was piqued.

The little convoy travelled up the driveway and they parked below the stone steps. Rosie's stomach lurched. She peered out of her window at the stone façade and saw a curtain twitch up in the green room, then a short while after, she saw Hettie and Edward walking down the great stone steps, coming to greet them. Her stomach flipped over. Michael and Clara stood by, in formal smart dress and looking stressed already.

She edged her way out of the back seat as the driver got out and opened the door. She smiled sweetly at him. Then she turned to watch James and his guest get out of his sports car. She noticed the trident logo of the Maserati and admired the car. It was beautiful. Then she looked at her brother, having rehearsed this moment a thousand times in her head. She was still blown away by how devilishly handsome he was, despite seeing him almost three months ago, and his smile made her

THE SECRET INHERITANCE 113

heart melt, as if they'd come home for the weekend, like they used to, to see Christian. To save him from Mother and Father.

'Sis,' James said simply, coming towards her, taking her into his arms before she could resist or stand back for a curt handshake. He squeezed her and she got sucked into his body and she recognised the familiar place of safety. He pulled away first. He smelled expensive.

'Sis, this is Sarah, my fiancée. Sarah, this is Rosie, my little sister.'

'It's so lovely to meet you, I've heard all about you,' Sarah gushed, as if she'd learned her lines. She did well, Rosie assessed, but she couldn't help wondering what this woman had done to turn her brother straight suddenly – or if it was all an act.

Rosie took her offered hand and shook it politely. Sarah's hand was warm and her shake strong. Rosie looked into her eyes for a moment and wished her life was as simple as Sarah's: in love, steady job, about to spend the rest of her life planning and nesting. She looked the type, but Rosie suddenly knew she wasn't. There was something about the way the guest looked at Rosie's body that told her she was here on a fact-finding mission, or something else entirely.

As always, James was oblivious to the inherent risks of bringing home waifs and strays. When Sarah wasn't looking, Rosie winked at her brother who looked away.

The three of them turned to look at the house and seemed to sigh in unison.

'Hettie,' James said sternly. He shook Edward's hand, like men who are desperate to avoid familial drama often do, while the women eyed one another up. It was Sarah who broke the ice.

'You must be Hettie. I've heard so much about you, too!'

Before Hettie could decide how to greet the stranger, Sarah had taken her into a hug and Rosie watched on with amusement. Perhaps the stranger might add much needed value to the whole affair, and it might not be that bad after all.

'Ready?' James asked his guest.

Sarah smiled at him and nodded. Rosie watched him take her hand, and she felt the icy fingers of jealousy course through her body, and she saw Hettie notice it. The sisters swapped curious glances for a brief moment, then the tedium of housekeeping thankfully took over.

Michael fussed over bags and Clara talked of food. To anyone looking on, they could have been an ordinary family reuniting for a holiday. However, Rosie was embarking on a pilgrimage to save her soul. A devotional journey towards enlightenment, which they wouldn't all survive. She felt Clara's body next to hers and they embraced, again, watched closely by Hettie. There was an awkward moment between Michael and James as her brother held onto his luggage and Michael tried to take it from him.

Michael looked much older.

He was still grieving Father, that was for sure, but Rosie wondered what else he still mourned. He was tall, with thinning hair, and wore a dark suit out of respect for his master. He was efficient and polite as James introduced Sarah, who hung onto James's arm for dear life. She was sweet, Rosie assessed, so it was a pity she was probably a liar, or Rosie might have warmed to her even more. It must be all part of the game. If Rosie had dared trust anyone, she might have done the same and brought a partner, too, to bolster her chances of survival.

They walked up the steps together and as they reached the top, they heard the sound of children.

'You're in the south wing,' Michael informed Rosie, then he turned to James and informed him of his sleeping arrangements and James nodded politely.

Rosie knew James never much cared for the hierarchy of grand room allocation at Warbury House; he'd have been happy with a sofa bed in the study. But it wasn't that which caught her attention. Hettie was also watching their brother closely and especially his interaction with Michael. Rosie smiled sweetly at Sarah, who hadn't noticed, and they went inside.

They dropped their smaller bags in the grand hall and headed to the back of the house towards the kitchen, from where they smelled baking. They left Michael to sort the bigger pieces of luggage. When Rosie felt Sarah link arms with her, her first instinct was to pull away, indignant that anyone would presume to be so forward, but then she remembered why James's friend was here. She was his safety blanket. *That's why he would have brought her here*, she figured in her head. Poor James, he'd never liked being alone. He was like Christian in that sense. He needed somebody to love and love him back. She was certain now that, rather than provide the romantic love her brother craved, Sarah was in fact a true friend, which could be even more valuable.

A host of aromas assaulted their senses and brought happiness out of the woodwork of Warbury House. It was Clara's way of bringing everyone together, as if they were one big happy family. It almost tricked everyone into thinking it was like old times, but Rosie couldn't ignore the peeling wallpaper and the general disrepair of the place. It left her feeling deflated, but that was soon replaced with something else as they entered the kitchen.

The three children who sat at the table could have been herself, Hettie and James, busy eating cake and drinking fizzy soda, and she caught her breath. Then she noticed the children staring at her, but they weren't children anymore. They were teenagers. The boy took Rosie's breath away. He looked just like Christian with his defined jaw and floppy blond hair. She held out her hand for each of her nieces and then her nephew, in silence. It had been years since she'd last seen them. She looked around for Hettie, who should have re-introduced them to her, but Hettie hadn't followed them inside. Rosie felt a pang of loss, which she was unaccustomed to.

'Kitty?' James stepped in to provide vocals for the children who were staring at Rosie as if she was an otherworldly creature. She'd expected it.

Kitty was tall, like her father, and she hid her body behind baggy, colourless clothes, but it was still clear she was a beauty like her mother, her dark hair falling over her face. She was unsure about the strangers.

'Auntie Rosie, I'm twelve.'

It was Pippa who spoke.

Her courage gave Benji a boost of valour and he held out his hand to James, who ignored it and swept him up into his arms.

'Hey, big fella!'

Benji giggled, but blushed at the same time.

'Do you want to play football?' he asked James.

'Let me have a coffee and some of Clara's cake, then I'll play with you.'

Benji smiled bashfully, then he looked at Rosie from under his fringe and she opened her arms. He reciprocated and a shot of electricity stunned her as she held him. She hadn't expected to feel like this. Finally, she pulled away and slid out a chair from under the huge oak table around which she'd spent most of her childhood. There must be seventy rooms in Warbury House but only one was safe, and always had been, and it was this one.

Rosie noted that the children were comfortable meeting strangers in the absence of their parents. They didn't display the tugging shadows of maternal glue, like many children did. She identified the absence of it straight away. It reminded her of her own childhood.

'Are you mute?' Kitty asked.

She nodded.

Clara coughed and Sarah laughed nervously.

Rosie took out her pad and pen and wrote Kitty a message.

She passed it to her to read, then Kitty took the pad and pen from her, and wrote a response.

She'd written, *I like your dress* on it.

Rosie scribbled a reply.

Thank you. I like your hair.

They'd overcome the hardest part. Rosie saw Clara turn her back and busy herself with the preparation of food, and the room settled into an easy quiet. James ate cake, after he'd got Sarah a drink, and the children gathered around Rosie, who wrote notes on her pad. She felt like a spectacle at the fair, but it wasn't an unhappy sentiment.

Clara sliced what was left of the cake and the two younger children took a slice each. Rosie thought she looked different somehow; her shoulders were lower and the lines around her eyes deeper, with sadness.

'That's your third, don't tell your mother,' Clara said, and the words echoed moments from Rosie's past when they kept secrets from their own mother.

Tiny secrets become big ones, she heard whispered inside her head.

The cake was delicious, and she sipped her tea from a china cup nestled on a saucer, collected by her mother from Italy. The clink of the cup reminded Rosie of her now, and she realised that Warbury House still held onto her shadow. Rosie was able to make up for the loss of her power of speech with her other senses, and her notepad, but the strongest medium was her instinct. She could *feel* her father was gone, because she could breathe more easily. The air inside the house was lighter and even the windows looked bigger as they proudly shone light into the space. But despite feeling safer, the house felt lifeless. The furniture was the same, and even the position of the pans, utensils, ingredients and baking tins, but even though her father rarely entered the kitchen, she could tell that his very being was absent, and even the house seemed to breathe differently.

She looked around as the children busied themselves with notes to her. They'd found a new and exciting game, with her at the centre. James and Sarah took turns asking the children questions. They all settled into an easy peace with its own unique rhythm. Benji bounced his ball impatiently and Pippa stared at Rosie's hands as she wrote. For a second, she wished Hettie had stayed but only because of their history, nothing else.

'Come on then, Benji,' James said, standing up. 'Do you want to come with us?' he asked Sarah, who shook her head.

'I'm happy to stay here,' she said.

Rosie flashed a look at James.

'It's OK, we won't go far,' James said to her.

Rosie looked at Clara next, who acknowledged her worry.

'Perhaps ask Hettie if it's OK?' Clara said to James.

'No!' Benji said. 'I mean, I'll be fine.'

'We're not going anywhere near the lake,' James said.

Benji stared at him and back to Rosie, who smiled, diffusing the tension.

'Right, that's settled then. No going near the lake,' Clara said to Benji, who nodded enthusiastically.

Pippa and Kitty were busy scribbling notes and Rosie wrote one to Clara.

Where's my father's body? she wrote, passing it to her. Clara took it and read it. It made her frown and peer at the huge Aga. James and Benji disappeared, then it was just the girls left. Kitty had found her own pad of paper from a bag, and she was busy writing.

'In the chapel,' Clara said.

Kitty ripped out a sheet of paper and passed it to her aunt, then stopped her hand as she began to read.

'Don't read it now. You can do it later and write me a letter back,' she said.

Rosie folded it and popped it into her bag. When she looked up again, Pippa and Kitty were staring at her.

'Warbury House is beautiful,' Sarah said, and Rosie suspected it was because she wasn't comfortable with silence. The children had adapted immediately, but Sarah was unsure. Rosie wondered why she hadn't gone with James.

'It's a fine home, not what it was once, but it could be grand again someday,' Clara said. 'It's fallen into disrepair a little,' she carried on, and Rosie glanced at her out of the corner of her eye. Rosie was used to her grumbling.

'Perhaps now everyone's home, the jobs can be taken care of. You know – the water has gone off in the west wing, and that's why it's shut off. The toilets don't work either.'

Pippa giggled and Kitty slapped her playfully.

Rosie appreciated that this was Clara's time to get everything off her chest, but her words was tinged with a mixture of anger and grief.

'What will happen to the house?' Sarah asked.

Clara turned around and the girls fell silent, joining Rosie in her quiet. Suddenly being mute was popular and Sarah blushed, so Rosie wrote her a note telling her that this was what everyone else wanted to know, too.

'It's going to be ours,' Pippa said. This time Kitty hit her hard and she cried.

They all stared at the girl.

Rosie was comfortable with gaps in conversation. The loss of her voice had taught her to compensate in other ways. The absence of noise was welcome rather than something that unsettled her. But she could see that Sarah was the opposite, and she fussed over Pippa's drawings and placated the child, soothing her after her faux pas.

Kitty, on the other hand, held Rosie's gaze and she saw in her a kindred spirit. It hadn't taken long for a pretence of calm to turn to chaos. In the midst of it, Rosie, as usual, was the observer, but, she realised, so, too, was Kitty, and a slow smile spread across Rosie's face. Perhaps she had an ally in this after all?

Clara turned back to the table and Rosie caught her stealing a look at her. It was an appeal, Rosie understood, but Clara needn't have worried. Should Hettie get her hands on Warbury House, then Clara and Michael would surely be turfed out, but Rosie wasn't about to let that happen. But the more interesting result of the little girl's loose lips was that she saw dissent in the older girl. All was not well in Hettie's camp, Rosie understood, and her eldest daughter was a potential mutinous soldier, open to delicately negotiated coercion.

FIFTEEN

James

Benji was a decent footballer and within half an hour, he'd outsmarted James, who found himself running after his nephew, unable to win the ball. Benji kicked it far down the lawn, as it sloped away towards the rear of the estate, away from the house, and the forest came into view, stopping James in his tracks. Benji looked behind for him and stopped playing when he saw that James was staring into the distance. James gaped at the view and beyond to the lake. He could just make out the lake house and the gable roof of the old chapel on the island.

'Is that where people are buried?' Benji asked.

'Yes, it is,' James replied.

Father had wanted Christian buried on the island in the middle of the lake, in his own plot, next to Mother, and it's where the old rogue himself would be laid to rest, if they ever got around to it after Hettie found out what was written in his will. A new plot had been dug to accommodate him, and James irreverently thought that the island was getting crowded.

'Who told you?'

Benji went silent and sheepish.

'You're not in trouble, I just wondered if you knew who was buried there?'

Benji shook his head.

'Is it Grandad?' he asked.

James smiled at the boy's innocence, and it reminded him of Christian.

'He will be, but his coffin will remain in the chapel until his funeral.'

'Why?'

'Tradition, I suppose. Do you know what that is?'

Benji nodded. 'It's a generational custom.'

James smiled. 'That's impressive and very… precise.'

'I study history.'

'And do they teach you how British convention is responsible for the most deaths in all of history?'

Benji froze into an awkward silence.

'Just toying with you,' James said, slapping his nephew on his arm.

Benji relaxed. 'How did he die?'

James envied his nephew's courage. Such bold enlightenment was met with a cuff over the head when he was Benji's age, or banishment to one's room without dinner. He considered the chance he was becoming old and brushed it away.

'It was an accident,' he said, before realising that Benji was asking about his grandfather and not Christian.

'I mean, he was old, and he had cancer. Everyone gets it sooner or later.'

'Do they?'

'I think so. Depressing, isn't it? You should know from your history that we shouldn't live for as long as we do now. We're a virus really, us humans. A simple organism, but deadly.'

James saw that he'd made his nephew uneasy.

'Come on,' he said, stealing the football away from him to get a head start.

Benji laughed and chased him.

'Is the lake dangerous?' the lad asked breathlessly.

James realised that this was what the young boy was digging for. Benji was scared of the lake because somebody was buried there, but he could see, too, that he was desperate to go there. Graveyards were fascinating to everyone.

'No! Not at all. I'll take you out on a boat. Do you want to see the lake house?'

Benji smiled, but it was tinged with trepidation. Then he nodded and James picked up his ball and walked towards the lake, forgetting his promise to Clara. Anyway, he owed no allegiance to Hettie, who'd broken plenty of promises.

'Come on, then.'

The lake was how he remembered it: serene and vast, though not as daunting as he'd expected. It was the first time he'd been here since Christian's death, and he was just as nervous as his nephew was. He glanced back to the main house and fleetingly thought about Sarah. Would she need him? She'd said she was fine on her own and encouraged him to go. But now he wished she was here with her breezy sensibility and knack for making any situation straightforward. He shook off the nagging doubts and carried on. He enjoyed the young lad's company immensely and wished, for a moment, that he could be that age again, but the fanciful silliness left him as soon as it had come. What a ludicrous idea. But this place did that to you. It made you forget, and dream.

Benji fell silent and James realised that the boy was taking it all in. The sun shone across the water, and he was taken with the stillness. Coming here from London was like listening to a piano concerto after attending a rock concert.

They walked to the boathouse and James found that it was

locked. He put down the ball and tried to move the huge door, but it was bolted from the inside.

'Wait here,' he said.

James went around the back and saw that the stone steps were overgrown with bushes. Sadness gripped him as he wondered why Michael would leave it like this. He swept the worst of them aside with his bare hands and they came away easily, revealing the rough stone underneath. He walked to the top and peered through an old window which was dirty with neglect. It was smaller than he recalled but he still reckoned he could get through it.

He forced the latch and it creaked open, sending thorns and small stones into the cavity. He heaved himself up and got a knee on the ledge. Holding the window with one hand, he scrambled through without much effort, and landed on a wooden platform. His eyes took their time to adjust, and he felt the wooden structure beneath him wobble with unfamiliar strain. Then it creaked and cracked, and he felt himself hurtling towards the stone floor below. But it wasn't slab, it was water, and he plunged into the icy cold dock. The shock of it, as well as the temperature of the water, took his breath away and he came up for air, gasping and gulping.

He laughed out loud and slapped the water around him. There were canoes and kayaks on the walls – hooked on by bolts and brackets – and in the middle was a series of rowing boats, as well as the single motor skiff that could take about eight people, if they pushed their luck. The water in the dock was only about eight feet deep and he found the steps where they'd always been and climbed out.

He shivered.

His leather Gucci loafers slopped on the concrete, and he peered down at them, suddenly not caring that they cost eight hundred pounds. He walked to the back of the boat house and unbolted the great doors, greeting Benji on the other side. The young boy's eyes widened as he saw the state of his uncle's appearance.

'I fell in,' James said.

They laughed together and James felt a sense of freedom stir in his chest.

'Come on, let me show you.'

Benji followed him and he pointed out the different vessels, from memory.

'Your mum used to flip in that one.'

'Flip?'

'Yeah, it's kind of rolling, you know, when you take it out to deep water and fall over sideways, using your paddle to get you back up the other side. She was good at it. Better than the rest of us.'

'She really did that?' Benji asked.

James understood that the boy probably might not believe him given the sensible and uptight adult Hettie had become, which is why he'd come down here in the first place: to avoid his sister for as long as possible. Pretending with Rosie was one thing, but Hettie was another case altogether.

'Will you show me?'

'Sure.'

James took off his shirt and wrung it out. He kicked off his loafers and socks and rolled up his trousers. He chose a canoe and took it off the wall, noticing Benji stare at his body. Muscles and hair to a pubescent boy were mysteries, he recalled from painful memory, and James smiled.

The water lapped at the sides of the docks as he threw it in and found a paddle.

'We should ask your mum if it's OK, but I suppose it wouldn't do any harm to take you for a quick spin,' James said.

'Yes, please,' Benji said.

'Get in.'

It was a two-man canoe and James held it while Benji slid in the front. He lowered himself into the back and took the paddle from the side and pushed off. They slid gracefully under the crumbling doors that once had been painted a bright blue. Benji was light – unlike Christian – and James paddled easily into the body of the lake.

Shafts of sunlight caressed his body, and it wasn't long before he grew accustomed to the temperature, and his wet trousers. He swished the paddle from right to left and soon they were right in the middle of the lake.

He stopped paddling and Benji turned around.

'You want a go?' James asked.

'Yes, please.'

James had to hand it to his sister; the lad was nothing if not polite.

James passed him the paddle and showed him the sweeping movement required to power the vessel. Benji did as he was told and soon they were spinning in circles. James laughed and threw back his head, peering up to the sky.

'Sorry,' Benji said.

'Hey, don't worry, is this your first time?'

Benji nodded.

'Didn't you visit Grandad?'

'We did, but I wasn't allowed on the lake.'

'Oh, then your mum won't be pleased I brought you here.'

'We don't have to tell her.'

At a tender age, the lad had already learned how to modify his behaviour for certain adults and a cloud of depression settled on James's shoulders. Benji sensed it.

'Please don't tell her.'

James leaned forward and patted Benji on the shoulder.

'Of course I won't if you won't.'

The deal was sealed, protecting them both.

'I don't want you getting into trouble and besides, it's my fault. It was my idea.'

'Thank you, Uncle James.'

After a few minutes, Benji got the hang of it and James sat back, allowing Benji to take control.

'There you go, look, you're a pro!'

'It's a long way to the island,' Benji said.

James followed his eye line and glanced back at the boy, who'd stopped paddling. The canoe swayed in the water. James peered into the ripples as they spread out beneath them and travelled as far as they could see and then died. He let his hand touch the surface and peered at the island, which was spitting distance away.

'We can come another day,' he told Benji, who nodded.

They sat still in the canoe.

'Are you scared?'

Benji shook his head, but said nothing, James couldn't see his face.

'Maybe you should be.'

James rocked the canoe slightly and Benji grabbed hold of the sides, allowing the paddle to fall into the water and drift away.

'Don't worry, we can swim if we need to.'

'I can't swim.'

'You can't swim? What has my sister been teaching you? If I tipped you out now, you'd learn, for sure – it's survival instinct.'

'Don't do that, please.'

Benji turned his head and swallowed and James saw his Adam's apple bob up and down. The afternoon sun twinkled on the water and shone in Benji's eyes, and he shielded them with one hand, looking back towards the shore. James could tell he was working out if he could make it, or not. He was a resourceful lad.

'Don't worry, I've got a spare,' James said finally, pulling a paddle from underneath his feet. He started paddling and Benji held on tight, reassured.

They reached the shore in silence and after they'd put the canoe away and James gathered his clothes, they walked back together.

There was a seriousness to the boy that James didn't recognise, but fourteen was an awkward age, he recalled with a shiver. His own childhood had been full of moments like this: stolen behind the backs of adults, glimmers of freedom in a world full of rules, and he'd inhaled every minute. Not so with Benji.

Like him, Benji had two sisters, but James had also had Christian to play with. Despite the age gap of nine years, Christian had been his partner in crime. They'd disappear for hours, down at the lake, or further afield, in the forest, making camps and building fires.

Never getting caught.

He could tell that Benji was never allowed to take risks. It was in the way the boy walked and talked. A few days wasn't enough to change that but perhaps he could show Benji what it was like to be free. A frisson of excitement coursed through James's body and a warning voice sounded in his head. It told him to be careful because pursuing the dream of freedom wasn't as straightforward as it seemed, and the path was fraught with danger.

James looked over his shoulder and back to the lake, where he promised to bring Benji back, and the warning voice disappeared.

It had been that of his brother.

SIXTEEN

Hettie

Edward paced up and down and stopped at the window.

'We shouldn't have left – it shows weakness, and it looks like they won,' he said.

'I just needed to think. I didn't expect to see both at the same time.'

'Come on, we should go back down, to show solidarity.'

'The children,' she said, suddenly panicked.

'Don't worry, they'll be force-fed cake until they roll out of there.'

Hettie nodded and became calm once more, but she knew she had to retake control. It was obvious her siblings had stayed in touch, and they'd lied to her.

'What is James doing, bringing a total stranger here?'

'They're all strangers. We don't know anything about their lives,' Edward said. 'Come on, let's go down. Are you ready?' He sat on the bed next to her and held her.

She took a deep breath and pinched her cheeks together, taking in air to calm her nerves.

'You look beautiful,' he said.

She smiled weakly.

'Right, here we go.' She stood up and he clapped his hands together.

She walked to the door, and he followed her.

Downstairs, the house was quiet, but Hettie heard sounds coming from the kitchen. Edward followed her to the back of the house, and they entered the kitchen together. Clara, Rosie, and their two daughters – as well as the stranger who'd arrived with James – were sat at the table. It was a cosy scene.

The buzz of conversation stopped abruptly.

'Well, this is... intimate,' Hettie said.

Rosie acknowledged her sister with a face that couldn't be read. Hettie was acutely aware of her daughters both watching her, and she felt under pressure to set an example and not get things off to an acrimonious start.

'Where's Benji?' she asked.

Kitty looked guilty. Rosie sat comfortably, sipping from a china cup. Pippa massaged what looked like dough. The stranger looked... awkward, but it was she who finally spoke up.

'James took Benji to play football,' Sarah said.

Hettie felt the warmth drain from her body and Clara dropped something in the Belfast sink, causing a clatter.

'Is something wrong?' Sarah asked innocently.

'Stay here, I'll go,' Edward said, leaving the room.

Hettie sat down and watched her sister.

'You're still not talking?' Hettie said.

'Mum! Rosie talks like this,' Kitty told her, holding up a pad and paper full of scrawls and drawings. 'We've had a whole conversation. She doesn't have to talk if she doesn't want to.'

Hettie read the messages and didn't know what to say. She'd only been there for five minutes and already, Rosie had brainwashed her children into thinking she was Aunt of the Year, and cool for not talking.

Kitty watched her mother and Rosie, then she tutted and pushed her chair back, making a screeching noise on the tiles.

'I'm going for a walk,' Kitty announced.

Pippa got up and followed her.

'Welcome to Warbury House, Sarah,' Hettie finally said. 'So, you and my brother are engaged?'

Sarah smiled and nodded.

'Was it all a bit sudden?' Hettie asked, staring at Sarah's belly.

'Ignore her, Sarah, she's teasing,' Clara said. 'Hettie, stop it.'

Hettie folded her arms and looked between her sister and Clara, whose conspiratorial club of two had always bothered her.

'Would you like me to show you around, Sarah?' Hettie asked.

'Oh, that's very generous of you. Yes, thank you,' she accepted graciously, and Hettie thought she might have some backbone worth investigating after all.

Sarah got up and Hettie gazed at the other two, who stared back at her.

'Somebody needs to look after our guest if James is going to abandon her,' Hettie said. 'Meanwhile, you two can plot my downfall,' she added.

Clara went to answer but Rosie stopped her with a gentle hand on her wrist. Hettie saw the gesture and smirked.

'Still thick as thieves, you two. United in grief?' Hettie said.

'Now, that's enough,' Clara said, striding towards Hettie.

'I can't wait to sack you,' Hettie leaned over and whispered in Clara's ear.

She led Sarah out of the kitchen and hooked her arm in hers.

'Come on, there's lots to see.'

She stopped Sarah in the hallway first and swept her arm

around. 'This grand entrance has welcomed royalty,' Hettie told her.

'Really?'

'Look, there.' Hettie showed her a framed photograph on the wall of her father with a young King Charles, taken at a dinner hosted for the Prince's Trust. 'Now, the house itself was built for the last Earl of Oxford in 1703, but it's been added to significantly since then, of course.'

'Central heating and electricity, I hope,' Sarah said.

'I bet you wish you'd gone to play football with James, don't you?' Hettie asked her.

'Not at all, I came here to get to know James's family.'

'You don't fool me. You don't have enough between your legs. But don't worry, your secret's safe with me. I do demand a trade, however.'

'I beg your pardon?'

'I'll keep your secret, if you tell me why James really brought you. Are you a policewoman?'

'No!' Sarah looked horrified.

'Lawyer?'

'No.'

'An estate agent?'

'No.'

'Then what?'

'I told you. His fiancée.'

Hettie studied her.

'This was Mother's favourite room,' she said, taking – almost dragging – her into a drawing room. It was decorated in fresh pastels and the wallpaper had birds on it, though it was peeling off. Hettie's shoulders sagged as she cast her eyes over the state of it and she could feel Sarah's pity oozing out of her. The colours on the walls had faded to smudgy beige and the birds looked as though they were fighting each other to the death to get out.

'It's been let go,' Hettie said.

'It looks like it.'

'Do you want to live here?' Hettie demanded. She was standing only a foot away from her.

'No.'

'Then what do you want?'

'Nothing.'

'Nobody ever just wants nothing. Especially James. I expect he's told you I'm horrid. It's not true. The eldest always shoulders the biggest responsibility, I see it in my own daughter. You know they were a handful.'

'Who?'

'Rosie and James, who else?'

'Oh.'

'Have you known her long?'

'Who?'

'Rosie.'

'No, we just met for the first time.'

'She hates me, don't listen to anything she tells you.'

'But she can't speak.'

'No, that's not correct, she can speak, she just chooses not to when she's scared. There's a difference. Shall I show you where Mother used to lock her up? Then you'll understand a bit more about why she's so odd.'

Hettie noticed Sarah pull away from her. It was understandable. Maybe she'd gone too far. Hettie watched her glance over her shoulder then look back.

'She was locked up?'

'Yes, it's awful, isn't it? The nuns did it to us at school, too. Bitches. We were all punished in the ways we were most terrified of. Sadistic, really. I was given puzzles to complete and if I failed then my knuckles were walloped with a bible. God, it was horrendous. Rosie was locked downstairs in a well under the cellar. James went to a boys' school... shall I tell you what happened to him?'

They were back in the hallway now and Hettie saw Sarah reach for her cardigan and pull it around her body, as if chilled by a passing ghost.

'What happened to James?'

'At home? Mother made the rest of us ignore him. We had to play around him, and he had to stay silent. We pretended he didn't exist.'

Sarah swallowed hard and Hettie pushed her face close to hers.

'It's amazing I'm normal,' she said. 'Wait until you see the cellar.'

'You have a cellar here? I thought you said that was at school?'

'Where do you think Mother learned it from? She went to St Mary's too. Local girl.'

Hettie walked away and Sarah followed her slowly. Hettie looked back over her shoulder and winked at her companion.

'Come on, it's down here,' she said. She led Sarah down a narrow set of stairs that was hidden from view behind the grand staircase at the front of the house, which headed two floors down to a door. There, she tried the handle and to her dismay it was locked.

'Shit.'

'Never mind! We can come another time,' Sarah said in a high-pitched voice.

Hettie was so close to Sarah she could have blown her hair with a tiny breath. She stared into her eyes and smiled. It was cold down here and Hettie was reminded how it felt when Mother dragged them under the house and opened the door with a key only she and Clara kept.

'Clara could have let us out anytime, she had a key, but she didn't. She let us rot down here. It's no wonder Rosie is scared of everything.'

She leaned in further. 'Don't let Rosie fool you. She got her revenge in the end.'

Hettie smiled sweetly then turned abruptly and disappeared back up the narrow stairs.

SEVENTEEN

Rosie

Time crawled into the afternoon, and they weren't expected in the library until three o'clock, so Rosie pulled on a thin-knit sweater over her summer dress and left her bedroom. She'd changed for the occasion of the reading of her father's will, and it was an ironic nod to him – who'd changed his outfits three times a day.

She headed down to the lake, to kill time, and to avoid another run-in with Hettie. It was always surprising to her how plenty of people could reside at the house and yet it was easy to avoid each other. She'd fully expected her time here to be full of clashes with her sister, but she hadn't seen her since the initial cold greeting in the kitchen. She had no idea where she'd taken Sarah earlier, but she had felt no desire to stop her from monopolising James's fiancée. Sarah might as well get to know them properly, and she was sure Hettie would have given her an exhaustive tour, as well as her own commentary. Warbury House was full of hidden corners to get lost in and Rosie considered for a moment if Hettie would be so cruel as to show Sarah some of them and leave her there, like they used to do as children.

Rosie felt her headache returning and knew she needed to take time for herself to rid her body of stress. Anxiety coursed through her, but she knew that with some peace and quiet and a little controlled breathing, she'd be fine. A walk amongst the flowers was just what she needed, and she stopped to smell them, shocked at how familiar they were.

She considered Hettie's family. Edward was as he always had been: controlled by his wife, meek and pathetic, and clearly here for the money. Kitty was interesting, she thought to herself as she plucked flowers from the bushes and picked them apart. Wandering down to the lake was just what her nerves needed. She felt like a girl again and expected at any moment, one of the boys to come tearing around a corner with a stick, firing it like a shotgun.

But nobody appeared.

Still, she had the distinct feeling that she was being followed. She stopped occasionally to bend over to pick a flower and look surreptitiously behind her, and she saw a shadow pursuing her. It would dart behind a bush every now and then, but it was there. There was no mistaking it. She lingered for a few minutes, hoping to identify the intruder but she saw nothing and carried on.

She reached the beach and checked her watch to make sure she had plenty of time to get over to the island before having to return to the house. It was a task she needed to complete before she could concentrate on anything else. It was an opportunity to say her own goodbyes in isolation, before the circus of the funeral commenced, after this was all over.

She took off her sandals when she got to the beach and the imported sand was warm underfoot. It sank between her toes like silk, and she scrunched them up like she used to. The water looked crystal clear and inviting and she was tempted to walk into the lake as she was, but she went to the boathouse instead. It was open and she suspected that James had brought Benji down here earlier. He was playing with fire and sooner or later, Hettie would surely find out. She went inside and the cool interior jolted her. The water reflected onto the ceiling above the boats and tricked her into thinking Christian was sitting in here waiting for her, as he had done for years.

After the camping trip, before he turned twelve, he'd come down here all his waking moments to build camps. He'd refuse to come back to the house, even for food, and Michael had to bring it down here for him. He hid if any of them tried to find him, and, at eighteen, she'd grown bored and given up. She had a life in London by then, and she'd got a job working for a prominent newspaper, thanks to her father's connections. She'd been too busy for the whims of a teenage boy.

She wished he was here now, so she could claw back the time.

When he didn't appear, she took a kayak down from the wall and grabbed a paddle, then carried it to the water's edge. That's when she saw Kitty on the beach, way over the opposite side to the boathouse. Rosie pretended she hadn't seen her and observed that Kitty was in her own world anyway – oblivious to the company she was in. Rosie disappeared under the bushes to the left of the boathouse, dragging the kayak silently behind her. The girl was a steam engine ready to blow, just like Rosie had been at that age.

The paddle over to the island wasn't taxing but it wasn't as easy as it had been when she'd been fifteen years younger. She wished she'd worn a hat and her sunglasses kept slipping off her nose. But finally, she made it and she pulled the kayak out of the water, noticing that Kitty had watched her silently all the way across.

The grass under the shade of the trees was cool and she found her way easily along the trail leading to the chapel. She emerged into the clearing and gazed upon it nostalgically, but also disappointingly. It was smaller than she remembered and less grand. It was a simple stone structure, with oak doors. She pushed one aside and went in.

She thought she knew silence, but the quiet inside the chapel had a depth to it that surprised her. She could smell it.

Then she saw her father's coffin and her throat gave way. She went to it and placed her hand gently on the lid. He was inside it, she knew, airtight and embalmed so he wouldn't rot. But still, it didn't seem real. She wanted to open the lid and wake him up and ask him why he'd left them like orphans, rudderless and lost, fighting for his affection and only finding hatred and viciousness. She thumped the wood, then did it again, then she spun around and left the chapel.

She stopped once more in the cemetery, which was full, their father told them, of the ancestors of those who'd built the place some four hundred years ago, but it wasn't them she'd come to see. They were strangers and unrelated to the family who'd bought into the ancients here at Warbury House. It was the memorial plaque of her brother, Christian. She stood over it and all the things she'd planned to say eluded her just then, right when she needed them. A sound escaped her throat, and she wiped her face with the back of her hand.

Then she marched angrily back the way she'd come, got back into the kayak and paddled to the shore, where she snuck up on Kitty without her realising. She watched the girl sat on her own for a full minute and read her expression. It was one of loneliness and confusion, but Rosie – who had no experience of children beyond the baby she'd had taken from her – figured she was witnessing merely a normal display of teenage angst. Everybody tired of their family at sixteen, didn't they?

Kitty saw her and smiled.

'What's over there?' Kitty asked.

Rosie smiled. *The family remains*, she wanted to say.

She beached the kayak and found her pad, then wrote Kitty a note, tearing it out and handing it to her.

The island is pretty, you should go over there.

'I will,' Kitty said. 'Is it haunted?'

Rosie smiled and shrugged. She watched as Kitty stared over the lake at the island and tried to remember what her fears told her when she was sixteen. She wasn't scared of ghosts by then because she'd already seen real evil.

She gestured for them to go back up to the house and pointed to her watch. She didn't want to be late for the meeting in the library.

'Why aren't me, Benji and Pippa invited?' Kitty asked. 'I guess it's because it's all about money.' The girl was getting used to answering her own questions.

Rosie nodded.

When they reached the house, Kitty said goodbye to her, and gave her a hug. The touch of another human against her body made Rosie freeze but she persevered for the sake of the girl, who'd done nothing wrong. Still, it felt uncomfortable. She'd expected some kind of affection from Clara, and even Michael, but not the children. They'd surprised her and reminded her how hopeful human beings were – and how open – when they hadn't yet seen terror.

On her way to the library, she paused in the long hallway and admired the paintings. She passed an open bay window and welcomed the breeze coming through the gap, but something in her peripheral vision caught her eye. In the distance, down towards the driveway, behind one of the magnificent, winged spindle trees which still clung onto its red canopy – the colour of blood – she saw a dark shape. At this distance, it was merely a speck of black against the claret, but it was there, nonetheless. Then it moved and disappeared.

It was too big for a crow or blackbird.

It was the outline of a man.

And she feared she knew who it was.

In the library, she was glad she'd put a jumper on. The room was cold and dark, overshadowed by thousands of books, collected by Rosie's father for no other reason than to show them off. She was the first to arrive. The only other person in the room was the lawyer Ian Balfour, who acknowledged her briefly. He was sat at Father's desk shuffling papers.

Rosie chose a seat impatiently and looked over her shoulder to the door several times, anticipating her sister's arrival.

The children would remain in the kitchen being entertained by Clara. She'd always been good at that, like she was good at most things. Rosie reflected on how charming Hettie's children were and she surmised that this was because children are uniquely innocent until later in life, when the truth turned them sour. After all, she'd loved Hettie, too, at some point.

James and Sarah arrived behind her and chose seats close to her. Sarah sat next to Rosie, with James on the other side. They waited without speaking for Hettie to make her entrance. There was no need for greetings. James had briefed Sarah well.

James and Sarah swapped idle chatter and the lawyer didn't look up from his work.

Then Hettie arrived and marched to the front row of chairs set out, sitting down with a sigh. Edward followed her like a loyal squire.

It was Rosie's opportunity to study her sister uninterrupted for the first time in years. Hettie looked different. Not just older and a little flabby, but more confident and reckless even, which she'd never been in front of Father. But it was pay day, Rosie thought uncharitably, and Edward had been dreaming about this day for years, thinking that today his patience would be rewarded. They both thought they were about to inherit millions, enough for anyone to live off for the rest of their lives.

She smiled to herself.

Ian interrupted her thoughts by coughing, and it was clearly his way of calling everyone to attention. Their father kept a close circle and Ian was alone, as expected. He was straight out of a Dickens novel: small spectacles on the end of his nose, a three-piece suit and white hair. Rosie loved Dickens and he was one of the reasons she began to write stories. His omniscient narrator had kept her in awe for hours, either under her duvet at home, or locked in the hole at school. After she grew used to the punishment, she began preparing by hiding books under her night clothes to keep her entertained. She felt heat rise up inside her chest as she recalled the book collection she'd created in the well, under the cellar, but it was just a snippet of a memory and then it was gone.

She noticed that Hettie had changed clothes, too. The habits of their childhood were impossible to rub out. James had been soaking from his jaunt to the lake, so he was the only one with a legitimate reason to change his clothes, but it also meant that no one noticed.

His secret was safe.

She wasn't supposed to know James had been to the lake. Kitty had told her by note, when they sat on the beach together after Rosie had been to the island. But that wasn't all the teenager had shared with her.

The message she'd given her in the kitchen was both beautiful and complex. Written by a teenager on the verge of adulthood, confused and alone. Rosie was trained to look for hidden meaning underneath words – it's how she survived – and Kitty's words were loaded with it. It had been a simple memo but said so much more. In it, Kitty had complimented her clothes again and told her that she enjoyed speaking through the written word, and she asked lots of questions. She wanted to know if Rosie could help her write stories. She also asked if Rosie knew anything about why, if her grandfather was so rich, did the toilets not work very well. They were the ramblings of a hormonal young woman who hadn't yet learned pace, but Rosie saw through the immature meandering and recognised a confused mind that wanted order. Kitty had all the qualities of a fine spy, though she didn't know how to process the information she was gathering, yet. That was Rosie's job, to make sure she didn't scare Kitty off.

Already, Warbury House was conspiring against Hettie, who didn't fit in. Even her daughter schemed against her, though she didn't yet know it. Now, Hettie looked laden down by her expensive designer outfit. Rosie wasn't familiar with labels, but Hettie looked like she was *styled*, not dressed. When they were kids, they'd worn wellies and higgledy-piggledy shorts and T-shirts, or whatever was shoved in their clothes drawers. Rosie had no idea where Hettie's love of fine clothing came from, apart from wanting to show that she was different and above everyone else. It also looked like armour, and a pang of pity washed over her. Hettie was scared of being ganged up on, like the old days. And perhaps with good reason.

James was in jeans and slippers. Sarah was dressed the same as when she'd arrived, in a long purple skirt, with a white blouse. Her bohemian fashion didn't suit James and Rosie smiled to herself: he could have chosen his fake date better, but they were doing a great job of pretending so far.

Finally, Ian looked up to scan the room and Rosie saw Hettie look down at her hands. He cleared his throat, and the library seemed to summon a large intake of breath, as if it was expecting the worst. Rosie wished she were somewhere else, but at the same time, she knew she wouldn't miss this for the world.

'Good afternoon, all,' Ian said at last.

Nobody replied. He avoided looking directly at Hettie, as they'd discussed. She wanted nobody catching on that they knew each other.

He peered down at the pile of papers on their father's desk, and remained standing. He assumed the position of superiority before them, and Rosie found it curious but understandable. His was not an enviable task.

'First of all, let me extend my sympathies to you all. Your father was a fine man, and his passing was a sad day for Radcliffe & Sons.'

Rosie knew just how sad a passing it was; she'd seen the figures. Father had been a loyal lifelong customer and they stood to make a killing from his estate. She daren't steal a glance at her brother for fear of them bursting into fits of ironic giggles. Somehow, being near to James had switched on a childlike propensity for silliness that they'd shared growing up, without Hettie.

Hettie tilted her head, which she always did when she was nervous. Rosie had watched her do it the day Mother had met with the nuns to see why Rosie had withdrawn from her studies and woke in the night with terrors. Hettie had sat with Rosie outside Sister Agatha's office, cuddling her and suffocating her with counterfeit concern. She'd bent her head then as she did now. She had been drowning in guilt.

'Your father's will is complicated...' Ian began. 'And I'm quite happy to schedule a private meeting with all three siblings this afternoon. It might take some time to... absorb.'

James glanced at Rosie, who shrugged. She was more interested in Hettie's reactions. At the front, Hettie couldn't see Rosie and James, but they could watch her shoulders twitch and her husband turn to her with concern. He was just as worried as she was. Rosie could almost smell the fear emanating from the couple, who had been certain they'd be inheriting the whole estate by the end of the day.

'We met several times before his death, together with a psychologist to confirm the full functioning of his faculties, and he had me draw up a number of documents that supersede all other contracts written regarding the Fitzherbert estate.'

'What?'

It was Hettie who stood up and Rosie braced herself for the initial fallout from their father's wishes. Ian looked at their elder sibling and Rosie watched him handle her with professional firmness.

Father had obviously warned him to expect protest.

James covered his mouth, but not in shock, Rosie assessed: in amusement.

'If you'll let me finish...' Mr Balfour said to Hettie.

Edward patted her thigh, but Rosie guessed his palm would be wet with panic. Suddenly, the late summer had come indoors, and the library was too warm.

'There is a series of deeds which must be worked through in order. The first is—'

'Excuse me,' Hettie spoke again.

James was now chuckling, but doing a good job of covering it up. Sarah was staring at him, then she turned to Rosie, who smiled reassuringly at her. She'd soon learn the ways of their family, Rosie thought.

'Are you expecting us to simply accept a new arrangement? I was given prior privilege by my father to arrange this meeting and I have brought documents given to me personally by him to keep these proceedings brief.'

It was quite a speech from Hettie.

The books surrounding them held their breath. A tiny part of Rosie felt sorry for her sister.

'That's what I'm trying to tell you,' Ian soldiered on. 'All documents arranged by Mr Fitzherbert prior to his death, except the ones he left expressly in my care shortly before his passing, are null and void.'

Rosie could see Hettie's neck turning pink from two rows back.

Now Hettie glanced behind her, and her stare could curdle milk, as her mother used to say about the nuns. James could no longer contain himself and he laughed out loud, then stopped himself with a snort. Everybody was looking at him.

'What's so fucking funny?' Hettie asked him. 'This is your doing, isn't it?'

'Hettie, why don't you just listen to what the man has to say? Father clearly changed a few things before he died. Let's hear it.'

'But he can't have done,' she spat.

Hettie was shaking, and Edward struggled to calm her. He used both his hands – one on her shoulder and the other on her knee – to lower the temperature in the room.

'Of course he could! And he did. It's his fucking property!' James turned to Ian. 'I assume all the recent documents are sanctioned and approved by independent parties?'

'They are, sir,' Ian said, on safer ground, with a fellow professional.

'So, let's hear it,' James said.

Ian drew a breath and began reading from a file.

'The last will and testament of Jude George Xander Wintour Fitzherbert II will be communicated to the three surviving children of the deceased when, and only after, a period of seven days from this day, after said beneficiaries have satisfied the criteria expressed in this document, see below, clause II, point thirty, and have remained at Warbury House, together, for said seven days, in harmony—'

'Jesus Christ!' Hettie shouted and stood up. 'Harmony?'

Like one of the more fiery characters in one of her own

novels, Rosie thought, Hettie was losing her shit. It was most entertaining for the others, except Edward, who'd gone pale.

Ian ploughed on. *'Should one or all of the siblings leave before the term has passed, that beneficiary shall cease to gain from the contents herein laid out, in accordance with the wishes of the deceased.'*

'What's going on?' Sarah whispered to James.

'Christ, he's really gone and done it,' James said.

'I thought you said no blaspheming,' Sarah whispered to him just within earshot of Rosie.

Rosie glanced at James, who was telling Sarah they couldn't last a night, never mind a week. Hettie didn't hear him, she was too busy wrapped up in her own tragedy. Rosie locked eyes with her brother and it took her back to a game they used to play down at the lake. They'd hold secret swimming races across it, to the island in the middle. The one who reached the island first, got out, ran around it ten times in the same direction, swam to the other side and raised a green flag James had cobbled together from cubs' uniforms, would dictate what the other sibling was allowed to do for the rest of the weekend. As they got older, the stakes got higher. They'd bet on a whole week, or even a whole summer.

Rosie spied the same hunger in Hettie's eyes now, and the same menace. Her sister was up for the challenge.

The corners of her mouth turned up a mere millimetre, and Hettie saw it, matching the facial movement. The contract was signed and sealed. The game was on. Both assessed their opponent, as James continued to complain to his fiancée about the strain of remaining at Warbury House for a whole week. Rosie held Hettie's stare and they might as well have been alone, so focused on the other were they. Each believing the other would lose. But Rosie had a secret weapon that Hettie didn't know about, and she stood no chance. She was the weakest link and the likelihood of her success was nil.

Like old times, when Hettie caught on to their games, and wanted to join in, they'd warned her that she didn't possess the resilience. Sure enough, when she'd tried, she'd failed to make it to the island before the others had already got out and run their laps.

She never played with them again.

EIGHTEEN

James

'You told me your family was fucked up, but this is crazy. How are you supposed to suffer this for seven days? Your sister is a basket case,' Sarah told James.

'Which one?'

'You know very well who I'm talking about. Rosie is lovely. Her silence is odd, granted, it was a shock at first, but now I've got used to it, I like her. We could all learn something from her. People talk too much. Hettie certainly does.'

'Welcome to the family,' James said. 'I'm glad you enjoyed your tour. Did she tell you all our secrets?'

'Is Hettie mentally stable?'

James laughed. Sarah sighed.

'Well, you don't need me for this, I should go. You've proved your point, and they believe you, I think, so it's perfectly reasonable for me to leave. I have a job and a life to pretend at, remember? Also, I could become suddenly afflicted with morning sickness. It would be entirely understandable. I might have mentioned my condition already, earlier, in the kitchen – they caught me out, sorry, Hettie guessed.'

James looked at her then softened.

'How did Rosie take it?'

Sarah looked puzzled.

'Never mind,' he said. 'It's one less job for me to do. But you can't leave – didn't you hear the grim reaper when he was reading out the document?'

'Which bit?'

'It refers to everybody at Warbury House, including the kids.'

'What does?'

'I was given a copy as we left. Hettie stormed out before getting hers, obviously, but look—'

He passed her his copy.

'It's null and void unless everybody who arrived stays for seven days.'

'What? That's ridiculous! I can't!'

'Yes, you can. It'll be fun. Aren't you dying to see how it plays out?'

'No!'

He jumped onto the bed and put his arms behind his head. 'You're staying.'

She read the paper he'd given her. 'This is so screwed up. Why would he do this to his children? And why would you want to be here?'

'Because this is what he did. He said it was character building, pitting us against each other to see who won. Besides, it's only a week, and we have the beach. Don't young lovers like to spend a lot of time alone? We needn't even see them – the will doesn't state how many hours we have to spend together!'

'Are you actually contemplating staying? You are! I can see you already planning. James! You can't. Seriously, don't let them do this to you. You came to face them, you've done that. Walk away. Let it go. You don't need the money.'

'It's not about the money.' His face darkened.

Sarah sighed and sat on the bed next to him. He pulled her down next to him and she stared at him.

'It's warped. Like some kind of experiment. Did he know you all detest each other?'

'Of course.'

'But you don't dislike Rosie, do you?'

He held her gaze. 'Of course not.'

Sarah moved away.

'Hettie told me your parents forced you to stand by while they played, and no one was allowed to talk to you. And that she was hit with bibles when she got puzzles wrong at school. Is that true?'

He fell silent, but it was enough for her to get an answer to her question.

'And Rosie was locked in a well under the cellar?'

'Ah, now that's contentious. We were all locked up, so she hasn't got exclusive rights on that one. School, here, it's all the same.'

'Oh, my God.'

'She told you a lot in half an hour.'

James was attempting to joke around but all the lustre and fun had gone from his face.

'She showed me, she took me down that creepy staircase in the dark.'

'Wow, you must mean a lot to her.'

She could tell that he was toying with her but underneath it, his eyes told her that he was still scarred by what had gone on here.

'You knew,' she whispered.

He didn't reply.

'You knew this was going to happen.'

'Good assessment,' he said.

'You knew he'd pull a stunt like this? That is why you came, not for the money, but to see what game he'd planned.'

He smiled at her, and she thumped him.

'What did you used to win?' she asked.

'What do you mean?'

'When your mother and father made you play these games, what was the reward?'

'It varied. Sometimes it was dinner. Other times we got to choose the punishment of the losers.'

She stared at him.

'And if you refused to play?'

Shadows danced across his face again. 'He had special penalties for that.'

NINETEEN

Edward

The piece of paper Hettie had treasured for years was worth nothing now. Warbury House wasn't theirs after all. They'd have to work for it. Edward brooded on his situation while at the same time trying to distract the children. They'd taken the news about staying here well. A week in a children's paradise wasn't too bad, even for Kitty.

He chased Benji across the grass, as his son outran him and dribbled a football at the same time. Soon he was out of breath and bent to his knees, resting his hands on them, catching his breath.

Hettie wanted to read the will alone. She was locking him out, he felt, but for now, there was nothing he could do about it. Earlier, she'd sobbed into his chest, then smashed a mirror in the bathroom. They'd both been shocked by her outburst. The last time he'd seen her cry like that had been when Christian died. It had been brief. She hadn't wallowed in misery, not like Beatrice had – Hettie's mother. And Rosie.

He reflected on the habitual self-pity exuded by his mother-in-law when she'd been alive. She'd been normally awash with emotions, whether she was supervising packing away Christmas decorations, at a wedding, or tasking Michael or Clara with something. Beatrice lived her life on the edge of a cliff, constantly switching between the precipice and the rock face. Her temper was incendiary and judging her mood was a full-time sport. Nowadays, it was called bipolar disorder, and Edward reckoned all women were afflicted by it to some degree. For Beatrice, it was only soothed by taking a bottle of something to her room and blacking out, but it took a terrible turn for the worse when Christian died. Her life changed, and along with it, the lives of her remaining children. She took to her room for days on end and refused to be moved. Only Clara had been allowed in to see her, and she'd kept her counsel. They were difficult days for the whole family, but at least Hettie and her siblings had lives to get on with. Clara and Michael had to stay and put up with Beatrice, an unenviable task.

Jude simply disappeared for weeks and months at a time, on business trips. A likely story. The late Jude Fitzherbert was a distant man who lived disconnected from his family, though Hettie told her husband early in their relationship that Christian had been an exception to that rule. Edward put that down to the youngest child syndrome. Your first brought with it a tsunami of fear and inadequacy, only alleviated by getting through another day. The second allowed some respite, because you'd done it all before. By the third or fourth – as in Christian's case – it was a walk in the park, and parents were free, seemingly, to enjoy the whole affair. The age gap between Hettie, Rosie and James, with their younger brother, was also likely a factor. Christian had been a surprise.

Perhaps Jude was punishing the others for Christian going first like that. It was disappointing, for sure, but he assessed that Jude was simply toying with them all, like he always did. He recalled his first meeting with his prospective father-in-law, when the man had grilled him over his commitment to his daughter. Edward had survived intact, just, but had been left a nervous wreck. That evening, Jude had laughed it off, but Edward knew that one never could relax fully around him. Jokes were only amusing if Jude was delivering the punchline. Should anyone else attempt pranks, then they'd be shot down in a bonfire of withering humiliation. He shivered when he tried to imagine what it might have been like to have him as a father.

Edward saw his role this week as keeping Hettie afloat and entertaining the children. Hettie must keep her wits about her and play the game like a professional. This was what Jude was testing, the old goat.

The girls were baking cakes with Clara, which, Edward figured, would be less taxing than charging after his son. He ended up chasing him into one of the workshops to the rear of the main house, and found James rooting around under broken canoes and old engine parts. When asked what he was doing, James informed them that he was trying to find an old go-kart. Hettie had expressly told him that their children were not to be left alone with her brother under any circumstances, but he didn't seem that bad to Edward at all, and Benji was enjoying himself, so he let it go. They all had to try to get along if they must suffer each other for a whole week, and laying the law down wasn't a way to begin to gain favour with his wife's estranged family. He'd be wise to get them on side and besides, the will made it clear that this was James's heritage, not his. He listened as his son asked incessant questions about the kart and Edward thought it would be alright to leave them. He felt rather a spare part anyway.

'I'm going back to the house,' he told his son, who barely registered him. Edward felt more than ever that he was an outsider as he retreated out of the shed and headed back to the house. It felt good to disobey his wife. On his way across the lawn, he noticed a few patches of pooling water. He tutted, cursing the ancient drainage, thinking it was yet another thing that needed looking at if they ever finally took over the house, then he made his way back, where he went straight to the library to speak to Ian Balfour who'd told them he was happy to answer questions.

The guy was an odd fish, Edward thought. A typical legal sort; all rules and no grey areas. As a banking man, one used to speaking plainly in high-level meetings, Edward figured he might get some sense out of him, man to man. He went in and closed the door behind him. Balfour smiled and got up out of his seat. Edward wasn't sure if it was because he was pleased that somebody wanted to ask his advice, or amused because he had guessed it would be one of the non-siblings to expect answers.

'I've come on Hettie's behalf, obviously,' he began.

'Obviously,' Balfour replied. 'Fire away.'

'How are the terms enforced? I presume you will stay here to spy on us?'

'I wouldn't put it quite like that.'

'Who do you report to?'

'Jude made arrangements. I have it covered, but I can't share the particulars with you.'

Another smile.

Edward imagined spies, or CCTV, around the place keeping tabs on them and it unnerved him.

'What if the children get ill?'

'You would follow the same procedure you would if you were a guest here ordinarily – call in the help you need, and it will be taken care of.'

Edward nodded slowly. He wasn't getting anywhere.

'What if somebody leaves, but comes back?'

'That would count as abandoning the wishes of the deceased, I'm afraid.'

'What if they were to act out of anger and regret it, though?'

'Same, I'm afraid.'

Balfour crossed his legs and perched on the side of Jude's desk.

'It's all in the file I gave to Hettie. If she has any further questions, then she can raise it in our private meeting later.'

'I know. It's all still very confusing, though. You and I know – being in the industries we are in – that face-to-face contact is invaluable for making that final deal.'

Balfour remained unmoved.

'What I'm trying to say is that Hettie can be... impulsive.'

'I think that's the point. You'll all have to dig deep and accept each other's company. Jude wanted to see his family together, properly, before his soul was laid to rest. The only way to do that is to give it time. He wanted the bonds between you to be genuine.'

'I see.'

Edward stood up and walked towards the door.

They were fucked.

TWENTY

Rosie

Rosie passed Edward in the corridor as she arrived at the library for her scheduled private meeting with the lawyer. She was toying with the idea of making Edward a character in one of her books. He had that stiff, half-dead look that came in handy when creating a wicked soul. She imagined him as a distant father, or a secretly gay professor in Victorian England perhaps, who killed for his lover...

Edward looked vexed, but then he'd always been a restless soul. She remembered when Hettie first brought him to Warbury House and the way his behaviour lacked authenticity around her parents, especially her father. But it was probably nerves. Edward was a misogynist of the worst kind. He was the type who nodded and smiled at a woman who spoke about politics or religion, or even business, but did so out of pity for the fairer sex, not believing they could possibly have anything pertinent to say. Her father had warmed to him, in so far as Jude Fitzherbert liked anyone. He had tolerated Edward and found him perfectly acceptable for Hettie, whose own ambitions had extended to motherhood and wifedom, but Rosie also sensed that Hettie was restless now, too. Perhaps she looked at Father's estate as the key to her independence. Hettie had thrown her life away on marriage when she could have done so much more, but that wasn't Rosie's problem.

She and Edward swapped brief glances and his smell lingered in the corridor long after he'd gone.

He tries too hard, she thought to herself.

But who wouldn't when fifty million pounds was at stake?

Rosie wagered he'd been to see Ian at the behest of Hettie – who probably couldn't face it herself – to convince him to change Father's wishes, and it wouldn't surprise her if he'd come up with some convincing arguments of legality. But she and James had already gone over it with Ian, many times.

The outcome was watertight. But the seven-day clause had come as a shock. Not insurmountable, but still, that's why she was here.

She knocked lightly on the door.

She entered and found Ian at her father's desk, and he smiled. The stiff, set and miserable visage was replaced by something approaching human. He looked relieved.

'Rosie, it's good to meet you in person finally. Your father had much to say about you.'

Rosie chose a chair and sat down.

'Zoom meetings are so sanitary,' he added.

She nodded in agreement and glanced at the mountain of paperwork on his desk.

He was prepared.

'Would you rather do this on paper? I have brought a duplicate MacBook, here.'

He fussed and produced a mini-Mac which he gave to her as he plopped an identical one on his lap. He smiled again.

'Look, I'll show you,' he said.

He was like a puppy, and it jarred her because he was

supposed to be in control. His waistcoat was unbuttoned, his jacket discarded, and he'd loosened his collar. She'd noticed all of this in the time it had taken him to explain how the technology worked, as if she was stupid. She was familiar with the format, using it for work all the time, but Ian thought the whole experience was novel to her – in fact, that he was doing her a favour. He was enjoying being helpful to somebody in need.

Rosie was the equivalent of the family cripple. She wouldn't be surprised if he slowed his words for her, too.

'Any general questions before we go over the documentation?' he asked.

She put the tablet to one side, getting her pad and pen out of her pocket, and considered what questions one might ask when you stood to inherit millions of pounds, dependent on passing a series of tests, set by a dead man, and judged by a bunch of lawyers.

Ian had done his job admirably, but he should remember his place, she thought.

In the absence of any questions, he placed his Mac to the side and asked why she'd come. She stared at him. She wasn't stupid enough to type anything that could be kept on a Cloud. Except what she might want others to see. So, she turned to her pad.

Are they James's or Father's thugs on the perimeter? she wrote.

He stared at her and the smile drifted off his face.

There could only be one winner at the end of the week. Rosie believed they were more likely to kill one another than get along, until there was one person left standing.

The ultimate outplay game. But to her it was simply a matter of endurance, and she was used to that. Missing one of the five senses made one disciplined in the others and waiting was merely another sensory task.

'I was of the understanding that you had put those men

there, with your brother,' Ian said. His response answered her question. Her father hadn't arranged the men, so it had to be James.

How well did you know my father? she wrote on her pad. Ian seemed irritated that he'd gone to all this trouble only for her to ignore his gadget, but Rosie wasn't about to pander to him.

His body was so easy to read. He touched his head when he was embarrassed, and he shifted his weight when he was thinking. His main task of reading the will had been completed. His hard work was over. He'd been of value to her and James over the last months of Father's life. He'd now become surplus to requirements. He'd gone the extra mile and stood to benefit from a small personal fortune for his efforts, including making their sister feel as though she mattered to him.

She couldn't help a tiny noise escaping from her nose as she reflected on the ease with which Hettie had been seduced. Ian froze.

'That's the first noise I've heard you make... it's beautiful. Why don't you talk?' he asked her.

Rosie's skin tingled with warning, and she recoiled. Her sudden movement away from him made him come to his senses and he sat back in his place. He'd fulfilled his usefulness and now he'd seen his mistake.

'I'm sorry,' he said weakly. 'I didn't mean to offend you.'

A shadow crossed his face, and he got up to walk to the library window, peering into the distance.

What happens if even after a week together, we still don't get on? Rosie wrote and joined him at the window to show him the message.

'A week is a long time,' he said, looking at her. 'If Hettie behaves as you expect her to, then there will be nothing for her to inherit.'

Is Hettie's document really null and void? she wrote, referring to the one Father gave her, signing over Warbury House.

'Yes,' he said. 'Your father gave it to her to make sure she never came back. He was very shrewd. It was a test to see if her visits were genuine, or she just wanted his money.'

Anybody could have told him the answer to that, she scribbled.

He studied her.

'Why did you come here?' he asked her. 'I know you don't need the money, Rosie. Your father told me everything. Why bother coming back?'

She was inches from his body, peering out of the window. She saw a figure in almost the same place as she had earlier. And this time she was sure she knew who it was.

She turned back to Ian and wrote another message.

Even though I'm not here for money, doesn't mean I don't want to inherit. I'm here for something else. Something more important.

He read the message and nodded.
'I'm glad you're not my sister,' he said.

TWENTY-ONE

Sarah

'All right, I'm in, I'll stay. This is better than *Real Housewives*, try getting rid of me,' Sarah said. She was standing next to the window. 'Who's that?' she asked.

James joined her and followed her finger, which she tapped on the glass.

'Who?' he asked.

'Down there,' she said.

She indicated towards the trees on the edge of the forest, but James saw nothing out of the ordinary.

'What did you see?' he asked.

'A man, all in black.'

James laughed. 'A tad paranoid, perhaps? I think this place is getting to you already.'

'No, I'm serious.'

'Well, it must either be Michael or one of the kids.'

'It wasn't a child, and it would take Michael all day to get down there, and he certainly couldn't dip behind that bush like that.'

'It could be press.'

'Press?' Sarah sounded alarmed.

'Dad's death has caused a small splash. He was quite the business mogul in his day, but we haven't had paps around here for years.'

'Paps?'

James burst out laughing and Sarah threw a cushion at him. 'Twat.'

'Seriously, though, Dad was famous back in the day. His death was in *The Times*. Or maybe Michael employed a new gardener. I don't know.'

'Let's go for a walk,' she said.

'Good idea, we can't stay in here until dinner.'

'Do you think we're being watched?' she asked.

'What do you mean?'

'Well, the terms of your father's will are that you must all stay here for a week and get on. Who is to know if you do, or you don't? Somebody must be watching and deciding either way.'

'OK, we'll assume that Father planted spies. So let's give everybody a show.'

'Really? Lay it on thick?'

'Absolutely!'

'Can we go to the lake for a swim? I brought my bikini especially.'

'Just what I was thinking,' he said.

They changed and packed casual bags, not minding their nakedness in front of one another. Neither was interested in the slightest in the flesh of another gender, and they were more like siblings changing after a swimming lesson, rather than two lovers sharing a bed.

'Nice tits!' James announced, seeing Sarah in her bikini.

She grabbed them with both hands and wobbled them up and down.

'Why, thank you.' She slapped his bottom playfully and they left the room. The house was quiet.

It was deliciously freeing to leave the main house and walk across the immaculate lawns to the lake, and Sarah began to sing.

'So, this is how you spent your summers? I'm beginning to think it wasn't as bad as you've told me,' Sarah said.

'Appearances can be deceiving,' he told her. He ran away ahead, and she sprinted after him.

They jogged through a clearing and down a grass path and the view to the lake opened up before them.

'Fucking hell,' she said.

James grinned and walked towards the beach in the distance. When they got closer, she saw that tables, chairs, clothes, towels, blow-up pool floats and various games had been laid out already. James waved his hand over the scene.

'Michael has it done every day when there are visitors – it's an old habit of my father's. He could never entertain anyone himself, so he paid to have others do it for him. This is the result. Everything you could need. If you lift the lid on that basket, it'll have a power source in there and chilled drinks and ice creams.'

'What? Are you serious?'

'Totally.'

'Is there a loo?'

James looked at the lake. 'There are two types of wild swimmers: those who piss in the open water, and those who lie about it.'

Sarah giggled. 'That's quite gross.'

'Not really. Fish piss in there, so why shouldn't we?'

Sarah rolled her eyes and set her towel out on a sunbed. She sat on it and lay back.

'I thought we were swimming,' James said.

'Right away? I bet it's freezing.'

'Don't let me down, come on! It'll be amazing.'

He ran away from her and splashed into the water, pretending to fall over in the depths and struggle to stand. She chuckled as she watched him and wondered what sort of a father could ruin such an idyllic place. Then James went under the water and the surface became quite still. She watched for signs of his bubbles rising to the top, but she couldn't see any and she tutted. After another half a minute, she sat up and stared at the spot where he'd gone in.

She heard screams behind her and turned her head sharply to see the children sprinting towards the beach, pointing and chasing one another. Her head darted back to the water, and she walked towards the edge, shading her eyes from the sun, looking for James.

The boy, Benji, made it to the beach first and ran to her side and asked what she was looking at.

'James went in and he's... holding his breath.'

'Is he seeing how long he can go without coming up, like Christian did?'

'Who's Christian?' Sarah asked.

'No one,' he said, too quickly.

The boy stared at her, but their attention was taken by a noise from the lake. James had surfaced with a flurry and was swimming to the other side.

'I'm going in, you want to come with me?' she asked Benji. He nodded nervously.

'Can you swim?' she asked.

He shook his head.

'Oh.'

'I've got buoyancy aids.' He trotted away and rummaged in a bag, finding bands for his arms, and pulling them on.

The girls joined them, already stripping off to their costumes. They shrieked and giggled as they splashed each other and pushed each other around.

'Dad won't let you go in without an adult,' Pippa said to Benji.

'Is that right?' Sarah asked him.

'Stop stirring, Pip! I can go in if I want, Dad said.'

'Did he?' Sarah asked.

He nodded.

Benji's eyes lingered on Sarah's breasts a little too long and she stifled a smile.

'Come on then, I don't need buoyancy aids,' she joked, pointing to her chest. He blushed and followed her to the water's edge.

'How old are you?' she asked.

'Fourteen,' he said.

She noted his shyness. He was awkward and acted way younger than his real age. And he should be able to swim at fourteen. His sisters could, after all.

'Maybe this is the week you learn to swim?' she said, smiling. 'Come on, I'll show you.'

He followed her into the water. She screamed in mock horror at the cold, and he splashed her. She dived under and he ran in after her. So did the girls.

'Come on,' she shouted. They swam away from the beach and into the deep water. She instructed Benji to control his breathing and to keep afloat, assuming the same positions she'd learned years ago during school swimming lessons. It was sad that a child of his age hadn't been taught.

'Did you know that if you relax and let all your muscles flop, you'll always float to the top? The key is to keep your face pointed up to the sky, like this.'

She showed him. Sarah noticed that it wasn't fear that had held Benji back – he was willing to give anything a go when she showed him.

'Come on, let's go deeper. That's it – just do breaststroke until we get deeper, come on, let's go to the other side.'

She saw James waving from the opposite shore, and he dived back in.

'Let's go to the island. James already took me there on a canoe,' Benji said.

'Rosie went over there, too, I saw her,' Kitty said.

They turned around in the water to glance at her, then they carried on swimming.

'You're doing brilliantly!' she encouraged Benji.

Sarah saw that he was on his way to becoming a strong swimmer and reckoned he didn't need much of a nudge to ditch the arm bands.

'I don't think you'll need those bands for much longer,' she told him.

They were almost to the island. James had got out already and was standing with his hands on his hips waiting for them, waving. He was a good-looking bloke and it saddened her to think of him hiding from meaningful relationships all his life. If she had swayed that way, he'd certainly have had her attention. His physique was lean and muscular, though he abused it with late nights, junk food and too much work, but he was still young and strong enough to get away with it. He looked the happiest she'd ever seen him as she and Benji reached the shore and got out. Benji threw his bands off.

'I'll try without them on the way back.'

'Good for you,' Sarah said.

'Look, here come Kitty and Pippa,' James said.

The girls had got into a race and Kitty was winning, but Sarah saw her slow down, to let the younger girl pass her. It was a sweet gesture. As they got closer, James, Sarah and Benji shouted them on and clapped and cheered as the girls reached the island. They got out, panting and smiling.

'I like your bikini,' Kitty said to Sarah.

'Thank you.'

She noticed Benji's cheeks turn pink, and James turned away.

'Come on, let's go and see if our old camp is still there,' James said, leading the way.

'You have a camp?' Benji said, distracted from Sarah's body.

'We had a camp. I think this is the perfect opportunity to do a bit of home improvement. Come on, we can even start a fire.'

As they followed James, one by one, through the bushes, Sarah couldn't fathom why on earth this family was estranged in the first place. But she did intend to ask James who Christian was.

'Kitty said Rosie came over here earlier,' Sarah told James.

'Really? That's odd.'

'Why?'

'I don't know. It's where my father's body is, that's all.'

'Oh.'

'Grandad's body?' Pippa asked.

'It's OK, he's in a coffin,' Sarah said.

But the girl wasn't reassured and stopped walking.

'I want to go back,' she said.

'Go back, then,' James said.

Sarah eyed him, his curt tone annoying her. They were only kids.

'I'll go back with you,' she told Pippa.

'Maybe I'll go back, too,' Benji said.

'Christ, you lot are no fun at all!' James said.

'I'll build a camp with you,' Kitty told him.

They high-fived and Sarah left with the two younger kids.

'Why is Grandad out here all alone?' Pippa asked her.

'Sometimes, those who die are left in peace for a bit before they're buried. It's quite nice, really. Not scary at all.'

'But it's dark at night,' Pippa said. Benji took her hand.

'Don't worry, it's not really him, it's just his body. His spirit is in heaven already.'

'Do you believe in God?' Benji asked her.

'Blimey... erm, no, not really.'

'Then why tell stories about heaven? We're atheists, so we know heaven doesn't exist.'

'But it still sounds nice,' Pippa said.

'I thought your mum was Catholic,' Sarah said.

'No, she said the nuns at her school were evil, and she thinks that religion is just a way to control people.'

'Deep. Things you didn't know you needed to talk about on a trip to the beach.'

'If nuns are evil then why do you think Grandad sent his daughters to school with them?' Benji asked.

'Did he?' Pippa said.

'Gosh, I'm not qualified in that department, I'm afraid. I don't know why people do things like that. Anyway, whether there is or isn't a God, your grandad is at peace now.'

'Mum said he'd never be at peace because of what happened here on the lake.'

'Really?'

They neared the beach and Sarah wished they had a boat. She was responsible for two kids, she realised, on her own, and it felt burdensome.

'I don't know about that either,' she said. 'Come on, let's take it slowly.'

'Uncle Christian died here,' Benji said.

'Did he?' Sarah replied.

TWENTY-TWO

Hettie

Hettie arrived at the library and knocked on the door lightly. She went straight in, not expecting to be intruding on anything, but as she opened the door, she saw her sister with Ian, sat closely together, poring over documents and smiling conspiratorially.

'Oh, excuse me, I wasn't aware you'd beaten me to it, Rosie.'

Rosie stood up and stretched. She'd obviously been leaning over the bunch of papers for some time. She excused herself, by way of a facial expression, and went to leave.

Ian looked panicked and made excuses for her to stay.

'Perhaps I could go over this with both of you?' he said.

'She's had her time, I'll have mine,' Hettie said.

Hettie held the door open for her sister, but before Rosie left the room, something passed between her and the lawyer and Hettie felt irritation stir in her stomach as she recognised a hot, fiery ball of jealousy rise inside of her. Rosie walked past her and smiled sweetly, as if she was the most pleasant and innocent of the gathered guests and it took Hettie all her strength not to expose her right there and then. After Rosie had closed the door, Hettie turned to Ian and glared.

'I expected you to have everything in order,' she said, controlling her voice.

'Well... your father was very thorough.' He backed away from her and sat behind the desk.

'Indeed, which is why I find it difficult to believe that he deviated from his strongly held values just before he died. It's... convenient. What exactly do you stand to gain from pulling this week-long stunt? How much are you being paid?'

Ian grinned at her, but it didn't last long.

'Hettie, this isn't a conspiracy. It's quite straightforward. Your father and I had long, recorded conversations before he passed, when he was aware he was terminally ill. He was keen to put his entire estate in order in this way, despite what he might have said before, verbally, to you or any of your siblings.'

She eyed him suspiciously.

'He made other agreements – not just with me?' she asked. Her heart fell to the floor like stone.

'Yes. He made all sorts of promises – to Michael, Clara, as well as to your brother and sister, and he scrapped every one of them.'

'I want my own lawyers to look over the paperwork.'

'Of course, but I do offer some word of caution. Your father's last wishes were drawn up with three solicitors. I wasn't there for the final draft for obvious reasons, and the verbal promises he gave prior to that are not binding.'

'But you promised me!' Hettie struggled to control the volume of her voice and Ian glanced towards the door.

'Be careful, Hettie,' he warned her. 'The conditions of the will dictate that you must display a solid relationship with your husband.'

'You bastard, you tricked me!'

Ian held out his hands in front of him. 'No, it wasn't like

that, I swear to you. It was genuine and I tried to do everything I said I would. Is the money the only reason you wanted to sleep with me?' he asked her. She couldn't tell him that the real reason she'd fallen so quickly into bed with him was because of her own husband's affair.

She realised her mistake and bit her lip, buying time. 'What had he promised the others?'

'You'll have to take that up with them, I'm afraid. You know I can't divulge private information like that.'

'For God's sake, Ian! Don't be so goddamn stuffy. Like you said, it means nothing now, anyway.'

She approached him and stood next to him, close enough to hear his breathing.

'Hettie, don't. This isn't the way—'

'You never complained before.'

Her hand touched his and he stared at it as it lingered and then traced his muscle up towards his elbow, then along his shirt to his neck. She smiled as he swallowed hard and the pulse on top of his carotid artery throbbed.

'I know what you're doing,' he breathed. 'But my hands are tied, just as yours are.'

'There's got to be a way,' she whispered.

She kept stroking him, around his shoulder now, towards his back, and with her other hand, she opened her summer dress slightly. He stared down at her breasts and closed his eyes.

'It's too risky,' he said. 'If we get caught...'

The chance of being discovered only made Hettie more focused. Here in Warbury House – her house – she could do whatever the hell she liked, just as she always had, and nobody could do anything about it.

'You're turning me down?' she asked.

She went to the door and turned the key in the lock. It clicked and she felt its power in her fingers, wondering how many times Father had done the same when he'd fucked Clara in here, on his desk. She turned to Ian and carried on unbuttoning the tiny pearl discs on her dress. Only this morning she'd felt frumpy, hormonal, unsexy and miserable, but now, after only a couple of hours at the heart of her father's power, alongside his desk where he screwed people's lives, and close enough to smell the money she was owed, suddenly she was turned on, and she sure as shit wasn't going to get what she wanted from Edward. Ian felt the same, it was written all over his pants.

She walked towards him, and he leaned on the desk. As she moved, another button came loose and revealed more skin, until it slipped off completely and she stood in front of him, reaching for his hand and putting it on her soft flesh.

He grabbed her and she unbuttoned his shirt expertly and, as he laid her back on her father's desk, she couldn't help thinking about Ian's signature, which she'd watch him apply to as many documents as she wanted, starting with the one her father gave to her.

Warbury House would be hers, even if she had to fuck Ian Balfour ten times a day to get it.

TWENTY-THREE

Rosie

Rosie always felt a waft of cold air when she was in the same room as Hettie, which is why she'd avoided her for so long. She felt that her sister's presence was followed by a dark aura that left her feeling like the frightened little girl she'd once been. She reminded her always of the times she'd been locked in the hole until one day, Rosie had excommunicated her from her life altogether.

She waited just around the corner from the library and overheard them talking quietly, then the door clicked locked, and Rosie knew exactly what was happening on the other side. Ian Balfour was easily led, which is why he was perfect for the task of distracting Hettie. She had no desire to listen to her sister's lusty efforts, and so she left them to it and hoped Hettie didn't tire Ian out too much or affect his good judgement. She hoped, too, he could be trusted. When James had first suggested using him as a Trojan horse, she'd laughed it off, but he'd impressed both of them with what he'd got out of their sister. Her plan to take the whole estate for herself on the grounds of being the eldest was ill-conceived and she'd underestimated her siblings.

The house was quiet as she wandered through the rooms on her way back to see Clara. Everybody else had gone to the lake. It struck her that Hettie and Edward's children had fitted straight into their estranged family as if they'd seen each other just yesterday. She begrudgingly acknowledged that Hettie must be a good mother. Better than their own, at least. She also had not witnessed any sign of her sister's mean streak in any of them. As children went, they were pleasant and intriguing. Though people might have said that about them as kids, too. Children often stuck together because they were supposed to, until they worked out why they shouldn't.

Kitty was a watcher and oscillated on a wave of teenage emotions beckoning adulthood to come. Her head seemed full of sentiments over the injustices of the world. Rosie could almost touch her inner turmoil, as she struggled to make sense of it all. Benji was a nervous sort, but sweet, and had taken a shine to James, which Hettie wouldn't like one bit.

It seemed for the time being that they were all in agreement that they'd stay and battle it out.

It was only seven days, what could possibly go wrong? Of course, they could all leave at any time, and were free to. But none of them would. The rewards were too great.

As Rosie approached the kitchen, she heard Edward's voice, and she entered the room and forced a smile. He was looking for his wife. Clara glanced at her, then picked up an empty picnic basket.

'Edward, will you help?' Clara asked him. 'I've made snacks to take down to the lake for the children.'

'I don't know where they are,' Edward said.

Clara looked puzzled. 'I saw them going to the lake with James and Sarah,' she told him.

'James? To the lake? Gosh, I better get down there before

Hettie or that'll be me walking home,' he said, laughingly, half joking but obviously not.

Rosie felt a pang of sympathy for him and wrote him a note hurriedly on her pad.

Hettie is in a very important meeting with Mr Balfour. I wouldn't disturb them. Help me carry the basket to the lake?

He gave a conspiratorial smile, and Rosie could tell he was pleased that Hettie was working on their fortune. Rosie wanted to add that she hoped it didn't exhaust her too much, but resisted. Clara handed over pies, cake and biscuits to wrap and they formed a production line. Soon, the basket was full, and they left Clara to her dinner preparations.

'I swear I'll put on a stone this week,' Edward laughed. She saw Clara turn her back on him and busy herself like she always did when she didn't want to speak. Rosie reckoned everyone could benefit from a spell of muteness, it avoided much unnecessary chit chat. She'd come to the kitchen to spend some time with the housekeeper, but it would have to wait.

Rosie and Edward walked across the lawn together in strained silence. Rosie was used to people assuming that because she didn't speak, they shouldn't either. It took time for them to relax in her company. Edward was chivalrous and offered to carry the basket. It had two handles, and the burden was meant to be shared, but Edward was like her father. Rosie allowed him to indulge his masculine ego to legitimise his self-worth. She was thankful she didn't have to live with someone like that, except for the characters she created in her books. Still, Edward struck her as a fragile beast, unused to the scheming ways of those with everything to lose. She'd met plenty of men like him; those who believed women didn't understand what it took to be the man of the house, but Edward hadn't known that she'd loved a man once, too, but her father had put a stop to it and she'd never felt the same again. Because she was unmarried, people tended to assume that she was incapable of romantic love.

She could tell by the way Edward looked around that he imagined himself Lord of Warbury House one day, but she was also convinced that Hettie – if she were ever to get her hands on the estate – had no intention of sharing. Even bonds made of blood sometimes broke when money was involved.

He soon relaxed a little more and asked her random questions about growing up here, then apologised for forgetting her muteness and answered them himself with supposition and hearsay – much of it from Hettie. She also suspected that he was testing her, like people tended to, to see if she slipped up and uttered a few words, thereby revealing herself to be a fraud, like Hettie would love to see her do.

'Did you spend much time down at the lake as a kid?' Edward continued making polite conversation.

Rosie looked at him and nodded. The lake had been their refuge as children, even though that memory had soured when Christian died there the summer after his last school trip in his final year – the one where he'd been found in another boy's tent in a compromising situation. Consenting, but awkward. But it didn't matter. His secret, like James's, was out.

That's when his quest to prove himself better than his older brother had begun, and Father being Father, had chosen sides.

'The children are loving getting to know their uncle, and his fiancée. What do you think of her?'

Rosie smiled. Edward was a natural conspirator and would have fitted into any medieval court with pride and aplomb.

'Do you ever think about learning sign language?'

She stopped walking and got out her pad and pen from her dress. She always chose skirts, dresses and jackets with pockets, in which to store her essentials, like now. She scribbled on her pad.

What is the point when no one else understands it? she wrote.

He laughed.

Let's get to the children if you're worried about the lake, she added.

A shadow crossed his face.

'You think it's dangerous? Because of Christian?' he asked, panic spread throughout his body.

Rosie shook her head and wrote more. She'd had enough of his chatter.

The lake isn't dangerous, but James was alone with Christian when he died. It left him traumatised. I don't know how he'll react, being there now.

'Jesus!' Edward dropped the basket and sprinted towards the lake. Rosie shaded her eyes, popped her notebook away, picked up the basket, which was heavy, but not overly so, and followed him, glad of the peace and quiet.

She arrived at a scene reminiscent of any Fitzherbert domestic argument from the past, and a satisfying glow resonated within her. From the water, James eyed her with suspicion, his brow furrowed. She winked at him. The kids were moaning about having to get out, and Sarah was playing mediator.

Edward looked at the basket she'd carried all the way on her own and apologised.

'All right, we can stay for snacks and to get dry,' he relented. 'But no more swimming without me.'

'Thank you for telling me,' Edward told Rosie quietly, out of earshot of the children.

Kitty approached her and already she looked different. Her layers of teenage angst were peeling off and she was becoming free. After a week in this place, she'd be almost healed. The two younger children played, chasing one another around. Benji reminded her of Christian with his wiry frame and lean muscles. His face was wide open and easy to read. Pippa giggled as he chased her and the noise of youth was just what the place needed, even though it had come too late.

'Will you stay the week?' Edward asked her.

There, he'd finally got around to it. He wanted to know if they'd have any competition.

Rosie nodded.

'Right, yes, we are, too.'

He waited before asking his next question.

'Will James stay?'

She nodded again. He raised his eyebrows.

'What really happened to Christian? Hettie never told me fully, not properly anyway.'

Rosie could see that it had taken a lot of courage to ask about her little brother, but still she felt as though he didn't deserve to know. She stared out to the lake and her body stiffened. The pain of memory was so acute that she felt the breeze clawing at her neck as the sun began its dip to the west, over Warbury House.

In the distance, next to the wall, which separated the estate from the main road to Oxford, she saw the figure in dark clothes, and she knew he was watching. The surveillance was to be expected, and now she'd seen the man at least three times, she was certain James had arranged it. Edward remained oblivious. He didn't know the estate like she did. She could spot anything out of place in any direction, just with a glance. This time of year, the gardens and wild trees and bushes were a chaotic symphony of colour. Black stood out.

She spread a towel on the beach, which had been layered with sand decades ago. Edward sat next to her, and they watched James and Sarah glide about on inflatables. She took out her notepad and began to write.

It was an accident. He and James were canoeing, and Christian's flipped over.

She handed him her pad to read.

'Hettie said he committed suicide,' he said quietly.

Rosie nodded. *Because the coroner found drugs in his system and that was enough to kill him. The drowning afterwards was considered misadventure because of the drugs*, she wrote.

Edward was getting used to waiting for his answers. Anybody could adapt, it seemed.

'Ah. That's what Hettie said. An overdose. I didn't know he'd gone canoeing and fallen in. And did James know about the drugs?'

I've never asked him, she wrote.

'I'm sorry to bring it up. Hettie doesn't like talking about it.'

Do the children know about him? she wrote.

'Yes, it came up and we told them... well, I told them. Hettie couldn't.'

She nodded. That sounded familiar, Hettie never could stomach the fallout of her own behaviour. Better to let others clean up after her.

Kitty was staring at them with suspicion and trying to listen to their conversation. For now, the discussion about Christian was over. Rosie smiled at the girl, who sat next to her and leaned back, allowing the sun to warm her after swimming.

Kitty stared at Rosie and then wrote her a note, asking Rosie what she was planning to wear to dinner. Her niece could easily have verbalised her questions, but it was touching that she wanted to communicate in the same manner as her aunt.

I'll show you, Rosie wrote. *I've got my own room so you can come back with me*, she added, which delighted the girl. Then she stared across the lake at the island.

'I saw the chapel and the graves,' Kitty said. 'James showed me.'

Rosie stared at her.

'That's where you went earlier, wasn't it?'

Rosie nodded.

'Why aren't they buried in a normal cemetery like everyone else?'

Rosie didn't feel like answering, and wished she could have just formulated some words to sum it up, but she didn't know how to tell her niece that she was glad her grandfather was being entombed there for the rest of his earthly existence, so he couldn't harm anyone else, but at the same time angry that her brother was trapped over there, on the land that had consumed him.

'It's tradition,' she wrote.

'Does that make it right?' Kitty asked.

Rosie stared at her niece and shook her head, trying to control the salty warmth threatening to engulf her eyes.

TWENTY-FOUR

Sarah

Later, as the sun went down behind the huge trees around the lake, James and Sarah walked back to the house.

'Those kids are so normal. They're not what I expected at all,' Sarah said.

'Give them time. The thing about kids is they all start off idealists and innocents, but adults always ruin them in the end.'

'That's dramatic,' Sarah said.

'But true,' he replied.

'But you were having fun with them, I could tell, so don't deny it. I went all doe-eyed, looking at my future hubby getting sentimental about kids.'

'Fuck off.' He tapped her playfully on the arm. 'Didn't you used to be that nice?' he asked her.

She slapped him back. 'I still am!'

'You never lie? Or twist the truth to get what you want? Or hurt people?'

'OK, you've got me there. I suppose we all end up hurting somebody. But does that mean that everybody turns out bad?

Isn't it the old case of yin and yang? You know, nobody is all good or all bad.'

'There are people like that, though.'

'Like what?'

'All bad, obviously, else I'd be out of a job.'

'What about mitigating circumstances?'

'Excuses, you mean?'

'James, I never had you down as a Victorian. Maybe this place has had more of an impact on you than I thought. Is coming back here making you more fascist as we speak?'

'That's so single-minded. The belief that all tradition, morals and ethics are outdated, and automatically wrong. Today, it's gutsier to stand up and remain loyal to tradition than it is to join a protest. Revolution is the new totalitarianism.'

'Deep. All I said was I like your nieces and nephew.'

They carried on in silence and Sarah put her cardigan on over her dress.

'Are you going to tell me who Christian is?' she asked. He looked away and she stopped walking. 'James?'

'He was my little brother. He died. It was thirteen years ago. My mother and father never got over it. Everything fell apart after that. He was eighteen.'

Sarah held her hand out and touched his arm. 'Christ, I'm so sorry.' She hugged him and he allowed himself to be held. Suddenly, their minor argument about human flaws seemed terribly insignificant. 'Do you want to tell me about it?'

He shrugged and they carried on walking towards the house.

'We think he went off for a late swim. I don't know if he was drunk or what, but he got into trouble. Hettie was the last person to see him. He was a strong swimmer, and he never would have got into trouble in the water normally, but... I wasn't there. I mean, we were all here at the house, but I wasn't at the lake. It's why Hettie is so paranoid about letting her kids swim, maybe I could have—'

'So what was different that day?' Sarah asked.

'Christian had just finished his last term at St Christopher's. He'd changed. He was angry and distant. He'd fallen out with Rosie, too. He was messed up before that, though.'

'What do you mean?'

'He was depressed, unhappy, lonely – I don't know. But he was also strong. One day he was alive and the next he wasn't. Rosie went back to London and Hettie went off travelling with Edward.'

'What about your parents?'

'They never discussed it with us.'

'What? Everybody just pretended it hadn't happened?'

'Pretty much. I told you what my family is like. They don't communicate – even if they do speak, they don't really. Nobody knows what really happened.'

'Somebody does.'

He looked at her.

'If it was an unexplained death, he'll have had an autopsy. Don't you want to know? Was there an inquest?'

James shrugged again.

'Come on, James, if you really wanted to know, you could get your hands on an autopsy report by saying it was for a case you were building.'

'I'd be disbarred if anybody found out.'

'Why would anybody ever have to know? Who's interested? Your parents are dead.'

'Anyway, there was no autopsy, my father forbade it. The other two blame me.'

'What? How could it possibly be your fault when you weren't even there?'

He stopped walking. 'Because he was like me. If he'd have

been normal, dad wouldn't have punished him and he wouldn't have been reckless.'

He walked away. She ran to keep up with him, but the conversation was over.

Now she knew what had brought him back here, as well as what had kept him away for all the years he'd avoided the place. She'd learned more about him in the last five minutes than she had in the last four years.

Her friend was walking around with the weight of the dead on his shoulders, and the people responsible allowed him to take the blame, so they didn't have to.

If it was the last thing she did, she decided to stay here at Warbury House until she found out the truth, and there was only one place to start.

TWENTY-FIVE

Edward

'You look nice,' Edward said to Hettie.

She was busy in the bathroom putting her earrings in.

'You smell divine,' he added, sniffing the air.

He was pleased she was in a better mood. Getting dressed up and ready for an occasion always made her feel better, he thought – dinner had always been an event at Warbury House. It was as if she had a purpose again, like she used to before the children. He knew she wanted to feel like a woman again and not just a wife and mother, but he didn't know how to make that happen. Especially after his stupid mistake.

'I'm glad you're refreshed,' he said.

She turned to him. She was wearing a green dress that made her eyes brighter.

'Why?' She was instantly suspicious.

'Because I have something to ask you.'

'Go on,' she said, sighing when she heard the children arguing in the next room. It was why she'd wanted the south wing, so she couldn't hear them. The green rooms were all together and noise travelled between them. It was, however, a good reason to tell Edward she couldn't possibly have sex or the children might hear.

'I was talking to Rosie earlier, well, not talking, you know, erm… communicating. She wrote on her pad and I asked questions, that sort of thing.'

'Why would you do that?'

'Being polite. We're here to get along, after all.'

'It's curious how nobody has even questioned it. The lawyer said we must all get along. But what does that even mean?'

'I don't know. I guess we'll find out. But it's what we must do if we want the house.'

'So, what did Rosie want?'

He knew he'd get her interest with Rosie.

'She told me that Christian's death was a kayaking accident. She said the drugs and alcohol were secondary.'

Hettie rounded on him.

'She's a liar!'

Edward flung up his hands in defence.

'Whoa, OK, don't shoot the messenger.'

Hettie's face twisted into something he didn't recognise, and he saw that in seconds, she'd lost control.

'It was Rosie who was with him. She knew he'd gone to the lake on his own and she didn't stop him. She should have been there when—'

'When what?'

Hettie stood before him, trying to find words but failing to come up with any. He watched her chest rise and fall as if she was battling something real and present in the room and not just a ghost from thirteen years ago.

'I remember being in London, you were here, Kitty was a toddler. I didn't mean to upset you,' he pleaded for her approval.

It wasn't the details of who was where, what happened, and

who saw, or the fact that they'd never discussed this particular set of details before tonight that intrigued him. What he found curious was the fact that Hettie had reacted so viscerally after thirteen years of keeping it all inside.

After Christian's death, she'd gone into a morose and distant state. They were dark times in their relationship, and it was why they chose to marry when they did – to cheer everybody up.

It had worked for a time.

But then he'd had the affair that changed everything. He didn't want to derail them again. Not now. So, he dropped it.

He knew not to push her, but Hettie had never opened up about what she knew of that night. And he'd dared not ask her mother. Who asks such a thing when one's child has just drowned in their lake?

Nobody, that's who.

Besides, the Fitzherberts were right to preserve their counsel and their privacy and Edward had always supported that. He handled press and photographers, offering to lubricate their bank accounts to stay away. He did that out of respect and because Hettie asked him to.

The funeral had been awful.

He recalled Hettie inconsolable, James's face cold and expressionless, and Rosie stoic and distant. Then Jude, dutiful but broken. Beatrice had gone to bed drunk. In fact, it was Clara who was the most dignified and who genuinely seemed to mourn Christian. And it was Michael who supported her.

A chill spread through his chest as he looked into his wife's eyes and finally understood her pain.

'Rosie was with him,' Hettie spat at him. 'She was with Christian, and it was her job to protect him, but she didn't and now he's gone. My mother never forgave her.'

TWENTY-SIX

Rosie

Rosie sought out Sarah's company before dinner. She'd worked out that Sarah was easily the sanest among them and thus the safest society at Warbury House, because she knew nothing of its history and even less about its inhabitants. It was obvious that Sarah knew her brother, but not like she did. So far, the woman had shown grit and patience in equal measure and Rosie was impressed. But the news about the baby had thrown Rosie into another cave of anxiety over whether she could trust her brother or not.

Was Sarah a one-night stand gone wrong? Had it been a result of James trying to prove himself to his father after all this time?

Rosie found her in the kitchen with Clara. They both stopped speaking when she entered the room. She sniffed deeply and smiled; it was her way of telling Clara she appreciated her. It smelled divine.

'Apple pie,' Clara said. Then she wagged her finger at Rosie and added that it was for after dinner, not before. Rosie was still full of cake, tea, snacks and ice cream from the basket down by the lake and she didn't think she could fit dinner in, let alone dessert. It was easy to forget how they were spoon-fed everything here at Warbury House and how easy it made their lives. Choice was stolen away from them because of excess. They had so much of everything that they ended up not knowing what they truly desired. None of them had any clue who they were until after they'd each left, and then it was too late to steal back a childhood that was never forthcoming.

When they were little, Christian and Rosie would pretend to be mother and child. She would drop him off to school in her pretend car (a couple of wooden boxes and a plate for a steering wheel) and he'd ask her to take him into the classroom to greet his teacher. James played with them for a time until he was too mature for such childish ways, but Rosie continued the game with her younger brother until he was a teenager. The seven-year age gap between them meant their relationship was weighted in her favour, she could admit that now. Christian was disadvantaged from the start. They played what she wanted to, even though Christian thought he was choosing. As a result, his ideals and values were really hers in disguise.

Christian had been her child. She raised him (with Clara's help), but she hadn't been able to protect him in the end. She'd failed him. It was a pain she'd carry forever, and no amount of inheritance would change that. But she wasn't staying for that. She chose to remain here at Warbury House for seven days because she could. For the satisfaction of seeing others miss out. In the meantime, she might as well enjoy herself and Sarah was an interesting companion. *Where's James?* she wrote on her pad, showing it to Sarah.

'Oh, he's having a snooze. He's exhausted from all the swimming he's done.'

Sarah was very pretty, not classically beautiful like Hettie, but more pleasing to the eye in a current and trendy way, Rosie observed. She had short, red hair and her earlobes were full and sensual. She wore four rings in each ear and had further piercings all the way up her left ear right to the very top. Her make-up was immaculate, even though they'd been swimming at the lake, and sunbathing in the glorious sunshine. Her skin was effortlessly sun-kissed, and Rosie was envious of her apparent freedom.

You make James happy, she wrote.

'Thank you... erm, I think I do,' she gushed and fiddled with her earrings. Rosie was making Sarah welcome, and she could see that Sarah thought she bought their story.

Where did you meet? she wrote.

'In London. It's a long story. My father was one of James's clients. I went along with him to help out and I met James. He contacted me after it was all over, and we went out.'

Her voice was well trained, but her timing was all off. It was rehearsed. Rosie was good at spotting it because of the way she studied people when they spoke naturally, and when they didn't. It was all part of the job of making her characters believable.

Rosie smiled warmly.

'James told me you write crime novels?' Sarah said.

Rosie nodded.

'Will I have heard of them?'

Rosie could tell by the way she was fiddling with her hands that she'd already looked up Roberta Todd and concluded that she was a nobody.

I doubt it, Rosie wrote, adding a few made-up titles below the message.

Sarah shook her head and her eyes glazed over with pity, which amused Rosie, but she controlled herself.

They moved on and Sarah asked her about Warbury House and the lake, and she wrote her answers quickly, not wanting her to think she was disabled or incapable of having a normal conversation, with punctuation, humour and flow. Sarah soon got the hang of it, like Kitty had.

When Clara emerged from the pantry, having prepared tonight's dinner, she looked at the two women, content that they were getting along. It was all Clara ever wanted: for things to be harmonious. It's what Jude's will echoed, and what Beatrice always used to say. Harmony sat tightly around Warbury House like a straitjacket, waiting for somebody to wriggle out of it.

And that's what Rosie had come to destroy: a myth. But for now, she continued to smile and answer polite questions.

'I love a good crime novel,' Clara chipped in. Rosie knew this information already. Clara was trying to make Sarah feel included. She'd known Clara's taste in fiction since she was a little girl. Clara had been employed by her family as far back as Rosie could remember, and before that, most probably, but she didn't look any different now to then. Her hair might be a little lighter, where the grey popped through under the chestnut brown, and her cheeks had sunk a few centimetres, but her eyes were just as bright and there was nothing wrong with her ears or her nose, as she continued to poke them everywhere and gather information. In all the years Rosie had known her, she'd never managed to quite work out if Clara was friend or foe: innocent gossip or worthy opponent. At one time, she'd fancied her as Mother's spy, but she'd learned that wasn't true when she'd kept Rosie's secrets close to her heart as long as she possibly could. In return, Rosie had kept some of hers, too.

She knew one thing, though, that all the times she'd been locked in the cellar, it was always Clara who came to get her out. She'd stand there, with open arms, telling her to be a brave girl and allowing her to stay inside one of her hugs for as long as she wanted.

'I do, too!' Sarah said.

They shared their favourite titles and Rosie listened with interest and found herself swept away on their enthusiasm.

They named classic novels that she also loved, and that she indeed learned from to shape her own craft. There was no need to jot anything down because she was enjoying listening to their shared interest. They were bonding.

Then Sarah said she'd read several of C.J. Dark's books and Clara stole a glance in Rosie's direction. Rosie wasn't quite ready to tell Sarah the truth, but she basked in the compliments. She enjoyed listening to tributes to C.J. Dark's books and this was no different. She was used to sacrificing direct praise from afar, receiving it indirectly, and she preferred it that way. She didn't write for adoration or obsession from a loyal fanbase. Rosie even thought that this was what made it even better because neither was holding back on their praise for her recent two books and both said they could see them on TV. Rosie went along with it, nodding or scowling at their suggestions for stars to play the lead roles.

Clara stopped talking abruptly as Ian Balfour entered the kitchen. Rosie looked for signs of his passionate tryst with her sister. His face was more open, but his clothes were arranged perfectly, and no one would guess what he'd been up to in her father's office a few hours ago.

'Are you joining us for dinner, Mr Balfour?' Clara asked him.

He looked torn, and Rosie saw that he needed some encouragement. She gestured to him that it was quite all right if he decided to dine with them. He looked to Clara.

'It's no bother setting another place,' she said.

Nothing was any bother here at Warbury. Rosie willed him to say yes, so she could study her sister's reaction to her lover and husband being in the same room together. Watching men like Edward squirm was ultimately satisfying. In a way, it made having to pretend she was a man to sell her books worth it. It had been her publisher that suggested coming up with a pseudonym, but the name itself had been cooked up here at Warbury House with Clara.

'I'm starving, actually,' he said.

No doubt his earlier exertions had left him famished, Rosie thought.

'Is it you who checks to see if we all stay for the week?' Sarah asked.

'It's all in hand,' he said vaguely, heading out of the kitchen.

'They're spying on us through recording equipment,' Clara blurted out when he was gone.

'Really? Is that true?' Sarah asked.

'How else can they know what's going on?' Clara asked.

'But that's ridiculous! Surely that's not legal?' Sarah said.

They both looked to Rosie for answers. She sighed and penned a response:

I think the easier, less dramatic, answer is that Radcliffe & Sons will treat us like adults and assess the situation at the end of the week. Whoever isn't here, won't be privy to its rewards.

They both read her assessment carefully and Clara went to check a pot on the Aga. Sarah sat back to absorb the new information. She seemed to believe it and no doubt would feed it back to James. Satisfied, Sarah left to change for the evening. It promised to be a tempestuous affair and they all needed to brush up on their acting skills. Dinner with Hettie would likely be a taxing transaction, and it was doubtful that her sister would last the evening without copious amounts of wine. But that was just what Rosie and James were banking on.

'All set?' Clara asked her.

Rosie nodded.

Is there any poison in the food I should be aware of? Rosie wrote, passing the note to Clara, who laughed.

'Tempting, but not yet. Not tonight.'

Rosie peered over her shoulder to listen for voices in the corridor, and when she heard none, she went to Clara and held her in a deep embrace.

'It'll all be all right, my love,' Clara said to her. Rosie pulled away and nodded. Clara wiped her cheeks and smiled, just like she used to when Hettie left her out of a game, or James didn't return from London when he said he would.

'You're a superstar, Rosie. One of these days, everyone will know who C.J. Dark is, and I'll be cheering you on. Christian Jude would be so proud, too, if he were here, God love him and rest his soul.'

Clara looked up to the heavens and Rosie pulled away and left the kitchen.

On the way back to her room, she passed several paintings on the walls and realised she hadn't looked at them properly for decades. They'd always been there, but she had lost interest in them when she was a child, knowing their stories and dismissing them as dull or downright depressing. Each scene was either a battle or a resurrection.

Both were equally as important to her father – the Catholicism he believed would save them all had, in the end, become their downfall in many ways. One of the paintings depicted a woman, half-clothed, being set upon by demons – Rosie knew how she felt. She'd been in that situation many times, but there was one glaring difference. In the picture, there was a shining light behind her, and it was supposed to depict God saving her with his righteousness. When Rosie had been set upon by evil spirits, there'd only been darkness.

She shivered and noticed tiny goosebumps on her skin, and it reminded her that her monsters were never far away, even though she'd left this house thirteen years ago and never come back. Until now.

Rosie held on to the stair rail and forced herself to breathe through the panic attack. Once it took hold of her body, she must ride the wave and allow it to subside, else it took hold and never gave up. She'd been down that road before and she never wanted to go there again. Whatever was preparing to emerge out of her memory, she must endure and allow it to pass. She trotted quickly to her room and climbed onto her bed, hiding under the covers and waiting for the images to enter her vision. Her breathing quickened and she felt her skin go clammy.

It was Sister Agatha leaning over her while the others held her down. Her body was forced open and she was exposed and naked from the waist down. Mean hands pulled at her and dug into her skin. Sister Agatha's hand slid inside her as she wriggled and screamed, though her shouts were silent because she had hands over her mouth.

'Dirty scum,' Sister Agatha spat.

She stepped away and the others let her go. She saw moisture drip off Sister Agatha's hand, and she opened her mouth to scream but she couldn't. She no longer wanted to make a sound.

There was only one person on the face of the whole of God's earth that she'd told about the baby. There was only one person who could have told the nuns, who then told her parents, who then forced her to give her baby away, and damn her to silence for the rest of her life.

As she shivered underneath the covers and allowed the vile images to pass, she felt locked inside that time forever, when she was only a girl and too young to understand the reason behind God's wrath. But it was different now. She was no longer locked inside the well as penalty for committing a sin punishable for all eternity. Only the memories remained. The hole was no longer real. She'd grown out of it and found the courage to look those who put her in there in the eye. Their faces were twisted and menacing as they grinned with self-congratulation.

It had only been when she'd seen Hettie standing there, behind them, that she'd known for sure, and it had been her laughter that was worst of all.

In nature, death was quick and functional. Inside St Mary's, it was slow and relentless. Only those with the capacity to withstand the pain survived.

A tap, tap, tap on her door made her dart her eyes in that direction and she was aware that her heart was beating out of her chest.

'Auntie Rosie, it's Kitty, can I come and see your outfit?'

Rosie sighed and got off the bed. She opened the door to find the girl standing there in a long black dress. Rosie's eyes widened in admiration, and Kitty did a twirl.

She stood back for her to come in, and wondered at her true innocence, and how she might cope if she were shut away in a dark damp hole for a whole night, on her own, without anyone knowing, just to see if she made it through.

TWENTY-SEVEN

Sarah

'Your sister doesn't talk much about her books, does she?' Sarah asked James when she'd returned to their room to change for dinner. Dressing up for what should be an ordinary function – that of eating – was a singularly curious concept, but she was going along with it and making the most of the opportunity to accessorise, with a full make-up and hair job, because she didn't make the effort often at home. Nights out in London were casual and easy and she hadn't been on a formal date in a good few years. She added, 'I couldn't imagine doing this every night for dinner.'

'It wasn't like this every night. What made you say that about Rosie?'

'We were in the kitchen discussing books – Clara is a massive crime fan, too – but Rosie was quite shy about her accomplishments.'

'It's because she doesn't sell many books as Roberta Todd, and she isn't the sort to brag anyway.'

'Hmm...' Sarah stopped searching for a particular bangle

she was looking for and squared up to him. 'I can see she's getting under your skin, they all are, and I understand that now, but maybe they're not as bad as you always tell me?'

James smiled at her. 'You're right, this place has bad memories and it's hard coming back.'

'I even like Edward, though he's clearly Hettie's lapdog. I feel sorry for him.'

Sarah stopped looking for her jewellery and stared out of the window.

'Look, there's definitely a man out there, I told you earlier. That's how they're spying on you! Jesus Christ, you were right.'

James walked towards the window. The early evening sun was turning the land orange and made shadows dance across the lawns, but it was clear to see: the shape of a figure wearing all black, walking along a row of bushes.

'What the hell are they doing?' Sarah continued.

'Whoever it is, they're not very good at it!' James laughed.

'James, how much money are we talking? I never asked, because it's fucking rude, but I'm beginning to think it's a bit more than you're letting on.'

'Why? You want a piece of it now you're here and doing your bit?' He was poking fun at her. She giggled and threw a wet towel at him. She found the piece of jewellery she was looking for and asked him to fasten it onto her wrist. He held the bangle carefully and worked out where the clasp fitted.

'Fifty million,' he said.

The clasp slid together and he went back to lacing his shoes.

'What the hell?'

'Exactly, and it's funny, isn't it, I don't even want a penny of it.'

'What? Hold on,' she said. 'You don't want any of it? It's yours! Well, a third yours. Also, what am I doing here pretending to be your pregnant fiancée if you have no interest in the inheritance anyway?'

He smiled at her. 'You haven't worked it out yet?'

She sat on the bed and spread her hands.

'I'm not here for the money,' he said. 'I'm here to finally say goodbye to my brother.'

Sarah's mouth opened slightly, but no words came out.

'Of course you are,' she whispered. 'James, how insensitive of me. Bloody hell. You're pretending to be interested in the money so you can use the opportunity to find out how Christian died. So, you're sure it wasn't suicide?'

He shook his head.

'I'm sorry, I should have told you my real reason.' He finished tying his shoes and sat next to her.

She stared at him. 'Yes, you should have. Not because I'd get mad if you didn't, but so I can help you, you dickhead.' She slapped him playfully. 'Why didn't you tell me?'

He shrugged. 'I suppose I wanted you to meet them all first and tell me what you think.'

'Get information without me realising it? You sneaky spy! I'm impressed. Right, new mission, what do you want to know? Oh! Do you think Edward was playing me when he told me that bullshit version this afternoon?'

'I don't know. I doubt Hettie has told him what really happened.'

'So, you really weren't there?'

'No, of course I fucking wasn't! Neither was Rosie – it was Hettie who was here with him.'

TWENTY-EIGHT

Kitty

'This place is so cool,' Benji said to his sister.

'It's good to explore, isn't it? It'll be even cooler when we live here,' Kitty replied.

'We're still going to live here?' Pippa asked from behind her.

'Do Auntie Rosie and Uncle James know that?' Benji asked.

'Who cares?' Kitty asked.

'I do,' Benji said.

'Me too,' Pippa chipped in. Kitty tutted and concentrated on her hair. When she'd been instructed to 'get dressed for dinner' she'd stared at her parents, not knowing whether to take them seriously or not. But she'd put on the only long dress she had – a black one – and had gone to show Rosie, who'd told her she looked beautiful and it felt nice.

Now, she headed for the stairs, leaving her brother and sister to finish getting ready. She'd poked her head into her parents' room, but they barely registered her, they were so busy fretting about what everybody else thought. What a waste of time, she thought to herself. Adults spent so much time choosing outfits, make-up and jewellery – well, her mother did, at least – that whatever they were excited about would have passed them by when they were finally ready. Ready for what? And who was there to impress? It was obvious that her mum hated her brother and sister. She knew from overheard conversations, whispers and arguments in the night, between her mum and dad, discussions they thought no one could hear.

And it was all because of Warbury House. Her mum wanted it, and she didn't want her brother and sister to have it. Her mum reminded her of one of the anti-heroes in a South American soap drama she watched on Netflix. All the female stars were beautiful and dramatic. They couldn't handle their emotions because everything kept going wrong, but everything kept going wrong because they couldn't see that they were causing it. They were so wrapped up in themselves that they failed to notice anything else, and their worlds crumbled with each passing episode because all they did was feel self-pity. The characters Kitty most aligned with were the ones who were quiet – who observed from the sidelines – but she figured the writers knew what they were doing when they included dumb ones who spoke rarely or were ridiculed by the main stars. Like Auntie Rosie: but she wasn't dumb, and Kitty betted the writers of the soap weren't either.

She'd lied to her siblings. She wasn't sure at all if they'd ever live here because Auntie Rosie didn't look like the kind of person who was a pushover. Besides, she wasn't sure if she even wanted to.

Natalia, her best friend at school, had sent through a link to her via email and she'd read the whole thing. It was the same article she'd told her mother about, sent by another friend, exposing her grandfather's wealth and how he came by it. After she'd read it, down by the lake, on her phone, she understood exactly what her mother wanted so badly. Natalia had read it, too, and suddenly became more interested in her family history.

The origins of the Fitzherbert fortune are disputed, with many researchers tracing it back to the sugar trade and links to slavery...

Kitty had felt ashamed when she'd read it, and Natalia had been sure to point it out, too. She worried that this sort of information could be used against her and leveraged to trap her into becoming beholden to Natalia in exchange for her silence.

She was related to slave traders, but Kitty wasn't at all sure that this was the worst of her worries. She had found herself in the middle of a bitter family wrangle to get hold of all the money that had been made on the backs of the vulnerable, and millions had died consequently. And the last thing she wanted was for her school friends to know about it. She knew one thing for sure: she wanted none of the Fitzherbert fortune, and she was mortified that her mum didn't care where it came from.

A tiny nagging thought pulled at her memory and it told her that her grandfather had made his money by trading with the family who owned Warbury House before them, so he wasn't to blame, but she dismissed it; the kids at school wouldn't see it that way. Her indignation had taken over and reason wasn't something that she was open to right now. What she did know was that in the few short hours she'd been at Warbury House, her mum's obsession with her grandfather's estate and what was left of it confirmed the immoral stink that made her stomach turn and she wanted no part of it.

It wasn't like that when she spoke to Auntie Rosie – or rather, wrote their conversations out, which was fun and different – nor was it like that when she spent time with James and Sarah. Maybe she was missing something, but they didn't appear to be here for the money either. It was in their eyes.

She'd seen it in her soaps. When actors were portraying greed – pure avarice so powerful it becomes like a drug in their brains – making them do anything for what they wanted, they looked a certain way, like they'd been taught at acting school, she concluded. But when they were depicting another desire, more personal and less materialistic, their eyes looked different. The dramatic pauses and the way they spoke and leaned into the camera shots was all different. Kitty studied them because she wanted to become an actress one day, though she hadn't told her parents. It was the one thing that allowed her to express her true self, which was ironic because when acting, she impersonated others.

She couldn't describe it, but she felt a freedom in her body that she hadn't been able to find by being who she was supposed to be – what everyone else thought she should be – and she wondered if that's why people did it in the first place: to hide in plain sight. The mastery of the art was what drove her. She studied people closely as part of her research into how people behaved. Only when she understood that would she be able to convincingly portray a character for an audience.

But one thing she was certain of already was that James and Rosie weren't here for the money; they were here for revenge, she just didn't know what for.

TWENTY-NINE

Rosie

Rosie passed the time before dinner strolling outside along the overgrown paths of her childhood. The house was in a terrible state.

She'd seen peeling wallpaper, damp patches, mud seeping through the stone steps at the back of the kitchen, and she'd heard sounds from the plumbing system that didn't belong in a sound structure.

Dispirited by the condition of the place she recalled as indestructible, she went back inside to see who'd finished getting ready for dinner. She found Michael in her father's study, with James. They stopped talking when she came in.

'Rosie,' James greeted her.

Michael nodded amiably and Rosie smiled at both of them. After the initial flurry of effort her face set in more of a grimace and they remained standing awkwardly for a few seconds before Michael announced he must leave to help Clara prepare the dining room.

Rosie watched him go and wondered how he could stand to

be in the same room as her brother for longer than a minute. His passion ran deeper than she'd expected, and it was a revelation.

'I wish you'd talk to me,' James said, after Michael had left.

Rosie walked to the door and peered around the frame, closing it and taking a seat on one of the Chesterfields. It creaked and sank in the middle and Rosie stood up again.

'Everything's going to shit, that's for sure.' James laughed. 'Even the Chesterfields.'

After growing fed up waiting for her to respond, he showed her a document. She took the file from him and read the details, then nodded her approval.

'It'll stop all allowances,' he said.

She nodded and shrugged. They didn't need words to get their feelings across.

'You know it'll tip her over the edge,' James said.

Rosie stared at him, and she felt her nostrils flare slightly. James looked away and took the file back.

'Right, all set.'

He went to leave, and she touched his arm.

'The kids?' he asked.

She nodded gently.

'We were kids, too, Rosie. Don't forget that.'

He left the room.

The clang of Clara ringing the dinner bell startled her and she jumped. She'd been sat in the study long enough for her body to become quite stiff. The sound of the bell reverberated around the house like those out at sea, sat atop a buoy, and it was just as forlorn, as if it was fighting the current in vain.

She made her way along the winding landing but something made her stop at the room which used to be her mother's. It was empty and soulless now, having been cleared out years ago. Rosie wondered why the door had been left open. Perhaps the children had been exploring. She went inside and peered out of the window, which afforded a view of the whole of the lawn down to the driveway, and she checked to see if she could spot any dark figures lurking under the trees. Father would have been horrified at the thought of somebody surveilling the place. He'd been many things, but scheming wasn't his *modus operandi*. Violence, yes. Abuse, force and fear, yes. But he'd never had need to play wily games behind the scenes like a master manipulator with his peers, only his children who couldn't fight back. He'd thrown out orders and people obeyed, and if they didn't, they paid the consequences.

Rosie was eight years old when she'd first witnessed him beating James.

She remembered at first not understanding what she was seeing. She'd always seen her father as a god: he was all-seeing, powerful and immortal. But that night, when she'd heard odd noises coming from the boating shed, and she'd tiptoed towards it, with her heart in her mouth, wondering if she was about to discover a new secret game, had changed her life.

It hadn't been a game, or at least no game she'd ever seen. She recalled how at first she'd thought James was having a good time, because his body had been floppy and he'd looked a part of what was happening. But then to her horror, she'd realised that her father was on top of him, and it wasn't a tickling game, and the closer she came towards them, she saw that James wasn't laughing or even smiling. He hadn't cried out or made a single sound, which was what had hoodwinked her.

It was as if her father had been playing with a toy, but nobody else in the boathouse understood the game. James had been like a mannequin, going through the motions of being a dummy, without feeling or thought. As her father's hand had come down on James's backside, again and again, she'd bitten her lip, knowing instinctively that if she made a noise, she'd be discovered and punished in the same manner. She'd backed out carefully, shuffling her feet one by one towards the door, until she reached it, and passed it, when her feet touched grass.

Still she never heard James cry out and that's when she knew – her body knew – that it wasn't something that was unusual or surprising.

It was normal. It was life for James.

And then, between grunts from her father's exertion, she'd heard him call her brother a girl.

'A son of mine will behave like a man!' she'd heard.

A noise dragged her back to the present and she sensed another person in the room with her.

She wasn't alone.

She turned around and Kitty was staring at her.

The girl smiled openly and broadly. It was rare that somebody understood they shouldn't launch straight into a barrage of questions with Rosie, the way other people did. Kitty had figured it out in one afternoon. She smiled back.

'I needed a walk,' Kitty said.

Rosie nodded.

'I don't even know why we're here,' Kitty said.

Rosie waited. A few seconds later, Kitty spoke again.

'I don't need to be here. It's only Mum who wants to be here. We're here for her, and it's not fair.'

Each time she blurted out an emotion-fuelled statement, Rosie saw that she expected to be scolded, or at least picked up or ticked off, and she could tell that this is what she was used to: adults always calling her out, challenging her position, shooting her down and shutting her up.

Kitty, in some form or another, wasn't good enough, or at least that's what she'd been told. *What was her secret?* Rosie questioned herself. James hadn't been good enough because he'd showed signs of being more feminine than Jude deemed acceptable. With Kitty, Rosie suspected her intellect challenged Hettie, and that's what was wrong with her. Flaws – both unwitting – that had shamed parents into rejecting their offspring to some extent.

Rosie felt the subtle shifts in the girl's energy. She'd learned to read somebody's vibration through the course of her muteness. It was like being with a horse or a dog – two of the most intuitive animals – and they felt changes in emotion and cognisance and behaved accordingly. People talked of dog and horse whisperers, but really, they were merely connected to the sixth sense of a more liminal world where innate urges spoke just as loudly as words.

'She forces us to do everything...' Kitty carried on. The information turned to a stream, falling out of her mouth faster than she could keep up with. Her feelings tripped over one another as they became words and motions and she gesticulated more until it all rushed out of her like a waterfall. Occasionally, she paused for breath and sucked in air, checking Rosie to see if she really was quiet and non-judgemental, or if she was pretending, or if she'd disappeared like a dream. Kitty was seeking a non-judgemental ally.

'I don't know why she wants the stupid house anyway. Look at it, it's a dump.'

Kitty checked herself and her cheeks flushed.

'I'm sorry, I didn't mean to... It's your home, too.'

Rosie shook her head in an attempt to reassure her niece. She scribbled on her pad.

I don't like Warbury House very much. Your mum is welcome to it.

The sun was dipping behind the house and Rosie's heart felt lighter than it had since she'd received the news of her father's death. It forced her to acknowledge that she'd been clinging on to the stress as if it was a dangerous ledge, a thousand feet up, with the knowledge that if she didn't hold on, she'd drop to the ground and be torn apart.

She glanced at her watch and saw she'd been listening to

THE SECRET INHERITANCE

Kitty for only half an hour. That was all. It wasn't a long time, but she felt her body releasing the tension of the last few weeks, and it felt exhilarating.

Kitty had no idea that she was such valuable company.

She was still talking and only paused again to walk towards Rosie and put her arm around her waist. Rosie reached hers out towards the girl and placed it around her shoulder. They moved closer and they remained entwined, growing used to each other's breathing and the tick of a distant clock in the hallway.

They'd be late for dinner, but Rosie suddenly didn't worry about it. She turned to her niece, and Kitty faced her. Rosie realised that they'd forged a connection. Kitty was speaking her language now. She understood her gestures so acutely that they didn't need words.

Rosie nodded and they walked out of the room together, towards the stairs. When they got to the dining room, Kitty went in first.

'You two are in the doghouse,' Clara said as she spotted them sneaking in. Rosie shrugged and Kitty giggled.

Everybody else was seated, though there was no sign of Hettie. They took their places and acknowledged murmurs of greetings from around the table.

'You're late,' Edward scolded Kitty. She ignored him and straightened her place setting.

'It's a good job your mum isn't here yet,' he added, emasculating himself before his daughter, Rosie thought. He clearly used that line a lot. He might as well have taken a knife and gutted himself, letting his insides spill out across the table.

But Rosie noticed Kitty's shoulders remain high and saw the power in the girl's posture, and she knew she'd broken free, if only for one day.

Ian Balfour sat opposite her and looked as though he'd had a few too many aperitifs. His cheeks were rosy, and he was chewing on a bread roll enthusiastically. He'd been dragged into an uncomfortable situation when his career had been at its lowest ebb. This was his last chance.

He'd had a nasty lifelong habit of bedding the wives of his legal clients, and that had been just what Rosie and James were looking for. A down-and-out who was desperate for money. The last thing they needed was an army of competent lawyers dictating what they could and couldn't do with their father's estate.

Rosie smirked to herself as she took her place and anticipated an entertaining evening. Just then, Hettie waltzed in and the air turned to glue. Rosie caught James's eye and an understanding passed between them.

He'd learned her language a long time ago and they communicated easily over the chatter of everybody else at the table. She understood what he wanted to tell her and it steeled her for the evening ahead. Getting through the meal was only the beginning.

James looked down at his starter.

His gesture communicated a message to her. The men he'd employed on the perimeter were doing their job. But what he hadn't told her, and what she now knew, was that Donny was here and part of the plan.

THIRTY

James

The arrival of Rosie alleviated the fogginess of the dining room air. James stared at her just long enough to confirm she'd spoken to Balfour and for her to reciprocate she understood.

Nobody noticed.
Nobody knew their language.
To anybody peering into one of the huge windows at the family sitting together enjoying a fine meal, under candlelight, with the gentle breeze of the summer caressing their bodies, they seemed a vision of beautiful union.

The dim lighting wasn't necessary, and the candles looked ridiculous and dramatic, but it all added to the mood and the realisation for James that, in fact, nothing in the house was useful at all. James was even surprised that the chairs were holding up.

He watched his older sister make her grand entrance, like she used to when she was the lady of the moment. Hettie had always had an easy confidence about her that unsettled Rosie, who he felt he ought to protect. It drove a wedge between them. Hettie, as the eldest, had held the ear of their father. She'd had the expert talent of being able to take their father's perspective and bend it to hers. Mother's absence helped. She was there physically when they were growing up, but emotionally it had been Clara who'd raised them. Hettie had stepped into their mother's shoes effortlessly, like Mata Hari at a Bedouin banquet pouring poison into the minds of unsuspecting prey. But now she was on her own and James saw her vulnerability.

Her isolation was palpable, and she had no one to help her. He watched her sit silently and it was Sarah who started the conversation.

'Whatever is for dinner smells amazing.'

'Hear, hear!' Ian chimed in.

With seven nights of this to look forward to, James resigned himself to getting inebriated to cope.

Rosie raised her glass while Edward poured water for the children.

Clara brought dishes in and set them on the table. James couldn't help thinking that Father was about to pop up from behind the old piano and surprise them all.

'In the spirit of the evening, can I suggest we discuss a topic that's acceptable to us all? We're stuck here, for better or worse, and we might as well make it fun,' James said, raising his glass in Rosie's direction.

The children stared at him and then at their parents.

'We have news,' James said, taking Sarah's hand and holding it. She smiled nervously.

'Sarah and I are expecting a baby,' he said. They looked at one another and James saw Hettie staring into her wine glass, then she shook her head and glared at Sarah.

James raised his own glass and gulped some wine down his throat as the others sat, stunned. It was Ian who broke the silence.

'Good luck!' he said, raising his own glass. 'You're braver than I am,' he added.

James caught Rosie's eye but this time, she wasn't communicating with him in a conspiratorial way, and his smile fell away from his face.

He'd hurt her. He should have warned her.

'Well, well, James, who'd have believed it?' Hettie broke the silence.

'Mum...' Kitty whispered. The girl was embarrassed.

But all James could think of was how badly Rosie appeared to be taking it. And the worst part was that Hettie had noticed, too.

'How far along are you, Sarah?' Hettie asked.

'Only a few months,' Sarah said.

'You'd better go easy on the poison, then. This is the most dangerous time – you know, one in three pregnancies end in the first trimester?'

'Thanks, Hettie,' James said.

'Pippa!' he then continued. 'What do you like to do outside of school?' James had changed the subject, but he saw Hettie still staring at Rosie, who'd withdrawn into her body, as if somebody had pressed her deflate switch.

The younger girl giggled. 'I like to buy clothes.'

'Really? Chip off the old block. Kitty, what about you?'

The eldest child flung herself into the essence of the task and thought hard. The tactless unpleasantness of her mother was forgotten.

'I investigate old buildings and who built them.'

'Crikey, have you learned anything about Warbury House?'

Kitty nodded. Clara busied herself at the table a little longer than James had remembered her doing in the good old days and he noted that she was eavesdropping. He found himself relaxing, now they'd offloaded their biggest lie, but guilt tore at him when he looked at Rosie. He glanced nervously at

Hettie, who hadn't managed to get a rise out of Rosie, and who was now bored with the conversation centring around her children rather than her. It was like when they had played board games when they were young, when she pushed over the pieces because she felt left out. He glanced at her, and saw she was sulking. It was as if the energy she'd spent getting ready had been a waste because no one was fussing over her, just like it had been when they used to sit around the table when they were all together. That hadn't happened for decades, but Hettie still wore the same bubbling resentment under her skin. She was no longer top dog and she appeared somehow less than she had before.

'I found out that the Fitzherbert fortune was built on slavery,' Kitty announced.

'Kitty!' Hettie exclaimed.

'It's all right, sis, let her speak, she's done some digging and she is correct on one count, give her that much. The ancestors of Father's business partners were brutal slave owners, funding their sugar empire. Slaves were picked up from the coast of Africa, then shipped over to the Caribbean where the ships were refilled with rum, coffee and sugar, then taken to ports like Liverpool and used to sweeten British society.'

Edward reached for Hettie's hand and petted it. *Like a dog,* James thought.

'But where your theory breaks down a little is that they weren't our family. Our father's – your grandfather's – wealth was earned from trading with the family who built this place, so technically we're not related to the slave owners, but I get your point, it's still dirty money.' James chuckled. He was enjoying himself. He was off the hook, for now. He carried on. 'Don't you think it's neat that the house was once a quintessential symbol of wealth and privilege that reflected the very fabric of society, and now that society has come full circle, so has the house and all its glory.'

'Yes! Exactly!' Kitty grew excited. 'That's what I thought. The house is rundown like the British Empire.'

'The house is not rundown,' Hettie complained. 'It's magnificent.'

'I'm afraid it is a little neglected,' Ian Balfour chipped in.

Rosie covered her mouth with her napkin, then buttered her bread. James assumed that the conversation about babies was forgotten, for now. Clara ladled soup into bowls and James noticed that she was finding anything to do but leave.

'What do you mean?' Hettie asked Ian. James noticed a look pass between them that Edward failed to pick up on.

'It's not that bad,' Hettie said.

'Children, you can start,' Edward told them.

James acted like a child and began slurping, making Benji smirk into his red pepper soup. James winked at him.

'The toilet in the green room doesn't work,' Kitty said.

'Neither does the one in the downstairs bathroom,' said Pippa.

'Can we change the subject? We're eating,' Edward asked.

'There's standing water on the lawn – is that normal during summer? Perhaps there's a problem with the drains in general?' Sarah chipped in.

Edward and Hettie glared at her, clearly to make her feel as though her opinion wasn't welcome as an outsider.

'I just noticed. I did an engineering degree at Nottingham, though I've never used it. There's damp in most of the walls all over the house,' Sarah added.

'You've been snooping all over the house?' Hettie asked her.

'For Christ's sake, Hettie, she's not snooping, anyone can see what a shit tip the place is,' James said.

'Don't swear in front of the children,' Hettie hissed.

'Why? Do you think they might catch something?' James retorted.

A piercing screech stopped their bickering. James stared at

Rosie as she scraped her spoon along the bottom of her porcelain bowl.

'At least the china is in one piece,' James said, making Rosie smile.

'Do you have to?' Hettie asked her.

Rosie scraped the dish again and Pippa covered her ears. Clara finally left the room, because, James noted, she was struggling to keep herself from laughing.

'Has there been a structural survey, Ian?' Edward brought order to the chaos, and everybody concentrated on eating their soup.

'Well, as a matter of fact, yes, it was completed a few weeks ago, though your father never saw it, he was too ill.'

'Who said he was too ill? Why was it kept from him?' Hettie asked.

'It wasn't kept from him, he couldn't read it,' Ian snapped.

'Maybe if you'd come to see him, you'd know for yourself,' James told her.

'That's rich coming from you.'

'I had plenty of meetings with him, via Zoom.'

'Zoom?' Hettie was amused.

'Yes, he asked my advice on investments.'

'Ha! *You*?'

Sarah reached her hand under the table and held his.

He was a grown man of thirty-nine years, he was a partner in three law firms and yet, Hettie's withering annihilation had him frozen in time, thirty years ago, as if her opinion was the only thing in the world to him. It was like a magic trick where the illusionist could stop time and paralyse their subject, leaving him easy pickings for predators.

She'd always been able to do it.

He saw Rosie's cheeks flush and she bent down to get something from her handbag. It was her notebook which she scribbled in furiously and gave to Kitty over the table. Kitty handled her moment with aplomb, clearing her throat.

'*Father had my help with investments, too,*' Kitty read.

'Well, this is quite the conspiracy,' Hettie said. 'Kitty, you know you don't have to be Auntie Rosie's mouthpiece, she's capable of talking. Being silent is a choice not an affliction.'

'Hettie, not now,' Edward told her.

'Why are we even here if all you're going to do is argue?' Kitty asked her mother.

Everybody stopped eating.

'If you don't make an effort to stop arguing all the time, you won't satisfy the terms of your father's will, Hettie,' Sarah said.

Rosie and James stared at her.

Hettie stood up and threw her napkin onto her plate. Edward reached for her arm. 'Not *now*,' he said with more force.

Pippa looked like she might cry. Benji stared at his soup. Kitty watched for what might come next.

'You're not even family,' Hettie told Sarah.

'Who is your family, Hettie? I don't see you treating your brother or sister as though they belong either – I'm in good company, it looks like to me. If you don't want to talk in front of your children, I'm more than happy to speak to you alone,' Sarah said.

James put a hand to his head and took a gulp of wine.

'Really? If you think you have the stomach for it.'

With that, Hettie left the room and Sarah pushed her chair back and followed her.

'Well, then... shall we finish our food?' James said.

'What do you think they'll talk about?' Kitty asked James, after her mother and Sarah had left the room.

'The weather?' he said.

She smiled at him.

'No?' he asked.

She shook her head. 'No.'

'Well, that was embarrassing,' Kitty carried on.

'Not a good start,' Ian chipped in.

Rosie, Edward and James glared at him.

'I'll try to be as lenient as I possibly can on you all, but I must file a report at the end of the week for Radcliffe & Sons, and it is my job to report the truth. If you don't get on, then it's out of my hands.'

'It's funny how Hettie is the one causing all the problems, as always, and she is the only person here who is interested in Dad's fifty million.'

Benji's eyes popped out of his head and Kitty's mouth fell wide open.

'James!' Edward said. 'I do not see my wife as the only person around this table who is arguing. If you back someone into a corner, they'll bite. And kindly mind what you say in front of the children, who love their mother, despite what you all think of her.'

James fell silent and his cheeks flushed. He caught Benji's eye and regretted taunting Hettie so much. A flash of recognition jumped into his head, and he realised that to kids, this wasn't a game, it was an awkward and uncomfortable mess. He felt like he used to when he was admonished by his own father for saying something stupid at the table.

Ian filled the silence by mumbling about the damage to the lawn. In the meantime, Rosie passed him a note. She didn't seem at all flustered by the spat. In fact, she seemed to be enjoying herself. *No wonder*, he thought, he deserved it for mentioning the pregnancy in front of her like that.

That went well, she'd written.

When he looked up and into her face, her eyes were twinkling with mischief like they used to when they left Hettie on the island without a canoe.

THIRTY-ONE

Sarah

Sarah held her hand out in front of her, as if in defence, when she reached the kitchen.

'Look, Hettie, calm down, this isn't personal, you're all adults trying to get along, or that's what it's supposed to be, else none of you get what you want. Why are you so hostile?'

'I know you're not James's fiancée,' Hettie said.

'Why would you say something like that?'

'Where's your ring?'

'I don't need one to make me feel validated by somebody else. I don't belong to James, I don't need to wear a label.'

Hettie fiddled with her own wedding bands.

'You're acting in front of the lawyer.'

'So are you. You all are.'

'James is gay.'

Sarah hesitated slightly. It was only for a microsecond, but it was long enough to invite Hettie's triumph.

'He's been gay all his life, so why would he even pretend he's not?' Hettie said.

'Because you made his life hell for being different. Just a wild guess. Besides, he's bisexual and I'm fine with that, not that it's any of your business. We are getting married.'

'That's absolute rubbish. You're a fraud and so is he. Tell him that I still have the photos I gave to Father to prove it.'

'What?' Sarah said.

They both turned at the sound of a rustle in the pantry and Clara emerged, carrying the huge pie for dessert.

'I didn't know you were there, Clara,' Hettie said.

'Don't mind me,' Clara said. 'It's funny, isn't it, how people apply labels to everything? James used to play in dresses when he was little and your father called him a nancy, beat him for acting like a girl, yet when he graduated with his first-class degree in law, he was so proud. I don't think people realise they're wrong until it's too late. Jude loved James in the end. He was old-fashioned, for sure, but he regretted what he did, he told me. No matter who James brought home, your father told me he wished he'd done things differently.'

'And who asked you?' Hettie said.

'Jesus, Hettie, who do you think you are? Didn't you get the twenty-first century memo? You can't treat the house help like slaves anymore. You really are a dying breed, thank God,' Sarah said.

'My father might have been brainwashed into forgiving him, but I don't think James's client base would appreciate being shown these.'

Hettie fiddled with her phone and held it up to show Sarah.

She saw a grainy photo which had been taken from an old-fashioned hard copy. It was of a very young James, and another young man. Sarah, for a flicker of a moment, considered how beautiful the image was: it was two men, gloriously naked and happy, but then the gravity of what she was seeing hit her. This was material with which Hettie intended to bribe her brother if she didn't get what she wanted.

'Nobody is interested in that sort of leverage anymore. Sexuality is a private choice; besides, it's sexual extortion, you can't use it,' Sarah said.

'Really? Watch me.'

She went to leave the kitchen.

'What do you want from him?' Sarah pleaded.

'What I want from both of my siblings is for them to accept that my father wanted Warbury House to be mine.'

'But that's not true, Hettie.'

Hettie snorted. 'How the hell would you know?'

'I've read the terms. Maybe you should, too. I came out here to try to talk sense into you – for the sake of your children, surely you can put aside your differences and be adult about this whole thing? I can see I wasted my energy.'

Sarah stood, expecting some thawing of James's sister and she did, for a moment, see a flicker of warmth.

'Sarah, you are in way over your head.'

'Aren't you, too? There'll be no winners here if you don't put aside your differences.'

Clara interrupted them by wielding a large knife from the block, above the sink. The blade was eight inches long and Clara held it expertly, walking towards Hettie, who held her breath.

'I need to get the cheese out of the fridge,' Clara said. 'The cheese course is always better at room temperature.'

They watched her open the fridge door and take out several lumps of cheese, as well as punnets of berries, carrying them to the counter. She began to slice them, and red juice ran along the wooden board and down the cupboard.

'You know you got what you wanted a long time ago, Hettie. If I were you, I'd take what was offered and never come back here,' Clara said.

'How dare you—'

'That's really not helpful,' Sarah said to Clara, suddenly privy to a different side to the housekeeper.

'Stop it.' Clara faced her with the knife in the air in front of her. Hettie froze. 'I spent your father's last days here taking care of him. He died of a broken heart because nobody came to see him. It's bad enough that you caused Christian's death. Now your father's. He never got over it. Now you have to come here and make a fool of yourself and squabble over what's left of him. Do everyone a favour and be happy with what you're given.'

'She what?' Sarah said.

Clara spun around and pointed the knife at Sarah, who backed away with her hands up.

'Can I go?' Hettie breathed. 'You're scaring me.'

'*You're* scared? Imagine what Christian felt that night? Your father knew what happened. Michael saw you ganging up on him, as usual, and your father blamed himself, because he knew deep down that it was his fault. He'd raised children who hated one another.'

Clara was a foot away from Hettie now and the knife pointed straight at her chest.

Hettie backed away, around the fridge and towards the door. Sarah could see that Hettie was as shocked as she was over Clara's outburst. Hettie was clear of striking distance from the knife now and seemed to find a glimmer of confidence to stand up for herself.

'It was Father's fault, you know it was,' Hettie said. 'You're in denial. It was his fault. Christian hated him. It wasn't my fault. I tried to protect him. I tried to protect them all!'

Sarah saw that Hettie was crying now and she felt torn apart by what James had told her and by what she was witnessing with her own eyes.

'Shall we all calm down?' Sarah said, looking at the knife.

'Yes. I'll bring the steak in shortly. Will you take in the greens?' Clara said to Sarah.

Suddenly, the housekeeper was composed and the rapid transformation worried Sarah even more. Clara lowered the knife, as if asking her to carry serving dishes in the circumstances was the most natural thing in the world.

Hettie searched the counter tops and spotted a terrine of green vegetables. She went to it and, after wiping her nose, picked it up, carrying it next door to the dining room, like a robot which had been given a strict set of instructions. Sarah followed, carrying nothing. The others stared at them, clearly questioning the possible outcome of their summit. Sarah avoided James's eyes and Hettie sat silently.

Sarah stared at Clara, having seen a possible new explanation for why the children of Warbury House were so traumatised. She saw the guests around the table in a different light to the one she had ten minutes ago, including James, and couldn't help wondering what Michael and Clara had to do with the disharmony of the place.

One thing was for certain... James hadn't told her the whole truth.

THIRTY-TWO

James

'Things better?' Clara asked James when he helped take dirty plates to the kitchen.

'What did you do?' he asked her with a grin. 'They came back in looking like they'd seen a ghost.'

They laughed and their bodies touched.

'Plenty of those around here,' Clara said. 'I just put Hettie in her place.' Her smile turned to a frown.

'What is it?'

'She has photos of you.'

'Hettie?'

'Yes. Remember when she showed your father?'

'How could I ever forget? He was willing to pay me ten grand to visit a hormone replacement therapist to transform myself into something more acceptable.'

'I know, I'm sorry.'

'What are you sorry for?'

'I suppose I feel responsible for some of your father's behaviour, because I was here and I could have stopped him.'

'You couldn't, Clara, he listened to no one.'

'He did in the end. After Christian died, he changed.'

'Because it was his fault?'

'No, it wasn't like that.'

'So, why did he lock himself away?'

'Guilt, yes, but grief, too. You know your father had a very hard upbringing.'

'We're going all Freud now? It's no excuse, Clara. He was a cruel bastard. He enjoyed it.'

James knew he'd gone too far when he saw Clara's face and the pain etched behind her eyes. He'd hurt her.

'I know you loved him,' he said quietly.

'I knew him for a long time. He was fair to me.'

She busied herself with pots and one clattered out of her hand and smashed on the floor.

'We're all grieving – well, some more than others,' she said.

'You mean Hettie?'

'No, she's just here to cause trouble, as usual.'

They both knelt to pick up the pieces.

'It doesn't take much, though, does it? These walls are held together by lies and deceptions.' He'd forgotten Clara's pain, now, and resumed his maudlin descent into examining the rot of the place.

'Can't you smell that?' he asked her.

She nodded her head. 'I can. What is it?'

They deposited the broken pot onto the table.

'I think it's the pipes. This place is falling down, Clara, but it's not before time. I think it'd do us all a favour if it did just that.'

'And you'd break your father's heart all over again.'

'Over again? The first time was because I was gay. Jesus Christ, how broken do you have to be to choose reputation over your kids?'

'So, is Sarah a lie? Or have you changed? You like women now?'

James smiled. 'I've always liked women, Clara, you know that.'

He smiled at her again and left, walking towards the back door to make a phone call. In the privacy of the back courtyard, James took out his phone.

'Donny,' James said, when he answered the phone.

'How's it going?' Donny asked him.

'So far, so good. My older sister is about to break into a thousand pieces. She's so fragile she won't last the week.'

'Be careful, James, wounded animals can still inflict a nasty bite at the end, even if they're dying. Remember the punch on the nose you gave Timothy Fawcett.'

James laughed. 'That was a good one.' Timothy was his bully at St Christopher's.

'You had a good teacher.'

'The best. I checked the stock price of Cairn Holdings last night and they'd revived again. The CEO can do no wrong.'

'Don't worry, his golden bollocks are about to be exposed. Same for North Sea gas – did you see Putin blew up another pipeline?'

'I did.'

'Well, then, stop worrying. More importantly, how are you doing being back here?' Donny asked.

'It's odd. Disconcerting. Clara and Michael are as tight-lipped as ever.'

'Of course they are, they've spent their whole lives protecting your father's establishment – they're institutionalised.'

'Brainwashed.'

Donny chuckled.

'Can you ask your men not to be quite so obvious?'

'It's a fine balance... what have they done?'

'Nothing, I've just spotted them a few times.'

'I thought that was the point.'

'They're dressed in black and loitering like cheap groupies at a Stones gig.'

'I'll have a word. I saw Rosie.'

'Did she see you?'

'I don't think so.'

'You sure you don't still have a thing for her?'

Donny paused, then laughed, but it was long enough for James to suspect he did. It had been years ago when the two of them were as thick as thieves.

James changed the subject. 'Did the Liverpool shipment go off OK?'

'Yes, we sorted it.'

'Good. How's the trace coming on?' he asked him.

'I have some news.'

'What?'

'I've located Christian's birth certificate. It took some ingenuity to get it, but you can get anything these days for enough money.'

'Obviously. And?'

'You were right. Your mother wasn't his birth mother.'

THIRTY-THREE

Rosie

Rosie got up to leave the table. The intensity of the evening was making her head hurt and she needed fresh air. The whiff inside and out of the house was becoming worse. But still, the air was bearable even if it was tainted with Hettie's self-indulgence. Kitty got up suddenly, too, and made excuses to leave. Rosie glanced at her elder sister as she walked towards the door. Hettie seemed to watch her all the way. Rosie felt a sliver of pity for her, always being on her guard and constantly plagued by the need to be right and to have the last word. She was curious as to what had gone on between her and Sarah in the kitchen to make Hettie return to the dining room so demurely. Perhaps she'd underestimated James's fiancée.

The news of their baby had knocked the stuffing out of her, but it was exactly the sort of situation where not speaking came in handy because no one expected her to articulate a response. She suspected it was a lie – one of James's ruses to satisfy the terms of the will –

but she had no proof of this and James hadn't confirmed it.

He'd simply thrown it out there at dinner without considering her feelings. She'd been able to keep her reaction to herself and shore all her emotions up behind a wall of control as her face held strong and froze into a mask like it did whenever she received bad news.

But this was her brother, whom she trusted.

She'd felt her abdomen ache and thought she'd imagined it, but decided that it was real and she couldn't eat another thing. The absence of her own infant caused her to grab hold of her belly under the table and imagine what it might have felt like to keep him. White-hot hatred towards her mother raged inside her. Her skin felt hot, too, and she was desperate to run away but she couldn't. She had to remain here like the others and face the shadows that taunted her.

She noticed Kitty ahead of her and decided to follow the teenager into the hallway. Rosie's body was accustomed to being quiet, it wasn't just her vocal cords that were unused. She utilised her body in different ways to other people to optimise communication without words. It meant that her movement could be manipulated to be loud or hushed.

Kitty had no idea she was being watched. She was absorbed with the paintings and vastness of the house.

The girl opened the door to one of the once-grand reception rooms and slipped inside. She left the door ajar so Rosie tiptoed behind her and stopped at the opening, watching her from the hallway. A draught of air floated out of the room and with it a whiff of damp. It wouldn't be long before the whole place was overcome by years of neglect, and it would fall down around them. It was curious how most people looked at their family home with nostalgia and longing, lodging it in their memories for all time as a place of succour and safety. But to her, Warbury House had become a diminished echo of its past. She felt uncomfortable in every room except the kitchen when she talked to Clara. That had been the only place where she could be herself as a child and she'd spent hours learning how to make bread and chop vegetables.

A wave of loss washed over her once more. Clara had been there that night, too. She'd wiped her head with a cold towel and had soothed her through the worst contractions. Mother had refused to attend to her. Clara had delivered the baby, then took him away – she hadn't even been allowed to hold him once. But she had got a glimpse of him and his black hair, and his tiny fat fingers. And he'd gurgled and hiccupped.

The ache of his absence hit her again as she watched Kitty in the lamplight against the window. What must it be like to have a child love you?

Kitty was beautiful, just as Hettie had been, though she didn't know it. The dim light around her head framed her like a creature from another dimension, and Rosie questioned her sanity for a split second. She found herself drawn to the girl not because of her ethereal, spiritual allure, but because of her innocence and her charm all in one. The girl was a fighter, just like her little boy had been. She remembered the tug of her heart when he was taken from the room and then he started crying for her. The feeling of it was like a deep traumatic wound in her chest. She felt it when she saw Kitty challenge her mother. The life inside the girl was almost overwhelming and drew Rosie to her.

Rosie placed her hand gently on the wall. She could close her eyes and feel her way around the house if she needed to. It was as if she sensed the house and its pain. Kitty had only been there for a matter of hours, but already she was discovering some of the house's secrets. Warbury House offered something to everyone who listened.

Rosie's eyes became accustomed to the dark as she peeked into the room and she saw that Kitty was staring at one of the windows, moving the curtain back and forth.

She was a clever girl.

She opened the door a little wider and Kitty spun around.

'Oh my God, you scared me,' she breathed, putting her hand to her chest.

Rosie smiled warmly to comfort the girl. Kitty looked behind her and pointed, walking to where she'd been peering.

'It's a camera,' Kitty said.

Rosie raised her eyebrows, but she wasn't surprised in the least by what Kitty was telling her. Her father liked to watch. It was part of his need to control, and it had been the reason he'd discovered their secrets. All of them.

The cameras hadn't yet been dismantled, that was all.

'I think it's how Grandad is keeping an eye on everyone.'

Rosie looked at her oddly.

'I mean, not him, obviously, but people who are in charge of his will. I overheard Mum and Dad talking about it. You all have to try to get along. Well, how else are they going to know? You could all leave and never come back and just say you liked each other, couldn't you?'

Rosie nodded.

'So, this is how. They've planted cameras. Look.'

Rosie did as she was told and it was true, Kitty had found a tiny device in the corner of the window, which looked like some kind of hearing aid.

'Who would have put them here?' Kitty continued.

Rosie turned to a portrait of her father hanging over the fireplace and Kitty followed her gaze.

'Before he died?'

Rosie nodded.

'There are more,' Kitty said. 'Come on, I'll show you. I don't want dessert, do you?'

Rosie shook her head.

She followed her niece into other rooms, and then to the door leading to the cellars beneath the house. She froze. Memories assaulted her senses and screamed at her to pull away, despite knowing that she must follow. Kitty wanted her to descend into the bowels of the house with her, to face the darkness where she'd been punished as a child. But her feet wouldn't work.

'Come on!' Kitty whispered.

'I can't,' she screamed inside her own head, but Kitty didn't hear a thing. The girl came back to her and took her hand.

'It's OK, I'll show you.'

The inside of Rosie's head pulsated, and her throat felt hot and prickly. Kitty tugged at her hand.

'Come on,' she insisted. Finally, Rosie inched forward and before she could back out Kitty had started to descend into the darkness. Rosie squeezed her hand.

In the long dark basement, where Rosie was sure she could hear animals scratching, Kitty flicked on a dim light and they found themselves surrounded by hundreds of bottles of wine and the familiarity calmed her. Her father had collected them as far back as she could remember. Michael had an encyclopaedic knowledge of what was down here, but she doubted the bottles would ever be drunk. She couldn't care less if the roof caved in over the lot, though she'd had it valued, via Ian, at over a million pounds. But she didn't care much for wine – she found it a vehicle for snobbery that irritated her. Some of the nicest people she'd met ordered the cheapest bottles of wine and the biggest bullies drank the ones with the fanciest labels and proper corks.

Hettie, of course, loved wine.

Kitty tapped her on the shoulder, and she jumped as she turned around to face her. Kitty's eyes widened and she giggled nervously.

'Don't you like the dark? Have you ever been down here?'

Rosie didn't answer. She was too busy looking around the cellar, trying to remember which rug covered the door to the well. At first, she had wondered if the place of torture at St

Mary's had been a replica of this one, or if it was the other way around. Or, if, indeed, it was simply perverse serendipity. Then she'd discovered that her mother had attended St Mary's, too, back in the 1950s, and it all made sense. After all, wasn't transgenerational trauma passed down through blood? Her mother must have got the idea from the nuns. Rosie hadn't been the first to be locked underneath the school.

'What are you looking for?' Kitty asked, jolting her from her bad memories.

Rosie shivered.

'I think this is where the feeds are collated, so somebody in the house must know it's here. Look.'

Kitty showed her a small box, on the underside of which was a series of switches. It was connected by wires to a Wi-Fi router on the wall.

'It's remote, so somebody can access it on their computer, or their phone.'

Rosie smiled and nodded. She took out her notepad from a pocket and wrote on it.

You're so clever.

Kitty smiled at her.

'So, who can access it?' Kitty asked.

Rosie shrugged.

'I interrupted Mr Balfour in the study, and he was secretive about what he was doing on his laptop, so I think it's him. He's creepy and odd.'

Rosie wrote another message. *They have to work out if we are who we say we are. Your grandfather was worth a lot of money.*

'I know, that's why my mum wants it all. I know what fifty million pounds is, I'm not a baby.' Kitty looked downcast, as if she'd just unburdened herself of a huge weight.

I know she wants it all, Rosie wrote.
'You do?'
Rosie nodded.

It's OK. Mr Balfour will be fair.

'I don't want any of it. It's disgusting that the whole of this place – and all the money – is on the backs of the oppressed.'

Rosie almost laughed but she knew the girl was earnest and didn't want to burst her bubble and tell her that the entire UK economy was based on the unscrupulous trades of bygone eras. Youngsters like her had yet to grasp the concept that her freedom to be outraged was as a direct result of the democracy that was built on the backs of others, but that was a conversation for another day, if Kitty ever spoke to her again after this week.

'Who shall we tell?' Kitty asked her.

Let's keep it to ourselves for now, Rosie wrote on her pad.

A smile spread across Kitty's face, and Rosie held out her hand for her to take, which she did. They clasped hands and shook on it.

It was their secret.

Let's get back upstairs, she wrote, and Kitty nodded with a conspiratorial grin.

On their way out, Rosie glanced back at the stone floor, as if mythical beasts might morph from the concrete and grab her from behind. She stayed close to Kitty but swore she heard the screams of innocents inside the walls and under the rugs, where water ran freely and candles wouldn't burn.

THIRTY-FOUR

Hettie

Hettie closed the bedroom door behind her, but she still didn't feel safe. All day, since they'd arrived, she'd had the feeling she was being watched, and she couldn't shake it.

She sat down at the small dressing table and marvelled at how little space women from bygone eras needed to see to their make-up and hair before and after a party. She remembered watching her mother fix her hair and puff her face with powder at a table identical to this one and she'd thought it vast and mysterious as if all the scents from an exotic paradise were piled up in front of her. But now it seemed minuscule and inadequate.

Tonight hadn't been a party, though dinner hadn't been as bad as she'd expected. There was the obligatory pushing and pulling between her siblings, but no surprises. In fact, it had made her thankful that Rosie was mute. Not having to listen to her sister had been a welcome relief – even that didn't irritate her half as much as she'd expected it to; she envied her the solitude and peace.

Hettie was used to being the odd one out: the black sheep. She'd never fitted in. She'd been left out of the younger ones' games, not invited to their secret hideouts, or their private spaces. But what had shocked her tonight was Clara's behaviour. Learning that Father thought Christian's death everybody else's fault was no surprise, but the viciousness in Clara's voice made Hettie think they blamed her and that was too much to stomach. The eldest carried the blame for everything, she'd learned, but it was her mission to set them straight, which was why she'd come. She refused to continue to carry the burden of everybody else's liabilities and soon she'd prove why.

But there were positives to being a survivor, too, like Kitty was learning. That was why the girl would survive, as Hettie had, through necessity. There were times when she'd protected Rosie at school, or James against Father, or Christian against Mother. She didn't shout about them. She got no credit, but that was her path; it was how she'd survived.

Rosie thought she was the clever, silent one, but there were more ways to be quiet than through muteness. And she had no intention of crying about it now either. Rosie and James had never understood what she'd sacrificed for them, but by the end of the week, they would.

Sarah was an unexpected fly in the ointment which had piqued her irritation. For that, Hettie was left feeling ashamed that she didn't possess better control over her emotions at times. She regretted using the photos of James against him. It was mean and cruel, but she'd had no choice if she were to expose the truth.

But now she had to put all that aside and concentrate on this week and how she was to achieve her aims despite the setbacks. Things were not going to plan.

Ian had made promises to her that he had no intention of keeping. And she saw collusion amongst the others every time she caught them whispering together when she entered a room.

They wouldn't let her in. They shut her out like they had decades ago.

She heard Edward come in.

'Are the children in their rooms?' she asked him.

He came towards her to kiss the back of her neck, but she recoiled.

He retreated and sat on the bed, undoing his shoes.

'Pippa said she saw men outside,' he said.

Hettie swivelled around.

'Men? What sort of men?'

'I don't know, I guess the type who aren't women.'

'Don't, Edward.'

He sighed and tutted, which was his way of communicating his desperate inferiority, which she couldn't help. Mother had told her not to marry him, the summer after Christian died. She'd told her to hang on and see how she felt on the other side of their grief. The other side had never come.

'Do you think they're people hired by the lawyers to keep an eye on the estate?'

'That's what I told Pippa, but she wouldn't have it, you know what's she's like. She came up with a conspiracy theory about them being security people to keep us in. I think Kitty has planted a seed in her head and she won't let it go.'

'How dramatic and suitable for her overactive imagination. Perhaps she should write fiction books like Rosie, but successful ones.'

Edward smirked.

'Rosie is incredibly theatrical, isn't she? The silence, and the facial expressions... do you think she even writes or just pretends to?'

'Apparently she does, under the name Roberta Todd.'

'Christ, really? How do you know that?'

Hettie touched her nose; she had her spies. 'I think it's just a hobby, though, which is why she needs my father's money.'

Hettie wandered over to the window and opened one of the curtains, peering out. The light from inside the room reflected on the glass and she could see nothing through the gloom outside, it was fully dark.

'What did they look like?' she asked.

'Who?'

'The men.'

'Oh, I don't know, Kitty said they wore black and hid behind a tree when she spotted them.'

'Do you think it's Father trying to spook us? A final game to test me? I wouldn't be surprised.'

'Probably,' Edward said, yawning. 'Or a figment of the girls' imaginations.' He took off his trousers and threw them across a chair, pulled up the duvet and turned over onto his side.

'Goodnight,' he said.

Hettie sat on the windowsill, with the curtain still in her hand. Their marriage had been a series of staccato monosyllables for a long time now, so it wasn't the sudden ending of the conversation that bothered her, but the desperate loneliness. Her solitude was almost visceral. She had only the thoughts in her head to keep her company and they weren't comforting at all. Soon, Edward was snoring gently, and she wondered how peaceful he was in his own skin; hers itched and irritated her like a scratchy nylon jumper. Or a nun's habit.

She got up and walked to him, peering over him to check he was asleep. He slept soundly and a flash of envy made her heart sink to her toes. She grabbed a cardigan and pulled it hastily over her nightdress, and tiptoed, barefooted, out into the hallway.

THIRTY-FIVE

James

James greeted Donny with a packet of cigarettes. They took one each and lit them, puffing into the night air. They chatted about the work that was being done around the place. It was extensive, and had been a nightmare to organise around Father's last few weeks. Clara had been easy to fob off with invoices and quotes for land work on sewers, drainage, boundaries and bushes, and Michael had convinced her not to worry. He'd taken his responsibilities seriously and was earning his freedom. With Michael on board, things were running smoothly – in fact, he was the reason they'd managed to come so far. They'd promised him that none of the things he'd done for Father would ever see the light of day, should he cooperate. He'd had no choice. He was easy to control. The spirit had been knocked out of the man the night Christian died and James knew it had never returned.

Donny measured the land with his feet, counting one, two, three, in between drags on his cigarette.

'This section is almost done, and when it goes, it won't be pretty,' he said.

James nodded, wishing he didn't have to be down here, close to the drainage for the whole estate. It stank. The effluent was almost up to the water table, and when that happened the whole place would be condemned and uninhabitable.

He looked across to where Donny pointed and saw another couple of men in the distance. His eyes grew accustomed to the dark and he made out clearer shadows as they moved swiftly across the horizon. It was a perfectly cloudless night and the temperature had dropped rapidly after dinner. Sarah had retired to one of the sitting rooms where Clara had built a fire and Rosie sat with her. His friend had settled well into her new environment, and nobody seemed to question her presence, but he knew that it wouldn't take Hettie long to sniff out the truth, especially after her performance at dinner tonight. And he needed to apologise to Rosie for not telling her about their phantom pregnancy.

The silhouette of the trees against the sky reminded James of his childhood, and the smell cast his memory back to nights when he'd sneak out with Rosie in the early hours and run down to the lake. Then, when he was old enough, Christian would go with them. They'd take a couple of canoes and paddle over to the island then pretend to hold ceremonies at the chapel, over the graves in the cemetery which had laid there for centuries according to Father.

They terrified each other by hiding and jumping out and telling ghost stories close to the graves and pretending to hear strange noises when the time nudged towards the witching hour, which Rosie said was three till four in the morning. It was when the spirits were most active.

After Christian's death, before he left Warbury House for good, James would sit down by the boathouse, staring over to the island, between three and four in the morning, wondering if Christian was restless and needed a friend. He'd swim across it in the middle of the night and, revived, shout out to the stars in the night sky, calling for Christian to hear him. But he never did.

'I said, it might be sooner.'

Donny's voice dragged James back to the present and he stared at him.

'The land is sodden, and there's ten years of sewage that hasn't properly been dealt with. This is the point of no return – you need to make that call now.'

'Go ahead like we said,' James said. 'It's what I'm here for.'

'And Rosie is good with it?' Donny asked.

Donny looked away and if it wasn't as dark, James reckoned he would see him blushing.

'You still got a thing for my sister? You're a happily married man, Donny,' James said, pushing him playfully.

With that, he walked away and took a last drag of his cigarette before throwing it into a bush. But instead of turning towards the house, he approached the direction of the lake and lit another.

The beach was deserted. Michael had tidied everything away: the toys, the sunbeds, the tables and the drinks. Any evidence that humans had been down here was erased. Just like any sign of his father having had four children, not three, had disappeared long ago, too.

Nobody spoke about him, no one mentioned him, and none of them remembered him like he did. The memories tugged at his heart.

He stepped out of his shoes and walked into the water, soaking the bottoms of his jeans, up to his waist. He finished the cigarette and threw it away, then dived under the water. The shock of the cold gripped his chest and made him desperate for clean air, rather than the toxin-laden shit he'd been inhaling, but he gulped just enough to calm himself down and went under again, this time swimming towards the centre.

Out in the middle, the lake was oily black and the surface

like a layer of silk. The water parted for him, and he pushed it away as he propelled himself forward towards the island.

The house, and everything in it, the crumbling walls and the damp, along with the people, and the memories, faded away behind him and sank to the bottom of the lake. He could see the island now and he pushed forward for the last few strokes, his knees scraping the bottom as he reached the shallows. Just a few yards more and he was wading out of the water, up on to the bank of the island. His wet feet turned the ground muddy underfoot and he squelched along, taking care to avoid the thorns and tangles of the bushes. He could navigate the island with his eyes closed.

The chapel stood in a clearing and was built out of stone. It had been there since before his father bought the property and all the land around it. He'd once told James that it was the island that lured him to it in the first place. James wondered whether it was the sinister loneliness of the place that attracted Jude, or the peace to be with one's own thoughts. Well, he had his wish now. Jude was all alone in the chapel, lying in a coffin, waiting for the family to tear itself apart before he could be lowered to his grave behind the stone structure, shaded from the rest of humanity forever. It was what Jude always wanted, James thought, to be on his own. And with Christian.

He went to Christian's grave first and knelt in front of it, touching the cold stone gently with his hand. His body shook in the night air, as his wet clothes cooled and stuck to him. He shivered.

He sat down and pulled his feet up beneath his body, adopting a foetal position, and hugging himself. He looked up above his head and watched the night sky for signs of divine company, then back down at Christian's grave.

He covered his face with his dirty hands. They were scratched and shrivelled with dampness, and filthy from his trek – though short – through the trees. He didn't care. His body rocked back and forth as visions of Christian jumped into his mind, all jumbled up and in no order. It was as if coming so close to his remains had triggered his body into remembering. But it wasn't displeasing, nor was it confusing or worrying. It brought him peace, though his body jerked back and forth and his mind whirred with images. He felt as though this is where he was meant to be after all this time avoiding it and pretending he didn't have the time or the energy to come home.

He lay down across the hump in the ground where Christian had rested for thirteen years. He touched the earth and stroked it, wishing it was Christian's vital body instead of cold grass and soil. He brought his knees up and placed his head close to the ground, as if he was listening to Christian's voice, but not really expecting it. A whisper caught his attention, and he paused his breath to listen harder.

It disappeared as quickly as it had come, so he closed his eyes and dreamed of the last time he'd seen his brother's smile.

THIRTY-SIX

Rosie

Rosie saw James leave and guessed where he was going. Her brother had always allowed worry to dictate his every move. At one time it had been endearing, but it was also what was slowly killing him. She made her way to the door and followed him outside. She'd been watching his emotional state since they'd arrived – he'd been sinking lower into a pit of despair by the hour. Dinner had been the final straw. She knew her brother could barely stand their sister's bluster at the best of times but tonight Hettie had been particularly awkward and stiff. And Rosie saw through James's attempts to hide behind humour and alcohol.

The opposite could be said of Sarah, who was becoming more confident and curious. The whole situation was threatening to unravel, and she was left feeling as though only a teenager had the resilience to see this through, and that was Kitty.

Rosie had watched Hettie and Edward retire to bed early, no

doubt to scheme and squabble over how they were going to get their hands on the estate. Kitty had sat with her and Sarah in the drawing room, the one that smelled the least of damp and was the most welcoming. Clara had puffed up cushions and served them coffee, then gone to bed herself. Rosie had listened to their conversation and for a moment had thought herself accompanied by two fellow intellectuals discussing things that mattered, like politics, world peace and climate change. She'd recognised herself in Kitty as she listened to her debating the merits of liberal democracy and damning the world's religions for their bigotry. It had made Rosie smile and almost forget why she was here.

Sarah had gone to bed first, suggesting they rise early to make the most of the weather. It had been Rosie who'd suggested, in a series of notes, that they should perhaps tidy the place up a bit, to occupy themselves. A week was a long time, when in the company of your enemies, and they had to do something to amuse themselves. It had been like arranging a girls' pact, which Rosie had no experience of. It felt deliciously conspiratorial and she'd sensed a notion of camaraderie between them.

They'd heard Michael helping Ian back to his room, drunk as a lord, and she'd exchanged glances with Kitty as they narrowed their list of suspects who might be responsible for the surveillance. Ian Balfour was useless, and he'd displayed it today, which was why James had selected him in the first place. He was an employee who was on his way out of Radcliffe & Sons, a subsidiary of James's private firm in St Paul's. The man's incompetence was second only to his capacity for booze and his eye for attractive women.

A sliver of guilt made her hesitate when she thought of Hettie falling so easily into his clutches, but then she reminded herself that they were adults with decisions to make and responsibilities to uphold. The days of her feeling accountable for her siblings were long gone and she gave herself immediate relief for not having to worry so much.

She bid goodnight to her niece and Kitty embraced her, totally by surprise – Rosie felt her stomach lurch. She hugged her like she might her mother – deep and sincere – until Rosie pulled away.

With the house quiet and deserted, she walked outside into the darkness, wrapping her cardigan around her body. The goings-on at Warbury House in the nocturnal clarity of the early hours had always held more allure to her than the daytime.

'Where are you going?'

She spun around and saw Clara standing in the dark, between the house and the treeline.

Rosie stared at her.

'I couldn't sleep. Don't follow him – if he wants to wallow over Christian, let him. It's about time he grew up,' Clara said.

Rosie took her paper and pen out of her pocket.

'You don't need to pretend with me,' Clara told her.

Rosie stared at her, then began to write a message.

Clara came close and swiped the pad out of her hand.

Rosie watched the pad and pen clatter to the floor.

'Speak to me, for Christ's sake,' Clara said. 'What are you and James up to? I know you're up to something, I can smell it, like I used to smell it on you when you'd been to the lake. You both stank of deceit then and you do now.'

Rosie stood devoid of ideas. She stared at Clara's face but made no effort to pick up her pad or pen.

'Dear God, the self-pity in your lot,' Clara spat. 'Do you have any idea what you did to your father?'

Rosie bent down and retrieved her pad and pen and scribbled furiously. She showed Clara her response.

Did he have any idea the damage he caused his children?

'That's rich. He did everything he could for you. He faced everything alone. Your mother did nothing – yes, that's right, look at me with your big eyes and your guilty stare, Rosie. I've known you since you were a tiny mite up to my knee. I've wiped your arse and fed you in the middle of the night. I know what your mother was; she could never be bothered but don't blame your father for it. Do you know how he died? In agony, alone, wishing you'd come to his bedside.'

Rosie didn't write anything down because her emotions prevented her thoughts from lining up.

'What are you up to? You and James and that woman he's pretending is his fiancée. Does he think I'm absolutely stupid?'

Rosie shook her head. Her anger was replaced with compassion, and she saw the pain in Clara's face. She'd nursed her father for years and tended to his whims after Mother died and he had no one. Money didn't rock you to sleep, nor could it make you feel somebody's love deep inside. Clara had done that, and Michael, too. She looked over her shoulder, half expecting to see her father's butler watching them.

'Whatever you're doing here, I think you're wrong,' Clara repeated herself.

Rosie looked at her feet and she felt as small as she'd been the first time Clara had caught her stealing cake from the pantry.

'You've always had fire in your belly, Rosie. I should know, I practically raised you. I remember wiping your tears when the boys picked on you. You'd had it at school and then here. I saw your sorrow, I remember your pain when I found you in the cellar. What are you doing? Is it revenge? For what? For whom? Yourself or Christian? He can't hear you, or see you, anymore.'

Clara looked at her hands then found a tissue in her cardigan pocket and wiped her eyes with it.

Rosie put her pen and pad back into her pocket and went to the housekeeper who'd fed and loved her all her life. She opened her arms and stood in front of her. Clara did the same and Rosie rested her head on her shoulder, allowing Clara to wrap her arms around her. She squeezed tight and she felt a breath escape from her, long and deep, as if it was what she'd been waiting for.

Clara knew why Rosie was here.

She pulled away.

'I've tried to find him, too,' Clara said. 'And I have more cause than many.'

Rosie nodded.

'You know your father didn't mean to be so hard. He was trying to protect you all,' Clara said.

Rosie turned away at this. It was too much. She heard Clara approach her from behind and felt her hand on her shoulder, but she shrugged it off and walked across the lawn towards the lake. Her body moved effortlessly forward, having made the journey a thousand times or more. It was as if the lake pulled her to it and she could have closed her eyes, but she wanted to look at the textures and colours of the trees and bushes as she walked. They were so different at night; more enchanting somehow, and full of warning, too, but she ignored them and ploughed on to the lake.

There was no sign of James, but she saw his shoes on the beach and knew he'd gone into the water. She bent over and touched her hand to it and shivered. The night was warm, but the water was chilly to the touch. She peered at the boathouse and contemplated her next move. She could leave him here, to his demons and self-pity, knowing he'd sleep it off eventually, or she could get out a canoe and paddle over to the island herself.

An unfamiliar knot of maternal protection rose in her belly, just under her diaphragm, and she realised that it was a desire to see if James was OK. Ghosts of the night Christian died taunted her. If only she'd checked on him. If only she'd stopped them going. If only Father hadn't chosen that night to tell her what he knew about her baby. He'd be twenty-three years old now, a man. Would he want to know her? Had he tried to contact her? To find her?

If only.

She toyed with her options, but realised that there were none. She was compelled to act, lest history repeated itself and James end up in the same trouble Christian had. She sighed and marched towards the boathouse, knowing that Michael would have probably locked it. She peered into the dark distance, where she knew the island to be, then back at the boathouse. It would take her half an hour at least to break in, launch a canoe and paddle over – possibly forty-five minutes.

'Jesus,' she mumbled to herself.

She risked a look back over her shoulder, checking no one had heard her. It had been a mere whisper, a murmur in the night, but it had been careless.

She made her decision and ripped her sandals off, then her cardigan, which made her shiver in the still night air. The sky was crystal clear and felt like a giant vacuum. The nothingness made her shudder and goosebumps covered her skin.

She waded into the water and the temperature took her breath away. She fought the urge to hesitate and launched herself into the water, not stopping to think about what she was doing.

She threw her arms out in front of her body, one after the other, and again, in an attempt to generate warmth. Soon, her efforts were rewarded and she felt calm pass through her as she got into a rhythm.

She still couldn't see the island, and the darkness in front of her melted into one mass of secret shadow. She couldn't afford to stop and think about what visions might await her if she peered into the blackness too much.

Suddenly, her leg caught on something and she went under. She gulped water and fought her way to the surface. It hadn't been a rock, or weeds; there weren't any in the lake here, or were there? No. She was adamant it hadn't been anything in the water.

Then she went under again, forced by a hand on her leg.

She tried to scream but the weight of the water prevented her.

She struggled to the surface again and spluttered.

'Speak! For fuck's sake! Talk!'

She found herself just out of her depth – he'd dragged her there – and she tried to swim away from him, but he caught her leg again.

'I'm not letting you go until you talk to me. Christ! Do it!'

The violence of James's voice caught her off guard and she panicked, forgetting her supreme swimming style and reaching too far too quickly, causing her to lose form and go under again.

She surfaced, spitting out water and blinking furiously, unable to get a full breath.

He was next to her and he was stronger, by far.

The water provided a levelling ground, where only brute force could triumph. It was going to be him or her. She felt her body weakening, but he wasn't going to let her go. He circled again, a seasoned swimmer – and stronger than her – and reached out to dunk her head under.

She came up, discharging liquid from her lungs, which were in danger of becoming overwhelmed. The gulping of breath and the retching of water threatened to overcome her. She felt panic rise in her chest as she saw yet another assault coming. He showed no signs of letting up.

'Stop!' she stuttered, barely audible. Then she closed her eyes and coughed uncontrollably, finally finding enough air to tread water comfortably. When she opened her eyes, he was smiling.

'Fuck off! Why did you do that?' she asked him.

'Because I was starting to think you were shutting me out,' he said.

'You prick,' she said, swimming away back towards the shore.

She heard him behind her and kicked harder but he caught her. His body was longer and faster. He pulled her under again, but her feet touched the ground this time and she was able to propel herself upwards, getting a mouthful of air before he pushed her under again.

'Stop!' she shouted at the top of her lungs. 'Please,' she begged.

He stood up and held out his hand. She was exhausted and struggled to stand so he helped her out of the water and she flopped onto the sand, panting and staring out to the lake, wishing she'd have held on for longer.

'Don't forget I'm stronger than you,' he said, as he walked away, and gathered his shoes.

'James, you're a fucking dickhead,' she said to his back as he flicked her the bird and disappeared.

She lay back on the sand and cried.

THIRTY-SEVEN

Hettie

Hettie stirred, thinking she'd heard a commotion outside but when she opened her eyes and felt Edward's body beside hers, and heard his gentle sniffling, she knew it had been a nightmare. She turned over and repositioned herself, regretting her inability to sleep soundly. She'd come to bed minutes ago, it seemed, and was cold underneath the sheets despite it still being warm outside. It felt like she was in an icebox, and she shivered. She'd wandered around the house aimlessly looking for something that she could never find.

Alone.

She'd found herself in the south wing, outside Rosie's door, her hand hovering over the handle, wanting desperately to go in and say she was sorry for leaving her alone, on her own, desperately clinging to the prospect of having nobody to come and save her, until the pain finally went away.

But it hadn't, she knew it.

Images of Rosie's baby haunted her waking dreams.

She'd watched her go down to the lake on her own and

figured she was meeting James down there to conspire and plot, like they always did. She'd been tempted to follow but had lost her nerve at the last moment and gone to bed, sneaking in next to Edward instead, but finding no solace there either.

'Jesus!' she sighed.

The silhouette next to her bed moved and came closer, and her daughter's face almost touched hers.

'Mum, we need to talk.'

Kitty was serious.

Hettie considered telling her daughter to take herself to bed and wait for her punishment in the morning, but something about her daughter's tone told her that she had something important to say and Hettie needed to hear it now.

She shuffled to the side of the bed, looking behind her to check on Edward, who was still fast asleep. She got out of bed and felt for a nightgown on the back of the door and pulled it on. The room was freezing, and Hettie smelled a weird smell in the air. It was a mixture of rotting food and soil. It made her gag, but the immediacy of her dilemma prevented a full realisation of the need to puke. Instead, she watched her daughter.

'Is everything OK? Is there a problem?'

Kitty ignored her question. 'Come on,' she beckoned, disappearing into the hall.

'What time is it?' Hettie asked, emerging into the dark hallway. Her eyes grew accustomed, and she made out the shape of her daughter in front of her. 'Where are we going?'

'To the cellar,' Kitty said.

'What?'

She followed Kitty to the stairs and they both went down. The house was in darkness and Hettie realised that it must be past midnight if Clara was in bed. Michael had always been a night owl, but it appeared that even he had retired for the night. The light from the stars and moon filtered through the windows and the smell grew stronger.

'What the hell is that? It's disgusting.'

'I think there's a problem with the plumbing,' Kitty said.

'What? How do you know that?'

'Rosie told me.'

'What, wait – she spoke?'

'No, she writes me notes.'

'Oh, of course,' Hettie said in her sleepy confusion. She followed her daughter past the paintings of her relatives, and past doors to forgotten rooms, all of which she and Edward had plans for.

'Wait!' Hettie said, louder now they were away from the bedrooms, even though the house was huge, and nobody would hear them anyway. Kitty didn't slow down but led her to the cellar door. In fact, in Warbury House, there were four cellars that all connected underneath the house, accessed from different staircases, and she wondered why Kitty had been exploring them.

An unsettled sensation hung around in her tummy and she couldn't help feeling that Kitty had been exploring on her own. Surely she hadn't found the well? If she had then she wouldn't be as calm as she was now, she'd be terrified. No, Hettie pushed the thought out of her mind. Michael must have sealed it off. It was lethal to have it down there in the first place, exposed like that – as children, they could have fallen into it at any moment, given how often they played in the cellar, pretending to be bank robbers tunnelling under the vaults to steal gold bars. The corners of her mouth turned up but then she reminded herself that they were doing something serious.

It *was* serious, she reflected, and an image of Rosie holding onto the lip of the mouth of the well flashed through her head.

Kitty flicked on a light switch and the brightness blinded Hettie for a few seconds. She froze at the entrance to one of the cold cellars, heard the dripping of water and smelled the stink of filth which was stronger down here. Eventually, she was slowly able to take her hands from her eyes and squint in Kitty's direction. She was stood next to a desk, which had on it a series of boxes that looked like electrical equipment.

'What's that?'

'It's surveillance equipment,' Kitty said.

Hettie laughed but the smile soon wore off when she studied the instruments and saw that Kitty was right. She walked towards the screens and wires and followed the trail of cords to a router on the wall.

'When did you find all this?' she asked Kitty.

Kitty fiddled with a few knobs and a screen came on. Hettie squinted and realised that the picture covered the front driveway. Kitty flicked some switches and the screen changed to a view of the kitchen, then a lounge, then a study.

'Is this all my father's?' she asked nervously.

Kitty shook her head.

'No, I don't think so. It's being used now.'

'No, surely not.'

'It is, Mum, I've checked the feed history. The files are up to date.'

'It's Michael, then, keeping an eye on the estate. Why have you got me out of bed for this?' Hettie sighed.

'Don't you think it's that lawyer watching us? He's the one who gets to decide what happens to Grandad's house, not you.'

Hettie stared at her.

'Everybody knows you want to live here, but maybe we don't.'

'What? Who have you been talking to?'

'It stinks. The grass is sinking, the floors are rotting .. Have you looked around? Why do you want it? It's horrible. I won't live here.'

Kitty exaggerated the emphasis on her words and looked around, as if playing to the imaginary cameras she assumed were spying on them all.

'You know it's all right if we live in an ordinary house, and me, Pip and Benji go to ordinary schools, and Dad has an ordinary job? Nobody will think any less or more of you if you don't win Warbury House after all of this.'

'What are you talking about?'

'The competition. It's what it is, isn't it? I remember you talking about Grandad's games, and this is one, isn't it? Whoever wins gets Warbury House, but you don't have to play. Rosie and James don't have to, either. Nobody needs to win. You can sell it. Get rid of it. Just be who you want to be.'

Kitty's eyes pleaded with her mother, but Hettie struggled to make sense of her words. She was torn between thinking Kitty was being insolent and giving unsolicited opinions on topics that were none of her concern, but also awed by the earnestness of her daughter's face and the mature words falling out of her mouth. She was telling her not to fight with her brother and sister.

It was sensible beyond her years, and not something Hettie wanted to hear.

'You don't understand, Kitty.'

'I do, that's where you're wrong. I do understand, you just won't talk to me. I know what you're all doing. You're all here to prove a point, but none of you will win, whatever it is you want.'

'What do you mean? You brought me down here in the middle of the night to tell me this? You have no idea what you're talking about. You've always had an overactive imagination, Kitty. I'm going back to bed. I don't want to hear anything more about it. I'll make arrangements for you and Dad to go home. You're not needed here and it's not fair, either. The lawyers will understand.'

'No! You can't do that, we all need to be here!'

'Calm down. Goodness, it's late. Go back to bed.'

Kitty held on to her mother's arm.

'You don't understand. None of you will win, none of you

can win. That's the whole point. If Grandad loved you enough to leave you a gift, he would have done it before he died. This isn't all yours – it doesn't even belong to the family. It was built with blood money. It should be destroyed.'

'Don't be ridiculous!'

Hettie lost her patience and folded her arms across her nightgown as she turned to leave the cellar.

'I found something strange,' Kitty said, desperate to keep her mother from leaving.

Hettie turned back. 'What?'

'Look.'

Kitty tapped some keys and opened a file on one of the computer screens. At first, it was a series of charts and figures, none of which meant anything to Hettie, though she did notice the locations which were all on the estate lands of Warbury House. There were dates and figures for the boating house, the chapel on the lake, the outbuildings and the garages. Then she read what Kitty had pulled up.

'What is this?' Hettie asked her daughter. 'How long have you been down here?'

'Long enough to know that whoever is using this system is also sabotaging the whole estate.'

Kitty looked over her shoulder and lowered her voice.

'I think it's Clara and Michael. They're trying to make out that the house is falling down, literally, and you'll hand it over because it's worth nothing. There'll be nothing left of any value by the end of the week. I'm telling you not because I want you to fight them, but because I think you should walk away – it's the best thing that could ever happen to it. We don't belong here.'

Hettie couldn't think straight.

'I told Rosie about the cameras, but I couldn't find James after dinner.'

'What?' Hettie snapped. 'Before me?'

'That's not the point, you were busy with Dad—'

'What have you two been discussing? She's tried to get information out of you, hasn't she? You know you can't trust her.'

'God, Mum, don't be so paranoid! She's my auntie. What is it with you two?'

'You don't understand.'

'That's all you adults ever say! At least Rosie listens to me!'

'Of course she does, she listens to everything, she's gathering evidence to use against me to make sure I don't get the house!'

'Mum!' Kitty took her mother by the arms and faced her head on, but she couldn't read her expression. It was no use. 'You're like children,' Kitty whispered. 'You don't care what happens, as long as you're all proved right. I'm trying to tell you that somebody is sabotaging this whole place and all you care about is beating Rosie and James in a game. I give up.'

Hettie softened her expression. Her daughter was onto something and it made sense. Perhaps James and Rosie didn't want Warbury House after all, but wanted to make sure she didn't get it either?

'I'm just worried about you getting hurt – it's my job,' Hettie said to her.

'I'm not stupid, I see things, too. I know parenting is hard, Mum. Does Clara have a son?'

'What?' Hettie replied.

'I overheard Clara say to Rosie that she missed him, like Rosie must miss her son, too, and Rosie seemed to agree. Did something happen? I didn't know Rosie had a child. I have a cousin?'

Hettie placed her arm around Kitty's shoulder.

'Rosie lost her son, a long time ago. It was a very tough time for her. Perhaps that's what Clara meant.'

'That's so sad. How did he die?'

'When he was born. There are many things about this family that I wanted to protect you from. I'm sorry I brought you here.'

'But Grandad made it impossible for it to happen any other way... Was he cruel?'

Hettie hesitated and she could tell that her silence was interpreted as an affirmative answer.

'It explains a lot,' Kitty said.

Hettie realised that her daughter was turning into a woman, but adulthood wasn't so much about age, as it was about accepting what had passed.

'Come on, it's freezing down here, and gloomy. Let's get you to bed.'

They walked back together, and the smell lifted a little in the main hallway. They heard a sound from the kitchen and Kitty turned to her mother. Hettie pushed Kitty behind her body instinctively and went to the kitchen door. She put her finger to her lips to keep Kitty quiet and peered through the gap.

Rosie was in there with a man. She could just make them out in the darkness. Hettie didn't recognise him. Kitty peered over her shoulder and tapped her arm rapidly.

'I told you there were people here.'

Hettie willed Kitty to be silent. She watched her sister hold the man's hands and then fall into an embrace, then she heard the pitiful whisper of tears.

THIRTY-EIGHT

Sarah

Sarah was waiting for James when he came back to their room.

'Where have you been? Jesus, you're wet through!'

'You're still awake, God. You know I'm a terrible sleeper. I went for a walk. Why do you ask?'

'I know what you're doing, James. It was your idea to bring me here, so I'm involved now, but it's wrong, what you're doing. You're playing with people's lives.'

'I never knew you were so dramatic, darling,' James purred at her, with the hope of sending her off-scent.

It didn't work.

'You might have your whole family fooled, James, but I know you better than anyone, we might as *well* be engaged.'

'Is this your way of telling me you've swung to the other side, and you want me to make love to you?'

'Oh, dear God, it doesn't matter if they're straight or gay, men always think about sex.'

'Of course, what else is there?'

'Life.'

'Life is sex. Sex is life.'

'Don't change the subject.'

He made his face into a sulking grimace, and she slapped him on his arm.

'Sit down,' she ordered him.

He did as he was told and went along with her playfully. 'Yes, ma'am.'

'What are you up to?'

'Nothing!' He spread his hands as if to hammer home the point and prove his innocence. 'Well, it depends what you mean. Nothing new, anyway.'

'So, tell me. Come on, then, I'm all ears.'

'I need a shower. I ended up going for a midnight swim.'

James walked to the bathroom, taking off his clothes as he went.

'What are those scratches?'

He looked behind him at his back and brushed her questions off, pretending they were nothing. She followed him into the bathroom. He turned on the tap for the bath and yellow water trickled from the nozzle.

'Ugh!' he said. He tried the sink tap and it was a little better, so he wet a towel under it and wiped his body with it. The room was almost pitch-black apart from a dim glow from a bedside lamp. The house was deathly quiet.

'A few years ago, I instructed my investment partners to approach my father about possible opportunities in the private sector,' James told her. He continued to wipe his body and he shivered in his nakedness. She sat on the bed and watched him.

'Did he know you were behind it?' she asked.

James shook his head. 'He was going senile by then.'

Sarah scowled.

'Why so judgy suddenly?' he complained. 'He bought into it and after a time trusted us completely. He holds almost all his wealth with us.'

Sarah's eyes widened. 'Holy shit.'

She waited for him to finish the story, but he didn't continue.

'Well?' she asked.

'Well, what?' he replied.

'Is that it? His investments are held in one of your companies and so they're worth a lot more now?'

He shook his head slowly and stared at the ceiling. His eyes were sleepy and they half closed.

'Oh my God,' Sarah said. 'You've run his investments into the ground so he's worth nothing,' she said.

James didn't reply.

'James! Answer me. Am I right?'

He turned to her and smiled. 'I wouldn't say they're worth nothing, but pretty close. He's had some bad luck over the years and his fortune has been diminished somewhat, let's say.'

'You did it on purpose?'

'That would be illegal.'

'So you're not admitting that's what you're doing. Why? Why would you do that to an old man – to yourself?'

'I don't need the money. Hettie does.'

'You hate her that much?'

'It's not hate, Sarah, it's past that. Besides, she'll benefit from having to fight for what she has.'

'And you think you have the right to dictate how she fights, and what for. You think you are justified denying her what's hers.'

'She doesn't deserve any of it.'

'And this is to punish her because you think it's her fault Christian died?'

'I know it is.'

She got off the bed. 'You're playing God.'

He walked past her and switched off the bedside lamp. She heard him get into bed. Her vision of them giggling under the sheets until the early hours had vanished with the first sunset over Warbury House.

'What if you're wrong?' she whispered into the dark.

But by then, he was purring through his nose and she knew that he was either asleep or pretending – either way, the conversation was over.

THIRTY-NINE

Rosie

Rosie stared at the constellations of stars above her head, which appeared to be making a pattern just for her. Her heart was filled with injustice. She hadn't expected James to behave in such a way towards her. She understood his dark side. She'd seen it in him before and knew he had the capacity to go to some awful places, but she'd wanted to believe that he'd left all that behind him. She should have known better. Regret filled her chest but there was no turning back now.

A sound disturbed her and caught her attention and she looked to where it had come from: near the trees surrounding the beach. Moonlight dipped in and out of clouds and shadows danced along the sand. Then she saw a silhouette and froze.

A figure stepped from behind a tree trunk and her body tensed.

He walked towards her and sat down next to her on the sand. He smiled warmly and she felt her heart pound.

'Hello, Rosie,' he said.

Donny had aged, but she didn't know why she was

surprised by it. He'd put on weight, too, but she'd always liked that about him, the fact that he was cuddly. It added to his charm. Since the first time they'd met, when she was eleven years old, she'd looked up to him as some sort of faraway hero. Because that's what he'd been to her, to James.

'Donny,' she whispered.

Hearing her own voice felt funny and she glanced around to make sure there was no one listening. Her outburst to James had unsettled her and she sensed her self-control slipping away from her and prayed that no one had heard it. She told herself that they'd been in the water, out of earshot from everyone, and it had been very late. Everybody else would be in bed. They all needed a good night's sleep to awaken fresh for tomorrow, which would be another punishing day together in the house. Day two.

But here, with Donny, despite not having seen each other in two decades, it seemed natural and she felt safe.

'I only caught the end of that, with James. I wasn't prying. I don't know why he would treat you like that. I'm sorry.'

She shook her head and tried to communicate with him via her face but the last time they'd been together, they'd laughed and chatted easily. Being silent was suddenly suffocating.

He reached out and touched her hand and she let him. His skin was warm, and she wondered what the rest of his body felt like. It had been so long, yet, sitting here, so close to him, she felt a yearning desire in her body that she had believed was dead. She allowed herself to slide across to him and he put his arm around her.

'James said you didn't speak.'

She shook her head, struggling to form any words after so long having not needed them.

'What happened?' he asked.

She bent her head and covered her eyes with her hands.

'Sorry, it's none of my business.'

Her mind played tricks on her and she questioned if she was really sitting on the beach, being held by him. How could she explain to him that the reason she didn't speak for so long was because her son had been ripped from her, cruelly and savagely, by people who told her they cared for her? She'd believed them. The betrayal was all-consuming.

Words had made her son disappear.

She remained silent, unsure if she trusted her new voice. He hugged her close.

'Where did you disappear to?' he said. His voice cracked and she looked up at his face, which was covered in pain. 'I missed you,' he said, forcing a smile.

Rosie opened her mouth, but again nothing came out. The combination of using her mouth, throat and vocal cords was too much. Something else stopped her from telling the truth. A reality she'd kept hidden for so long.

'Never mind,' he said.

She didn't know how long they sat there together, but she sensed her bottom growing numb and her body feeling the effects of the night air. She felt stiff, but she didn't want to leave the refuge of Donny's arms.

'I can walk you back,' he said.

She gazed into his eyes and smiled, shaking her head.

They stood up and she faced him, holding both of his hands. She wondered if she closed her eyes and willed it enough, she might travel back in time to the boat. It was one of Donny's few pleasures – even back when they were teenagers – and she wanted to ask him if he still sailed. She remembered the smell of the bunk, the polished wood, the sensation of moving with the tide and the sound of Mersey seagulls screeching at them to get up. She wanted to be there now. In his arms again, in that bunk, where she had fallen in love.

She touched his face and turned to leave, walking away from him, leaving him staring after her.

When she reached the path, she glanced around but he'd gone. He'd disappeared again into the treeline, but she knew she'd see him again.

When a man – or a boy – is the father of your child, you never forget him.

The walk back to the house was cold and lonely, and she felt her own silence keenly. Suddenly, the incident with James made her want to scream and shout and wake everybody up. But she settled for slamming a door instead, then regretted it, thinking she might have to share her thoughts with someone else who couldn't sleep.

She padded along the hallway to the stairs, shuddering at the paintings on the wall, which seemed, in the dark, to come alive. Their subjects moved hauntingly and seemed to watch her as she headed to the stairs.

She sensed fingers reaching out to her and checked behind her in the darkness, just in case somebody had emerged out of the wall to pull her into blackness. They were the same voices from the dark when she'd been locked away in the hole at St Mary's. She shivered and drew her cardigan tight. But she knew that she must face something even worse here, inside the walls that were once her home. She cursed her paranoia for doing this to her body and mind: she couldn't wait to get away from this place and close the chapter of her life that had brought her so much pain, and had cut off her voice, like a guillotine chopping off a limb. James making her talk had undermined her and thrown her off balance.

The smell was getting worse.

Soon, the sewers would overflow and reach the house. She'd already spotted patches on the lawn, where the ground water was bubbling up to the surface, as it tried to find a way out of the earth. The waste pipes must have burst weeks ago.

But that's what they'd intended.

And Donny was a part of it.

She couldn't change her mind now. She was witnessing the results of months of work, and she couldn't go back. It was too late.

She had no idea why she was suffering a crisis of confidence now. Perhaps it was because of James's behaviour at the lake. He'd scared her. He was out of control and different to the person who'd approached her last year with a plan to pay Hettie back once and for all.

But she also knew that seeing Donny had derailed her.

Perhaps the reality of what they'd done was beginning to set in.

The dark silence, and the spectre of the shadows racing across the hardwood floors, galvanised her sense of reality and her eyes became accustomed to the darkest corners of the hall.

Who would throw away fifty million pounds?

Had it been her or James who'd come up with the plan? She couldn't remember. It had grown exponentially once they'd decided upon a trajectory of action, and now it had adopted a life of its own. Her worry was that it had taken hold of something inside James and his obsession with it threatened to send him off the edge of the precipice.

All they had to do was hold it together until the final reading of Father's will, then they could leave this place and never come back. Hettie would be forced to settle the debts on her own and get rid of Warbury House for good.

But what damage had they done? What if the house was so badly ruined that they each had to find funds to repair it? What if they pushed their sister too far and another tragedy then engulfed them? One that they didn't intend.

And what about the children?

Rosie tried to calm herself. She and James had spoken about this. It was like writing off a car. The debts would be settled by handing the estate over to probate. Besides, if there were any residual costs, they could both afford it.

She stopped at the stairs and decided instead to go to the kitchen, where she always felt out of harm's way. And she stopped abruptly as she saw Donny standing in the doorway. He'd followed her to make sure she was safe. The least she could do was make him a cup of tea. The warmth of the Aga and the feel of the slate under her feet calmed her nervous system and she was able to clear her head a little. She forgot why she was here and instead embraced the opportunity to simply sit with somebody she'd loved fearlessly and completely, until he was taken away from her. The betrayal of her body by others left her in pieces, unable to ever speak to anyone ever again.

She realised, as they sipped their tea in silence, that all she wanted was to leave this place, and forget any plan she'd agreed with James. It wasn't worth it. She couldn't go through with it. She couldn't trust him.

And she didn't hate her sister enough.

Or was it that she didn't love James enough? Love and hate had become mixed up years ago when her emotions had been put into a giant pot and thrown up into the air. When they'd come crashing down again and hit the ground, she'd been unable to fix them back together again.

Only her stories had got her through. But now, seeing Donny's face, she realised that she'd sunk into a world of nothingness when actually what she'd craved was companionship, and love. And she'd been searching for the wrong thing in the wrong place all this time. It was a noise in the hallway that made Donny decide he should go, and he'd disappeared into the night, like the phantom of her past he really was.

. . .

By the time she got back to her room, she heard no sound in the house. Everybody must have been fast asleep. But she still wasn't tired and so she reached for the notebook that she'd been keeping next to her bed, where she kept all her musings and story ideas.

It wasn't where she'd left it. She checked the cupboard by her bed. It wasn't there, either. Panicked, she flicked on the light and checked her suitcase, the drawers in the dresser, under her bed and in the bathroom.

It was nowhere to be found.

Then a hot, tingling sensation grasped at her throat.

She was sure she hadn't misplaced it or taken it from the room. But if she hadn't, then who had?

FORTY

Hettie

It couldn't possibly be.

Hettie flicked through the pages over and over again. She'd been so engrossed by what she read that she'd gone into the bathroom to sit on the toilet with the lamp on until the early hours, reading pages and pages of Rosie's thoughts and confessions. It was like an outpouring of an adolescent who missed nothing. It was as if she'd stumbled across her own diaries as a fifteen-year-old and discovered a cascade of emotion more suited to a teenage magazine than a grown woman.

But most interesting of all were the notes Rosie had written about her writing career.

After years of despising her sister and wishing her out of her life, so she could be free of the incessant complaints about her childhood and questions about what had happened to Christian, Hettie suddenly found her interesting.

Rosie had gone from victim to curiosity in a matter of pages. She felt a mixture of fascination, pride and envy that her sister was in fact the hugely successful – and rich – novelist CJ Dark.

As the dawn light penetrated the bathroom, Hettie realised that she was stiff from sitting hunched up over the book and she stretched, making her body ache even more. It had been in the same position for so many hours that changing now, when it was cold and stationary, sent pains through her shoulders and neck. She stood up and realised that her feet had gone numb, and they were blue.

She walked up and down and rubbed her hands together and tried to massage her shoulders, then decided to have a shower. She placed Rosie's notebook carefully on the side, as if it was a precious treasure, which, to her, it was. The plumbing must be a hundred years old, she thought as she listened to the clunking and moaning of the pipes. A splutter of water shot out of the taps and she turned the function to the shower head, but it didn't work so she filled the bath instead.

The moment was a nostalgic one because it reminded her of sharing a bath with her siblings. They must have been young, perhaps five or six. Then when Christian came along they took it in turns to wash him and change him. Rosie did most of it and didn't like anyone else taking an interest in the baby. He was something to love, Mother said. Being the youngest, Rosie never experienced what it was like to play with her own toys or be given responsibility for herself – there was always either Hettie or James in charge. She must have found the new baby to be some kind of relief, to have her own plaything, Hettie supposed. And then later, when she had him all to herself, he became the son she was denied.

Babies figured a lot in Rosie's notes. She wrote everything down, from what it felt like to give birth to the experience of losing her son before he'd taken a breath or been put to her breast. Hettie's heart had felt pulled through a knot in her chest when she'd read that. Hettie had experienced trouble-free pregnancies and straightforward births, and her children had never been in any real danger. The closest she'd come to family tragedy – if she discounted the death of her brother, which she'd trained herself to do – was the near-death experience of their pet rabbit yesterday morning. The notion that one of her children could be taken away from her appalled her and it reignited the tragedy anew. Hettie had been nineteen years old when Rosie had laboured through the night to give life to her son. The son that was so cruelly taken away by their mother.

All that was in the past, but she knew that each person dealt with things differently. There was no code, just instinct, and some children, like James, were fighters. He still was. Others froze, like Rosie, who thought sacrificing her voice was some kind of revolutionary stand; some tried to run away, like Christian tried to, and some fawned, like her, trying to morph into shapes to blend in and keep the peace. She shivered remembering Rosie's screams as her baby was wrapped up and taken out of the house by people she trusted. Back then, she'd seen the baby through her father's eyes – as something that was going to ruin Rosie's life. She'd been brainwashed, too.

In Rosie's notebook, there were pages and pages of feelings that Hettie guessed Rosie couldn't articulate out loud because she'd punished herself so many years ago by cauterising her desires – for what are we if not our voices?

Suddenly, Hettie realised that she'd never connected with her sister properly because they'd colluded in her silence. She felt more emotion from the notebook than she ever had from her sister in the flesh. Rosie had lived her life since losing her son through the written word and Hettie acknowledged that it's what made her so good at it. C.J. Dark, now she knew was her sister, wasn't just successful, he – she – was extraordinary.

The book was full of diagrams of plots and stories, notes on the appearance of characters and made-up names. The book in her hand was her sister's best friend, her mother and her father, her brothers and sisters, and her child all rolled into one.

She remembered Rosie's belly growing and her trying to

hide it, until she no longer could, and Mother's face twisted with disgust. The incessant questions about who the father was. The nuns pushing her into the hole and calling her names like whore, harlot and prostitute. Sister Agatha's face mangled in rage.

Rosie kept the baby because she loved it, like Hettie had loved her unborn children. But it was ripped away from her minutes after the birth, at Father's wishes. That night, Hettie had watched her mother take him and had followed her.

She turned off the bath tap. The water was warm, at least, but a strange colour, and she put it down to the age of the pipes. She expected hefty renovation costs when they eventually moved in, but it would be worth it to see her family home returned to glory and she'd do it as much for James and Rosie as she would be doing it for herself.

The bathroom door opened a crack and Edward peered around it.

'Did I snore? I didn't hear you come to bed. Did I disturb you?'

'No, it was fine. I couldn't sleep anyway.'

'You know, I think I prefer these rooms to the south wing. We should make them ours when we move in. Did you think any more regarding talking to James about your proposal?'

She shook her head and undressed, stepping wearily into the water.

'Christ, look at the colour of that. Do you think it's clean?' he asked.

'I have no idea, but I'm sure it's just rust from the pipes. The shower isn't working so I'll make it quick. The thought of lying in my own dirt isn't greatly appealing.'

'Or somebody else's dirt by the looks of it.'

'Stop it, Edward, you'll put me off. The house needs more work than we thought.'

'There's no rush, we can do one wing at a time, and make it a project.'

Hettie winced inwardly as she considered again if she truly wanted Edward to be a part of her future here at Warbury House. Ian wasn't only an excellent probate expert, he knew a superb divorce lawyer, too, and she'd already had three or four meetings with her. Edward's affair last year had ripped out her heart and she'd turned to Ian in desperation rather than passion, at first. He'd made the initial move, when they'd met to discuss her father's affairs and he'd told her that he'd been asked to reach out to all three siblings. Ian had been a helpful ally, and he was straight with her, or so she'd thought.

She looked at her husband and the familiar disappointment crept into her brain, and she looked away. She couldn't rely on anyone. He saw her recoil, and he backed away, obviously hoping that one day she'd forgive him.

Alone once more, she couldn't wait to keep reading Rosie's notebook, so she washed quickly and stepped out to dry herself, noticing a whiff from the water as it swirled down the plug hole.

The smell was rancid and it made her gag. She ran the tap in the sink and soaked a flannel and rinsed herself, making sure she removed all traces of the bathwater, then she wrapped herself in a towel and went into the bedroom.

'I've let the water out. I'm not sure I'd repeat that again,' she told Edward.

She got dressed quickly and sat at the dressing table to apply her creams and make-up and heard the bathroom door close behind her.

As soon as she was ready, she slipped the notebook in her bag and pulled on a pair of trainers. Her plan was to go down to the lake and finish reading Rosie's notes, so she'd know exactly what her sister had been getting up to since leaving Warbury House.

Before she left the room, she googled the net worth of C.J. Dark and whistled.

No wonder Rosie wasn't interested in money.

FORTY-ONE

James

James was bored of counting the passage of time. Days two and three, out of seven, had passed in a summery haze of chatter, beach swims, and restless nights. Clara had kept them stuffed full of food. Hettie laid low, always with her head in a book. The kids were having the time of their lives, and Sarah spent more time with them than any of the adults. And Rosie avoided him, which, he supposed, he deserved. Only Edward focused on why they were all here and commandeered Ian Balfour's time, asking him incessant questions about Warbury House.

Talk of the worsening problems facing the fabric of the place was becoming the focal point of everybody's days.

James found it excruciatingly dull.

It was mid-afternoon when he found Michael in the boathouse. Almost four full days under the same roof had been agonising. James had caught Michael staring at him several times and he felt old emotions stirring every time he saw him, even from a distance.

'Have you been here all night?' James asked.

Michael didn't reply.

'Christ, I'm surrounded by selective mutes. You know what? Rosie can talk, and so can you.'

Michael turned around and squared up to the younger man fully. He'd been fixing brackets on the boathouse wall and was dressed in shorts and a T-shirt. James could see the older man's muscles through his clothes and couldn't help but study his body.

He'd looked up to him for half his life, he still did. Michael had taught him to fish, to build campfires, to row, to paddle, to dive and to love. The age difference hadn't meant anything to him. Michael must be in his late fifties, James realised now, but it had never mattered to him back then and it didn't now.

'You haven't changed,' James breathed.

'Neither have you,' Michael said. He held a wrench in his hand and tightened his grip. James laughed.

'You're scared of me?' James asked.

'Shouldn't I be? You break promises, James. You're a grown man now, you can handle me telling you the truth.'

'It was my father who broke promises. He was never loyal to you, yet here you are, doing his dirty work still.'

Michael turned away and busied himself with fixing another bracket.

'What truth are you even talking about? You're a damaged and disgruntled employee who wanted my father out of the way to get your hands on the scraps of what's left.'

'I know there's nothing left, and your words fall on deaf ears here. They mean nothing anymore. I know what you're doing, and I'll have no part of it once it's over and I'm dead and buried like all the rest of them. You lot haven't changed.'

'And why should we? Besides, Father made us who we are. We're survivors, remember?'

'How could I forget?'

James moved closer and Michael backed away.

'I did it for you, Michael.'

'No, you didn't, you did it for yourself. Your father turned his disgust to me because you pointed him in my direction.'

They faced each other. James saw Michael's chest rise and fall. He recalled being held in his arms, inside this very boathouse, a lifetime ago. And what had happened when they'd been caught. It had been his sister Hettie who told Father about their affair, and James said then he'd kill her one day. He hadn't known then that death can come in many guises, not just physical. To Hettie, being poor could do the same thing. Since those days, he'd learned more effective methods of execution.

'Why didn't you leave?'

Michael looked away.

James stared down at his feet. His father had a file an arm's length on Michael's history. James had offered to rub it out for him, once he'd learned the ropes and become entrenched within Donny's family. He believed he could have pulled it off, but by then Michael no longer trusted him and he couldn't blame him. He'd left him here, abandoned to spend the rest of his days beholden to a man who belittled him and turned him into a shadow of himself. James almost recoiled at the stench of guilt on the man's body, but he couldn't quite turn away and now he was here, he felt something pull him towards his old love.

'Where will you go when we all leave?'

'I've lived here for forty years, James, I'm not going anywhere.'

'You haven't lived. You've remained, you've existed; it's not living.'

'I didn't think I was trapped until your father reminded me I was. Now it's too late. No matter. I don't worry about it anymore and neither should you. It's all in the past.'

Michael got on with his repairs and turned his back on James. He took a few steps towards him as if he couldn't be in the same room as him without stepping closer to him, but Michael turned around and warned him with his eyes to stop.

'Don't. You have no idea what you're doing.'

'But Michael...'

'Don't, James. It's been too long. The sore never went away – in fact, for me it got worse. I'm happy for you, with your new fiancée and a baby on the way, truly I am. You can love the baby like none of you were loved.'

'She's fake. Sarah is fake. She isn't my fiancée, I brought her here to satisfy the terms of the will.'

Michael stared at him, unable to speak.

'And Christian *was* loved. He was the only one who was.'

'Yes, he was, by you and your sister, and Clara. My mistake. You're a grown man, James, are you not? Your family will never make sense to me. All these games. So... you are not getting married?'

'No.'

Michael had always been a hopeless romantic. He'd taught James how to feel. Not just love but to exist in a state of tenderness, experiencing the consciousness of desire.

Michael would have been around the same age James was now when they'd first touched, right here in the boathouse. That first kiss, and the explosion of passion and guilt inside James's head had changed his life forever.

It had been beautiful, and it still was, but his father had turned it into something gross, vile and undignified.

'So, you care now?' Michael asked.

'I've made myself legitimate and worthy overnight,' James said. He fiddled with his fingers and thumbs and looked away from Michael's stare.

'You, of all people, running scared of your father.' Michael laughed and the pain it caused almost bruised James's heart.

'Why are you laughing at me?' James asked.

'You still care? You still care what I think of you? No, it's not that, is it? It's what your father thinks of you, even though he can't see you, even though he's cold in that chapel over there.' Michael pointed to the island. 'You're still scared of him, like I always was, but you pretended you weren't and I believed you.'

James was five feet away from Michael now and he could hear his breath. The older man's eyes were softer and surrounded by deep lines that James had caused when he'd left him here for good. He held out his hand and Michael looked down at it and shook his head.

'I'm dead inside. I have no love left,' Michael said.

James uttered a sound that was a mixture of an animal in despair knowing that it has run to the very edge of a cliff and has nowhere else to go, and a mother whose child has disappeared from sight. It carried harrowing pain as it escaped his throat, and Michael's face almost cracked in response. His eyes flickered and tears formed at the corners; his mouth, though, didn't move.

'It's too late,' he said.

Michael left the boathouse and James turned to watch him.

'There won't be anything left,' he shouted.

Michael stopped and turned back.

'Any of what left?'

'This, money, everything, it's all gone.'

'I don't care, James. I've done what you asked. I set up the cameras and I've turned a blind eye to all your workmen.' He came close enough to James for him to see the perspiration on his skin. 'I never cared about money.'

Michael walked out of the boathouse and disappeared into the sunlight.

FORTY-TWO

Rosie

Rosie dressed quickly after her strip wash. The shower had completely packed up and the smell was getting worse. The house was in a poorer state than she'd imagined.

Everything was fixable, she'd tried to tell herself, but it was so much easier to do it in stories. Inside her own fictional worlds, she could make her characters do what she wanted.

They could kill, love, betray and sacrifice.

Here, at Warbury House, they followed the same rules they had for almost forty years. The rules of survival.

The anger she'd felt building inside her since arriving at Warbury House was threatening to bubble over and spew out of her if she wasn't careful. She could feel it burning underneath her skin and she didn't know who to direct it to for maximum benefit. But for the past few days she'd been distracted by the loss of her notebook. Without it, she had nowhere to deposit her thoughts.

She'd fantasised about this moment, coming back, seeking revenge on those who'd caused her harm. But it hadn't been like that at all. She'd lost all perspective on where to direct the worst of her rage. She thought she knew who deserved it and the very clear reasons why but now she questioned even that. The last few days had found them all settling into an unhappy routine, but a routine, nonetheless. The children played in the sunshine, like she had with her siblings so many years ago. Clara never tired of looking after everyone's physical needs and they were made as comfortable as they could have been under the circumstances. She was beginning to believe they'd see the rest of the week out in one piece.

She'd rallied the children around, and Sarah had joined in, to tidy the place up a bit. They'd asked Michael to hand out jobs and show them tools, and they'd made the place more habitable. Clara had taken offence when they'd suggested throwing away some of the clutter in the kitchen, and they'd learned their lesson and left her alone. As for the rest of the house, they'd washed, tidied, fixed and sorted. It kept them busy.

And it masked the root of Rosie's true pain.

It's just a house, she told herself.

But the reality was that their lives were dominated by the tendrils of Warbury House wherever they went. It was why Clara had never left, and why Michael still hung around like a corpse in a graveyard, haunting those around him but unable to depart completely, despite how Father had treated him after he found out the truth about him and James.

She wondered if her father would haunt them, too, once he'd been buried on the island.

She'd half expected the formidable Jude Fitzherbert to come to her at night and list all her failings, how she'd disappointed him. She'd been prepared to fight an invisible ghoul in her sleep, to keep him away from James and another beating, to stop him shouting in her ear and deafening her with his voice. But it hadn't been like that at all. Each person here was fighting their own battle. Even the children wrestled their own demons; big or small, it didn't matter. The point was, it wasn't just she who struggled. She'd kept a keener eye on her brother since the night at the lake and she'd seen him in a way she hadn't before. He was vulnerable, too. Despite his bluster, and confidence, she'd seen the way he pined after his lost love. And the way Michael looked back in return.

It wasn't just she who'd lost something dear to her within these walls.

They all had.

Even Hettie. Rosie saw it in the way she truly loved her children: Hettie had lost her own childhood because of their mother, and she was trying to prolong such a loss of her own children as long as she could.

And in the privacy of her bedroom, Rosie had been practising using her newfound voice. It was creaky and painful at first, but it was there. The truth was that it wasn't the first time she'd used it since losing her son. She'd tried to speak many times before since leaving Warbury House, but she'd simply found it more comfortable not to. But now, she toyed with the idea of rediscovering it, not just for herself, but for those who she might want in her life in the future.

Clara, who so desperately wanted to talk with her. Donny, perhaps. Her nieces and nephew.

She'd begun to desire a voice, as if that is what might finally give her more substance, more meaning, like one of the characters in her books. Without it, she had no more vitality to her than Father did, or Christian. She felt dead inside, she realised, and speaking had confirmed everything she worried about it. Her voice had all but disappeared and taken with it her very being. Since being forced to shout out at her brother at the lake two nights ago, she had hidden it once more and kept it to herself, keeping it safe until she felt as though she could truly trust it. Even James had looked guilty over what he'd done. But she couldn't help feeling that eyes were upon her now, expecting her to snap.

Once she was dressed, she headed downstairs.

Everybody would be at the lake, she assumed. The house was silent, though it was to be expected as this morning she'd slept late and missed breakfast. Her deep slumber had surprised her.

The house seemed to breathe the same as it had when she'd first arrived; it moved the same way and it looked the same, but everything had changed. She'd come expecting a climactic war, and a clash of enemies, but that hadn't happened. The skirmishes had been mostly benign and here they were, halfway through the week, existing beside one another, living.

She headed towards the cellar, making sure that she wasn't seen, before closing the door behind her. She shuddered at the thought of being left in here all alone by her mother. As the door closed, she pulled on it to shut out the last connection with the rest of the house, but a hand forced its way through and she saw Clara standing in the doorway defiantly.

'Where are you going?' Clara demanded.

'You know exactly where I'm going.'

'Finally! She speaks! What took you so long?'

Rosie glared at the older woman. This wasn't the Clara she knew. The woman forcing her way through wasn't the loving guardian she had relied upon for a huge chunk of her life.

'You won't find what you're looking for down there in the dark. You're looking in all the wrong places, Rosie.'

'You have no idea what I'm looking for. Now please remove your hand.' Her voice felt strong, and it startled her.

'Oh, but I do. You're looking for him, like I look for Christian in every dark corner in the middle of the night when I can't sleep. Like I do in the early morning when I see the sun rise and I go to the last place I held him.'

Anguish anchored the two women in pain, and they stared at one another, each rooted to the spot by their torment.

'On the beach,' Rosie said quietly. 'Why didn't you stop them?'

'No one could stop your father.'

'It was Mother who took him. Like she took my son.'

'She was terrified of her husband. She'd do whatever she was told.'

'But Father loved you. You could have changed his mind, to save your son.'

'Don't.' Clara's face screwed up with loathing.

'At least you knew what it felt like to love him, and to raise him.' Rosie allowed her resentment to bubble over. Clara had suffered the indignity of having to pretend her son wasn't hers, but at least he'd lived, for a time.

'You were only fifteen, Rosie. I agreed with him. You were too young. It would have ruined your life.'

'How do you know?' Rosie's voice cracked and she thought that it might be because she was so unused to using it. The sound of it was unfamiliar and her throat felt tired after just a few sentences, and she realised that this was why she'd stopped talking in the first place. Because it was pointless. Nobody ever got what they wanted by asking for it.

'Leave me be, Clara.'

'I know how it feels.'

'No, you don't. You had Christian for eighteen years.'

'Not really. I watched other people have him. He never knew he was mine.'

At this, Rosie stopped, and her heart softened its hard edges suddenly. Her resolve was close to crumbling, but she couldn't abandon everything she and James had worked so hard for. They were almost there.

'What are you doing in here? I've seen the surveillance equipment.'

'I don't know what you're talking about.'

'You're not fooling me. What do you think you'll achieve?'

'Let go of the door.'

'No.' Clara stood firm and came inside the doorway, shutting the cellar door behind her.

'Clara, I'm warning you.'

'Ah, be quiet, you were barely speaking a day ago and now you're warning me? I'll take you over my knee – you think you're too big and I won't? Is this what you're looking for?'

Clara held her notebook in the air. Rosie went to take it, but Clara moved it out of the way.

'Where...?'

'Where did I find it? Your sister had it. You're in trouble now.'

'She had it all this time? I haven't been able to find it for days.'

'She's read the lot. See it as a good thing. Now you don't have to creep around pretending! I never knew why you always had to act, you and James. Always playing at being something that you're not. What a waste of energy – just be who you are! Do something good with all this energy you have. All the passion your father gave to you.'

Rosie held her hand up and closed her eyes. She couldn't bear to listen. 'Father gave me nothing, he only took it away.'

'Oh, away with your drama, you're as bad as Hettie. Always making up stories in your heads. That's why you're such a good novelist, Rosie, your stories were always the best. Hettie only wanted to copy you, that's all. You know I've read every single C.J. Dark book there is. I gave you the name, so I thought it only right to read them, but you have something, Rosie. A talent. It's incredible, you make people feel something. The world wants to know who you are, tell them! Don't keep it a secret. Shout it out loud! Be proud of yourself.'

Rosie stared at the housekeeper. Was she really telling her

to let it all go? Was she standing in front of her, after what they did to Christian, and encouraging her to forgive?

'Let it go, Rosie. I've watched you all your life – well, most of it, and from afar, too, and your brother and sister. What were you coming in here to do? Lock Hettie in here like you used to? You and your brothers? I'll have your hides, you know I will. Leave her alone, you've driven her half mad as it is.'

'You can't talk to me like that, Clara, I won't allow it.'

Memories flickered inside Rosie's head and burnt her temples. She'd lived inside fiction for so long, she couldn't work out what was true and what wasn't.

'Here, take this back. I've told Hettie to avoid you like the plague. It's best for all of us.'

Rosie took a step toward Clara and puffed her chest out.

'Threatening me now? We've all lost. You, your baby, and me, mine. Leave it be. Did you try to find him like I told you?'

Rosie shook her head.

'Why not? You have a chance I don't, at least. He might be alive and well, thriving – what'd he be now? Twenty-three? Twenty-four? He might have children, you might be a grandmother! What are you doing wasting your time on hate?'

A hot fire burst up through Rosie's body and she launched a punch with all her weight behind it at Clara. She connected with her cheek, knocking her down. Rosie stared at her on the floor, not knowing where the aggression had come from. Clara didn't move. Rosie knelt down and took the housekeeper by the collar and realised with horror that she'd knocked her clean out. She reached over her limp body and took back her notebook and then stood up and locked the door from the inside, making sure they were alone.

She knelt again and reached her hand to Clara's neck and felt a pulse. She was staggered by her own strength and could only think that it had come from deep inside her where the hate Clara talked about had been stored up. It was a loathing she couldn't erase, like Clara had so breezily suggested. It was part of her, and was all she'd relied on to get her here, in this place, to carry out her intentions. But the edge had been taken off it and she stared at Clara with huge remorse burning inside her heart.

The only thing she could do to stop the terrifying disgrace punishing her was to ignore it. She backed away, mindful of why she'd come down here in the first place.

She went down the stairs behind the wine bottles and to the basement level where the CCTV equipment was collating the events of the last few days. Suddenly, her peace was shattered, and she couldn't think straight. But before she could gather herself and decide how to undo what had already been done, she saw Hettie sat in front of the monitors.

She froze.

Hettie saw a reflection in the screen and jumped, turning round and seeing her sister stood behind her, like a terrible statue, having been placed there by an unseen hand.

'Jesus, Rosie!' Then she began to laugh.

Rosie stood where she was and tried to figure out how she could make all this go away.

'You're the true crime sleuth like in your novels, aren't you? Skulking around the halls and cellars looking for plot lines. And you've stolen all of ours already, except the final one. What will it be? Poor Christian? Or maybe your own baby stolen away from you in the middle of the night while you were still aching from pushing him out?'

Her sister's words were laced with venom. Rosie found herself desperate to get out words of her own but was unable to pinpoint the ones she needed, so unused she was to articulation.

Before sense clarified any other option, Rosie found herself crossing the rough floor and slapping her sister across the face. As soon as she'd done it, she withdrew her hand to her mouth and gasped in disgust. Something had taken over her body and was forcing her to do cruel things. It was the house, she thought.

But then she heard a voice telling her that she was right to defend herself.

Hettie had hit her with words. But she'd retaliated with violence. Something she'd suffered from terribly but detested in all its forms. She'd hurt Clara, now her sister. Hettie held her face in shock and sat bewildered. Neither knew what might come next.

But then Hettie exploded.

FORTY-THREE

Rosie

'It's too late, little sister, I've sold your story to the press. I thought they might be interested in it.'

Rosie remained rooted to the spot. She couldn't work out if Hettie was bluffing. Suddenly, the slap didn't seem so bad. Exposure was her worst nightmare.

Rosie took a step forward, but Hettie was out of her chair and they met somewhere in the middle, fists swinging, hands clawing, and feet kicking.

The eruption of savagery lasted mere seconds but when the two sisters stopped to catch their breath, they panted and sank to their knees, eyeing each other with suspicion lest they start up again. Neither did.

They looked at one another and Rosie thought she saw tears in Hettie's eyes. After years of not wanting to hear the incessant opinions of others, Rosie now wished Hettie would speak.

'I never thought you had it in you,' Hettie said finally. 'They wanted to pay me five hundred grand for the story. C.J. Dark the recluse is big news.' Hettie managed to laugh in between assessing the damage to her face.

'You didn't,' Rosie said.

'She speaks! Hallelujah, I knew it!' Hettie laughed hard. 'I did, but I gave it to them for free. I didn't want a penny. I see you have your book back now. Clara saved the day as always. She came charging around trying to find me and scold me like she used to, for not looking after you, even though you were old enough to do that yourself. You were certainly old enough to fuck somebody but apparently not to look after your little brother. Who was the father?'

'I'll never tell you.'

'Of course not. I reckon it was the gardener at St Mary's, he was dishy – actually, all the girls wanted him, we used to flash our bras to him at break. Is that why you did it? To get back at the nuns?'

'Stop it.'

'Maybe it was James's friend from Liverpool, the one Mother called common? He was a hunk.'

Rosie opened her mouth, but this time no words came out.

'It *was* him! Suddenly, you're mute again.'

'Happy now?' Rosie asked her sister.

'Not happy, no. After all these years I still don't know what you and James think I did.' Hettie's voice wavered and a sob escaped her throat.

'You stole from me,' Rosie breathed. Anger seethed out of her.

Banging on the cellar door jerked them both out of their present circumstance and back to the present.

They both looked towards where the sound was coming from and heard faint voices. One of them was Kitty.

Rosie's chest heaved and fell with exertion. They were both exhausted and Rosie saw a shift in her sister's demeanour. They locked eyes and there was an exchange of something they'd lost many years ago and it surprised them both.

'I didn't tell Mother about your pregnancy,' Hettie said.

'Stop it, you're lying,' Rosie said.

'And I didn't tell Father about James and Michael. Christian did.'

'Stop!'

The banging grew louder.

Rosie sensed rage consuming her once more.

'The house is ruined, it's worth nothing. Did you see the documents?' Rosie said the words with something approaching joy in her voice, but she didn't feel it inside.

'What do you mean, the house is worth nothing?' Hettie asked. She'd straightened her clothes and was stood up, facing her sister.

The change of subject seemed to give Rosie a new rush of purpose. 'Ian Balfour didn't tell you when he was bending you over Father's desk? There's nothing left. The grounds are condemned, the piping is destroyed, the whole foundation of Warbury House is fucking demolished.'

'You're lying,' Hettie said.

'Am I? Have you seen the survey? Ian lied, we've had it for weeks.'

'We?'

'Ian works for James and me.'

Rosie watched Hettie gather her thoughts and observed her struggle with this new information. She backed toward the stairs.

'What else do you think is on that hard drive?' Rosie asked her.

Hettie peered at the screens. 'I've searched it. It's just surveillance set up by Michael years ago.'

'Is it? It was Kitty who worked out the whole system and told me. I have no idea what she might have watched, or if she might have seen the footage of you and Ian fucking in the library.'

'You're bluffing.'

'Am I? It would crush your daughter, wouldn't it? Like it ruins all children who discover the true reality of their parents. She looked very upset when I saw her leaving the cellar earlier. I tried to speak to her, but she ran away, and Benji ran after her. I think they went to the lake, with James.'

Now she'd started, she couldn't stop, and the pent-up frustration came rushing out of her in a torrent. She watched Hettie struggle to swallow to clear her mouth. Fear gripped her and she looked suddenly weak as if the life was draining out of her. It was cool in the cellar, but there was no air.

'He's angry with you, sister. He never forgave you for handing those photos over to Father.'

'I had no choice,' Hettie whispered. Panic was setting in and restricting her ability to talk clearly. Rosie knew exactly how that felt.

The banging grew louder and they heard the shouting more distinctly now. Hettie went to the stairs and ran up the first few, but Rosie was close behind her and tried to get ahead of her.

At the top of the stairs Hettie saw Clara lying on the floor in a heap. She turned around but she was too late, and Rosie caught her by her hair.

'Get off me!' Hettie screamed.

Rosie put her finger to her lips to warn Hettie to stay quiet. Hettie forced her body to go limp and give herself up to her sister's hate.

'Aren't you tired?' Hettie asked her sister.

'Me?'

They stood at the top of the stairs, Hettie holding onto the rail, feeling like she might pass out, and Rosie clenching her fist around the neck of her blouse.

'Pretending to be something you're not. Your anger has

consumed you, even I didn't know how much. I didn't tell Mother about your baby,' she repeated.

'Shut up!' Rosie screamed.

'C.J. Dark. *Christian Jude*? Who came up with Dark? Did it make you feel clever?' Hettie asked.

'Clara chose Dark.'

'Figures, she was always rooting for you because you kept each other's secrets.'

They fought, fist to fist, tangled in a web of limbs. It wasn't clean and each became disoriented, lashing out blindly at the other, or where they thought the other was. After a few minutes' effort they collapsed in an exhausted heap and sat back staring at one another, admiring their opponent's strength and resilience.

'You're a noisy fighter,' Hettie said. 'Making up for lost time?'

'Fuck off.'

'You're not going to gag me, it'll be the last thing you do,' Hettie told her sister.

'Try me,' Rosie said, getting up on her hands and knees and crawling towards Hettie with a look of murderous hate on her face.

Hettie scrambled in the other direction, desperate to get away, then she felt a tremendous weight crash into the back of her head, and everything went black.

FORTY-FOUR

James

James walked briskly ahead of the three children.

Like he and his siblings had been, Hettie's kids were left to their own devices a lot, though it didn't seem to affect their childhood like it had his own. And they loved their mother, that was plain to see, though try as he might, James still couldn't understand it.

No one knew they were heading down to the lake, except Michael, who had prior knowledge because of his computer surveillance system. James accentuated his walk, as if performing to a hidden camera, just in case Michael was watching in real time and saw him half naked, in his swimming costume, swaying his hips from side to side, on his way down to the lake.

If Michael was determined to wither and die here, then at least James could show him what he was missing.

Rosie was supposed to be here, but he'd given up waiting.

It had been the same with Christian. His whines and

nagging had driven James crazy with resentment at his younger sibling who everybody seemed to pander to.

He turned his head up to the hot sun and allowed the feeling of pleasure on his skin to soak into him. It wouldn't be much longer now. Three more days and it would all be over, though he doubted, looking around the place, if the house itself could last that long. Clara and Michael were doing a good job of holding things together, but James wouldn't be surprised if the ground itself opened up and covered them all in shit. And that wasn't the only thing falling apart. He'd checked with Ian this morning, first thing, who'd confirmed that Jarrow Mining was out of the game. There'd been a total collapse of the south Peruvian silver trade and their father's stock had lost thirty million in two hours.

But the news had elicited mixed feelings in James, and he was beginning to see why his father had requested them all stay here for a whole week together. The old fucker knew exactly what he was doing. It was as if each passing moment he shared with what was left of his family, the more he pined for a happy ending, which he knew would never come. But Ian didn't understand, of course.

'I just can't fathom why anybody would be happy at the loss of all that money. You clearly have too much,' Ian had said.

'Well, I had too much yesterday,' James had joked. 'Now it's time to break the news to my family.'

'I don't envy you that. In fact... can we talk about your sister?'

'Which one?'

'Hettie.'

'Ah, you did a good job there, Ian, you should consider acting,' he'd told him.

Ian had winced, and James concluded that it was his recollection of everything he'd done to deceive Hettie – at James's request – that made him squirm. James had come across countless criminals who took to deception like a hobby, but Ian seemed to struggle with it. The last thing James needed was the lawyer grappling with his conscience last minute.

'She's fragile,' Ian continued.

'Who?'

'Your sister.'

'Which one?' he repeated.

'Hettie!'

'Fragile? What, you mean she's beginning to realise the damage she's caused and what it might cost her?'

'No, I didn't mean that. I meant... I think you have her wrong.'

James had sensed mutiny then and reckoned that Ian was losing his bottle, after everything they'd paid him. James had always known that if you wanted a job doing properly it was always best to do it yourself. Michael had taught him that. It was strange how being back at the house had revived in him a desire to use his hands, and get things done directly.

'Leave Hettie to me,' he'd told him.

'That's what I'm worried about. I don't think she can cope with it. What you're doing, I think it'll push her over the edge.'

James had become angry then and his patience with Ian had run out. 'That's the fucking point.'

So he'd started the day in a bad mood, but to his shock, and at Sarah's insistence, time with the children eased his fury. She'd come here as a visitor and now it seemed she knew more about his family than he did.

The kids ran ahead and screamed as Benji chased the girls. The three of them had relaxed in their short time here at Warbury House. And he remembered feeling the same when he was young, until he learned to hate it. The house seemed to wrap you up in a blanket of wholesomeness and then when that ripped, it didn't have the strength to hold it together and it fell apart, letting you fall out and suffer irreparable damage. He watched them skip ahead and the girls scampered out of Benji's way as he chased them.

He called Donny. 'Are we all set? This place stinks.'

'Done, it's a sinking ship, literally. If you look outside your window, you'll see that the lawn is almost underwater,' Donny said.

'I'm walking through it.'

All the way down the drive, as far as the eye could see, surface water sat stagnant in puddles, and was beginning to flow down the slope. He felt his shoulders tense and then go loose as months of planning came together. The lake seemed the only place that had escaped the stench, which is why he was taking the children down there.

'I owe you, brother,' he told Donny, and hung up.

'James!'

He spun around and saw Michael panting behind him. He'd been running and for a split second James thought he was going to scoop him up in his arms and carry him off, but then reality hit and he could see that Michael was distracted.

'You have to come back to the house – it's Rosie and Hettie.'

'What?'

'They're fighting.'

James wanted to laugh out loud, but curiosity won over as he imagined his two sisters battling it out in a boxing ring. Who would win? His money was on Rosie who was like a wounded animal kept in captivity for too long and at the end of its rope. But then Hettie had an edge of her own, and the grace of the wild, with the wits of experience.

He glanced towards the lake at the children.

'I'll watch them,' Michael said.

James eyed him.

'It's probably best,' Michael added.

James toyed with asking him what he meant but he saw the earnestness in his eyes. He turned away instead, trusting him with Hettie's children, and marched back to the house.

FORTY-FIVE

Rosie

Rosie stood panting, her chest heaving up and down.

Somebody had found a spare key and suddenly the tiny space in the wine cellar was full of people. Edward stood protectively next to his wife and demanded to know what had happened. It was his idea to call an ambulance for Clara, while Sarah tended to Hettie's wounds.

Rosie was in no mood to explain why violence had suddenly exploded inside her and she was herself shocked at how quickly her rage had taken over. She stood in front of them, watching them fuss over the two women she'd attacked but afraid to speak in front of too many people.

Clara began to wake up and Rosie felt secretly relieved. She'd never meant to knock her out.

'She assaulted Clara and then me – she's gone crazy,' Hettie told Edward.

Rosie's heart rate was slowing down, but adrenaline still rushed around her body, keeping her fired up, although as she looked at the people in front of her and realised her part in it, she didn't know what to say. No noise could be found inside her throat, and it was as if she'd frozen in time and her body had stopped functioning properly.

Again.

'Is that what happened?' Edward asked Rosie.

'Why the hell are you asking her?' Hettie demanded. 'Clara! Tell them what happened.'

Clara sat up with the help of Sarah, who cradled her from behind, but she said nothing to back up Hettie's story.

'I think we should all calm down,' Sarah said. 'It looks to me like Rosie and Hettie each had a good go at one another and they've years of business to settle – perhaps they're finally even. Let's go back upstairs, where we can wait for the ambulance, sort this out once and for all, then we can all go home. It sounds like it's been a long time coming.'

'We can't go home, we've still got three days to go,' Edward said.

'Cancel it,' Clara demanded. 'Cancel the bloody ambulance. I don't need one!'

'Jesus, you're brainwashed, too!' Hettie said to her. She pushed Edward off her and went for the door. 'She could have killed you,' Hettie said to Clara.

'I'll be fine, just get me out of here,' Clara said.

'Where's James?' Rosie said.

Everybody stared at her, unaccustomed to her voice. She felt herself blush a little.

'Michael went to find him,' Edward said, unable to take his eyes off Rosie, as if her voice was a physical presence.

Hettie marched past them, stepping over Clara, and stomped up the stairs, closely followed by the others. In the kitchen, she went to the sink and doused her head with water. Rosie watched her, with a feeling of shame slowly spreading inside her. Her sister's wounds looked painful and she was shocked at the damage she'd caused. It had been the same when they were small. James and Rosie ganged up on Hettie and she'd had to fight her way out of it, alone. Michael and Clara had always sided with the younger two. An overwhelming sense of guilt washed over her, and she ripped a towel off its hook to give to Hettie to dry her face with, but in doing so she caught the handle of a pan of food and it crashed onto the floor, spilling everywhere.

Clara came into the kitchen and stared at the mess, thinking it was Hettie's doing.

'For goodness' sake, you can't be left alone for five minutes without causing trouble!' Clara scolded Hettie and the others gathered round.

Suddenly, Hettie burst into tears. The injustice of being blamed for all the ills of their childhood home was too much, Rosie saw it plainly now. Rosie believed that she'd been the one who'd been overlooked, and it had been her voice that was never heard, but Hettie had felt it too. Nobody gave a second thought to the impact on Hettie of taking all the blows herself, so her younger siblings didn't have to.

They all stood in a row in front of Hettie: her husband, her little sister who'd just tried to kill her and Clara, who was also hurt but not by her hand, with Sarah and James rushing in behind to complete the team for the prosecution.

Hettie covered her face and turned away from them. Rosie thought she'd never looked so alone in all her life.

FORTY-SIX

Clara

James burst into the kitchen to find Clara with a nasty swelling on the side of her head, and Hettie with a puffy eye, which was rapidly turning purple.

'What the hell happened?'

Sarah looked at him gravely as she examined Clara's head and pressed a flannel to her temple, but the housekeeper, who hated fuss, pushed her hand away.

'I'm fine.'

She took the flannel herself and wiped her face with it, putting a kettle on the Aga to boil water.

'Which bowl should I use for hot water?' James asked her, wanting to help her the way she'd helped them. She'd been their nurse and surrogate mother. She'd patched them up when they were broken, yet James thought he could repay her with a sticking plaster.

'It's for tea, you moron. Everybody needs to calm down.' Clara glared at Rosie as she said this and Rosie, in turn, morphed into her teenage self again, staying quiet and looking into the distance as if the answers they all sought could be found somewhere out there, away from Warbury House instead of inside it – perhaps at the lake where she had buried everything else in her life. Clara watched her as she pulled a chair out from under the table and plopped herself on it.

'What the hell happened in there?' James repeated his question.

'Rosie is C.J. Dark, the novelist,' Hettie said, with the last of her strength. Everything was an effort, even rage. She slid a chair out and sat on it heavily.

Rosie's secret was out. Clara eyed Hettie, and Sarah's mouth gaped open.

'Oh, I've read him,' Sarah said.

'*Her*,' Clara corrected her.

'Her,' Sarah repeated, turning to Rosie. 'You've sold ten million copies worldwide.'

'What?' It was an audible collective gasp, but James spoke the words. Rosie looked at her feet and picked her nails.

Clara looked at the woman Rosie had become but saw a girl and knew she'd never be satisfied, not after beating Hettie half unconscious, and knocking her out. None of it was enough to make the pain go away for Rosie. She could dig a knife into Clara's body a thousand times, and nothing would ever bring back her baby. Clara knew because she felt the same thing herself, which is why she wanted no police or doctors involved. She'd played down the assault to keep their secret one last time. She wasn't even sure if it mattered anymore. Whatever they'd come for, James and Rosie had surely got it now. She glanced at Hettie with pity and was almost thankful Christian hadn't had to suffer the toxicity of these three siblings.

Clara breathed deeply and at length, and it felt good. The air in her kitchen at Warbury House was clearer than anywhere else, despite the stench of sewage seeping into the fabric of it. It was as if the end was in sight and soon, they'd all be able to leave. Despite the obvious problems of the damn septic tank and the ground water, which was oozing through the grass inch by inch. It was the first fresh lungful of air she'd had since the children had arrived, and now perhaps they could all have a sensible, grown-up conversation about what they all wanted. She watched the siblings around the table, as James took a seat. Hettie winced in pain, but Clara noticed how Edward didn't tend to her – he was too busy thinking, no doubt calculating how all this affected him.

Clara thought the siblings looked twenty years younger suddenly – children again, sat together in the kitchen – and she half expected Beatrice to shout from upstairs for another decanter of sherry to take away the pain of a man who ignored her, shoved her aside, trashed her beliefs about true love and took another woman to his bed, making a child and asking her to pass it off as her own. Anybody would turn to drink. But she couldn't explain this to the children. As she sat there, waiting for somebody to take the lead, like she had decades ago, Rosie withdrew into herself and the person who'd attacked Clara and Hettie in the cellar vanished before their eyes. Clara could forgive the physical violence.

James, on the other hand, found things to distract himself. He made jokes and acted the fool, always the one to divert attention away from himself to make sure that no one discovered who he really was underneath it all. But he hadn't fooled Clara then and nor did he now. She saw him trying to take charge.

But they all missed their father, or at least his authority – they were just babies without him. Jude was like a powerful dictator whose departure resulted in a power vacuum and everything turning to shit.

Even worse shit.

Then Clara looked at James differently and felt a deep maternal responsibility for him. She'd watched him mature and turn into a man. Now he was barely a shadow of himself as he struggled to find something to do to keep busy. He didn't belong in here. His world was outside, and he looked out of place inside the belly of Warbury House, where all the rot was. Underneath the silly comments, James's face ached with longing and regret – and Clara wondered briefly what might have happened if Jude had never found out about him and Michael.

James's sexuality had been obvious to her from the moment the boy found the first hair on his chin. Clara gave him extra loving, additional care, supplementary mothering, to make up for the hurt building up inside of him. Jude thought it could be beaten out of him, but Clara knew better. She'd tried to make Jude see reason, and see past what Jude said was God's effluent. It still made her cringe to think of it, and the way he took the lad and beat him, in the hope it'd make him a real man.

James turned to look at Rosie. Was it guilt she saw pass over his brow? Or panic? She knew they were up to something, but she still hadn't figured it out.

They'd been thick as thieves: James and Rosie. Always shutting out their elder sister, and then using Christian when he came along, like a toy to be bargained with and manipulated. She'd hoped Rosie breaking free and finding a different voice might help, but she saw now that it had only made her harder.

Clara shivered at the memory of them together, plotting and planning into the night, about what trap they would set for their little brother the next day, and he fell into it every time. But the extent to which Clara could intervene to protect Christian was limited because Beatrice had taken him on as her own. Clara could never show that she loved him more than the others. But now she wished she had.

She'd kept everyone's secrets, but Jude's was the biggest and most damaging. Her silence when she saw Jude pleading with his wife to take on another woman's child as her own – and the shadows it created behind her every step from that moment on

– were hard to bear. But it meant that she could at least see her son grow.

She'd hidden the pregnancy from her employer because Beatrice took no notice of her figure, or dress, or health, but Jude arranged for her to be taken away for his birth. She'd spent a week in a private hospital in London, where she'd held her boy and fed him. It was the most precious week of her life.

But now she wished she hadn't cared what anybody else thought and kept him for herself. He'd still be alive for certain.

None of it mattered now, though, and that's what Jude had seen clearly on his deathbed; all his regrets and wasting of his time on things that meant nothing in the end. He put what he thought was right over what was good and once those two things got mixed up, they could never be unpicked again. One became the other and Jude believed what was right was good, until the end, when he learned that what is right and good is different for everyone.

What a waste of life, she thought. She got up wearily.

'Tea?' she asked no one in particular.

She got a few grumbles in response and forced her worn-out body up to arrange it. She ached, but she could take it and more than that. Her body had been battered before and she'd survived. But she was running out of the energy to fight. These kids had been destroying each other since they crawled out of their mother's belly and no one had stopped them then, and nobody would now. All animals need looking after and if nobody does that for them, they'll find other ways to survive. Jude and Beatrice had pitted their children against each other without even knowing it, and their offspring had found a way.

Christian had tried desperately to find his way, too, but the odds against him were too great. Clara never believed what they said about him at camp. That's when it had all started to unravel for her boy. It was as if Christian disappointed Jude more than the others ever could just by being a boy. From that moment on, Christian had turned spiteful.

She turned away from them and concentrated on the tea.

'Is nobody going to say anything?' Sarah said.

'Leave it,' Clara told her.

Sarah wasn't used to the way the family here at Warbury House had always buried their feelings. And Edward had never got the hang of it either, mistaking secrecy for tact.

This sport would only end when they were all lying in coffins over on the island where they belonged.

Clara placed the tea things on the table and pressed her hand into Hettie's shoulder, acknowledging her heartache.

'Where are the children?' Hettie asked.

Clara noticed that she didn't address Edward, their father, but moved on.

'I told the children to busy themselves – they've gone to the lake.'

But it was the worst thing she could have said.

'What? No—' Hettie said. She sat up straight but winced as her injuries prevented her from moving too suddenly. 'Rosie said they were with James, but he's here,' she said.

'Kitty will supervise, she's more than capable,' Edward said.

'I asked Michael to watch them,' James chipped in.

'You knew about this?' Hettie glared at her husband.

Rosie flushed. Hettie glared at her. Clara watched as cruelty and scorn floated across the room between the two women.

'Now, now, ladies,' James said. 'Maybe it's a good opportunity for Benji to learn to swim?'

Hettie glared at him, then stood up and winced in pain. 'I'm going to the lake.'

'I need to be here,' Edward said. 'If there's a family conference,' he added.

'No, you don't,' all three siblings said in unison.

'Edward, if you put my father's money before your son's safety then you've told me all I need to know. You'd be better off packing right away and leaving,' Hettie said.

Rosie let a scoff escape from her throat and Hettie rounded on her.

Clara saw something change in Hettie's face and she realised what was coming before she could act.

But it was too late.

Hettie went up close to Rosie. 'You want to know what happened to your baby? Father told you he'd help you find him, didn't he? But he lied. The night you gave birth to him—'

'Hettie, don't—' Clara said.

Rosie glared at her. 'Clara?' she said. It was a low growl, as if she was preparing to defend herself against prehistoric predators.

'Mother dealt with him. He never survived the night,' Hettie said.

Silence gripped the space between the two sisters. Clara took a tiny step forward, as did James.

'Oh my God,' Sarah gasped.

'Don't,' Clara begged her.

'I watched her bury him – you want to know where?' Hettie said.

Hettie moved out of the way, just as Rosie went for her, and missed, ending up crashing into a chair.

FORTY-SEVEN

James

'Hettie, stop it,' James said.

'You knew, too, you hypocrite!' Hettie screamed at him.

Rosie spun to look at her brother, who refused to look at her.

'But you're the great C.J. Dark. It's all right, Rosie, you'll survive, just like you always do. Go and write a book about it!'

'The house is worth nothing, Hettie,' James said. But his ploy to distract her didn't work.

'I know! Your sister kindly told me. You think I care? You think this is about the house?'

Edward stared at her, then James. 'What?' he asked meekly.

James turned to his brother-in-law. 'The investments, the house, the infrastructure, the insurance, nothing, there's nothing left, it's all worth nothing.'

Edward looked like he might faint. James enjoyed the moment and found it difficult to stop now he'd started. Suddenly, he felt powerful and realised that's why he'd come home. 'What?' Edward repeated.

'There's no money. Father's stock took a tumble over the last few days and is virtually worthless.'

Now, Hettie paid attention, too, as did Clara.

'You knew this?' Hettie asked Clara.

'No.' She'd never lied to any of the children. She might have massaged truths to soften blows and she'd certainly remained silent, but she'd never told a barefaced lie. She stared at James, whose look of triumphant glory was fading to something else. He knew this was it. Crunch time. This is what he'd been waiting for, the opportunity to tell everybody that he was in charge – that everything that had been done to him was being repaid a thousand-fold. But it didn't feel good at all. He'd imagined this moment feeling triumphantly glorious, but it didn't.

Watching Hettie in particular, he tried to muster up some sense of achievement –

some satisfaction – that he was finally challenging his father and his legacy on his terms. But even the sight of his older sister – who'd been the most aligned to him in character, had been the living embodiment of what he stood for, had obeyed him even when at his cruellest – wasn't gratifying at all. Everybody watched him.

'James has been devaluing the house and the investments,' Sarah said.

It was now her turn to attract everybody's attention and they all turned to her.

'Sarah!' James said.

'What? If you were willing to do it, then at least own up to it.'

'I couldn't put it better myself,' Clara said.

'Neither of them needs the money, I get it now,' Sarah added.

'I don't understand. Father told me he'd invested all the money and it was watertight,' Hettie said.

James looked away.

'James?' she asked. 'Rosie?'

'There's nothing left, Hettie. You'll never live at Warbury House. The survey recommends demolition and the sooner the better,' James said.

Silence whirled around the room like an uninvited guest. It skipped and danced between them until slowly, the pieces fell into place. Clara looked between James and Rosie and then to Hettie, who understood it, too. Edward put his head in his hands.

'Why? Why would you do such a thing?' Hettie asked her brother and sister.

'Where is my child?' Rosie replied calmly. Her voice was more measured now and she was getting used to moving her mouth around the vowels and consonants.

'Wait – you knew?' Clara now addressed Rosie. 'You did all of this to make a point because you were angry?'

'She told Father about my baby,' Rosie said, indicating Hettie.

'No, I did not!' Hettie screamed.

'Yes, you did,' Rosie screamed back.

Clara wasn't the only one who jumped at the noise. Rosie's voice was powerful, shocking and irrevocably back.

'No, she didn't, Rosie, your mother did,' Clara said.

Rosie's face crumpled. Clara looked between the two sisters, finally understanding what caused all the hate.

'She told the nuns,' Rosie said.

Clara put her straight. 'No, she didn't, that was your mother, too. Hettie fought your corner.'

Hettie couldn't take her eyes off Rosie. James ceased his fiddling, too scared to breathe while his sisters went head to head.

'She watched while I was held down and examined.' Rosie was becoming breathless. Clara saw that James was beginning to panic. His fiancée grew more shocked by the minute as revelation followed revelation, making the family she was to marry into – if that's why she was really here – an abomination.

'I tried to get in to stop them, that's what you probably saw,' Hettie said weakly. Her voice was now quiet and resigned. 'You've ruined everything.' She got up and held on to the back of her chair. 'You two planned all this? Together? It must have taken years. The investments, the lawyers, the house. Those men on the perimeter are yours?' she asked James. 'You did it all to get back at me for something I didn't do? And what did I do to you, James? I protected you from Father. I stayed here to make sure he let you go.'

James's face was set and unmoved. Nobody said a word.

Clara had run out of words. For so long, she'd held the family together with her wisdom and sensible grace. But now James saw that it had deserted her. She was confounded by the spite of these two children whom she'd raised.

'What is it with you two?' she asked weakly.

'You're lying about my baby,' Rosie said to Hettie.

'You think so? And all this time you went along with James's plans. You idiot. You have no idea what he's capable of,' Hettie said, pointing to her brother.

Rosie turned her hateful face to James, who threw up his arms in self-defence.

'Sis, I have no idea what she's talking about.'

'I want to know, too,' Clara said.

'So do I,' Edward chipped in.

'Shut up!' the others said to him together. He stood back.

'Why don't you ask him what he was really doing down at the lake the night Christian died?' Hettie said.

'What?' Clara asked. It was a whisper. Her throat sounded as though it had seized up.

'Hettie?' Edward said. She ignored him.

'Christian told Father about your affair with Michael, didn't he, James?' Hettie asked.

'Hettie, stop,' James said to her. He took a step towards her.

'What is she talking about?' Clara asked.

'So, you went to the lake to find him,' Hettie continued. 'Mother told me before she died.' She turned to Clara. 'James held him under, Clara. Your son, our brother, was killed by James,' she said.

'Her son?' Sarah asked.

Rosie stared at her brother.

Clara's head felt hot and she leaned forward on the table but scalded her hand on the teapot. She cried out in pain. Suddenly, it hurt more than the bruises Rosie had given her.

'Ask Michael, he'll tell you,' Hettie said. 'I'm going to find my children.' She stood up and turned to Rosie. 'If you want to find your baby, I'll tell you where Mother buried him when I know mine are safe.'

Hettie marched out of the kitchen, closely followed by her husband.

'Is it true?' Rosie asked James, after Hettie had gone.

Everybody turned in his direction and waited to see what he would say.

'You lied to me? You were at the lake, with him?' Rosie asked him. 'Tell me it's not true, that you didn't hurt him.'

James rose from his chair and backed away slowly, bumping into a chair, which scraped along the floor, and Clara's face crumpled.

She watched James back away further and then he turned and ran out of the door. Rosie shot up and followed him.

Clara turned to the only person left in the room, Sarah, but the outsider couldn't ease her agony. She appealed to her to make the pain go away, and the thoughts in her head disappear. She told herself it was just babbling – the result of decades of these children falling out, they'd say anything to hurt one another –

but the way Hettie spoke was such as Clara had never seen before. It was so final. So brutally honest. And James had not denied it. He'd done what he always did when he was caught out: he ran away.

But Clara also realised that deep down she had always known that her son hadn't drowned or committed suicide. She'd done what Jude had told her to, and carried on as normal, believing it was a terrible accident. It was a dark shadow in her gut, and she'd never had the courage to ask Jude what really happened, but she knew now that the day he died, he'd told her everything she needed to know when he'd said sorry.

They weren't the dying regrets of an old man. It had been a confession.

FORTY-EIGHT

Hettie

'Wait, for God's sake, Hettie, wait!' James caught up to her, but Edward put himself between them.

'That's enough,' Edward said. Hettie ignored both of them and continued to the lake. Her pace sped up and her feet splattered in the wet grass.

'What the hell is all this?' Edward asked, looking down. 'This is your doing? You flooded the place as well? Dear God.'

James ignored him and ran past, catching up to Hettie. He took her arm, but she wriggled away.

'Get away from her.' Edward pushed him and James stumbled but recovered quickly and swung for Edward – but missed. Edward dodged his efforts a second time and caught up to Hettie. They were getting close to the beach when Hettie saw Michael and began to run. Edward caught her up and James followed behind. They arrived on the beach and Hettie looked for the children.

'They're having a great time, Hettie,' Michael said.

'How dare you! I can't trust you!' Hettie said to Michael.

'You're just as bad as him!' She pointed to James. Then she spotted a dinghy out on the water and heard shrieks of laughter.

'Benji!' she screamed.

She saw Kitty and Pippa on a canoe, but couldn't see her son. The girls were splashing and pointing at something in the water. The adults huddled at the shore, and James stood helplessly lost as he saw Clara and Sarah walking down from the house to join them.

'Edward! Where's Benji?' Hettie said. Her legs moved blindly in rhythm to transport her to the water, but she wasn't aware of them.

Edward shaded his eyes and the girls' voices drifted across the lake.

'There they are!' he screamed.

James ran to the water and dived in, not stopping to take off his clothes. Michael followed him. Hettie pointed to the canoe, and her children, but her legs had stopped moving.

From behind her, Sarah ran into the lake, followed by Edward. Hettie saw four swimmers closing in on her children and felt arms around her. She turned to see Clara holding her and their eyes met.

'Get a canoe!' Hettie screamed, coming alive suddenly. She ran to the boathouse and dragged a vessel out to the water, jumped in it, and began paddling. There was no way the swimmers could beat her in a canoe.

She passed them and the screams of her girls grew louder.

'Benji!' they shrieked. 'Benji?' she heard.

She was almost there. As she got closer, she saw Pippa was holding a set of armbands.

Hettie's body ached and her shoulders screamed at her to stop, but she kept going. James appeared from under her canoe, and she watched as he dived underwater, over and over again.

Time stood still and she tipped herself over in the canoe and swam underneath it, but the lake was murky, and she struggled to see. Out here, she knew it was over twenty feet deep and she kicked downwards, desperate to find her son.

She resurfaced and lifted her head up above the water's surface and gasped for air as she treaded water.

She twisted around as she heard James shouting behind her. He'd surfaced again and was taking huge, deep breaths, preparing to go under again.

In her brain, she saw her little brother fighting for air, in the middle of the night, held under by the brother he'd betrayed. She went under again but all she could see was Christian's face and not Benji's. She surfaced once more, and her head banged the girls' dinghy.

'Mummy!' they screamed at her.

Pippa was shaking with fright and her face was creased up into a ball of terror. Kitty held onto her little sister and reached out to her mother. Their faces were frozen in agony.

Then they saw James surface again and that he was holding onto something.

It was Benji.

She swam to him and helped keep her boy's head above the water. They cradled him and kicked for the island. She saw Edward reach the girls and knew they were safe, so she looked to the island and held onto her boy for her life.

They reached the shore and she and James dragged him out.

Benji was blue and cold, and his eyes were closed.

No, no, no, no…

They rolled him onto his back and James started CPR.

'Come on, darling,' she whispered to her son.

James counted: 'One, two, three…'

He heaved his body weight onto his chest.

Hettie sat back on the mud and her hand lingered on her son's face, where she traced his profile.

James counted once more.

Then Benji spluttered to life and his body rocked back and forth as he spewed water out of his lungs. Hettie held onto him like she had Rosie when she had had her baby taken away from her. She went to take her brother's hand, but her hand fell onto the mud. She looked round for him, but he was getting back into the water.

'James,' she whispered.

He shook his head and went into the water.

'James,' she said.

'I didn't mean to,' he said.

'James, come back,' she pleaded with him.

'He fell in, I couldn't find him,' he said, backing away into the water. Hettie knew he was talking about Christian, not Benji. She hadn't meant to blurt it out and accuse him like she had, and she felt wretched.

'James, don't. I didn't mean... I want to know what happened,' she said.

She turned back to Benji as she heard his laboured breathing, and the lapping of the water on the island as her brother's body made ripples and tiny waves. She remembered teaching Christian to go under the surface and swim with his eyes closed. She turned again to try to beg James to stay with them, but she watched his body disappear. She called to him once more, but she wasn't sure if her voice was real. Benji held her hand and she turned to him. *James is swimming back to the others*, she told herself. *Yes, that's what he's doing.* He's going to reassure them.

She cradled her son in her arms, warming his body with hers.

Behind her, James took one last look at the island and slipped under the water.

FORTY-NINE

Hettie

Hettie sat on the beach, her son draped across her.

She was aware of somebody close to her and turned to see Michael and Rosie approaching in canoes. They jumped out and pulled their boats up onto the shore. They both looked relieved to see that Benji was OK.

'I'm sorry I spoke to you like that, Michael,' Hettie said. He gave her a look that signalled he understood a mother's anguish when she's pushed. Rosie knelt next to them.

'You weren't lying, were you?' Rosie asked her gently. Hettie felt an unfamiliar welling up of emotion inside her. Hettie looked at her sister but didn't answer, then Michael knelt in front of her and took Rosie by the shoulders tenderly.

'Were you here, Michael?' Hettie asked him.

He nodded.

'You saw what happened to Christian?'

Another nod.

'Mum?' Benji murmured.

'Michael, is the ambulance here yet?' Hettie asked him.

'Not yet, it's on its way.'

'We need him checked over,' she said.

Michael nodded and produced a bag he'd brought with him in the canoe that contained a blanket which he threw over the boy.

'Where is James?' Michael asked.

'He's not here?' she said, confused.

'My throat hurts,' Benji said.

Michael took a bottle of water out of the bag and gave it to Benji, who sat up and sipped some.

'Thank you, Michael,' Hettie said.

'Where's James?' he asked again.

'Hettie, what you said back there at the house, about Christian's death... I must know what happened. Michael, is it true? Was James responsible for Christian's death? Did he really do that? I can't...' Rosie asked.

Michael's face darkened.

'Has he gone to visit the grave?' he asked. 'That must be where he's gone.'

'He went into the water after he saved Benji. He saved Benji,' Hettie repeated. Her mind was still befuddled with what was going on. She knew that Benji was safe, but she wasn't quite sure where everyone else was.

'The girls?' she asked, panicked suddenly.

'They're fine,' Rosie said. 'They're in shock, but Clara is looking after them.'

Her sister's voice was soft and gentle, and Hettie hadn't heard it like that for a very long time. Well, not since Rosie had stopped speaking, at least. The last time they'd been true sisters, before she saw what Mother did.

'I don't know why I never told you,' Hettie said to her sister. 'I heard him cry, I knew he was alive. I should have told you.' Hettie stared at her own son.

Michael stood up. He walked to the water's edge, searching for James.

Hettie turned to face the water. 'He went under.'

Michael waded in and walked past the canoes. They watched him go out of his depth.

The sisters stared at Michael, who dived in, then disappeared.

'Remember when James used to hold his breath for four minutes and he told us he'd seen an underwater world?' Hettie asked.

Rosie nodded. Then she got up and walked to the water's edge. She turned.

'How could he do that to his own brother?' Rosie asked.

'But he wasn't his brother, was he? Half-brother. He shouldn't have been the favourite. James was in love with Michael and Christian ruined it for him. He never got over it,' Hettie said.

'How long have you known?' Rosie asked. She sat down again and held Benji's hand.

'What about?'

'What James did to Christian.'

'I got it out of Mother when she was drunk. It was a couple of years after Christian died and you two had left for good. She deteriorated quickly, even after my wedding, she just went to her room and slept and drank, drank and slept.'

'I remember her like that. It's why I never came back, that and Christian, and...'

'I'm sorry.'

'Mum?' Benji asked. Hettie stroked his face.

'It's okay, darling, the ambulance is on its way.'

They sat in silence for long seconds and saw Michael surfacing and catching his breath.

'Did Michael know what James did?'

Hettie turned to her. 'Of course he did. So did Father.'

'Why did Father keep it to himself? How could he bear it?'

'Denial, fear, dread? Not wanting to admit his child was a murderer? Who knows? Most likely he was protecting Clara. If she'd known, it would have broken her.'

'Maybe it will now.'

'Maybe she can get help.'

'Nobody can bring her son back.'

'And nobody can bring yours back either.'

'Will you show me where he is?' Rosie asked.

Hettie understood that her sister was talking of her own child, and a fresh wave of shame engulfed her as she held onto Benji.

'He was healthy and strong when they took him from me,' Rosie said.

'I know.'

'She took on another woman's son but couldn't allow mine to live. To our mother, her own daughter was more shameful than her husband.'

'She was weak, Rosie, she could never stand up to him, and we were the ones who suffered because of it.'

'What is Michael doing?'

'I think James went under,' Hettie said.

'Of course he didn't, he'll be somewhere, tell Michael to stop.'

'Is that an ambulance?' Hettie asked.

Rosie stood up again and peered into the sky. An air ambulance helicopter circled above, then descended into the field behind the lake. It was where Father used to leave for trips to London via chopper, when he was lucid and in charge of his empire. They'd huddled as children, watching him take off and zooming into the sky like Superman.

They heard the motor of a boat and soon Edward appeared close to the beach, with two paramedics in the old skiff. They approached the shore and the paramedics jumped out, with Edward close behind.

Hettie allowed the medics to take charge of her son, and Edward went to hug her, but she moved away. She turned to Rosie.

'I'll show you. I put a stone over him. Mother didn't know I followed her.'

'He's here? On the island?' Rosie asked.

Hettie nodded. She watched the medics put Benji on a stretcher and examine his vital signs. She turned to her husband.

'Do this for me. I need to go with Rosie. Don't take your eyes off him, do you understand?'

He nodded. She went to her son and kissed his forehead and Benji smiled up at her, then looked to his father. Benji was loaded onto the boat and Hettie walked away, towards the chapel, and Rosie followed.

'I know where you hid my blanket,' Hettie said to her sister. 'I didn't take it back because I knew you needed it more than me, after yours went missing. When I took Christian off you because you held his nose tight shut, I thought you'd kill him. It wasn't just James who wanted to. You were acting out because you couldn't understand what had happened, I know that now. Back then, I guess I just saw you as self-indulgent – you didn't understand, and it was my face you saw coming out of Sister Agnes's office, but you didn't see my backside when I left there after she'd belted me for allowing my sister to get pregnant out of wedlock. As if it was my fault!'

Rosie stared at her sister's back.

'Did you keep in touch?' Hettie continued.

'Who with?'

'His father?'

'I never told him.'

'What?' Hettie spun around. They'd both dripped lake

water on the ground and created a trail of mud between them. Their legs were filthy.

'You stopped talking in so many ways, didn't you? It was your way of saying nothing at all and evicting everyone out of your life. Even him.'

'He's here,' Rosie said.

'Here? Now?'

Rosie nodded. 'He and James remained best friends. He's the one coordinating the surveillance.'

Hettie shook her head. 'You belong in one of your books,' she told Rosie. 'Remember you told me once you were scared of monsters, and I comforted you like you were my own? Then you became the monster, Rosie – you and James, equally. That was you. That is who you were to me. A voiceless beast.'

'That's poetic, Hettie. You always told the best stories.'

'*The Bones of Cameron Beck.*' Hettie referred to Rosie's *New York Times* bestseller published last year.

'What about it?'

'He's buried on an island and the sisters steal a boat to save the little boy who stumbled across his grave.'

Rosie nodded, and as she did, she slipped and landed right next to her sister, who grabbed her arm to steady her.

'And that's the one being made into a TV programme?'

Rosie nodded.

'So you kept your family with you really,' Hettie said, turning towards the chapel.

They carried on walking.

'You followed Mother all the way out here?' Rosie whispered.

'She rowed, I swam. I was the strongest, remember?'

'Always.'

Hettie stopped next to a tree; they were almost at the chapel. She looked at the ground.

'Here?' Rosie asked.

Hettie nodded. She bent under a branch and Rosie followed her. Underneath the canopy it was fresh and cold, and Hettie knelt and moved away dirt. Rosie bent over and helped her. Together, they exposed a round stone. It looked out of place, as if it didn't belong there.

'I brought it from the workshop,' Hettie said.

Rosie knelt next to her and read the inscription on the stone. It was made from scratch marks as if Hettie had done it with a knife.

Sleep, baby, it read.

Rosie put her hand over her mouth and lay down on the earth, moving the stone to one side and digging her fingers into the soft mud. The soil on the island was a mixture of peaty loam, and easy to dig, which is why the owners of long ago had chosen to build a cemetery there. Her fingers sank into the mush. Hettie saw what her sister was doing and bent over to help her. They removed a good foot of soil with their bare hands and then Hettie looked around for a tool, finding a medium-sized branch with a sharp end. She dragged it across the earth, loosening the mud, and took handfuls out and dumped them to the side.

'How did Mother do this?'

'It took her all night,' Hettie said.

After a few minutes, they'd dug two feet down and Rosie stopped.

Hettie looked into the hole.

There was a grey wrapping of cloth which looked like a dust bag.

'Oh, no, Hettie, please, I can't look.'

Hettie took Rosie's hand in hers. 'We don't have to. We can leave him in peace.'

'You heard him cry?' Rosie asked.

Hettie could tell that Rosie was trying to be brave, trying to hold back the torrent of anguish that had tormented her for over twenty years.

Hettie hesitated. 'I did, then he stopped.'

Rosie bent her head and pulled on the grey material. It came loose with both of them pulling and they dragged it out of the hole. It was about the size of a small cat and Rosie held it in her arms.

They sat back.

'Do you want me to?' Hettie asked.

Rosie shook her head and began unravelling the wrapping. Then she threw the blanket away from her body as it was revealed what was inside.

Hettie gasped and held her sister.

The skeleton was tiny, but perfectly intact. They peered at it then Rosie crawled towards it and stared down at it. She spotted a lump next to him, which had fallen out of the bag and picked it up, knowing what it was. She brushed the worst of the mud off it and held it up. It was her bear, a stuffed toy that had gone missing after she'd given birth, but maturity gained in such a way had dissuaded her from looking for him, thinking herself childlike and foolish – never knowing it was here, with her baby.

'He needs a proper burial,' she said.

FIFTY

Rosie

They sat next to the grave for a long time, Rosie holding the bear and Hettie trying to tidy the hole, as if that might make things less brutal somehow. Hettie wrapped the baby back in the blanket he'd been buried in and placed him inside the bag, handling him gently like she would if he were her own. They heard faint shouts from the lake and Hettie looked at Rosie in panic. She jumped up.

'Benji!' she cried.

Rosie got up, too, and stared at her son's remains.

'Do you want me to put him back in the grave?' Hettie asked.

Rosie shook her head and went to the bag, placing it carefully back into the hole.

'Come on, we need to see to your son,' Rosie said. 'I can come back later.'

They rushed back the way they'd come, insensitive now to the state of their clothes and skin. When they emerged by the beach, they looked like two castaways, recently discovered on a desert island, having endured months fighting to survive.

The paramedics were working on somebody, but it wasn't Benji.

Rosie and Hettie approached the stretcher and saw Michael sitting next to the patient. The paramedics sat back, and one shook her head.

Michael let out a sob.

Edward approached Hettie and looked solemn. He shook his head and held out his open arms to her. That's when they saw that it was James who lay on the stretcher on the ground, and he wasn't breathing. Hettie covered her mouth with her hand, and she watched Rosie rush to him and kneel down.

'Where's Benji?' Hettie asked Edward.

'He's safe, they took him back by boat.'

'Why didn't you go with him?' she asked him angrily, but she couldn't work out if the pain was more about her son or her brother. 'You thought it more important to stay close to the benefactors?'

Edward glared at her, puzzled and hurt, but she ignored him and went to Michael, who was facing away from them, at the water's edge, staring into the distance.

'Michael,' she said gently. He turned to her and shook his head. His face was creased in pain.

'What happened?' she asked.

'There are no reeds in there,' he told her.

She knew that was true.

'And it's not cold enough for him to cramp.'

She shook her head.

'And he isn't injured,' he said.

'No,' she whispered.

She turned to Rosie, who was holding James's hand, then she let it fall and joined Michael and Hettie.

'Can you tell us what happened?' Rosie asked him.

'No, I don't know. He saved the lad's life, then he went in of his own fancy. And went under.'

'Michael, I meant what happened the night Christian died,' Hettie said.

He looked at both of them. They sat either side of him. Then he began to speak.

'Christian told your father about us, me and James. It was innocent enough, we just...'

'Go on,' Rosie said.

'Jude was incendiary, inconsolable. He beat James half to death, here by the lake. I swam across when I found out where they were and pulled Jude off him. James swam back to the beach – I'd never seen him like that. It was as if he turned into an animal. Christian was on the beach, drunk. He and James argued and fought in the water. By the time me and Jude rowed back, it was too late. James had disappeared and Christian was in the water.'

'That's when I came down and found Rosie here?' she said.

Rosie nodded. 'I got down here just before you,' she said.

'I thought you gave him the drink because you were jealous of him after what Father did to you,' Hettie said.

'I thought you'd told him to tell Father about James and Michael, because we left you out,' Rosie said.

They turned to Michael. 'Why did you stay? After everything?' Rosie asked him.

'Your father had a way about him. He had a knack of making people feel guilty and that they owed him payment for something. My debt was enormous, almost unrepayable.'

'But it was James who caused his death,' Hettie said.

'If I hadn't had been... like I am... James never would have fallen out with his brother.'

Michael walked away toward the chapel, from where Hettie

and Rosie had just come and they looked at each other, both thinking the same thing, that they should warn him what he would find, but they couldn't move. They both were rooted to the spot, and then they stared at James's lifeless body in the hope that he just might wake up. After everything he'd done, they didn't want to be the sisters of two lost brothers.

FIFTY-ONE

Ian Balfour

Two Days Later

The library was silent.

Ian Balfour stood at Jude's desk and looked across at the gathered guests. The children weren't present. Kitty watched over Pippa and was under strict instructions to make sure they stayed in the kitchen out of harm's way. Benji was still in shock but well. He'd been taken to the John Radcliffe Hospital in Oxford. Edward had accompanied him. He didn't need to be here.

The four women sat in a row, facing Ian, waiting for him to start. Rosie, Hettie, Sarah and Clara.

Michael had packed up his things and left.

Ian coughed. 'Strictly speaking, we're only on day six,' he said.

'What? Are you serious?' It was Hettie who spoke.

'Mr Balfour, that is ridiculous,' Clara joined in.

Ian held up his hand.

'I understand your frustration, but if you will allow me to speak.'

The women calmed down.

'There is no provision for this particular set of circumstances in your father's will. However, I do believe that we have grounds for a suspension, and the conditions could be satisfied at a later date.'

'Lawyers. Empty as an old tin can,' Clara said.

'James left this in my bag,' Sarah said. She stood up and passed an envelope to Ian, watched closely by the others. She sat down again and Hettie patted her hand. Sarah smiled weakly.

'He'll have provided for you, as his fiancée,' Hettie said.

'I think we all know that's not true. I'm James's neighbour. I loved him, for sure, but not like that. He thought it would help his father love him if he turned up as straight and in impending fatherhood.'

'But Mr Fitzherbert had already passed on,' Ian said, stating the obvious.

'James was superstitious like that. Perhaps he thought he'd still be able to absolve himself,' Sarah said.

Nobody responded.

Ian opened the envelope and read the note that was inside. Then he scratched his chin and nodded.

'What does it say?' Clara asked.

'It's a case from 1982 – similar to this one in circumstance, and a precedent to allow me to override the terms of the will, providing I'm satisfied that everyone remaining in the house at this time is under amicable conduct.'

'Lord, help us,' Clara said. 'Can you say that in English?'

'I think what he's saying is that James found a way to get this charade ended, as long as we look as though we quite like each other.'

'That's a bit strong,' Clara said.

Hettie glared at her, but Clara was smiling, and she softened. Rosie stared at her, hands on her knees.

'Rosie?' Clara asked.

She turned to them and then to Ian.

'Amicable? Absolutely. There is nothing for us to fight over.'

'Well, that's why I wanted to call you here – partly, anyway. James also left instruction on several get-out clauses, should the circumstances of the house's condition be so materially different by the end of the seven days than at the beginning. My assessment today will be my final one, and it's not looking as bad as we thought. James arranged for a site manager to take charge and he's given me a report. I have it here.'

'Who is that?' Rosie asked.

'Mr Donny Salvatore. He's waiting in the adjacent study if we need him to clarify your position.'

Rosie took a sharp intake of breath and Hettie watched her.

'I think we'll talk to Mr Salvatore ourselves, thank you, Ian. If you can just get to the point and tell us if this is all over, we can go.'

'Yes. Quite. I do apologise. Yes, I can confirm that the period of condition is now at an end.'

There was an audible sigh of relief.

'And I can confirm that the estate will now be split between the two remaining siblings: Henrietta and Rosamund.'

The women stood up and Rosie left the room.

FIFTY-TWO

Rosie

Donny turned to see Rosie come into the room.

'Rosie, I'm so sorry about James, I can't believe it,' he told her.

She could see his eyes were red and his face had aged. In the light, now she could see all of him, he looked much older.

'Donny, are you all right?' she asked.

'It's a shock. We'd been planning this for some time, as you know.'

'Not all plans are good just because so much energy goes into them. James and I were seeking something from here that we will never get. Though maybe he's at peace now.'

'Is it true he drowned? I can't believe it. Not James. He's too strong, Rosie. Was it that Michael? I have connections. I can find him.'

'No, Donny, stop. You have it all wrong. I need to explain it all to you, but not now. It's been the worst week of my life… well, perhaps the second worst.'

'Of course, I'm sorry, you need time.'

'And there's something else I must tell you first.'

'What is that?' he asked her.

She led him to a sofa and sat down. He joined her and they sat close. In the late-afternoon sun, Donny's face looked yellow and pale. She took his hands. She couldn't help thinking that the pressure of working with James all that time, and what he'd been asked to do had put so much strain on Donny, he'd aged years more than he should have done. But she also saw something else, something she'd seen in her father, when they'd video-called before he died. It was in his pallor and the way his eyes drooped. Could she be losing Donny, too? When she'd only just found him again?

'I never apologised for ignoring you after that last summer,' she said.

He nodded and looked away. Something passed across his face, and she knew he was reminiscing because he smiled. She joined him – recalling the times he'd beamed at her just like that, many years ago, when their faces were close and their bodies warm, made her tingle all over.

'I had a baby,' she said.

His mouth fell open and she instantly regretted her decision to tell him. But then he recovered and began to grin.

'You had a baby? Wait, was he... she... mine?'

'Yes, Donny. Yes, he was.'

'He?'

'I called him Christian.'

'After your brother?' He frowned then. 'But James never told me. Is he here? I have a son.'

'No. You don't. We don't. But I can tell you what happened to him.'

FIFTY-THREE

Hettie

One Week Later

The sun shone over the chapel on the island and Hettie heard birds chirping in the trees above her as she held onto her children. Rosie walked with Donny. Edward accompanied Sarah and Hettie, and then Clara and Michael finished the procession. He'd returned one last time for the funeral. They'd taken the eight-seater to the island, driven by Michael, and he'd done several trips to get them all across.

Nobody knew if having a priest present was the right thing to do, but Donny had sorted it out.

He'd waited for his mother to arrive before escorting her across the lake, and she hung back, apart from the others. It wasn't that she was aloof, or even judgemental, though everybody acknowledged she was entitled to be. They also recognised that she was the one person here, with the exception of Donny, who had been the closest to James. Nanny Salvatore had politely introduced herself and accepted the offer of an overnight stay graciously. Ian Balfour was not attending the funeral but busy arranging contractors and building specialists to reverse the damage done to Warbury House these past few weeks. They'd been told it was salvageable.

At a price.

The funeral of Jude Fitzherbert was to be a joint affair, to include a ceremony for Donny and Rosie's baby, Christian. She'd named him in her heart decades ago, but with the blessing of Clara, had articulated it out loud. She was getting used to things becoming real, more authentic somehow, if you said them out loud.

As they walked, Hettie felt strangely closer to life than death, despite the occasion. A huge weight had been lifted off her, and she held her children close. Paramedics had worked for forty minutes on the body of her brother, after they'd dragged him out of the lake where Michael found him, but he'd remained unresponsive.

They'd had conversations around the table in the kitchen, as Clara cooked and made tea, about how it had happened. Hettie knew, as did Rosie, that James was a strong swimmer, and it seemed impossible that somebody could drown themselves on purpose. Surely panic kicked in and made one kick for the surface?

Michael said not. He knew it was possible.

All Hettie knew was that she'd seen James go into the water by himself and he hadn't resurfaced. Nobody else had been there. There were no dangerous reeds in the lake, Father made sure of it. James hadn't been drunk.

But he had been mad with loss.

And guilt.

Hettie never even had the chance to tell him that she'd invested money for their father too, but wisely, and it had done very well indeed. Enough to start again. It'd take time and patience, but with help, she was sure she could restore Warbury

House to her former glory. Rosie, with the wealth of C.J. Dark behind her, had agreed to help.

The air ambulance had struggled to get airborne again, once they'd loaded her brother's body onto it and it had whipped up so much effluent that the trail of sewage across the land as it flew over Oxfordshire had been reported in the press. But James's legacy wasn't only to be a pile of excrement, like he wanted – the draining of the sewage had revealed new tubers of native lotuses, which loved humid heat. The crap had fertilised them.

Now, Hettie looked at her father's coffin.

You selfish old bastard, she thought, and she wanted to say out loud, *If only you'd known what your children were capable of, you might have lived to see them thrive instead of destroy one another.*

Hettie wondered what monsters sounded like when they walked, if their skin felt prickly when they shuffled in wet pants, and if their feet squelched on the mud when they went barefooted. Theirs had. But James had been silent. He'd lived with what he'd done for thirteen years.

He'd also saved Benji and had loved his sisters once, too.

They'd all come to face their demons and exact revenge. And each had met a bigger and more frightening one. James paid for what he'd done to his brother with his own life, Rosie had her control stripped away from her and Hettie's reckoning was accepting finally that she was able to let Warbury House go. She'd agreed with Rosie to renovate it, then they would sell it.

They'd each lost themselves, but in doing so had discovered the peace that had eluded them for all the time they'd lived at Warbury House.

The family paused in front of the three new headstones, alongside their mother's, and Christian's. Rosie put her hand inside Hettie's.

'What do the sisters do next?' Hettie asked her. 'In your books?'

Hettie didn't expect an answer. She'd read so many of C.J. Dark's books, she already knew it. They moved on. To the next chapter. To the next part of their story.

Together. As well as celebrating the end of a case with a glass of champagne on the roof of their cottage. A place totally made up by Rosie, or that's what she told the press. Hettie knew differently.

'I reckon we can get a ladder up to the south wing and take some of Father's wine stash from the cellar onto the roof,' Rosie said.

'And a couple of blankets,' Hettie said.

Rosie looked over her shoulder at her nephew and smiled at him.

Benji was losing his voice as a result of the trauma he'd suffered under the water. Rosie had told him that a period of muteness wasn't all that bad, but when his voice came back, he'd be stronger, and clearer.

Hettie squeezed her sister's hand and then let go as the priest took his place. Rosie looked at Donny and saw the pain on his face. She didn't know which was worse, losing a baby after you'd laboured to bring him into the world, believing him healthy and happy, or losing a son you didn't even know existed.

But she was glad she'd told him, despite the pain. There'd been enough secrets kept in the walls of Warbury House to last for the next hundred years. They didn't need any more.

A LETTER FROM THE AUTHOR

Dear reader,

Huge thanks for reading *The Secret Inheritance*. I hope you were hooked on the Fitzherbert family's story. If you want to join other readers in hearing all about my new releases and bonus content, you can sign up here:

www.stormpublishing.co/rachel-lynch

If you enjoyed this book and could spare a few moments to leave a review that would be hugely appreciated. Even a short review can make all the difference in encouraging a reader to discover my books for the first time. Thank you so much!

Thanks again for being part of this amazing journey with me and I hope you'll stay in touch – I have so many more stories and ideas to entertain you with!

Rachel Lynch

x.com/r_lynchcrime

ACKNOWLEDGEMENTS

I loved writing and researching this book. It started with a vision of a beautiful country house on a hot summer's day and ended up being a story of family tragedy and betrayal. The setting of the English countryside alongside the dark secrets of the siblings of Warbury House is an arrangement I have come to love exploring. As always, I could not have written this without the support of my incredible family. My children, Tilly and Freddie, are constant sources of joy and pride, and as far as teenagers go, they're pretty damn fantastic. They support me in everything I do and I hope I show them every day that you can follow your dreams. My husband, Mike, listens to strange and disturbing storylines on idyllic walks in the countryside most days and I commend his patience and imagination. His contribution to my stories when I'm stuck is scarily wonderful.

Thank you to Kathryn Taussig at Storm whose belief in my work has allowed me to explore new breadth and depth to my writing. She's a joy to work with and I'm very lucky to have such talent beside me when crafting something so different and new.

I also want to thank my agent, Peter Buckman, who said this is my best work yet. Peter always has my back and has guided me from the very beginning of my career in this industry which can be a terribly tough place to navigate. His wisdom and experience have allowed me to grow as an author and his advice and guidance is invaluable to me.

Thank you to all the readers and reviewers who love books so much that you shout about them from the rooftops, just in case nobody heard the first time. Your support is everything. Without you we wouldn't have jobs.

Printed in Great Britain
by Amazon